Table Money

Table Money

Jimmy Breslin

TICKNOR & FIELDS · NEW YORK

Portions of this book have appeared in different form
in the *New York Daily News*.

The quotation on page 106 from "Prisoner of Love"
by Clarence Gaskill, Leo Robin, and Russ Columbo is
used by permission of Edwin H. Morris and Company, a division of MPL Communications, Inc. International copyright secured. All rights reserved.

The identities of all the characters in this book are
fictitious, and any resemblance to any living person is
unintentional.

For Ronnie Myers Eldridge

1

THE FIRST WATER for a civilization moves slowly, perhaps a couple of inches a second, as it runs through the woods in the night, the brook widening at the end of the woods and the water now moving at a foot per second and then much faster as it runs downhill on land that drops one foot in each ten thousand over the 115 miles to the city.

Black night rain falling on a ridge in the Catskills. In the morning sun the water becomes brown against the mud bottom of the brooks, which join into streams running past the backs of stores, through old towns that sigh in the afternoon, over the gravel alongside dead railroad tracks, and then around suburbs of lost laughter. Each day, over the eight months the water takes to run to the city, the color lightens more and more to the eye and the streams become swift creeks pouring into basins that look like lakes. The water leaps and spins in the sun: pure rainwater with oxygen counts of eleven and twelve when the most oxygen water can hold is fourteen. Water flowing on natural gravity, the drop of one foot in each ten thousand bringing the rain into the cupped hands of a city that requires a billion and a half gallons a day.

This pale treasure caused a city, and it brought the Morrisons to the boroughs of New York, where they live as one of the nation's oldest families of people who work with their backs and hands for a living.

There was a time in 1800 when Alexander Hamilton and Aaron Burr envisioned climbing a night ridge in the Catskills and placing a foot in the way of the water, or shoving a board into the wet earth and causing the water to back up and sink into the ground. Meanwhile, in the small city, people feared that to drink brackish water from its own wells was to gulp yellow fever. Hamilton and Burr saw a city staring at them with dry tongue hanging out. Which caused Burr to go to the legislature with a bill that would give his Manhattan Company control of the city's water, with the subclauses buried in the middle of the bill, paragraphs past the attention span of any local politician, speaking for Burr's craving for national control: all profits from selling water a glass at a time would be consigned to a new bank to be owned by Burr. How marvelous, he told himself. The bank would become so powerful that he, Burr, would step outside one day and buy the Presidency as if it were a frock coat. In the midst of his scheming, Burr dug a water well on Spring Street in New York as a display of good intentions. Then the body of a murdered woman was found in his well. Both Hamilton and Burr arrived in court as lawyers for a man named Rackmill, who was the woman's boyfriend and suspected of doing the killing, although in defense-table conversations it was Burr who clearly seemed to know more about the killing than the alleged killer. The client got off, and the records show that it was Burr's first public involvement with homicide, and his last with the people's water.

Seventy years later, the city was run by "Boss" Tweed of Tammany Hall, whose thought it was that New York's future could be guaranteed by the purchase of 375 square miles of upstate watershed, including the night ridges of the Catskills, and the water properly managed by building a system of the highest quality concrete and cast-iron aqueducts and tunnels to carry the water from Catskill ridge to Bowery faucet. The water, Tweed explained, was delivered by gravity, without pump, and thus cheaply, so that the high initial cost would be offset by low water expenses for the public over many years, while at the same time these construction costs would ensure that no growl of hunger would come to a Tweed belly for at least a century. Tweed, however, was a limited man, who thought that all stolen pots had to be of a size that would fit in a steamer trunk. It never occurred to him that the city would not end up owning the watershed land. Within his political circle, however, there was Albert Cardozo, a judge who kept both hands off the gavel, the better to receive, and his mind on enormous projects, for, having pored over the past, particularly Burr, a most stirring thief to study, Cardozo wanted to buy the watershed privately, thus giving Tweed and group a firm hand on the city's throat. Cardozo felt that with this money, and control over the nation's main city, they would be able to name Presidents. Tweed, with a clerk's vision, was afraid to try this. He decided that his city would buy the land and he would build the system: tunnels and aqueducts running hundreds of miles and taking decades to build, which would last for more than a hundred years without failure as they turned a city into the most influential on all the earth. While the marvelous system was being built, money magically dropped to the floor, and Tweed, whose belly was so big that he couldn't get his hands below his shins, allowed Cardozo to pick it up. Cardozo took great care of himself, then passed the bulk to Tweed, who threw it into the sky. Cardozo left his secret money to his son, Benjamin, who was brilliant and became as famous as he was reluctant to return the illicit money that founded his career. Of course, Tweed's name became synonymous with stolen goods, although he left a city with water and, by his own estimate and that of the sharper newspapers of the time, Tweed also made some fifteen hundred whores rich.

"No woman climbed out of my bed in need of anything for the spirit or purse," Tweed declared.

As riches from the water system spread among Tweed's outfit, they began to broaden their special program of mass public improvement: they now tried to make all the whores in the city rich. As the number of women who, if able to evade disease, rose to the positions of honor that came with money, Tweed's Tammany Hall became one of the few vehicles for the advancement of women prior to the Nineteenth Amendment.

One woman so assisted was Florence Morrison, who was born in Ireland and seemed destined to remain there. She lived in a stone cottage that was chilled by the cold mists of Burtonport, a fishing village in County Donegal. Her father fished for a living in the North Atlantic, her mother swept and sewed, and Florence worked in a tannery, which she had done since the age of fourteen. Her brother, Johnny, four years younger, cleaned fish.

At night, her father, Eamonn, walked up the rutted, sloping path to Mrs. Curtin's grocery store, where men sat around a small peat fire in the rear of the store and listened to the town's storyteller, Dan Joe, as he kept the legends of his land fresh. Dan Joe could not read or write and spoke with a slight lisp that was caused by both missing teeth and teeth crumbled into yellow stumps. But his ability to tell a story, with a beginning, middle, and end, and to dramatize it, made him perhaps the most important figure in Burtonport. He was the town's university, lecturing nightly on the power of mystery, the belief in mystery, the reasonableness of mystery, and because of Dan Joe the importance of mystery never waned in Burtonport, where the Irish understood that the matters known by humans, when placed together in all the libraries and written in all the languages of the world, were meager in comparison to all that is not known, and because of this they were able to form beliefs in the un-known, in the mystery of God in Heaven, and in such vital matters on earth as coincidence. Dan Joe, through stories, taught people in Mrs. Curtin's grocery store that some coincidences were not that at all, that they were events that announced their presence in ways that only fools did not recognize. In Burtonport, Dan Joe insisted, anyone from all the ages past knew enough to flee the sound of a wagon going down a bumpy road at night, for each hoofclop, each rattle of the wagon, was an an-nouncement of the presence of death. At first sound, the only defense was to run and hide, for to actually see a wagon on a bumpy road at night was to ensure death. It would happen at any time thereafter.

And then one night Florence Morrison's fisherman father, Eamonn, tarried too long over stout in Mrs. Curtin's store. When he came out into the darkness and walked unsteadily down the road, with a North Atlan-tic gale blowing in his face, hearing nothing but the gale's howl as he walked down the sloping road to his stone cottage at the edge of the ocean rocks, suddenly behind him came a roar and Eamonn Morrison teetered for a moment and then threw himself off the road and into a ditch. He heard the loud rattle, and he knew he should hide his head, but something—the stout, or worse, subconscious disbelief—caused him to look up and watch a runaway wagon roll down the road, milk cans on the back rattling loudly. He watched the wagon plunge into the darkness and then he got up and trudged home. In the morning, he awoke to the sound of the sea splashing high over rocks and he knew that this meant there would be no way for a Donegal fishing boat to last in such water. On the next morning, the sound of the ocean was slightly muted and Eamonn Morrison put on his white fisherman's sweater, oilskins, and heavy boots and got into the drab twenty-six-footer and, with two cous-ins crouched in the small cabin, started out into heaving gray water. They were two miles out, heading for water that ran over a ledge where turbot and Atlantic salmon darted through the darkness, when suddenly waves began to roll into the boat, each one gathering more power, and the bow disappeared into the water and the stern rose as high as it could and then the bow rose and the stern dropped with a smack into the water. The boat shook. Suddenly, there was a new sound, that of a loose board in the stern and the bow went into the water again and then rose, and the stern started to drop and Eamonn Morrison clenched his teeth and began to open the front of his slicker. His fisherman's sweater underneath would be helpful for at least a few moments against the freezing water and was certainly worth its weight. The oilskin slicker, however, was so loose and heavy that it would pull him to the bottom of the sea; therefore he prepared to pull it off. Eamonn had made the decision many years earlier to learn how to swim, something unheard of in Burtonport, where common sense ordered that no child of a fishing family be taught to swim, for if, when grown, he ever fell into the North Atlantic, the sooner he drowned, the better. The fisherman's belief was "Take a good breath of salt air and use it to say an Act of Contrition. And that's it." Eamonn, however, lived in more hope than that. And now he had one hand on the side of the fishing smack and the other starting to remove his slicker. He then would strike out into the waves if required. The stern was high in the air and then dropped. When it hit the wild ocean this time, the stern broke into pieces and the ocean rushed into the small boat.

A glance to the left showed dark sky, foam, and the masthead of Syl McGuinness's smack. Morrison was elated. Just stay afloat and McGuinness will go through any storm to pull you out, he thought. Eamonn lost footing and fell, and as he did he clutched the side and found wood still there. He saw his two cousins gripping it. We'll all be saved, he thought. Then he saw one of the cousins, Jack McClosky, start to wash away with the cold water. Eamonn dove for him. He missed, and his head went into a tub of rope, which twisted around his neck. He stood up to get the rope off and then he slipped and fell backward into the water. His foot hit Jack, who was hanging onto the side of the boat, whose planks had enormous strength, so much that when the wet thick rope caught itself on a piece of the wood that jutted out, the wood held the rope, which then snapped Eamonn's neck. Syl McGuinness's smack made its way over and he pulled Eamonn Morrison's two cousins in. Syl was pulling on the rope in the water, with Eamonn Morrison's form shimmering as it came close to the surface, and then the head came up, flopping over with the neck broken, and suddenly a huge wave washed Syl McGuinness off his feet and he dropped the rope, and Eamonn Morrison, who had heard the wagon at night, and then had made the mistake of looking at it, was gone forever.

Eamonn left his family an inheritance of the wagon story, and thirty pounds in a kitchen pot. The year was 1869. Florence Morrison, twenty-five, took her share of the inheritance, and the only good dress she owned, a long clinging dress knit by the women of her village, and went to the docks at Magilligan Point, where the steam packets slid out into the North Atlantic for the trip to New York. As the ship approached the dock at Castle Gardens, the predecessor to Ellis Island, Florence put on her dress and joined a crowd on deck that appeared dressed for Easter Sunday. Throughout all of immigration to America, virtually no one—from Irish maid and farmer to German brewery worker to Jewish seamstress from Poland—debarked at New York in anything less than frills and flowers. These were not huddled masses in torn clothes; they were men in shirts and ties and women in holiday finery, who understood the show of dignity.

Florence Morrison lived for months on Mulberry Street in the Five Points slum of Manhattan and did so poorly she began to think of Burtonport as livable. She scrubbed floors in a bank and gave it up as a bad job. One night, her red hair brushed till it blazed, she walked many blocks to the Blind Beggar on Rector Street and brazenly took a place barside, where she had just started a pint when a Tweed politician, Gerry Corcoran, a bulky man with dark, mean eyes whose political duties consisted of beating up people, sauntered into the bar. At first, he smirked at this low-class woman at the bar, for he was used to standing alongside the rich. Condescension subsided as his prick rose. Corcoran bought Florence a drink, inquired of her background, and then boasted of personal influence so great that it spanned the ocean. Anybody in Ireland need only board a ship armed with Corcoran's name, the mention of which in New York, at the Board of Water Supply, created immediate employment. Corcoran then decreed that Florence Morrison was so beautiful that he was in love with her and wanted to buy her a new wardrobe for city life. He swept her out of the bar and into a room at the Hotel Piedmont, where he subsequently fell asleep. Florence Morrison remained awake. Some regard this as an advantage. Florence slipped out of bed, dressed, and, rather than risk awakening the thug and have him find her going through his pockets right in the room, took his suit, shirt, underwear, socks, and shoes and went downstairs, to an alley alongside the Hotel Piedmont, where, in his pockets, she found two hundred dollars, money for a lifetime. She took the clothes back to Five Points and sold the suit for two dollars. By the time Gerry Corcoran, snorting like a bull, appeared on the street in bare feet, the big toes sticking up so as not to step on a broken bottle, his bare body wrapped in a blanket with the name Hotel Piedmont emblazoned across the back, Florence Morrison was in her room at Five Points, writing, with tremendous effort, a letter to her brother in Burtonport. She told him that wealth was everywhere in New York and that he had only to appear and use the name of her friend, Gerry Corcoran, to obtain a job paying high wages. The job, she wrote, was digging a water tunnel.

Six months later, wearing a gray suit jacket belonging to his late father and with a long scarf draped around his neck and not twirled around it as a muffler, despite the cold day, as he wanted all to see his immaculate new shirt, the only shirt with a starched collar he ever had owned, bought from a girl at the factory gate in Derry only hours before boarding the steam packet to New York, here came Johnny Morrison, age twenty-two in the year 1870, walking off the ship and past an immigration officer who said he was a grand lad and needed no papers or questioning. Florence Morrison led her brother to the Board of Water Supply, where a clerk said that Morrison could start work the moment he reached the construction site at Beacon, New York. Which delighted his sister, who felt that if Johnny had one night in a dance hall in Five Points, he would be a permanent guest in her room, an intrusion she intended to go without.

And so Johnny Morrison walked into the construction camp three miles outside the town of Beacon, so delighted with himself at being in America—by Jesus, working already!—that he danced as he walked through the camp gates. Of course, the job he had obtained was so abominable and perilous that the only people who took it were those who belonged working with slaves: Irish fresh off the boat, blacks from the West Indies, and Italians. If he had used Tammany politician Corcoran's name once more, he would have won a night job in hell. As he was Irish, Johnny Morrison was hired at the highest rate of pay, seventy-five cents a day, along with bed and meals. The West Indians, being black, were paid sixty-five cents a day, but as they spoke English, furthermore spoke it with a British accent, they were paid more than the Italians, who couldn't speak the language and were regarded as subhuman, and were thus paid sixty cents for the ten-hour day.

Morrison was shown to a bunk in a hut that slept sixty, including a thin Italian in the next bunk who wore a heavy jacket in bed. The Italian tried to sit up, gasped for air, was exhausted by the effort, and fell back. Morrison was summoned outside, where he boarded a wagon that took him to the shaft and the fourteen-hundred-foot ride down to the tunnel, which most of those working it referred to as "the mine." His first job was to help a man from County Kerry who drilled holes in the rock face. The holes were then stuck with dynamite and the rock face blown up. After the first explosion, Johnny's head became heavy from the nitroglycerin fumes hanging in the air. As Johnny began cleaning up the muck from the explosion, the water dripping onto his head from the coarse-grained roof of rock made him apprehensive. Johnny, growing up in a fisherman's family, had settled on one vision of death: being strangled by freezing water under a wide, nasty sky. Here in the middle of the earth, Johnny suddenly was terrified of death from this gray rock overhead.

When he came out of the mine after his first day, sick from nitroglycerin and claustrophobia, he went to bed without washing. Beside him, the thin Italian was inert.

In the morning, the Italian still would not move. Morrison said to him, "I'd like to be doing the same t'ing." When Morrison returned that night, the Italian's dark eyes were coated. His breath noisily sought cracks in caked lungs. Touching the Italian's forehead, Morrison felt a high turf fire. He went to the camp office to get a doctor. But as it was after six o'clock, only one person was in the office. A fat man armed with a shotgun blocked the door. When Morrison said he wanted to report illness, the guard stepped aside and allowed him to enter. The person at the desk, a rangy man with snowy hair, looked up quickly.

"Don't come too close to me," he said. Frozen blue eyes inspected the dirt on Morrison. "The doctor went home for the night. Be back first thing tomorrow morning," the man said. His eyes returned to his papers.

"I'll go get the doctor," Morrison said.

"Oh no you won't," the clerk said. "He lives all the way into Beacon."

"Is that far?" Morrison said.

"Too far for you," the clerk said. He stood up. He was a full six inches taller than Morrison. "I'll give you something that will get the man through the night," the clerk said. He went to the closet and brought out a heavy gray blanket. "The sick rate some concern," he said, handing the blanket to Morrison and dismissing him at the same time.

At the door, Morrison turned around and said, "I'd like to thank you by name."

"I'm Mr. Frayer."

"Thank you, Mr. Frayer."

The clerk went back to his papers. Morrison went to the hut and placed the blanket over the young Italian, who was barely conscious and unable to respond to soft word or touch. Throughout the night the Italian wheezed and intermittently gasped. Once, a huge black got up cursing and padded over to the Italian's bed. He grasped the Italian's nose between his fingers.

"I got to teach this *mon* how to breathe."

"Your *mon* here is sick," Morrison said, his accent as thick as the black's, each with the heritage of colonization by the same harsh-accented people from northern England.

"Let him be sick by hisself," the black said, still holding the nose. "He makes me wake up."

Morrison swung out of bed and pulled the black's hand off the nose. For a moment, the two stood on either side of the bunk and speculated on the outcome of a fight. Then both stepped back in the darkness and flopped back in their bunks, which had grown cold in the night air. Morrison fell asleep to the Italian's irregular wheezing. Awakened at dawn for work in the tunnel, Morrison hurriedly said to the Italian, "The doctor should be here any minute." Then he went outside and caught the horse wagon for the mine.

When he returned later that day, the bunk was empty. Got him into a hospital, Morrison said to himself. After dinner he walked to the office, stood in the doorway, and called in to Frayer, "How is my *mon?*"

"Who?" Frayer said, not looking up.

"The Eyetalian."

"Oh. Poor boy died today. It was too late by the time the doctor saw him. The boy was dead by noon, they tell me."

"Is it after telling me that he'd be here sooner than the sun?"

"He arrived at his usual time. First thing after he finished rounds of his own patients. At least that's what I'm told. I wasn't here, of course; I was home in bed as all this was happening. I sleep during the day. Now I must tend to my work all night." With a wave he dismissed Morrison.

Outside, Morrison went to the front gate where two armed men sat in front of a fire.

"Where's a pub?" he asked.

"Two miles down."

"That's for me," Morrison said.

"You sure can't go," the guards said.

"You can be full sure I will."

"Not while we're here. None of you can leave the camp at night."

Morrison walked through the dark toward his hut, then simply strolled off into the woods and came out on a road that, after he had walked fast for several minutes, brought him to a crossroads, on one corner of which sat a low building with amber gas lamps in the windows and a sign advertising whiskey. Inside, two men sat at the small wooden bar, which was tended by a young woman whose ease in her surroundings indicated that she probably was the owner's daughter.

"Stand back ye," she said, both hands waving, as Morrison approached.

"I'll only be havin' a pint."

"Not here you won't. Back off now."

For the first time in his young life, Morrison's feet were uncertain on a barroom floor.

"We serve no tunnel workers," the barmaid said. "Please get out. You'll bring us Fenian bugs all around."

"I'm a bug, am I?" Morrison said.

"You carry bugs. You Fenians go down in the tunnel and come out covered with bugs. Roaches. You brought roaches to every house in Beacon. We never had a roach in Beacon until you Fenians came. You're just dirty people who don't mind being covered with roaches. Well, you can't stay here. It's against the law for you people to be out of the camp anyway."

"Law?" Morrison said.

"We had to start a police force around here to keep the lot of you away from the town," she said. "Now be off!" Her voice rose to a shriek.

Morrison left and stood outside for a moment. He saw lights in the distance through the woods and he walked toward them. Soon he was on the first streets of Beacon, hard dirt streets lined with clapboard houses, the dirt streets turning into cobblestones and the houses into shops in the downtown part. Morrison walked through shadows with his eyes searching for a light that would indicate a saloon.

"Here now."

Two men were standing under a streetlamp. Morrison glanced at them and started to walk on, but then he saw one of them raise a rifle.

"Stand fast, scum," the man said.

Now Morrison saw that the two of them wore silver badges.

"You're from the water tunnel?" the one holding the gun said.

"I don't know," Morrison said.

"Why, I know by looking at the dirt caked all over you," the gun man said. "Don't you know it's against the law for you people to be in this town? Stand clear of me, covered with mud like you are."

Morrison was thrown in the back of a wagon, and the two Beacon cops drove him to the camp, where the night clerk, Frayer, came to the office doorway, his thin lips arranged in a snarl. One arm was kept inside the doorway. "You were specifically told by the gate guards that you were not to leave this camp!" he shouted at Morrison. "It's bad enough that I must sit here exposed to your bugs. Now you've walked through my town. God knows how many roaches you've left. Maybe on the very street where I live."

As Morrison started to walk away, he heard the noise coming through the air behind him and he wanted to throw himself to the ground, but the most he could do was duck his head as Frayer's bullwhip shrieked and struck his back, shredding the jacket and the shirt under it. Morrison's body jerked straight, and he howled into the black night sky. The whip whirred through the air again and tore at his back. He went black with pain and stumbled away, but now the whip came again between his shoulder blades and onto the back of his neck and he threw his hands into the air, reaching for God's help, for he could not endure the pain.

They carried him to his hut and threw him in front of it. Dazed and whimpering, he clung to a tree outside the hut as the pain stung his shredded back. Finally, he made it into his bunk, where he rolled in torment throughout the night. It was not until the afternoon that somebody pointed Morrison out to the doctor, who came over and swabbed and bandaged his back. Six days later, Morrison was able to walk out of the hut. It was morning and he was wearing his new shirt from Derry; his work clothes had been torn to bits by Frayer's whipping. Shivering, he watched as Frayer left the office at the end of his overnight stint and rode off in a brougham. Morrison then walked into the office and told the day clerk on duty that he had promised Frayer that he would do personal work on his house in Beacon, but that he had misplaced the address.

"Has he gone mad?" the day clerk said. "You'll leave Fenian bugs all over his house."

"He told me to take a shower first," Morrison said. "We understand each other now."

"I guess you sure should," the day clerk said. "Harry Frayer lives at Fifteen Selby Street. Yellow house, two in from the corner of Haymarket."

"I'll use the shower," Morrison said.

He walked through the gates, left unguarded by day, and went into Beacon and found Frayer's house. The front door was unlocked and Morrison slid in, listened for house noises and heard none, and then crawled upstairs. Frayer was asleep on his back in a bedroom dark from thick-draped windows. He had a shotgun next to him on the far side of the bed. Morrison thought that if he tiptoed to the bed, the wood might squeak and awaken Frayer, who would grab for the shotgun. Morrison thought about rushing the bed, but felt this noise, too, would wake up Frayer in time to grab for the shotgun. Morrison tiptoed downstairs and started a roaring log fire on the wood floor in front of the living room fireplace. He went into the kitchen and started a second log fire on the floor alongside the stove. Morrison left the house on a dead run, the fire's first crackling sounding behind him. He had no idea whether Frayer lived or died in the fire. Either way, that's the last time that whore's get will be whipping somebody. He went to the railroad station and, using the last of his money from Ireland, bought a ticket to New York.

Morrison fell asleep with his face pressed against the window. He awoke as the steam train was inside the tunnel under Park Avenue. When he arrived at Grand Central Station, his eyes were dazzled by the crowds of men in rich overcoats who strode through the pale, smoky light coming from glass panes hundreds of feet overhead. Morrison went downtown by trolley and found his sister on Mulberry Street. Morrison told her about Frayer from Beacon. "Maybe I didn't kill him," Morrison said with eyes that were fairly exploding with hope.

"Maybe he died and they'll come hang you," the sister said.

"You best loan me some money and I'll take the boat home," Morrison said.

"I loaned you money to get here," the sister said. "You'll have me goin' without food now."

"Then I stay here and risk my neck," Morrison said.

He walked the streets of the Five Points neighborhood until a bar owner named Divers, who was from the town of Muff, in Donegal, hired him as a bar boy. The owner's last name, and the town he was from, a small village stuck into a hill above Loch Foyle, created much schoolboy humor in the barroom. Morrison, fearful that each stranger walking in was a policeman from Beacon, spent most of his time ducking his head under the bar, arranging bottles on shelves. "He's a muff-diver all right," the customers shrieked as they saw Morrison's head disappearing. At first, Morrison didn't understand what it meant. When he did, he was vaulting over the bar to defend his honor so often that he wound up with the face of an old tomcat.

At the same time, his insides winced every time he thought of his possible murder of Frayer up at Beacon. He dared not confess the act, as he thought the priest, as penance, would command him to face the authorities. Occasionally Morrison had to receive communion, a sacrament for those purified by confession, lest all in church stare at him and then whisper furiously to each other that he had committed some monstrous sin that prevented him from walking up to the rail and receiving the Lord's body. Therefore, Morrison now and then made a bad communion, which is perhaps the darkest act of all.

Late one spring night, a few days after making a bad communion at Easter, Morrison was morosely mopping the saloon floor after closing hours. A waitress named Annie sat in the darkness in the table area and sobbed. Morrison walked over and sat down with her. "What's the matter?" he asked.

"I'm pregnant," she cried.

"That's wonderful."

"I've no husband."

"Well, did you tell the boy?"

Annie's voice rose to a full wail. "I can't find him."

"When is this baby coming?"

Annie pulled her sweater up and showed a bulge. "The doctor says I'm five months gone."

"Why did you wait so long?" Morrison said.

"I thought it would go away if I didn't look at it," Annie said. She dissolved in tears.

"Stop crying," Morrison said. "I'll marry you."

She looked up in astonishment.

"Meet me at eleven o'clock tomorrow morning in front of City Hall and we'll buy a marriage license. Now stop crying. I've got to be about my work," Morrison said.

The next day Annie stood in front of City Hall, certain the bar boy would not show. But at eleven o'clock, his smile as good as his word, Johnny Morrison skipped up, grabbed her hand, and led her to the marriage clerk's office. They were married on a Wednesday in St. James' Church by a priest who saw that the bride had her future well in front of her by now, and therefore he gazed only at her face to avoid embarrassment for all. Four months to the day and hour later, she gave birth to a daughter, whom she named Jean.

Annie clutched the baby in her hospital bed and looked up at Morrison and thought of him as totally heroic. Johnny, who had trouble standing still for more than a few moments in such circumstances, went for a walk. His sister Florence remained.

"I have to say to you," she said.

"What's that?" Annie said.

"That his heart is good but it also wanders."

"He's young," Annie said.

"He's part of this family. Jesus, there's not a one of them ever behaved."

"The drink," Annie said.

"Oh, they can't get enough of it. Then they disappear. They're great, but they're not reliable."

"How can you be talking? You're one of them."

"That's why I'm telling you. They drink and then they disappear either with a woman or with more drink. Who knows it better than me?"

Florence Morrison was telling the truth. By now, she was married to a man named O'Gara, who had a grocery store over in the Chelsea section. Waiting for her downstairs in the hospital lobby was a cheap but thoroughly enjoyable horse bookmaker from Brighton Beach in Brooklyn, with whom she intended to spend the afternoon while her husband was busy selling cold cuts and potato salad.

Pacing in the hallway, Johnny Morrison, new father, was assessing his fortunes. First, his soul felt cleansed; by marrying Annie and saving her daughter from a life of illegitimacy, he had made amends, just in case the night clerk Frayer actually had been killed in Beacon. Furthermore, as Annie had not been a virgin upon their marriage night, he was entitled to snuggle with women whenever his chase was successful. Had she known this as she lay in her bed with her baby on this day, rather than idolize him, she would have wished upon Johnny Morrison some form of torture.

Annie took her daughter home to rooms on Catherine Street and Johnny Morrison blew down the streets like a bright cloud. He was generally ecstatic, because he was in love with several women, and at home he had a wife who cared for him very much, and who had been told of the Morrisons' habits but had neglected to retain the lecture. Instead Annie thought the marriage was composed of kind notes. Meanwhile, Johnny Morrison managed saloons and, deep in the night, while drinking so much that his legs buckled, he kept hearing the sound of a wagon, but in his mind he changed this to a gay pony trap, pony festooned with ribbons, the back seat of the trap taken up by a large jug of *taus an puta,* which is the top of the home-distilled whiskey, the moonshine, the first whiskey through the copper tubing and thus of such strength that Johnny could drink it in the heart of winter and look at a snowbank and see flowers.

He laughed one night when he heard the rumble of a wagon outside the saloon on Fulton Street and then, looking out the window, saw a garbage wagon going by slowly. "Be off with you," Johnny said, waving in disdain. To prove he had no fear, he walked home that night in the middle of the street. When nothing happened to him the next day, he proclaimed the old story out of Donegal was a lie. As he drank, the whiskey turned to cement inside his liver.

He and Annie had had a son, Kevin, born in 1872. Added responsibility meant added whiskey; the hardened liver now slowed every part of his body except the glass hand, which moved so swiftly that Johnny always appeared to be in a rowing race. Of course, by 1880, at age thirty-two, he turned as yellow as a crocus and was buried in Yorkville. He had not been around long enough even to leave dreams.

Annie Morrison came back from the cemetery to her rooms on Catherine Street, put her black veil on the dresser, looked at her son and daughter and wondered what they were thinking of, how they saw their tragedy, and then she knew it was time to look ahead; there was no food for dinner on this same night. There wasn't a dollar in the house. At the funeral, several bar owners and bartenders had been generous in offers of buying drinks for the bereaved family, but all fled at the suggestion that more substantive assistance was needed.

Her sister-in-law, Florence Morrison, by now a mother of three, and firmly attached to O'Gara's grocery store and its world, knew enough to bring food, and later paid the rent a couple of times. She helped Annie get a job at her old trade, saloon waitress. The children went to bed early each night and the mother went to a saloon until dawn. Her short but tiring years, and the grief they had brought with them, had weakened Annie's underpinnings so much so that on many nights she simply had neither interior spirit nor legs free enough of pain to allow her to work. She began losing jobs.

One day, Florence took the daughter Jean far uptown, to a great stone mansion on the corner of 69th and Fifth, a place with a wrought iron fence and a gate in front of a high stoop that led to a doorway lit by lamps. It belonged to a family named Bigelow. Florence Morrison stood in front for a moment, checked the address on the slip of paper in her hand, and then walked Jean around to the back. She banged on a door on the side of a high stoop. A young boy, fourteen perhaps, hair falling into his face, looked out.

"What is it you want?"

"Mrs. McCallum."

"The chief kitchen maid, is it?"

"I think so," Florence said.

The young boy looked at Jean. "Jesus, you'll hate it."

"Hate what?" Jean said.

"Hate here."

He was gone and a husky woman with red cheeks and auburn hair, her wide midsection covered with an apron, appeared. Florence Morrison immediately began to sell Jean's ability to work speedily, to pay attention, and to show humility at all times. The chief kitchen maid was quite interested. At this time in New York, it was common to hire a ten-year-old girl for kitchen work, for factory work, or for any work that paid almost nothing and could be done by someone who did not have a powerful body.

Ten-year-old boys often went to work at their fathers' jobs. It was common to see a father and son shoveling concrete into a wheelbarrow, or for a father and son to be unloading bananas from a freighter. Sometimes, the boys stumbled a bit under the loads, but as they grew older, to be twelve and thirteen, and their shoulder widths increased, they were able to work with less strain.

Now, in the kitchen of this Fifth Avenue mansion, the chief maid, Mrs. McCallum, said that, yes, she thought the household could use this promising girl worker. Jean Morrison, clutching her doll, was given a paper bag full of underwear and nightclothes by her aunt, and then a kiss and the aunt was gone. Jean was astonished at the size of the stoves and number of brown wooden iceboxes in the large, gloomy kitchen. The maid walked Jean to a windowless room that was so narrow only a child could fit between the bed and the wall. She pulled a long string to light a small bulb high up on a ceiling that was dark with smoke. "Don't you like it?" Mrs. McCallum said. She was a fat Scotswoman.

"When is my auntie comin' to fetch me?" Jean said.

"First, you'll put your dolly on the bed and you'll come with me," the maid said.

She led Jean to a large wooden icebox, one of three in a pantry. "First off, ye'll take everything out of the icebox. Then ye'll get yourself a brush and pail of water and soap and ye'll scrub the box till ye can hold yer dolly's face to the insides and see how she looks."

"Will me auntie be here by then?"

"Be off with your auntie. Ye'll start earnin' yer keep now."

The fat Scotswoman handed Jean a pail and brush and left. It was two in the afternoon. The girl opened the icebox and emptied the milk and beer bottles, butter, boxes of strawberries, vegetables, huge steaks wrapped in butcher's paper, and a large turkey. She placed them all on the floor. At the top of the icebox there was a large cake of ice.

"Ye'll take that out, too," the chief maid said. Jean tugged at the ice, found the piece was too heavy, and then looked at a young man, who was almost fourteen, who had on a neat white linen jacket for serving. "Help me lift the ice out?" Jean said.

"He'll do no such thing," the chief maid said. "He's dressed for servin' in the parlor."

"I can't lift it out," Jean said.

"Then ye'll wait till it melts."

Jean sat on the floor and waited while the block of ice diminished in the muggy kitchen air. She never looked down, where the drip pan under the icebox became full and the cold water slopped over the sides, until suddenly Jean found all her food on the floor, the vegetables and steaks, sopping with ice water.

The chief maid let out a shriek. "Ye've ruined the food! That'll come out of yer pay."

Jean was scrubbing the icebox and the floor around it until six o'clock at night. At which time she was summoned to a wooden table in one corner of the kitchen and given a piece of bread and an egg mixed with turnips. When she finished, she stood up.

"Thank you," she said. "Is me auntie comin' now?"

"No. But the dishes'll be comin' soon. Set ye down and wait for them."

That night Jean stood on her tiptoes at a large sink and scrubbed pots. Once, walking a pot over to the stove, she brushed against a tray of crystal glasses, causing one of them to drop to the floor and break.

"The Waterford!" Mrs. McCallum yelled.

Her hand spread and she hit Jean on top of the head and caused the little girl to black out for a moment. Later, the chief maid walked Jean to the narrow bedroom, opened the door, and said, "In you go."

Jean fell asleep with her doll in the crook of her arm. She was awakened at six-thirty in the morning and was given the job of slicing oranges and squeezing juice.

On the following Thursday, at noon, her aunt arrived and Jean yelped in joy. The aunt held a finger to her lips to indicate silence and then went in and spoke to Mrs. McCallum, who was inspecting the food shelves. The aunt then came back and took Jean by the hand and led her out of the house.

"Why did you leave me?" Jean said.

"Oh, I didn't leave you, child. That's where you stay from now on.

That's yer job. I have to tell you, you can't afford to break any more glasses. They're paying you sixty cents a day, but the glass cost three dollar twenty. They charged ye fer it, and the food you ruined, too. So ye got no pay."

Jean was at home with her mother, Annie, from one in the afternoon until five in the evening. When her brother, Kevin, returned from school, Jean was elated to see him and they ate dinner together and were talking about going out to play when their aunt arrived and said it was time for Jean to get back to the Bigelow mansion. Jean screamed and tried to cling to her mother, and then reached for her brother, but Florence yanked her away and led her, bawling, out of the rooms on Catherine Street and back up to the mansion, where the Scotswoman greeted her with a smile. "Yer in time for the last of the dishes. Shooo."

She was to remain in the mansion for five years and become part of the children's asylums in the shadowy kitchens of nearly every great mansion in the city. The rich acclaimed the style of their butlers, and were proud of their number of maids, but they never spoke of the kitchen children, illiterate, faces without color, spirits splintered by the drudgery of the days.

Once, she poked one swinging door in the kitchen and when it swung open, she found herself in a short passageway, which she stepped along silently and then found herself in a long room with burning lamps in the corners and a long dining table, covered with crisp linen. Maids in new uniforms were setting places under the direction of the butler, a short, chunky man with black curly hair. When the butler noticed Jean, he was instantly offended.

"Will someone please *remove* this child?"

As Jean retreated from the burning lights, she heard the butler snap, "Next you shall allow the *hairdresser* to pass through the front of the house."

In her years of servitude, this was the closest Jean came to being in the presence of the masters of the house, the Bigelow family, or the elegance in which they lived. They were unknown gods, unthinkable that she would ever see them, and with the only reminders of them in the kitchen being the silverware and Waterford crystal.

As Annie Morrison grew weaker with an illness nobody could determine —and as a result she worked only sporadically—the aunt, Florence, assumed more control. One day when Kevin, the son, was almost ten years old, she took him out of school at lunch and brought him to a lumberyard on Water Street, where he was hired for $1.40 a week. He had a sister in a kitchen and he was in a lumberyard, thus making the Morrisons a family of American workers.

There were no child labor laws at this time; nothing really effective was passed until 1938. There was only the spirit of Horatio Alger, which was advanced as the national answer to sorrow. The great Horatio Alger story formula told of young men like Ben the Bootblack, who glanced up from shining shoes to spot a runaway horse that was about to trample to horrible death the beautiful young daughter of a multimillionaire banker. Ben the Bootblack dropped his shoeshine rag and rushed gallantly into the street, risking his meaningless life in order to save the banker's daughter. Of course, Ben the Bootblack then kept his eyes down in the daughter's presence, rather than taking the opportunity to molest the banker's daughter, as he certainly had the right to do. As a reward for all this, the multimillionaire banker praised Ben the Bootblack, ordered him to throw away his shoeshine rag and report to the bank, where he worked happily ever after as one of a hundred thankful clerks who put in fifty hours a week at desks in dusty air and for a rate of pay that was never mentioned, as the numbers looked too small in print.

In the lumberyard, Kevin Morrison struggled each day with long pieces of wood; sweeping was his only relaxation. He found it difficult to understand that the big men, some of them as old as thirty, working in the lumberyard did not much like it when Kevin threw wood chips around to have fun. A couple of clouts across the legs with a heavy stick taught him to tend to business, just as a whip smacking a racehorse between the ears is supposed to make him concentrate on running. Kevin walked home at night, his hair white with sawdust.

One night in her fifteenth year, one of the kitchen boys, an eighteen-year-old, slipped into Jean Morrison's bedroom at the mansion, fell atop her, and pushed her legs apart. The act was unknown to her and the pain and the boy were gone quickly. On another night, after a huge party in the mansion, the job of polishing silver and putting away Waterford vases lasted until two A.M. Jean was sweaty and exhausted and a man in a tuxedo opened the bedroom door and, preceded by the smell of wine, walked in and removed his pants and got into bed with her. He reached for her, then fell asleep with his hand on her stomach. Jean was afraid to hurt the man's feelings and remained still. Sometime before dawn, the man awoke, eyes red and watery, and seemed appalled to find himself where he was. He immediately resumed pawing her. He got on her, had intercourse, and then stood up to dress.

"Thank you, dear."

That Thursday, when she went home, she wailed upon entering the rooms on Catherine Street. Her mother, who was, as usual, in bed sick, asked her what was the matter, but got only tears as an answer. Then her aunt Florence came over and the two women talked to the girl and finally Jean wailed out something that caused the two women to gasp. Kevin Morrison, trying to listen, couldn't make out what they were saying. Then his aunt stepped out of the bedroom, and told him, "Don't you worry about it. This has nothing to do with you. Some evil people up there touched her, that's all. I'll have something to say to *them.*"

Kevin went into the bedroom and said to his sister, "Somebody hit you?"

She nodded. He ran out of the Catherine Street building with change in his pocket and took a horse-drawn trolley toward the suburban section of the city, to the corner of 69th and Fifth.

Where, at the noon hour, he rang the front doorbell of the Bigelow mansion, not understanding there was a rear door, and when a footman opened it, Kevin slipped past him, ran into the house, was momentarily stunned by the furniture and rugs and chandeliers, and then raced about, looking for the kitchen, while the shouting footman chased. Kevin went through the dining room and a short passage to the swinging door, which he exploded through, looking for someone obviously evil enough to hit his sister. There was one scullery maid and a young boy of fourteen or so. Now the footman entered the kitchen and Kevin grabbed a large knife from a carving block and swung around.

"What is it?" the footman said.

"One of ye hit me sister."

A smirk came on the footman's long face. He walked up to Kevin Morrison, ignored the knife, and slapped Kevin on the left side of his head. Slapped hard. The footman intended the next slap to be even harder. Kevin stabbed the hand before it got to him. He tried to push the knife right through the hand and the footman started a long scream.

In the noise, Kevin went out the back door and was soon racing down streets he never had seen. He did not get to Catherine Street until late evening. His sister was still there, and the aunt was trying to get her to return to the mansion.

"I stabbed the fooker that hit her," Kevin announced.

At this point, the aunt realized that there was no way to take Jean back. She left her on Catherine Street. Where, outside on the street, ten days later, she met a young man named Willie. As she had nothing to do, and neither did he, they strolled down to the docks and after quitting time for the men, at four-thirty, the two went onto Pier 44, East River, and had sex in the late afternoon sun on the coffee sacks.

It didn't take Jean very long to become pregnant by somebody, and four months later, she was living at Catherine Street with a bulging stomach, a mother who by now was completely bedridden with her mysterious ailment, and a brother, Kevin, who was still doing boy's work in the lumberyard. Florence Morrison, summoned to the house, took one look at Jean's midsection and clapped a hand to her mouth.

"I guess the lot of us is grandparents," she said, sighing.

She then took Kevin Morrison to the office of the Board of Water Supply, whose clerks listened as she told of the family heritage in the city's water supply, omitting the news that her brother, Johnny, had worked only long enough to incinerate, or certainly singe, the night clerk at Beacon. They hired Kevin for a job at the Croton site. Two days later, he walked through the pale light of Grand Central Station, as had his father, Johnny. Kevin looked at the shirts worn by the men who rushed through the crowded station. Spotless and stiff. They make thousands and don't even get the shirt dirty. He wondered how many shirts men such as these owned. Probably no more than two. Look at this one fellow here. He can make it through a week with what he has on; doesn't even move enough during the day to get the armpits moist.

He took the train to the Croton Reservoir, which was fifteen miles into Westchester County, and became one of hundreds of laborers building a gravity dam with cyclopean masonry. Plans called for the dam to go down one hundred fifty feet into soundrock, widening at the base. The top of the dam was to climb one hundred forty feet up from the water it held back, twenty million gallons of rainwater that ran to the reservoir on the magic land that dropped one foot in each ten thousand as it sloped toward the city.

He lived in a work camp, and on the first payday he went with a crowd down to Willis Avenue, in the South Bronx. There was a line of bars, and the streets were crowded with Irish. He was instantly at home, and he never made it below 138th Street and Willis Avenue again, except for the funeral of his mother. It was held in Chelsea and his aunt Florence and her husband, O'Gara, the grocer, were in charge. Jean was there with her baby. She had been tending the grocery store counter while Florence cared for the baby. After the funeral, he went back to his job in Croton and his life on Willis Avenue. He was eighteen when he met Kathy Gallagher, who lived in a brownstone on Willis Avenue that was inhabited by tunnel workers, who called themselves sandhogs, and unmarried schoolteachers of some age. One of them, Rose O'Neill, who lived in the apartment next to the Gallagher family, taught their prospective son-in-law, Kevin Morrison, the forgotten art of reading. Working at the kitchen table at night, she noted the speed with which Kevin stepped from being able to pick out the words "can't do it" to realizing immediately that "can't" meant that whatever it was they were talking about could not be done. He could be suited for more, she said, but then she looked over at him. He was rubbing against Kathy Gallagher, plainly yearning to get on top of her right at the table. When he talked he concentrated on the money he could make as a sandhog. Sufficient that he can read and write, the old schoolteacher decided.

When Kevin Morrison married Kathy Gallagher a year later, they moved into a rooming house whose owner, in need of a superintendent, offered the job to Kevin, who refused, since shaking down a furnace at night and putting out ashes was in direct conflict with his nightly occupation of being a paying customer at the Keeper Hill Lounge, number 412 Willis Avenue. When at work one day, deep in the tunnel under the dam, Morrison's friend, Jerry Barry, who was here three months from Donegal, turned off his acetylene torch at the tip but left the tank open. Lit up like he deserved a good smoke for himself. Lit up in a tight chamber far under a reservoir. Barry blew straight up through the roof and into the water. Later, standing on the gravel shore, somebody spotted Barry out in the reservoir. The head was bobbing along, the face looking up, with sometimes no water covering the face at all, looking up at the sky as the water swept it toward the gate in the dam that led to the tunnel to the city. Somebody handed Morrison a pole with a small net on it and said, "Well, this is about all you'll need to fish Barry out of the water." It was. When Morrison picked it up in the net, the man rowing the boat looked at the head in the net and said, "I guess he sure left a sour taste in the drinking water."

That night, Morrison carried out the ashes from the rooming house for the first time. He felt that if anything happened to him on his regular job, his wife of six months could take over as janitor and have a place to live. He may have thought about her at other times during their years together, but he had an extraordinary ability to mask such things.

Kevin Morrison had auburn hair and blue eyes, and was of average size for an Irishman, five foot five. At this time one could always tell an Irish saloon, for the ceiling lamps hung dangerously low, yet only by leaping upward could any customer ever hit his head. Kevin Morrison became famous on Willis Avenue for his tactic of remaining docile at the bar, no matter what words were hurled at him, and if fists were thrown, he always slipped the punches and walked away, and then at six the next morning, auburn hair neatly brushed, he would knock on the offending party's door and, depending on how he felt, might or might not say something before throwing a punch at the man with a hangover who answered the door. Kevin Morrison also carried the water bucket for and worked in the corner of the most famous person in the neighborhood, Frankie McCann, a bantamweight fighter who, seeking aid from those places far beyond the sky, took the name of his parish church, St. Immaculata, as his ring name. Fighting as Frankie Immaculata, and weighing 116 pounds, he was thrown in over his head with a man named Jack McAuliffe, from Cork city. When Immaculata came back to the corner at the end of the ninth round, during which he had absorbed a frightening number of punches, Kevin Morrison jumped up the steps and swung into the ring and held the bottle of water to Immaculata's mouth. Immaculata had trouble finding the neck of the bottle with his mouth. Kevin Morrison then held out a tin pail so Immaculata could spit out the water. Immaculata bent toward the bucket, but then spit the water into the canvas several inches to the side of the bucket.

"Is he all right?" Morrison said to the manager.

"Mind your business," snarled the manager. He then started to snarl at Immaculata for not landing more punches.

In the middle of the twelfth round, Jack McAuliffe hit Immaculata with three left hooks and the drops of sweat and water from Immaculata's head sprayed out into the seats. Kevin Morrison, crouched at the bottom of the steps, suddenly flew up to the ring and was going through the ropes with his hands out to stop the fight by himself, when McAuliffe, working close to Immaculata, his shoes squeaking, threw a right hand that sent Immaculata onto his back. His head banged against the canvas. He died in the ring.

That night, Morrison sat in the fighter's kitchen and ate potatoes with the jackets on while the parents prayed in the living room for their dead son and waited for St. Immaculata's to open for the day.

At six A.M. Kevin Morrison left for work. At eleven that morning a cable slipped and a stone weighing many tons crashed onto Eddie Leary, who had been trying to guide the stone down. Leary's right arm was under the stone. His left arm was free. The left arm whipped once through the air like a windmill. Leary's scream ran across the rocks on the roof of the tunnel. Then Leary's voice died and the arm stopped swinging.

They kill us all over the lot, Kevin Morrison said to himself.

He had three daughters who would be married, but of course, that was the mother's worry. He waited until finally a son, Harry, arrived with the new century. A second son, Jack, was born a year later, but Kevin concentrated on Harry, who attended St. Luke's Grammar School on East 138th Street. At night, Kevin Morrison paced the kitchen floor until Harry was finished with his homework, something Kevin had never done himself. Kevin then initialed it, placing his K.M. directly alongside the "J.M.J." for Jesus, Mary, and Joseph, which his son was obliged to use as a heading for each homework page. At graduation, Kevin Morrison stood with another proud father, a plumber. The man's arm was draped proudly around his son George's shoulder. George had graduated with Kevin Morrison's son, Harry.

The man said, "He goes right into the union apprentice program. He'll be a plumber, won't you, son?"

George nodded happily.

Kevin Morrison said loudly, "Mine goes on to more schooling. He's going to be the first to work in a shirt."

He sent his son to All Hallows High School in the Bronx, and demanded that thoughts of beer, or the wrong side of a girl's skirt, should be kept out of his mind.

Then one day in 1917, Kevin Morrison, forty-five, the second male Morrison to work at tunnels, was on a job that started in the Van Cortlandt Park section of the Bronx. One morning, the man working next to Morrison, Eddie Hughes, was walking toward a water hose, not bothering to pick his way over the rocks, but walking quickly, for he knew he had to hurry to keep his job. He slipped and fractured an ankle. Two days later, an electric cable caught fire and as smoke poured into the tunnel, the younger workers ran for the shaft and made it out, but a worker named Larkins, in his fifties, his belly heaving, collapsed and died in the fumes before they could carry him out. The miners blamed poor safety precautions. The foreman and contractors blamed Larkins's age and weight. A month later, Kevin Morrison didn't get his hand out of the way of a mud bucket quickly enough, and he lost the tips of two fingers. White with pain, he took the lift up to the top.

On Willis Avenue later that day, Kevin Morrison, his hand thickly bandaged, ran into Johnny McGuire, one of the foremen, who was from Donegal and thus a friend. "My kid, he can work like the wind," Kevin said.

"That's what a boss wants these days," McGuire said.

At four the next morning, Kevin Morrison woke up his son Harry and handed him the rubber boots and oilskin slicker of a miner. "You can pass up school for a time; we've all we can do to eat in this house, even with me working," he told the boy. Harry Morrison, seventeen, went up to the shaft, was sent down to work by McGuire, and never left the job. Following the family custom, he made it to Grand Central Station once: remaining too long at a bar near the job in the Bronx one afternoon, he fell onto a New York Central local intending to ride two stops. He fell asleep and the train came down through the Bronx and deposited him in Grand Central. As he had not showered after work, he was still covered with mud as he stood at the bar alongside commuters heading for Westchester and Connecticut. Growing more resentful by the swallow, Harry Morrison announced, "You're all a whore's get."

"And you're through for the night," the bartender said, removing Harry's glass.

Harry, too young for World War I, worked in a bullet factory in Yonkers, and when the shooting ended he returned to mining tunnels. He was a bit backward on dance floors, but bold in Willis Avenue saloons and downright famous for his demeanor in hallways when escorting girls home. One night, the prettiest girl on 144th Street, Emily Daly, fell in love with him even as he pushed against her so hard that she was afraid her back would splinter her own doorway. They were blessed, as were the bartenders on Willis Avenue, with only one child, a son, Jimmy, born in 1925.

Five years later, Harry's foreman, McGuire, ran for union office and Harry Morrison participated in the election as a highly trusted worker— his young jawbone was stout enough to withstand the usual flurry of punches that was the highlight of any election meeting. Because of this, McGuire, when victorious, chose Harry to drive with him to St. Louis for a union convention in which the New York miners were attempting to break away from an international laborers' union that was run by hoodlums out of Chicago.

After checking into the hotel in St. Louis, they drove over to the West Side, the black neighborhood, to the Castle Hotel, a three-story wood structure with a wide porch. Seated on the porch, a beer in his hand, and a couple of women looking at him speculatively, was Amos Mabry, the black delegate from the New York sandhogs. Mabry had taken the train out, for the idea of driving into a white town each night and being unable to find a room was more than he could handle. Mabry was from the island of Grenada, and he was the largest and most vocal of the blacks working the job, who kept entering the union during times when there were enough jobs atop the ground to allow whites to sneer at mining, leaving vacancies for someone like Mabry, whose first thought was a meal, not the danger involved in obtaining it.

McGuire then drove back to their hotel, and in the lobby he cautioned Morrison, "These fellows around here would take the milk out of your tea." Later, the hoodlums from the international brought a suitcase full of money to McGuire's hotel room. Either take the money or we come back for you with a machine gun, they intimated.

"I never took a nail off the job," McGuire told them.

"What's that supposed to mean?" one of the hoodlums said.

"It means you got a whore's pay in your hands. Go out and give it to some whore."

At that moment Harry Morrison became so overwhelmed by the purity of the experience that he was certain it would govern the rest of his life, which he felt would be an immaculate and glorious one. He then went to a speakeasy behind the hotel, where he ordered a drink. He was insulted when the bartender said that a man on the other side of the bar, one of the hoodlums from Chicago, wanted to pay for the drink. Harry Morrison threw a five-dollar bill on the bar. He immediately gagged when the bartender took a dollar five out for the drink, twice the price of the best drink on Willis Avenue. Harry Morrison finished his first drink, then sure felt like another. As he decided that his honor had been well established by now, he said to the bartender, "Now I'll take that drink with that fellow." Harry nodded his head toward the hoodlum on the other side of the bar.

The next day, at the opening of the convention, Harry walked into the old, smoky Labor Lyceum Hall alongside Mabry while, sitting in the rows of wooden folding chairs, squinting in the heavy smoke, strangled by shirt collars, wanting to hit somebody, the delegates from places like Cicero, Illinois, felt their insides swell in aggravation at the sight of this black nigger bastard walking down the aisle wearing a delegate badge.

Instantly delighted, Harry pushed his way through a crowd and found

McGuire, who was standing with his ear cocked as Melvin Wise, the labor lawyer he had hired, spoke to him.

"I got something important to say," Harry said.

McGuire looked at him.

"All the guineas are going crazy because we brought a nigger."

"Then we ought to have more niggers," McGuire said.

The lawyer's lips pursed in distaste. "Don't use that language, please."

"What language?" Harry said.

"The type of language you just used."

"What? That I said nigger?"

"Exactly," Wise said.

"What else are you supposed to call them?"

"Negroes."

"I never heard that word in my life. All I ever heard is niggers. Let me ask you a question. What am I supposed to call you?"

"What do you call me now?" Wise said.

"Jew lawyer. What do you want me to say, Catholic lawyer?"

McGuire kept his attention on the Italian delegates from Cicero who were openly rebellious at a seating arrangement that had them within a thousand yards of a black.

"If it drives them this crazy, then we should have come out here with a half a hundred niggers," McGuire said.

He and Harry Morrison then sat on either side of Mabry and were so openly solicitous of him that an Italian from Cicero in the next row turned red as a streetlight and, clutching his chest, had to be assisted out of the row and to a water fountain in the rear. When the convention ended, McGuire returned to New York filled with resolve to see that the sandhogs not only would keep the blacks they had, but would get more, thus placing a dark spear in the side of all these labor leaders who, regarding the sandhogs as ignorant ruffians, would now have another reason to shriek. Best reason on earth, too. If there was one thing that brought everybody together, Irish bricklayer, Italian mason, Jewish cutter, it was the sight of black skin. No Gael or Spartan, no Tartar or Hun, ever was able to strike the terror that the mere sight of a black face, lips appropriately thickened, did at this time to the white labor movement. "Niggers are beautiful," Harry Morrison declared.

In the 1930s, the sandhogs' union in New York had an enrollment of almost thirty percent blacks. This was two decades before the subject was fit for religious sermon or political speech, before the muted expressions of conscience, sense, and then hesitant legislation. Two decades before anybody in America did anything, the sandhogs of New York had blacks all over their jobs, blacks working with whites, for the good and just reason that the blacks aggravated everybody else so much that it saved breath. The sandhogs didn't have to shout "Fuck you!" to anybody.

"Just show them our members and watch them all fucking die," McGuire announced at a union meeting. The members applauded, particularly the blacks, who, in the grinding thirties, were being paid the same wages as the white sandhogs.

Because of their blacks, the sandhogs suddenly became the strongest gods to the Communists in New York. The union lawyer, Wise, who throbbed at the thought of smashing industrial society, brought McGuire and Morrison to a Communist Party meeting at the Hotel Fairfax, Broadway and 93rd Street, where a room packed with about a hundred, a mixture of the very old and high school students, was elated at the presence of two rough tunnel workers.

A smiling girl in flat shoes and no make-up asked Harry Morrison, "Can I get you something to drink?"

"Yes, anything you got," Harry said.

She ducked into another room and returned with a bottle of Dr. Brown's Celery Tonic. Harry thanked her and went into a corner of the room and dropped the bottle into a wastebasket. He did not, however, leave the Communist movement that night; a distribution system for the party newspaper, the *Daily Worker,* was discussed, and Wise, the lawyer, asked McGuire and Morrison to collect monies for the paper. They began that night, picking up fifteen dollars at the meeting, which they threw onto a workers' bar on Willis Avenue. At the end of the week, Harry Morrison went to a Young Communist meeting in the basement of a building at Columbia University, where students first asked him for his autograph, as he was the first workingman they ever had seen at a meeting, and then put up twenty dollars for subscriptions to the *Daily Worker.*

"Here's to the Communists," Harry Morrison said later that night.

"What's so good about them?" the man next to him, McLoughlin, said.

"They're buying us drinks."

"That makes them good," McLoughlin said.

When the Communists did not get their newspapers, and found that the *Daily Worker* circulation department had no record of their payments, there was a squall from the hierarchy, and Harry decided to leave the movement.

*   *   *

Harry Morrison stayed in the Bronx and worked on tunnels and lived on Willis Avenue, which had four funeral parlors and eight bars in order to keep each side of the family separated at a wake. His bachelor brother, Jack, was the first in the family to get away from mining and the Bronx. Jack became a messenger boy for a rich lawyer in Manhattan named Quinn, who was assisting with the pocketbook of William Butler Yeats, who, treated with the high honor the Dublin Irish reserve for their greatest successes—utter despisal—had arrived in New York, where lawyer Quinn had heart flutters upon being introduced to Yeats at a dinner party. Yeats moved into Quinn's thirty-room apartment on Central Park West. The job of delivering an allowance to Yeats was given to Jack Morrison; Quinn did not want to embarrass Yeats by giving him money directly, and Yeats would perform no such demeaning act as picking up his own allowance, particularly from a lawyer, a man who had to read a rulebook to know what to think, while he, Yeats, had body fluids of madness and genius. Quinn also had a much younger woman who held his arm but kept eyes on Yeats, which caused a certain amount of unease. But Jack Morrison still was given envelopes to rush to Yeats, who would stand in the doorway and immediately rip open the envelope to make sure the insides were in order. This ripping sound stuck like a burr in Jack Morrison's ear.

Of a spring afternoon, a Friday, Jack Morrison, the envelope for Yeats in his pocket, walked the streets toward the apartment. He remembered the ripping sound. At Columbus Circle, he took two steps to the right and into Nugent's Gaelic House, where, rather than perform the dishonest act of steaming open the sealed envelope, he ripped it open and spread the money onto the bar and, with a nod to the bartender, put himself in business. At sunset, a most delightful time, with the interior of the barroom the color of old gold, Jack Morrison was demanding speedier service of the bartenders. He stared at the somewhat depleted stack of money on the bar, and said grumpily, "I could make words rhyme, too, if I tried."

Somewhere in the heart of the night, the remnants of both envelope and money were shoved under the apartment door, while Yeats inside bellowed that a grand party had been waiting for him for hours and he had been unable to join it. Yeats, a scholar of the helpless, never demanded that the messenger boy be fired, but as the deliveries thereafter became slightly sporadic, Yeats one day did say to Quinn, the benefactor-lawyer, as Quinn's diary noted: "I just received your envelope in time and completely intact. This day therefore shall be truly known as the 'Second Coming.' "

By the time the lawyer died, Jack Morrison was so influential in the office that he was placed in charge of the lawyer's thirty-room apartment for several days. He had his brother Harry's wife, Emily, come to the place and told her to take something for herself. Quinn had covered his walls with so much art that he had had to keep a stack of Renoirs under his bed. Emily Morrison looked at the Renoirs, but then saw an original Yeats manuscript, with Yeats's editing marks on it. "Anything Irish got to be better," Emily Morrison said, pushing a Renoir back under the bed and walking out with the Yeats manuscript. The manuscript, a sixteen-page one-act play, was folded and placed in a plain white envelope and taken back to Willis Avenue in the Bronx, where Harry Morrison looked at it with a sandhog's eye and wondered if he could sell it.

The Yeats manuscript remained in a cupboard and Harry Morrison assumed his place in the life of Willis Avenue, which had the highest rates of infant mortality and tuberculosis in the city. At breakfast one morning in 1942, his usual morning cough shook his body so much that the ribs sounded. He brought up enough blood to fill the bottom of his coffee cup. Seeing this, his wife Emily gasped, "You caught TB." Her large, sad eyes could see only the shadow of the neighborhood disease. Harry Morrison, however, had been spitting blood in private for three years. He now became numb, refused to talk, and slowly forced himself to stand up and leave for work. He left his wife to clean the stove and keep the linoleum floors glistening, and three months later when Harry began to hiccup and could not cure the condition with water taken in short gulps or even with entire pitchers of icy beer, she rose to the pinnacle of usefulness and nursed her husband until his death from cancer of the esophagus.

Afterward, in a daily black dress and gray face, Emily sat waiting for her son, Jimmy, to come home. At seventeen, he had left school and thought of no other business but urban mining. As the great-grandson of Johnny Morrison, who had come from Donegal to start a line of tunnel workers in New York, with cousins in the sandhogs and in allied construction unions all over the city, he was not inclined toward accounting. Nor did his bloodlines cause him to race directly home from the job each day. If there was a family crest, it was a raised glass. So his widowed mother sat, and he threw money on the bar, holding out only enough for her household needs.

During World War II, Jimmy Morrison swaggered into the draft board on his eighteenth birthday and announced that they were in luck, that he wanted to go that day. The board checked him and found him the sole support of a widow. He felt inadequate and began to go into strange bars. Then on St. Patrick's Day over in the High Bridge section of the Bronx he met Agnes Hayes at a dance and, filled with beer, he told her that he was losing his manhood because of the 3A draft classification. She sympathized with him so much that he fell in love with her and married her forthwith.

A year later, working in High Bridge, Jimmy Morrison and three others got on a lift that dropped like a flowerpot off a windowsill, dropped down a nine-hundred-foot shaft with the four men on it trying to scream out but unable to make a sound. Jimmy was on his hands and knees and forcing an Act of Contrition through his frozen mind when the elevator cable caught and the elevator stopped at once. The four were thrown against the steel sides of the shaft with bones breaking and the first cries coming from them. Then the lift broke free again and dropped the last fifty feet to the bottom. It splintered and the four men were pulled out and had to remain in the shaft for several hours, until a new lift was fashioned and sent down to them. One of the four, Gene Cooney, went berserk and, when healed, had to be put away. The other two left sandhog work. Jimmy Morrison, with fractured vertebrae, was in a ward in Bronx General Hospital for six months. When he came out, he was given paperwork duty in the union office. He tried to enlist, but the Army now found him physically unfit for military duty and even in 1944, when they were accepting anyone who could make it to a physical while breathing, Jimmy still was turned down. At the start of 1945, however, he went on his own and found a bored doctor who certified him. Elated, Jimmy Morrison bought flowers for his wife and kept a protective arm around them so they wouldn't be crushed on the subway ride home. At eleven that night, he was still protecting the flowers, which were in a water pitcher on the bar at the Galtee Mountains, 144th and Willis. Deep in the night, he left the bar; the flowers did not.

In the morning, he went around to the bar and retrieved them, and was so parched that he had a glass of tomato juice and three beers to get everything going. On the street on his way home, he suddenly became ill and, in throwing up, thought he held the flowers clear but did not. As they were covered with puke, he tossed them into a garbage can. Still, his intentions were good and he almost became the first Morrison in America to bring flowers to a wife in the kitchen.

Twenty-year-old Jimmy Morrison was in armored training at Camp

Hood, Texas, when the war ended. He returned to Willis Avenue, where his wife had been working in a dry goods store, and pulled her out of the job; no woman works while a Morrison can stand, even if the mining jobs were nonexistent at the end of 1945.

Agnes suffered several miscarriages but finally produced a son, Owen, known instantly as Owney, who was born in 1949 into a neighborhood where less than five percent of the Catholic school graduates went to college, causing most of these Bronx Irish to spend the most glorious part of the day, their mornings, in gloomy depression and resentment on the subway ride to jobs they despised. Jimmy went for years without a steady job, surviving on odd work around construction yards and a small weekly payment for being an officer of the sandhogs' union, an organization that at the time appeared to be dying.

"I met Krantz from the bakery on the street today," Agnes Morrison told her husband one night.

"So?"

"He said if I needed work, he could use me afternoons."

"Forget it."

"I think that's silly."

"I work and you take care of the kid," he said.

"But you're home most afternoons," she said.

The rage ran into Jimmy Morrison's eyes and the subject was never brought up again. Except deep in Jimmy Morrison's mind, when he sat alone at the bar and thought that the family trade, the work that caused the body to tingle with effort and that set him apart from all other laborers—as the miner's trade is the most hated, it also is a revered trade, and a miner's behavior is always acceptable—was of the past. If somewhere downtown, in Manhattan, a whole lot of people were making money as they sat and did nothing, then his son Owen would have to be pushed in that direction.

But then in 1955, work on a new water tunnel picked up. Soon, Jimmy Morrison was swinging into the places on Willis Avenue again, covering the bar with all the money he could pull from his pocket, toasting himself in his glorious line of work. Up the sandhogs. I'll never be broke again, he promised himself in the mirror each night.

In 1955, the first Puerto Ricans came into the South Bronx, and shots were fired on 141st Street during a dispute between two Puerto Rican families; the dispute was over a dispute. At the same time, in the Keeper Hill Bar on Willis Avenue, an Irish hoodlum, Reilly, walked in and shot a guy named Hynes over gambling territory. The bartender, Corbett, held up his hands and said to Reilly, "I don't see anything." To ensure this being so, Reilly shot the bartender. Jimmy Morrison then decided it was time to leave the neighborhood.

He found a six-room apartment on Central Avenue in Ridgewood, in Queens, with rooms as clean as a fresh shirt, but with a landlord named Kunzman who was insufferable: he wanted to get paid.

"The rent is eighty-six dollars," Kunzman said.

"I'll be the super for the building," Morrison said.

"What does that mean?" Kunzman said.

"I'll keep the hallways clean."

"My wife does that," Kunzman said.

"I'll make sure the garbage cans are in and out," Morrison said.

"That's my job," Kunzman said. "Your job is to pay the rent on the first of the month."

Morrison moved the family in, although he woke up on the first of each month with a hot iron bar inside his chest. As the sleep went out of his eyes, the bar pulsated and expanded and shoulder to shoulder his torso was afire. Immediately, he wanted to squall for a doctor. Then he realized that the pain was beyond medicine: today, he had to pay rent. On other days, in searching through Ridgewood, he found the low-rise buildings ably attended by the German couples who owned them. If they could find a free apartment, they would have moved into it themselves.

Then one day, when Owney was eleven, his father took the last thirty dollars out of the house, muttering that he needed it for rent. The mother, Agnes, still in bed, nodded. When she awoke fully and realized her supermarket money was gone, she let out a wail. Twenty minutes later, the mailman changed all moods when he delivered an income tax refund of four hundred seventy-five dollars.

"I'm going to buy a couch with it," she announced to her husband when he arrived home fairly late that night, filled with beer.

"Yeah, but we need some of it here," he said.

"For what?"

"For the rent. What do you think, we live here for nothing?" The beer had robbed him of short-term memory.

"You stole the rent from me this morning," his wife said. "You can just go out to where you lost it and get it back." She waved the check. "This goes for the couch."

That Saturday, when she started out to buy the couch, she found Owney's father, holding his son's hand, walking with her. As she understood that he was there to steal the change from any purchase, her eye remained fixed only on couches costing close to four hundred and seventy-five dollars.

Late in the afternoon, she decided to look in one more place downtown and they were standing on the IRT subway platform at Grand Central Station when the mother said something about dying before surrendering any more money and the father got so mad he said he would walk to the next station. The father waved to Owney and the mother began to yell, but the father led Owney to the end of the platform and down an iron ladder to the grease-pit train tracks.

The father went first and Owney followed him into the black tunnel toward 33rd Street, Owney shrieking in the darkness. They were deep in the tunnel, trying to stay out of the puddles of dirty water, when the father looked back. Owney remembers the laugh stopping on the father's face. The father said, come on, let's run. He pushed Owney in front of him. Owney was dog-trotting, trying to keep his shoes out of the puddles. Owney remembers his father yelling, "You can fix a pair of shoes but you can't fix a pair of legs." Owney loved that. He began running directly through the water, howling, his feet throwing up splashes. The lights of the 33rd Street station were tiny in the distance. Owney's father banged into Owney from behind and Owney remembers turning to see his father's mouth open, sucking in air. "Don't look!" the father said. Old family stories suddenly threatened. Behind the father, back in the blackness, making the first noise of movement, the rumble of a wagon on a bumpy road at night, was the train coming out of the 42nd Street station and starting after them.

Owney's father, face crimson, said, "Want to sit down and rest?" Owney put his head down and started running as fast as he could. Legs flying out, running through puddles. Behind Owney, over the sound of his father's heaving for air, he could hear the train. The tunnel they were in had no notches or cutouts for trackwalkers. The train behind them was running through a series of green lights. The running became serious and sapping, and then Owney and his father finally broke out into the glare of the station lights at 33rd Street. They scurried up the ladder and Owney remembers his father, wobbling, holding out his arm, palm flat against a post for support, heaving and spitting as the train rushed past them and stopped quickly far down the platform. It was a three-car train used for trash collection from the stations. The porter working the 33rd Street station walked up to the train, threw in the trash bags, and the train quickly pulled out.

Several minutes later, the regular downtown local from 42nd Street pulled in. Owney remembers how he danced back and forth, arms waving, as he looked through the windows for his mother. When she stepped off, she was furious, but the hands remained clenched on her purse. It was one of the few times in her life when she stood her ground financially. Which caused the pain to be all the sharper when, on the third day of the couch's reign in the living room, her husband spilled beer over most of the right side.

2

O WNEY ATTENDED Fourteen Holy Martyrs School, where, as always, the Catholic religion made its fiercest fight against nature's call, suspending this only to honor the dead. The Catholic religion's doctrine on the subject of sex, from impure thoughts and desires through masturbation and intercourse and thence to the homicide of abortion, has as much give as a tree trunk. In many places, Catholics may suggest a thought considered modern, but in Owney's family blood, and in the cold churches where the family prayed over the decades, Catholicism remained as it always was, a form of worship that suggests flashing swords and velvet cloaks.

When Owney was in the fifth grade, his job was to look out the classroom window and count the number of mourners walking to the nine-thirty Mass. There was one morning when he watched an usher, who was bending over to take the last drag of a cigarette, open the door of a lone car behind the hearse. Out struggled parts of an old lady. After her came two more people. Nobody else. "Three people, Sister," Owney called out.

The nun put the chalk into the gutter of the blackboard and had the class chant a Beatitude: "Blessed are those who mourn, for they shall be comforted." Then the nun took the class down to church, and everyone knelt in rows behind the three mourners as the nun paced the aisle and led them in prayers for a man who, even by taking his last gasp, could raise no crowd of his own.

Owney attended Bushwick High School, whose concentrated field of study was its cement schoolyard. And during these years, Owney Morrison was fashioned by the neighborhood where he lived, Ridgewood, which sits like a stone fort on the border of white Queens and black Brooklyn, with the line separating the two showing only on tax maps of the city of New York. There are no official markings on the streets to show which is Queens and which is Brooklyn and none are needed; the skin tone and living habits of the people on a block marked the address. The intersection of Myrtle and Wyckoff is the boundary, in fact. On the eastern side of the intersection, the gleaming Queens German streets run to the border as dentine to a cavity. Across the intersection, past the subway kiosk and bingo hall, into the all-day darkness under the low, dirty el tracks, along streets that run downhill from the intersection, run downhill so far that they narrow in eyesight, on these streets are crowded the most feared of all people: the sons and daughters and grandchildren of field-hand niggers and Puerto Rican hill people who stand on streets of concrete in a city of office workers.

When the blacks first edged out of Bedford-Stuyvesant and toward Ridgewood, they followed the bus routes and subway lines; the poor do not travel privately. First, the Bushwick-Aberdeen stop on the LL subway line, then Wilson Avenue, where in Carmine's Bar, across the street from Fourteen Holy Martyrs Church, the owner put a shotgun under the bar. Then the blacks reached Halsey Street, and the whites there formed a gang called the Halsey Bops in order to protect their rights in the park, a place with benches and cement tables for checkers and a basketball court. The basket at the west end of the park was loose and if the shot was a little high and hit a dead spot on the backboard, the ball simply dropped through the hoop; there was no chance of it kicking off into the air. Owney always played in that park, and used that dead spot, and he joined the Halsey Bops, whose leader, Tommy Clarity, eighteen now, had been in trouble since he was twelve. The enemy of the Halsey Bops soon was the Head Stompers, run by brothers called Big Cheese and Little Cheese.

When the time came that the Bops had to sit down and negotiate with the blacks, Owney was there, standing with his arms folded, to make sure Tommy Clarity didn't give away his favorite basket.

"Down the middle," Tommy Clarity was saying at the park bench.

Tommy Clarity had lived with blacks in Elmira Reformatory, but it had done nothing for him. Dark hair slicked straight back, eyes narrowed, he showed contempt for the Cheese brothers, who were accustomed to scaring whites.

"You wants the park and we wants the park," Big Cheese was saying. "We both intends to do, we goan cut it right down the fuckin' middle."

"Split it right down the middle," Tommy Clarity said.

"Fahn." Big Cheese gently patted his big high nigger pompadour.

"Then nobody fucks with our people," Tommy Clarity said.

"And nobody fucks with *mah* people."

"Anybody comes up your end of the park is—"

"—is *prey.*" Big Cheese grinned. The scar on his face, long enough to be the result of a duel, became wider and resembled webbing as his face opened into a smile.

"Same as us," Tommy Clarity said. "Any of your fuckin' niggers come up our end of the park."

At the end of two hours of bargaining, a peace treaty was confirmed with a handshake.

"You owe me, I saved your ass, you can still be a star with the backboard goin' for you," Tommy Clarity said to Owney.

Under the peace treaty, the Halsey Bops kept the west end of the cement basketball court and the Head Stompers were allowed the other half. And then late one Friday afternoon, several days after the treaty, Owney was out on the Halsey Bops' end of the court, the white man's end, the end with the dead loose tin backboard, playing in a four-man game. He took a shot from the top of the keyhole and didn't even need the backboard. The shot went through clean. Turning in triumph, he faced the other end of the court where a black man in his forties played with two boys of about fourteen. Owney then walked out of the park as Tommy Clarity came along with two whites he had met in the reformatory, Jackie Scanlan and Crazy Carl. The three of them were drinking canned beer. Clarity sat on a park bench and watched the black man laugh as he kept missing shots that his kids were making easily. Clarity got up and walked to the brick Parks Department house and came out with a hammer. He walked out onto the court as the black man was bending over, bouncing the ball on the foul line before taking a shot. Tommy Clarity hit the black man on the head with the hammer. Jackie Scanlan punched one of the fourteen-year-olds in the face. The other kid was running to help his father and Tommy Clarity spun around like a shot-putter whirling and hit the kid in the chest with the hammer, sending him onto his back.

Somebody yelled that a police car was coming down the block. Owney, on the sidewalk outside the park, began running, along with the others he had been playing basketball with: Jimmy Reilly, Mike Minelli, and Victor Koenig.

It happened the next night, Saturday, and it happened very fast. The black kids came out of the park at the white end, the end with an exit onto a street called Knickerbocker Avenue. The blacks came up the block toward the pizza stand on the ground floor of a four-story tenement. There were eight or nine of them and they all had their shirttails out and in their hands they were holding these folded newspapers. They walked through the screaming and music and the other night noises coming out the open windows of the tenements on both sides of the street. There were twenty Halsey Bops in front of the pizza stand.

"What do they got in the newspapers?" Jimmy Reilly said.

"They got shit," Tommy Clarity said.

"What could the niggers have in there, fuckin' long rifles?" Crazy Carl said.

"They got fuckin' bats and they think they're tough," Tommy Clarity said. He walked out to the curb and ripped an aerial from a car. He whipped it around.

Salvatore, the eleven-year-old kid who had a job mopping the floor in the pizza stand, came out and grabbed his bike, which he had leaning against the front of the stand. He pushed the bike through the crowd of the Halsey Bops and into the chalk-marked green doorway next to the pizza stand. Owney was in Salvatore's way. Owney had a bottle of orange soda on the floor in the doorway and he was bending down to pick it up and Salvatore was trying to tug the bike into the doorway when the two of them saw the blacks in the middle of the street tear the newspapers off the machetes they were carrying.

The bike fell as Salvatore raced upstairs. Owney's foot kicked the orange soda over as he ran to the curb, pulled and ripped at a car aerial, and then began moving on the sidewalk, moving on his toes, the aerial switching back and forth in front of him.

"We down, you motherfuckers," Big Cheese said.

"Nigger shit," Tommy Clarity said.

Clarity was pulling on the door of the pizza stand. He wanted to get inside and get knives, but the man who owned the stand, Mario, had the door locked and he was trying to hide behind the counter.

"Open the door!" Tommy Clarity said.

"Who hit Lester and his kids last night?" Big Cheese said.

"Lester got his ass kicked, same as you get yours kicked, nigger," Jimmy Reilly said.

The black closest to Jimmy Reilly swung the machete crazy in his right hand. Jimmy Reilly ducked. The black took the machete in both hands and brought it up over his head and then the machete came down and dug into Jimmy Reilly's skull.

"Shooooo!" The blade passed three feet from Owney's face. "Shooo!" Still three feet. The black coming around the car swinging his machete was afraid of the car aerial. The black kept swinging his machete, hoping to strike the aerial and shear it. But Owney held the aerial down and then up and he timed his swish with the passing of the machete blade through the air.

He caught the black once. Just grazed him on the corner of the mouth. It must have stung the black because he made a gargling sound and came at Owney with the machete slashing back and forth, forehand, backhand, and Owney jumped into the green doorway next to the pizza stand, jumped over the bike and started up the stairs. The black came charging in and tripped over the bike. Owney came crashing down the stairs to jump on the hand and grab the machete, but the black pulled back. Owney went halfway up the stairs. The black started up, then hesitated— could he go up the stairs without getting trapped? Now there were car doors slamming out in the street and the black turned and ran. Cops always are close in a neighborhood like this. Owney went up the stairs; the last time there had been a fight, Owney was at the movies when it broke out and he never made it; the cops arrested everybody, whites and blacks. Fuck that. Owney went up to the roof, walked over three rooftops to the corner building, went all the way down to the cellar and out the back way and ran home.

Jimmy Reilly died that night in the hospital. Tommy Clarity was in serious condition. He had been caught in the doorway and held up his arms to protect his face and the machete blows went chunk-chunk-chunk into the meat part of his forearms. Four others were seriously cut. The black from the park was in a coma. Crazy Carl told everybody that he was going to get guns and blow the niggers away for real.

Two days later Owney came into the park wearing a sports jacket and fresh shirt.

"Where you goin'?" his buddy Ralphie Schmidt asked him.

"I'm going to join the Army," Owney said.

"Why?"

"All I'm going to do is get in trouble around here."

"I'll go with you," Ralphie said.

They met two others on the corner and the four of them went to the Army recruiting office in the Post Office on Tillary Street in downtown Brooklyn. The year was 1967.

Owney trained in three hot Army camps, after which he was given fifteen days home in Queens and a voucher for a flight to San Francisco and then to Vietnam.

At the end of his leave, he met Dolores Kaufhold, who was a year younger, had long brown hair and brown eyes, and whose walk, a swing that suggested more of shoulders than hips, was an announcement of her determination.

A second-grade teacher, a nun at St. Matthias School, noticing that Dolores was left-handed, tried to turn her around. Dolores wrote with her left hand when she finished second grade, and she wrote with the left hand when she graduated from the school.

At St. Barbara's High School, she took the commercial courses demanded by her mother, but she spent hours in the library in Glendale reading science books. She never learned to type. She complained her fingers got in each other's way. The only thing she learned in shorthand was to take a number two and put a big tail on it, which transformed the number into "Dear Sir." She told her mother one day, "Do you call this something to learn? I call this stupid that I can take a good number and make it into something stupid."

She soon added so many academic courses that in May of her senior year she was accepted at Queens College. Where, in typing papers in her first year, her fingers suddenly darted across the keyboard. Biology was her best course. She took the new words from the course and made them her own. She lived at home in Glendale with her mother.

One afternoon, Dolores went up to Myrtle Avenue to buy curtain rods for her mother. She wore blue Landlubber hip-hugger denims from Revelation on Austin Street in Forest Hills, and a blue work shirt. On the way home, she stopped into Oting's, the soda fountain on Myrtle Avenue, which the owner, an Italian, kept as if Norman Rockwell was not a reason for throwing up. The owner sat behind a candy counter along one wall in the front of the store and watched the Mets play baseball on television while mostly high school students sat in booths in the back and listened to an all-Motown juke box that was so loud that the owner many times winced at the high notes. The juke box was the reason why Dolores and most of her friends had just started going into Oting's.

She sat at the counter and ordered a Coke.

There was a cardboard display on the fountain counter on which were pasted the pictures of the customers who were in the service. There were ten of them. The young guy behind the counter, Glenn Paulson, who wore his black hair in a ponytail, looked at the pictures and rocked his head to the Temptations, who wailed out of the juke box.

"They'll have my picture in the Post Office," Glenn said.

"You going to rob banks?" Dolores said.

"No way. I'm going to be the most famous draft dodger in Ridgewood. They'll have my picture over the special delivery window. In a big heavy coat with a fur hood. Where I'm going to in Canada, the dogs won't even come out."

Three days before, she had been in the crowd at an antiwar rally in the quadrangle at Queens College. The rally had ended when the students running it had to take down the sound equipment and get to a lecture. Just as well. It had been an hour of arguing against the air, for nobody at the school would get any closer to a uniform than at a discount store. Glenn was real. At nineteen, just as most everybody else in Ridgewood and Glendale, he was one mail delivery from a war. "No way to get a deferment?" she asked him.

"Nope."

"What about college?"

"What about I get a job as a lead singer in the opera?"

"College isn't as hard as you think."

"I had trouble in grammar school."

"It's the best way to stay out of the Army. Go to school."

"My best way is to put on heavy clothes and do what I have to do."

The owner looked up from the Mets game and waved to a guy walking into the place. "I got it right up there," he said, pointing at the cardboard display.

"Let me see," Owney Morrison said. "Excuse me," he said to Dolores. He looked at the board and picked out his picture. Serious, chin high.

"That's it. They told me it was here."

Owney was standing at the fountain counter. His auburn hair was cut short and his face, neck, and arms were dark from long weeks in Louisiana swamps. Only the bottom of his neck, as white as milk in an open shirt collar, showed that his color was not gained sunning himself at Rockaway. He had a small, square chin and amused brown eyes.

"You look good," Glenn said.

"I'm looking at where they're going to put your picture soon," Owney said.

"I have to tell you the truth, we were just talking about it. I don't think you're ever going to see it."

"No?"

"Not me."

Owney looked at Dolores. "What do you think?"

"I'd hide him in my house."

"Is he your boyfriend?"

"No. I'd hide you, too."

"I don't want anybody to hide me," Owney said.

"Then I won't hide you."

"Hide Glenn if he wants."

"Do you think Glenn is scared?" she asked him.

"I don't talk like that. Glenn is my friend. He can do anything he wants. Run, hide, fight. Whatever he does is fine with me. We're cool."

"The only reason I won't hide is I'd get bored staying under the bed," Glenn said. "I'll go up where there's tundra."

"All right with me," Owney said.

"I'll send you letters," Glenn said.

"Where from?"

"Wherever there's ice."

"Who wants to hear about some glacier? I want her to write me." Owney was looking at Dolores.

"I'll write," Dolores said. "Where to?"

"I don't have the address yet."

"When you have it, I'll write. I know you. You used to play ball in the park down from my house. I live on Sixty-sixth Street."

"I live on Central. We used to come over to that park to play ball. Were you one of that mob of girls used to watch?"

"Sure." Dolores often walked down to the park in the early evenings to watch them play softball on the asphalt for ten dollars a man. She was not about to say that she used to stand outside the fence and look over the fronts of each of them.

"I don't remember seeing you," Owney said.

"I was there." She remembered seeing him, all right.

"How could I miss hair that pretty?"

"Thank you." She knew that the neon in the fountain window put points of light in her hair.

"They shouldn't've taken me in the Army if I couldn't see you."

"How long have you been in?" she asked him.

"Almost a year."

"So you've got a year to go?"

"Right now, I'm in my last two days at home."

"Where do you have to go back to?"

"To Vietnam."

Her hand rose involuntarily and touched Owney on the arm.

"What do you do, work?" he asked her.

"No. I go to Queens College." She had her water buffalo sandals up against the next stool.

"That's pretty good."

"I think so."

"That's a good way to beat work, go to school."

"What kind of work could I get? Make sure everybody in an office has coffee?"

"Then you don't work in a place where they do that."

"My friend Kay Seibert got a job in the city. She thought it was the greatest thing in the world. Do you know what she does? Every morning she has to go into the boss's office and fix the flowers. She has to make sure the flowers are fresh and they have water."

"But how old is she?"

"Same age as I am. We were in high school together."

"Then she's just starting at a job."

"Starting what? To be a slave?"

"And what do they have you taking up in school?"

"Regular courses. I like biology."

"Oh, that's different. You're going to school to become a nurse."

"I'm not so sure of that. Maybe I can go past that."

"Like what?"

"Why can't I be a doctor? Or something else. Let somebody bring me coffee."

"That I like. You got to think you can do anything."

"Absolutely. I had to talk my mother out of making me go to work. I'm not going to college because somebody thought it would be nice, the family could talk about it and all. I know I don't want to be another woman on the block. Standing there. That's all they do. Stand. Anyway, I'll figure something. I'm beginning to think you go to school to find out something about yourself."

"What'd you find out so far?"

"I'll let you know when I hear something."

"Tell me ahead of anybody else."

"I will. And tell me what you're going to do."

"The day I get out, I go to work with my father in the sandhogs."

"Digging tunnels."

"That's it."

"Isn't that dangerous?"

"Sometimes."

"Can't you think of anything else?"

"I like the union work. My whole family helped run the union. I want to get into that."

"That sounds better. I was afraid you were like everybody else around here. The family tells you go out and get money and be glad that the boss is nice enough to pay you."

"That doesn't happen with me."

"Good. Now what do you do in the Army? I'm afraid to ask."

"Nothing special. I guess they want me to kill a lot of people," he said. Then he asked, "What are you doing with yourself all day?"

"Taking these home," she said, touching the curtain rods.

"Want to go to the beach for a while?"

"It's three o'clock already."

"I want to catch some waves."

"Surf?"

"Sure."

"Yeah, but until what time?"

"I don't know. Six, maybe."

On the way home, they got as far as the Grassy Point, which is a bar in an old wood house on the road right after you come across the bridge from Rockaway. She was sipping the first beer, as always bitter to her mouth, and he had half of his gone with one swallow. He smiled and swallowed the rest of it. He put the glass out and the bartender snatched it.

"What are you going to do about school if you get married and have kids?"

She didn't answer. Whenever she thought of how she was going to be different, she never put children into her mind. There was, of course, no way you could have any other kind of life then except a mother's. Just think of your own life, how you got here, she would tell herself.

"Then I've got my arms full," she said finally.

He swallowed the beer and said he wanted just one more and he had that. On the way home, Dolores said, "I forgot the curtain rods. I left them at Oting's."

When they got to the place, it was empty and Glenn was sweeping the floor. "The curtain rods are behind the counter," he said. "I'll be right with you." He bent down and picked something up. "Look at these." He held out two orange pills.

"Downs," Owney said.

"Are they?" Dolores said.

Glenn nodded. "Last year I swept the floor here, all I got was Marlboro butts. Look at what we got now."

"I'll take beer," Owney said.

"Where do they get them from?" Dolores said.

"That old bastard sells to the whole neighborhood," Glenn said. "Old Jack. You heard of him?"

"No," Dolores said.

"I have," Owney said.

They got back to her house around nine. She got out her keys and opened the front door and then went into the vestibule, spun around and faced him, and he took her in his arms and kissed her softly.

"Am I going to see you again?"

Owney laughed. "I sure hope so."

As she realized what she had said, her hand involuntarily came up to her mouth. She pulled it down.

"I mean, you told me you had two days."

"That's right. Today was one day. And then tomorrow I go to San Francisco. I have to be there by six."

"That means I won't see you?"

"I'll write you," Owney said.

Dolores went into her purse and took out a sheet of paper from a small pad and wrote down her address. She leaned out and kissed him again and then shut the door and ran upstairs quickly and flew to the front window so she could watch him walk up the street. He went two street-lights down, and then he turned around and looked up at the house and Dolores stood at the window and her arm waved back and forth and Owney's right hand came up and then he turned and was gone.

When she woke up in the morning, she ran across the street to Nancy Lucarella's house. Dolores burst through the open front door into the Lucarella apartment. Nancy was in the back, sitting at the kitchen table with a Tab, a cigarette, and a stack of paper.

"I just met a boy I'm in love with," Dolores said.

"I already finished writing my book," Nancy said. "You're too late." She placed a hand on the stack of paper. With the other, she brushed uncombed black hair out of her eyes. A face as pale as newsprint contained large dark eyes and a small, thin, colorless mouth. A loose black T-shirt and black pants that were even looser did little to hide the fact that spaghetti goes to the hips of even a twenty-one-year-old. Nancy was the sole woman who tried to live with the calendar and not with the trolley tracks on Myrtle Avenue, which stood for so much of everybody's lives.

In 1949, the trolleys on Myrtle Avenue had been replaced by buses and the tracks were covered by asphalt, with tar over the asphalt, and it was supposed to be this way forever, but then snow water seeped into the tar and froze and expanded and the tar eroded and the asphalt under it cracked and in the spring the old shiny trolley tracks gleamed in the sunlight. Steamrollers would arrive and fresh asphalt would be thrown over the tracks and rolled tight and then the winter would crack the new asphalt, and in the years that followed, the city workers did less repairing and finally there were places on Myrtle Avenue where the old trolley tracks showed their silver spines permanently. And on the blocks running off Myrtle Avenue, the ways of life being taught by old women to young women were as old as the trolley tracks. Let the people in Manhattan have their loose lives and multiple marriages; here in Queens, the man still works and the woman is raised to get married and then walk children to school and come home to fix dinner. Through the '50s and '60s and later even into the '70s, paste over the Glendale housewife a thousand magazine covers proclaiming the changing role of woman in society, and steam from a teapot wilts the covers while, in an opening, there appears a hand gripping a potholder.

When Nancy was deep in Catholic high school, she would walk out onto the top of her stoop with nothing on, wiggle her young breasts, give a great yawn, and go back inside. When she graduated, she went to St. John's University for a week, after which she came home and said she was leaving.

"They made one of the deans a federal judge," she told Dolores and her mother, "and they put in the note on the bulletin board that it was a lifetime job. The school took off for the whole afternoon. Let me go someplace where people try to count because of themselves, not because of the fucking job they have."

She got in an old car and drove out to the University of Iowa, where they had a program for creative writing. Nobody knew whether she went to school much, but when she returned to Glendale three years later, she announced that she had sold a novel. She did this by standing on the stoop one morning, naked, in a Statue of Liberty pose. Holding up as her lamp what she announced was the publisher's check. Nancy said she was home only until her apartment in Manhattan was furnished. While she was home, however, she was the only one who ever caused Dolores to feel and listen for something else on these nearly deserted daytime streets whose sameness causes people to suspect anything different, who must see the trolley tracks in order to be comfortable, and who silence so many sounds of encouragement.

Now, Dolores pulled a Tab out of the refrigerator and sat at the kitchen table with Nancy.

"Who is he?" Nancy said.

"Owney. Owney Morrison."

"Where is he?"

"He's in the Army but he's home."

"Where?"

"On Central."

"If you love him so much, what are you doing here?"

"You're right. I ought to go right over there."

"When does he have to go back?"

"He has to go to Vietnam today."

"Today? You'll go with him," Nancy said. "We'll pack you in a big trunk and mail you to him."

"Right now!" Dolores said.

"They'll send the trunk to Hawaii first. Late at night in the Post Office you can push open the trunk and get out of it and go for a walk on the beach in the moonlight. Waves. Somebody will play a ukulele around a big fire. You can sit with them and sing and then go back to your little trunk, fold up your legs, and pack yourself up. The next face you see will be your boyfriend in Vietnam. Can you imagine his look when he opens his trunk? Standing right there on a battlefield, and you jump up at him?"

"Wow!"

"How long have you known him?"

"I met him yesterday."

"Then he must be very much in love with you."

"Sure, he is."

"And you're so in love with him."

"I can't eat."

"Then we better pack that trunk right now."

"I can't get packed today. I got finals next week."

"Oh."

"Can you imagine?"

"What?" Nancy said.

"That I'm sitting here and I have a boy going away to war. Did you ever think of such a thing in your whole life?"

"No. I only write about sodomy and things like that. I never wrote about anything as dirty as that."

That day, Owney flew to San Francisco, took the bus up to Travis Air Force Base, where he sat through a Northern California evening, staring through cigarette smoke, waiting for the military flight to Saigon. When the waiting room became tiresome, he put on his field jacket and went out into the chilly darkness. A couple of others came out, saw a cab pulling up to the terminal, and asked Owney if he cared to take a ride with them. They told the cab they wanted pizza, and the cab took them to a pizza stand and beer bar just outside the base gates. Owney drank beer and for a moment he saw Dolores in her jeans and work shirt. When they got back to the waiting room and were standing outside the cab while they put together the money to pay for it, there was a sound coming from the darkness on the field. The others went inside the terminal building and Owney, listening to the sound, walked around the building and to the start of the tarmac. The sound defined itself now, a rumbling sound, the rumble of a wagon on a rutted road. It grew louder and Owney went out onto the tarmac looking for it.

Coming out of a bumpy side road on the base was an electric cart and behind it were wagons that bounced over the bumps; on the wagons were silver metal coffins. As the wagons came into the light from the terminal windows, Owney could see the stenciling on the coffins. HR. Human remains. The airman driving the electric cart got out to open the gate in the low wire fence.

"What you got?" Owney said to him.

"Remains from Nam. Had them here in the base mortuary. They got here yesterday."

"Where are they going now?"

He pointed to a freight plane that sat with its lighted insides showing.

"Dover, Delaware. These are East Coast bodies. Fly them to Dover,

Delaware, and then I think they put them on the train to their hometowns from there. All right. See you."

He drove out onto the runway, with the wagons rumbling behind him and the aluminum military coffins bouncing on the rumbling wagons, and they disappeared into the darkness between the fence and the plane with the lighted insides that was far out on the field. The sound of a rumbling wagon was constant.

As Owney walked back to the terminal building, his fingers dug inside his jacket for his scapular medal, which was there to protect his throat. It was a silver medal of the Sacred Heart, worn on a chain around the neck, although traditionally there are scapulars that are two cloth medals, bearing pictures of the Sacred Heart on brown cloth, worn on brown cord around the neck, one cloth medal at the base of the throat, the other at the back of the neck. As Owney needed something more substantial than cloth, the head of the ushers at Fourteen Holy Martyrs got him the metal scapular medal, a reduction from the usual two, but permissible and practical.

Then a transport plane rolled up outside the terminal and a noncom bawled out names and Owney walked out to the plane. Twenty-six hours later, he landed at Ton San Nhut in Saigon, on the military side of the field, and as he walked off the plane from Travis he was directed to a C-130 that, moments later, took off and flew in and out of thunderstorms and landed in the mist at Pleiku, in the Central Highlands. On the wet ground alongside the runway there were two Vietnamese army officers squatting down and chattering to a thin man who had an old face and a young, nasal voice. The thin man wore black pajamas and rubber thongs. One of the officers took his hand. They all kept talking and the officer holding the man's hand kept looking straight into the man's eyes and he made no extra sound or effort as he pushed the man's index finger straight up, then simply kept going and made it snap as he pushed it straight back, like a hinge. The man in black pajamas let out a nasal howl.

Owney walked by without hesitating. He had been on the ground in the country for a total of only a few minutes and already he did not give a fuck for anybody. Any dates he had to keep had to do with his own throat and neck, and not some gook's finger.

On his first day in Pleiku, with the afternoon thunderstorms lighting the sky for miles upward, and turning the ground into ankle-deep mud, he sat in a bunker and wrote a letter to Dolores Kaufhold. For four days, her kiss had lingered.

*   *   *

The first Kaufholds in New York were a young bakery worker named George and his wife, Bertha, who arrived here from Cologne in 1889, holding hands and wearing festival clothes on deck as the new city presented itself in the first sunlight of a June day. They moved into a room at number 116 Clinton Street in the downtown East Side neighborhood that was at the time as German as a new lathe. That summer, the sound of Wagner and polkas came from the open windows of five-story tenement buildings that were overcrowded with Germans, who formed the largest migration ever to reach New York. The Irish, Jews, and Italians arrived here in fewer numbers, and kept shrieking that theirs was the true saga of the New World. The Germans, too orderly as they worked through years of the poorest conditions, were all but forgotten.

George Kaufhold became a bread baker in a large new business owned by a man who called himself Count Gengler and who knew nothing about baking but quite a bit about human tolerance for greed, of which there usually is none. Count Gengler was of common coinage, but in coming to America he took on a royal name in anticipation of charges that would be hurled at him, similar to those in his native Mannheim, where he became the city's first bowling hustler and was forced to leave. In Manhattan, Count Gengler strolled about in a white suit and in search of indoor or outdoor bowling matches. He would hold the ball as if it were a garbage can, totter forward, and drop the ball. The Count would laugh good-naturedly with the crowd and then say, "I giff you bets." At which point, there would be those who would shuck off latency and actively try to rob this foolish German Count, who as always would totter to the foul line, but now would release the ball as if it were the product of an explosion. The Count won himself a bakery.

George Kaufhold, the sweat pouring off his thin body, pushing bread about with long wooden sticks, wondered how long it would take a man to learn to bowl in a league with the Count.

He tried once, going to a bowling tournament in a place on Park Row and betting half his week's salary of twelve dollars against a man with a withered right arm. Upon completion of the deal, the man with the bad right arm picked up the ball with his left, which had the muscles of a snow tiger, and each roll caused pins to leap into the air.

When George Kaufhold had to get a salary advance at the bakery, and was required to give the reason for it, the owner, Count Gengler, sneered at him.

"Make the door open for yourself by hard work. You don't know how to do what I do. In Mannheim, I practiced bowling fifteen hours a day until I could giff bets and win them. You only have the will to steal. That is not enough. You must have the ability to steal, too."

George Kaufhold took the advice, although his blood was restless.

In the meantime, he had a daughter, Frances, and a son, Eddie. On May 20, 1904, his wife gave birth to another son, Billy. On June 15, she went out for the first time, taking Frances, then thirteen, and Eddie, fourteen, to the spring outing of St. Mark's Lutheran Church, which was on 6th Street in Manhattan. The outing was a boat ride around Manhattan on the stern-wheeler *General Slocum*. The boat departed from Pike Slip, East River, with children waving and mothers carrying flowers and food, and it headed up the East River, into a fresh spring breeze. Opposite East 95th Street in Manhattan, the *General Slocum* caught fire. The captain had the ship on the Manhattan side of the river, with miles of pilings and rocks and concrete shoreline to choose from, but rather than stop the boat and attempt to drift to the Manhattan side, the captain increased speed. His high old wooden boat went right into the breeze, turning into a fireplace. The mother, Bertha Kaufhold, was separated from her children. Frances and Eddie found themselves holding hands and surrounded by flames leaping out of the wooden deck. Everywhere, mothers and children were leaping overboard and, nearly all unable to swim, caused the water to turn white as they flailed at it. From the shoreline the white water looked like that caused by baitfish being pursued by regiments of striped bass. On the top deck, Eddie Kaufhold lifted one of his hot shoes and put it on a foothold on the ship's flagpole. This gave him an idea and he began to climb the flagpole away from the flames. Frances Kaufhold looked up at her brother and wondered how he would be safe in the sky. He turned and held a hand out, but the deck under her feet was showing smoke now and she had to do something and she looked at the flames around her and was about to start climbing to her brother's hand when suddenly the sheets of flames along the rail stopped. It was as if somebody had thrown a great rug over this part of the deck. There was flame everywhere else, but none along this one patch of deck. Frances Kaufhold ran for the opening. The boards were black and smoking and they burned through the thin soles of her shoes, but she did not break stride. The rail was gone and nothing was in her way as she slipped between two white-hot metal spokes used to hold up the rail and jumped high and out as far as her wounded feet could cause her to go. She landed feet first in the water and went down so far and so fast, she was afraid that she would not come up. Arms and feet struggling, she ended the plunge and started the long way up toward the vague light at the top of the water, her chest bursting with need. She came onto the surface with her mouth sucking in air and her hands keeping her afloat; she was one of the few who had attended summer swimming lessons given by the Steuben Recreation League. Now as she looked at the ship, which was still tearing upstream into the wind, flames rising higher into the sky, she saw her brother climbing the flagpole. Climbing, climbing, climbing, and behind him the flames licking and, in moments of anger, suddenly leaping at him. Her brother Eddie went higher and now the flagpole, weakened by the fire, began to bend backward. Eddie Kaufhold still was climbing with his feet and knees, but the flagpole was bending him back into the flames. He was a little figure in the air and Frances, frozen as she watched him, started to slip under the water. She put her face into the water and took a couple of strokes to regain her buoyancy. Now when she looked there was no flagpole and no brother. Only fire.

Frances floated on her back and shrieked to the sky. Hearing her, a tugboat captain guided his boat over and picked her up. Frances Kaufhold became a rarity: a child who had survived the *General Slocum* fire, which had taken more than a thousand lives in the bright June morning. Hardly a tenement on the downtown East Side was left untouched. The Germans buried their women and children in the Lutheran Cemetery in Ridgewood, in Queens, and then nearly all the Germans moved from the East Side to Queens, in order to be closer to the graves they visited each Sunday by the thousands. And as they left the streets of the East Side, they were replaced by Jews from Eastern Europe who quickly made the street names, Ludlow, Attorney, Eldridge, Rivington, Allen, Orchard, Delancey, part of American lore. The Germans who had preceded them now lived in Queens, which could be seen clearly from Manhattan, although it was actually a thousand miles away.

George Kaufhold was left with his daughter Frances and a son, Billy, who was only weeks old. He moved to Onderdonk Avenue in Ridgewood, and while outwardly able to carry the tragedy, he became ill and missed work for the first times in his life. In the middle of the second winter in Queens, he came down with a cold that became bronchitis and suddenly one night he had to be taken to St. Catherine's Hospital on Bushwick Avenue, his breathing sporadic, and doctors said there was no reason why he could not breathe, but his lungs simply stopped working and he died. His daughter Frances, at fifteen, was left with a two-year-old baby brother and a job in a knitting mill. She paid neighbors to watch the baby during the day, leaving her with nights of washing by hand while a baby squalled. She was nineteen, and with eyes that sometimes indicated her mind was in strands as she tried to cope with a six-year-old, when she met Arnold Fink, a plumber. He promised Frances a protected life, but upon their return from a honeymoon at Schmidt's Farms, Earlton, New York, Fink made it plain that he still expected her to go to work. He would, however, save her money by having a relative care for the baby, Billy Kaufhold. On Frances's first post-honeymoon shift at the knitting mill, she found that the same people who had treated her as a gardenia only two weeks before now indicated by an amount of indifference that she was merely one of them, somebody who had to work for a living and was not awaiting an important event, a marriage, to lift her away from this. They despised her for having used up their hopes, and then reappearing as a failure, just as they were, people who must work grimly, breathing lint, for just enough pay to keep them from sleeping on the sidewalk. When Frances Kaufhold, now Fink, got home from work that first day, she looked at the baby brother being returned to her in time for bathing and feeding, and then at her husband, who was washing his hands and inquiring about dinner.

Frances Kaufhold took a deep, angry breath and muttered to herself, "I just guess I'll have to get by without true love."

She did. There was to be no stare, glance, whisper, discussion that would cause the risk of a fight that would leave her alone. This was a winter of her life that she recounted for all to hear and learn from, through all her years. She got out of work by the simple method of becoming pregnant with the first of four children she was to have with plumber Fink. Her brother Billy, who was placed in the role of the oldest child in the family, and who attempted to fight with Fink as soon as he was tall enough to reach him with a punch, left Grover Cleveland High School at seventeen, worked at a job he hated in a machine shop for a few years. He studied for the police department exam, which he passed in 1925, and went on the job in 1926. During the Depression, when the pain of being out of work was at its highest for the most people, Billy Kaufhold, with his city check guarantee, still regarded his job as one of opportunity rather than security. He became known as a patrolman with insides cold enough to allow him to walk into a speakeasy that was under the protection of captains and lieutenants and attempt to use his silver shield as a lance and shake the place down. In 1928, he met Ellen Kearns, and, against his better judgment, married her in 1937. Ellen lived at 107-82 101st Street, Ozone Park, an attached two-story white frame house that was across the street from the side entrance to John Adams

High School. Behind the high school was a rutted athletic field that ran into a large farm. From her stoop, Ellen Kearns could look beyond the athletic field to groups of Czechoslovakian women with kerchiefs on their heads who worked the farm by hand. Then beyond the farm were the old green stands of Aqueduct Race Track. In the spring and fall afternoons, when the horses ran at Aqueduct, the people of 102nd Street—whose speech ran to the Queens "Jeet yet?"—listened to the voice of the track announcer, who, as part of a sport originally English, cried out in traditional tones: "They're at the haaalf."

Ellen Kearns was one of only two girls in a family of heavy-equipment union men, with the one closest to her age, her brother Matty Kearns, a member of the Operating Engineers Union before he finished high school. Ellen was brought up as both a strict Roman Catholic and also a woman who believed that you took the man's name upon marriage and were a limited partner thereafter. She and every other woman in the area knew the value of male opinions: they only had to watch the male on the block as he walked back from the racetrack, with gills white and eyes frozen.

The first time her brother Matty went to the track, he told Ellen, "I'm not going to work today. I'm going to make money without going to work."

"How can you be so sure?" Ellen said.

"We're smart today," he said.

In 1921, Tom Welch, trainer of the horse Naturalist, stepped out from the stable area of Aqueduct Race Track and onto busy Rockaway Boulevard and mentioned to at least a couple of people that he was delighted by the training moves of his horse. He felt the animal would shoot home ahead of everything in the big race coming up, the Paumonok Handicap. Naturalist was a seven-year-old, but those listening to Welch assumed there was nothing unusual about that, for the horse was owned by a rich man, Joseph D. Widener, who discarded nothing of value: Widener wore his grandfather's suits, and ordered his kitchen help to save all empty egg shells for possible use as fertilizer.

As horse trainer Welch's conversation began to circulate through Ozone Park, many working people began to plan the acquisition of sudden fortunes. They bet the living room couches on Naturalist, which had a fine price, 4–1, and of course could not lose.

On Paumonok Day, women out on the stoops on 101st Street listened to the loudspeaker as its sound drifted across the farmland. Naturalist was on top all right, running magnificently, and then jockey Charlie Turner found himself on an animal who was looking about for a soft bed of hay. At this point, the track announcer blurted out, "That is On Watch . . . coming on!" This caused spectators to sag. On 101st Street women's knuckles turned white as they gripped their brooms. The horse On Watch ran past the aged Naturalist and won the race by half a length. Naturalist went back to the barn and slept with all four legs sticking straight up in the air. Many of the horse's Ozone Park supporters crept home and took seats on the floor, for there was no furniture left in the front room.

When Matty Kearns got home that night, he said to younger sister Ellen, "You got any money hid?"

"Bus money for Rockaway."

"You better give it to me. I need bus money for work."

Ellen Kearns was raised to yield to a man on every issue, except, in her case, her religion in a mixed marriage. When she married Billy Kaufhold, her Catholicism remained firm and his Lutheran belief, watery at best, became part of his past. All children were to be raised as Catholic as possible.

Four years into their marriage, on December 7, 1941, Billy and Ellen Kaufhold were in Charlie's Oriental Bar, on Metropolitan Avenue and 62nd Street. The bar was crowded and both the owner and his wife were serving. The pair spoke with heavy German accents, not unnatural in Ridgewood, and seemed happy and relaxed, although now and then Charlie kept ducking through a doorway that led downstairs to the basement. "Tap the keg," he said. There was a radio on the back bar that had on music and a football game and then over it came the news about Pearl Harbor. The bar became silent and excited, with people indicating with their hands that they needed drinks in a hurry and then Charlie said he needed a breath of air. He went out the side door of the bar, leaving his light-haired wife to handle the crowd. Suddenly, she sighed, wiped her hands on her apron, and said she best retrieve her husband. She went out the side door. As all attention in the bar was on the radio reports about the war, nobody noticed the lack of a bartender until an empty glass was involved. Long minutes passed, with neither the woman nor her husband returning, and there was some grumbling. Billy Kaufhold looked nervously at his empty glass, went into a pocket, brought out his silver shield, pinned it to his lapel, and shouted, "This place is under martial law." He got behind the bar and served drinks with his badge on.

Later, here they came through both doors, squads of FBI agents, and one of them ran up to the bar and called out to Billy, "Officer, is there anybody here we should detain?"

"Not that I know of," Billy said.

"All right. On with it." The agent followed the others down the basement stairs. Billy Kaufhold, fingering his badge, went down after them. There was a short-wave radio that took up most of the basement wall. A German submarine commander was bitching over the radio that nobody was answering him. The FBI agent in charge congratulated Billy for having the street sense to come to this bar and, a mere New York City patrolman, try to arrest these dangerous spies. "It's too bad you didn't get here in time to catch them," the agent, who gave his name as Bowman, said to Billy. The agent then said that he would notify Billy's superiors about his work in defense of the nation.

When the FBI man made good, Billy was awarded a detective's gold shield and a post in the 103rd Precinct, in Jamaica, which had the greatest concentration of bookmakers in Queens County and therefore the greatest challenge to law enforcement: when Billy arrived, the question in the 103rd was whether detectives should become partners, at a percentage, with bookmakers, or simply take a fixed payoff each week. When one of the bookmakers, Tony Buffalo, said the police could be his partners if they shared in his losses, too, the police voted to retain their fixed weekly payments.

Kaufhold immediately used the detective's pay, plus extra money from bookmakers, to move into a new apartment on 66th Street in Glendale. And right away, he was more comfortable in better bars. The nicest place to drink in the 103rd Precinct was in Constantine's Restaurant, which was on Hillside Avenue and Parsons Boulevard. The restaurant was popular and crowded, but the barroom had a tile floor that urged you to take a drink. Over the months, Billy spent long hours in Constantine's, even though the place often committed the most serious sin of charging him for a drink.

One night in March of 1942, while he was supposed to be protecting the citizens of Queens during the hours from four to midnight, Billy was in Constantine's. He glanced about as the FBI agent, Bowman, walked in, lips tight, brown Glen plaid suit unwrinkled, carrying a brown hat in one hand. When Billy roared a greeting, the agent jerked his head vigorously and went to the men's room. Billy followed.

"The man parking cars," the agent said. "We have an agenda for him. His name is Kleinstuber. Do you know him?"

"Oh, sure I do. What does he do?"

"Spy."

"Oh, I thought he was acting quiffy."

"You know we had three Germans land from a submarine out at Amagansett," the agent said.

"The ones the Coast Guard guy caught."

"They were supposed to come here and get money from this guy parking cars outside."

"Grab him!" Billy said.

"Not so fast. We're waiting to see just who comes along. The Director himself sent orders that we are not to summarily lift him. The Director wants us to get other bodies."

"I'm trying to remember who he talks to," Billy said.

"Oh, we overhear him talking. The trouble is, we don't have anybody who speaks German."

"Well, I do," Billy said.

"Then why don't you go out there and see what you can get for us? The Director would be pretty pleased, I'll tell you that."

Billy went to the bar, threw down his drink, wiped his mouth, and sauntered outside where the parking valet stood at the narrow entrance to the lot.

"Stell dir mal vor: der Typ da drinne hinter der Theke ist Jude," Kaufhold said.

"Don't do that," Kleinstuber, the valet, said. "Talk in English."

"Was kümmert's mich?" Kaufhold said.

"I said, speak in English. If someone hears you speaking German around here, they suspect."

"I guess so," Kaufhold said.

"My job is bad enough as it is," the valet said. He jammed the red cap with the gold lettering "Constantine's" down over his eyes. "All right, I go to my work now." He walked back down the narrow driveway to the parking lot.

Billy sauntered across Hillside Avenue and went around a corner to a newsstand, where Bowman stood nervously with two other agents.

"Who's watching him?" Billy said.

"We've blanketed the area," the agent said.

"That's good. Because I don't want him getting away."

"He won't. Believe me. Now what did he say?"

"He asked me if I knew anybody who worked on the docks. He wants the times troop ships leave. He says he is going to blow up every fuckin' troop ship they load in New York."

"Why, that monster," the agent said.

"I'd get him now," Billy said.

"I think we've got to move up our agenda for this monster," the agent said. He went into the newsstand and got on the phone.

At midnight, when Billy was going off duty at the 103rd, there was a commotion downstairs and when he walked in, there were over a dozen FBI agents around the booking desk and then a few more crowded into the captain's office, where Bowman was seated, and across from him, in handcuffs, covered by drawn pistols, was Kleinstuber.

When he saw Kaufhold, Bowman beckoned.

Kleinstuber glared at Kaufhold. "I say nothing to him."

"Yes, you did," Billy said.

"I said hello and good-bye," Kleinstuber said.

"You told me you wanted to blow up a ship with President Roosevelt on it," Billy said.

"Liar!"

"You told me you wanted to see Roosevelt swim in the ocean with his braces on."

"You lie!"

"You fucking Nazi!"

Billy went home enthralled. The *New York Mirror* the next day said that Kleinstuber, the master spy, was in America on a sworn mission to personally kill President Roosevelt, and that he boasted of this to members of the German community in Queens. When he reported for work, Billy was informed that he had been raised to detective second grade on orders coming directly from the police commissioner's office.

"You must have some fucking rabbi," the squad commander told Billy.

At the zenith of his career, Billy spent so much time cavorting about Jamaica, mostly in Constantine's, but also in the Paddock Bar under the el at 165th Street, and with the horse trainers and sportswriters at the Hotel Whitman, that his presence at home amounted to that of a boarder. One day, his sister Frances arrived and, as always, Billy Kaufhold was silent as the strong one of the family spoke.

"I can't tell you how to live, because I don't know the half of your life," she told him. "Besides, from what I do know, you can't live any other way. I can tell you that I worry, and I think so does your wife, that you don't have any children."

From then on, Billy and his wife attempted to have a child, and when none materialized over a couple of years, they tried the medical information of the day.

"There seems to be nothing wrong with you. Perhaps it's simply a matter of time," a gynecologist said to Ellen.

"We've gone through a lot of time," she said.

"Well. Oh, come in," the doctor said, pointing to Billy, who was peering in from the waiting room. "We're just saying that everything seems to be in order. Ah. This is just a thought." The doctor pushed his glasses up and rubbed his eyes. "Ah. Perhaps you should be tested," he said to Billy.

"There never was anything the matter with me," Billy said.

"We're thinking of the present," the doctor said.

"I've only gotten stronger as a man," Billy said.

"Wouldn't it be sensible to be certain of that?" the doctor said.

"What's sensible is for her to go home and calm down and have a baby," Billy said. He walked out of the waiting room and grabbed his coat.

By 1950, with the baby boom in full swing, and so many young women in Queens morning sick that pregnancy dominated the precinct conversation, Kaufhold was still unable to father any children. Mention of anything bearing on the subject made him defensive. The use of the word *sire* at the racetrack caused him to turn his head. Then one day at the precinct, the mayor of New York arrived for an inspection tour. Billy Kaufhold positioned himself on the staircase leading to the detective room so the mayor would be certain to notice him. Which he did.

"When did you come on the force, lad?"

"Twenty-six, Mister Mayor."

"And when were you married, lad?"

"Thirty-seven."

The mayor's eyes narrowed. "Well, if you're living by the rules of your church, you've got three at home by now. Haven't you?"

All the inspectors and captains accompanying the mayor laughed. So did Kaufhold. Now feet shifted, as the mayor's party began to move on. The mayor did not. His eyes narrowed and he looked intensely into Kaufhold's.

"How many are there now?" he said to Kaufhold again.

"None," Kaufhold murmured.

"Are you a Protestant, lad?"

"I am. The wife isn't."

"Tell her I was inquiring." The mayor's eyes widened in amusement and he clapped Kaufhold on the shoulder. "Good lad!" He went up the stairs and Kaufhold left the building and walked the streets with his face red with embarrassment.

Six months later, he was in the Sea Grill on New York Boulevard, a few doors down from the side entrance to Gertz's department store and across the street from the Terminal Pants Shop, which had become famous as the place where the musician Fats Waller bought his clothes. The Sea Grill had a circular bar, and seated across from Kaufhold were two young people, a chubby guy who was under twenty and a young girl with a child's face but a powerful little body almost cut in half by a thick brown leather belt.

"I had it," the chubby young guy said.

"What do you mean, *you* had it?" the girl said, with a Southern accent.

"I can't go no more."

"What is that supposed to mean?"

"That I can't go no more."

She put a cigarette into her small, pouting, tough mouth and then, exhaling, said nastily, "*Way*ll, I expect you ought to be poisoned."

"What are you saying that for?"

"Because you just ought to be poisoned, that's why."

She was looking at the beer in her hand as she talked. Easily, with no particular haste or new sound of anger, she flicked her hand and the beer went into the guy's face. She slid off the stool and walked out the door. The chubby guy remained on the stool, the front of his yellow shirt dark and wet from the beer. He stared at the bar for long moments. Then his hand slapped the bar.

"I had it with that bitch!"

The bartender, watching the guy leave by the other door, said, "Oh, they'll have some more trouble."

"They're young to be fighting like this," Billy Kaufhold said.

"They come in here to do their fighting, I guess," the bartender said. "They live in a room on the other side of the trestle. I don't know what they're doing here. I know she's from the South. They got a new kid. You'd never know, looking at her."

"And they do fight," Kaufhold said sadly.

"Sure do," the bartender said.

An hour later, as Billy Kaufhold was leaving the bar, a patrol car was moving slowly down the street. Billy waved and the car stopped.

"What address is this, anyway?" the cop asked him.

"Ninety-one something," Billy said.

"We're looking for an eighty-four number," the cop said.

"Other side of the trestle. Don't you know your own precinct?" Billy said.

"We're from Brooklyn. We just got put here."

"It's down there two blocks," Billy said. "What do you have there?"

"Family disturbance. What the hell else is there out here?"

The car went on and Billy started to walk to the left, to the bus that ran under the Jamaica Avenue el and out to the trolley up to Ridgewood. Then he turned around and walked back toward the railroad trestle. He passed the Green Bus Lines terminal on Archer Avenue, where there was a line of faces, loafers from all over, inside the double glass doors. He was under the trestle when he saw the patrol car parked in front of a three-story wooden house the color of tree bark. It was one of five houses that were atop a bare slope. Cement steps led up to each house. Loud noise from the house the color of tree bark caused Billy to look up. Standing with his back to a second-floor window that had no shade, in a room lit by a bare ceiling bulb, was one of the cops. He was holding up his hands for silence, but this only made the noise inside the room louder.

The front door to the house was open and Billy stepped into a dark entranceway and went up creaking old stairs to the musty room on the second floor. In the doorway with her back to him was the young girl.

"I told y'all, I'm leaving," she said.

"What about this?" the young guy said.

"I'm sure I don't know."

Billy looked over her shoulder and saw a baby, about as new as a baby can get, on the bed.

"You better take her," the guy said to the girl.

"Good-bye," the girl said.

"I said you better take her."

"And I said, good-bye."

Kaufhold stepped past her and into the bedroom. "Don't you want this baby?" he asked her.

"I'm leaving."

He looked at the guy. "You don't want this baby, either?"

"*Hay*ell, no."

"The two of you sure?"

Both nodded.

"Don't fool yourselves," Kaufhold said.

"I sure don't ever want to see this place or anything in it again," the girl said.

"You're a winner," Kaufhold said. "All right. The two of you don't want this baby, then I'm taking this baby."

He picked up the baby and told the patrolmen, "Give me a ride." The young girl already was walking down the old staircase. She was out on the sidewalk, lighting a cigarette, with a small suitcase at her feet, when Kaufhold and the cops came out of the house. She picked up the suitcase and started walking up toward Jamaica Avenue.

"Hey," Kaufhold called.

"What y'all want?" she called back over her shoulder.

"What's the baby's name?"

"Dolores."

When she was about six, in the middle of the summer before she went to first grade, Dolores stood at the counter of Lutzen's delicatessen on Catalpa Avenue with a note and money to hand to the owner. Standing in front of her, one of the neighborhood women looked back, then said to the owner, who was behind the counter, "She's starting to look like them now."

"Looks like the father," the owner said.

"Oh, I think the mother."

"I suppose you're right," the owner said. "Whatever. It sure proves that even when you're a stranger, you live with somebody long enough, you get to look like them."

The note and the money were clenched inside Dolores's little fist as she went out the screen door of the store and went home.

"Why didn't you go to the store?" Ellen Kaufhold asked her adopted daughter.

"Who do I look like?" Dolores said.

A fire alarm sounded inside Ellen Kaufhold. She gave vague answers and waited for her husband to arrive home. At first, he felt the truth would weaken their authority with the girl. Ellen also noticed that her husband had an inability to put connected sentences together on the subject, thus indicating that he had not been able to think the matter out clearly enough to speak unhesitatingly. Billy then called his sister, Frances, who was still the dominant figure in his life at times such as this.

"She told me to tell the baby the truth," Kaufhold told his wife after he hung up.

"I could have told you the same thing," Ellen said.

"Well, now I'm going to do it," Billy said.

The next day, he and Ellen took Dolores to Myrtle Avenue for a gleaming blue lunch box, a leather school bag made for students of college age, and then, with Dolores impatient to run out and show her presents to her friends, they forced her to sit in the living room while Billy Kaufhold told of how she had entered the family.

"What happened to my real mother?" Dolores asked.

"She went away that night and nobody ever saw her again. But we wanted you so much that we brought you into this house that very night. It was one of the happiest nights we ever had."

"My real father went with my real mother?" Dolores said.

"No. He went in another direction. Something was the matter. I couldn't ask them. I was too much in a hurry to bring you home and make your mother happy."

Later that night, when Billy spoke about this to Frances, he heard her voice rise to a scream. "Why did you say the mother and father ran away?"

"Because that's what happened. You told me to tell the kid the truth."

"But I didn't tell you to tell her more truth than you had to," his sister said.

"What do I know? I do as I'm told," Billy said.

"I wish you'd tell yourself what to do sometimes," Frances said.

One day a year later, Dolores was on Myrtle Avenue with her mother and as they windowshopped at Empire Dresses, Dolores asked for change to buy a scissors for school. She went into the little Woolworth's and bought shears and then went back to the mother at Empire Dresses. The mother then decided to go into Muller's Shoes next door. Dolores said she wanted to remain outside. "But don't wander," the mother said. Dolores slipped into Empire Dresses and waited until the saleswoman was busy at the far end of the store. Then with the scissors, she carefully cut large pieces off the hem of each dress on the rack in front of her, and one blue dress, the one she had decided that her real mother was coming in to buy, was cut to ribbons.

"Where is your mother?" the saleswoman said to her softly.

"Shoe store," Dolores said, hiding the scissors behind her back.

"I see."

The woman walked into the shoe store.

That night, Dolores was in bed, but Billy Kaufhold, who had had too much to drink, talked so loudly to his wife that Dolores heard him.

"All we have to do is tell her that her mother went to a place way down South or something and that she never comes up here to buy a dress or anything like that. Then the kid'll have no reason to cut everything up."

"Think that'll work?" his wife said.

"I hope so. I tell you, I'm starting to love her so much that I can't handle it if she gets unhappy."

At the delicatessen two days later, the counterman caught Dolores stealing a family-size package of Fritos.

When it came time for her first confession, she was uncertain of what to say to the priest. She had been doing wonderfully in school, but didn't think he wanted to know about that. When she got in the confessional the first time, she couldn't figure out what to do. To stand. Or kneel. She didn't even know which way to turn in the darkness. Then a wooden panel slid and there was the priest's face.

"I said *bum* three times," Dolores told the priest.

"Is there anything else?" he asked.

Dolores felt she needed something more, so she said, "I stole some money from my mother's pocketbook."

"How much?"

"Fifty cents."

"Will you put it back?"

"Sure."

"Where will you get the money to put it back?"

"From her other purse."

3

IN VIETNAM, the first time Owney Morrison was shot at, from trenches under a tree line that rose from the hot, stunted grass, he headed toward the fire. Springing, flopping, springing. He sidestepped an old Vietnamese face that was covered with orange sand and had the tongue hanging from one side of the mouth. He continued through grass and bushes that had wet bandages and torn shirts hanging from them. In a trench dug into the soft dirt he found himself for a suggestion of an instant looking at a regular North Vietnam soldier, in khaki uniform. The North Vietnamese was scared and did not move and Owney's senses were clear and his hand and shoulder moved. The North Vietnamese went down on his back. There was no hesitation or sound. The body was gone before Owney could see the face or the wound. The body was in the dirt with one arm stiff in the air. Straight up in the air as if saluting. One ankle was behind the other. Only a few times did Owney see in his mind this ungainly form. Never did he give a fuck for the guy. Nor for the others. Always, his hand went inside his shirt and touched the scapular medal.

He met John Wayne one day. Or, at least he got close enough to John Wayne to thrust his hand through the crowd and Wayne, shaking each hand that came at him, grabbed Owney's. Wayne was making a tour, like a general, and showed up at Duc Co, standing in the middle of a hot field that was several miles from gunfire. His helicopter was behind him and old, gray, smiling officers nobody ever had seen accompanied him. As some sort of walking music, there was a Frank Sinatra tape playing over the loudspeaker.

"That man got a slow voice," Goat Gregory, a black from Lafayette Avenue in Brooklyn, said.

"It's Sinatra," Rulis, who came from New Jersey, said.

"I don't care who it is. He sings *draggy*. Get on some Aretha Franklin. Who wants to listen to this old man motherfucker *draggin'* away?"

Now here was Wayne with a circle of grunts around him. Big, all right, but old as hell, and he had on a blue baseball cap with admiral's braid from the carrier *Enterprise*.

"Mister Wayne!"

He looked around, his face amused.

"You can't wear that here. You're with the grunts."

Smiling, Wayne took the Navy cap off, revealing sparse hair over a red forehead. Somebody handed him a fatigue cap and he put it on, letting it sit on the bridge of his nose. Everybody clapped.

"You're all a lot younger than I am," Wayne said. "Seems to me, every time I see a war, the guys fightin' it get . . . younger."

"You still could fight with us, Mister Wayne," somebody called out.

He smiled. "It would be my . . . honor. It's an honor just to stand with you men. When I think of how some of my country is supportin' you." He bowed his head and shook it slowly. Then raising it, and looking around at the crowd, he said, "They hide in school. Do you know what's their idea of somethin' to read? John and Mary goin' around San Pedro Bay. Mention to them about fightin' for their country and you know what they do? They run to Canada. They run so fast you can't even . . . see them. Even that's not far enough. Somebody in Canada says to them, 'Why don't you go home and fight for your country?' So they hightail it some more. They don't stop runnin' until they see polar bears. That's how far north they go. The poor polar bear, he got to mosey off because he can't stand the sight or the smell of the crummy-lookin' bastards."

"Mister Wayne!"

"Yes, son."

"What did they do to draft dodgers in your time?"

"That was another time."

Now Owney yelled, "Tell us what did they do to those guys?"

Wayne held up a hand in disdain. "Let's not talk about those scum. I want to get around here and meet some real men." He began stepping and grabbing hands and Owney thrust his hand between shoulders and he felt this big hand grab his and then Wayne stepped on. Smiling gray heads and silver eagles and stars around him. Behind Wayne, this chubby bald man in an expensive khaki hunting shirt was twisting one way and the other to help answer some of the questions that everybody was shouting at Wayne.

"He wore the eye patch in *True Grit*," the chubby man said. "What's that? No, no. John Wayne never got laid on camera. Ha!"

Owney called to the chubby man: "We were asking him what happened to the draft dodgers in his time. Do you know?"

The guy shook his head. "I can't even remember them."

"What war was that?" Owney said. "What war was John Wayne in? World War Two, right?"

"Korea!" a voice yelled.

"You're nuts. He's older than that. He was around in World War Two."

"What was he in, the Marines?" Owney asked.

The chubby guy shook. "No, he wasn't a Marine. We wouldn't bring a Marine here to get you guys mad." He smiled and clearly tried to curtail the subject.

"A flier?"

The guy shook his head and shuffled after Wayne.

"He had to be infantry," Owney said. Then he yelled, "Mister Wayne!" Wayne's big head turned.

"What were you in, Mister Wayne? Infantry, World War Two, right?"

Wayne smiled and waved his hand and then began some vigorous handshaking with a group to his right.

When he was gone, and it was getting dark, Gregory was smoking dope and insisting to a circle of guys, "I doan think that fucking man ever was in anything."

Everybody, Owney included, laughed at that.

"Then why doan the man tell us what outfit he was in?" Gregory said. "You ask *me* what outfit I'm in, I tell you, George W. Gregory, RA 11817415, D Company, 17th Cav, 173rd Airborne Brigade. I tell you *that*. Now what did he tell you? You hear him give his outfit?"

"Sure, he did," somebody said.

"What outfit?" Gregory said.

"Marines."

"He never said Marines," Owney said.

"Then what did he say?" Gregory demanded.

When nobody answered, Gregory said, "The man doan give an outfit 'cause he ain't got one to give. He never was in no military service. He a hero in his mind."

"Bullshit," Owney said. It was irritating to hear a nigger against Mr. John Wayne like this. That night, he got half shot on a bottle of Seagram's and he made a tape recording to send home. He and everybody else with him felt puffed up, and capable of extra violence, because they had shaken hands with Mr. John Wayne. For the tape recording, they fired guns and screamed and then Owney spoke into the recorder. His words were only the least bit slurred. He said that they had had Mr. John Wayne with them all day and that he stirred things up.

"I didn't expect it to be this dangerous. The reason I am sending you this on tape instead of writing you is that I need both hands tonight. I can talk into a microphone I got set up, but I need my hands. I'm going to strangle a gook tonight when they come near me, which they sure will."

He mailed it, and then when he realized a day later what he had done, he went around trying to get the tape back, but it was too late. As they were out in the field and wouldn't get to Pleiku, where there might be a chance to patch a call to New York, he could do nothing but hope the tape was not as bad as his memory told him it was. It was. When the tape arrived home, his father went to Kings Plaza in Canarsie and bought a player. That night, he had people over—Chris Doyle and Delaney from work, Owney's cousin, and Owney's mother's brother and his wife—and they all had a drink and then Owney's father stood in the middle of the room and told everybody to be quiet, that he had something special for them. He turned on the tape.

The first gunshot sound caused Owney's mother to wail.

"Holy Jesus," the father said. He tried to turn the tape off, but he got nervous and was still pulling at it when now, mixed with the shots on the tape, came screams. Finally, the father simply yanked the plug out. He carried the tape out of the house and when he made the turn to go to the bar on Putnam Avenue, stopped and threw the tape into the trash can.

The letter that Owney wrote to Dolores that affected both the most was the one he wrote early one morning. He drank beer until as he wrote he could not feel the pen in his hand. The setting, lonely and threatening, demanded that he love someone, and he wrote page after page to her about the depth of his love.

"Everything here is small. The cows are half the size of regular cows. The men are as big as school kids. Why do such big things happen here, then? I guess it's just another test of a person. On earth, waiting to see someone you love makes every moment seem like an hour. In Heaven, the time races while you wait to see someone you love. But the time stops when the person you love walks in. The time stops forever. So what happens to me here doesn't matter. I'll just sit in Heaven and wait for you. I know that when you do come, I'll have forever with you. So when I do get killed, it'll be temporary."

Ten days later, his outfit was brought back to Pleiku, and he was able to get a phone call through to Dolores, who did nothing but cry because she had just finished reading his letter about death again. Owney then received a letter from Dolores that said that she appreciated his thoughts about being together in Heaven, but right now she preferred him alive in Queens.

One day, when he had been there for seven months, Owney was sitting on a bunker and suddenly his throat tingled and his fingers scrambled inside his shirt and there was no scapular medal. He became nervous and started walking until he found the chaplain, who was saying Mass on an altar of sandbags. The moment the Mass was over, Owney asked him for a scapular medal and the chaplain went into a bag and came out with the ordinary kind, with two cloth medals.

"I'll have to take care of them," Owney said.

"And please God they'll take care of you," the chaplain said.

Three days later, in the midst of the fight that brought him his honor, something blew up in his throat and he wound up on his back in the dirt in the sun, bleeding to death. The blood caused the front scapular medal to stick sopping to his chest. Nobody was able to stop the blood and Owney lay with his eyes glazing and then out of the dirt and the sun came a medic named Friedman, who had taken premedical courses in Brooklyn. Who knows how he got there, a Jew drafted out of Brooklyn and sent to Vietnam. Friedman dropped on his knees and told Owney not to move and to breathe as shallowly as possible, but not to hold his breath, and as he said this, he reached into Owney's throat and simply clamped his fingers on a vein and stopped the blood from spurting out into the hot air. Friedman's fingers holding the vein were a couple of inches above the sopping wet scapular medal.

He was picking up his money, keys, and the rest of his belongings from the bed while the guy from the next bed, Robards, stood next to him and stared out the window.

"They're all your people out there," Owney said.

The St. Albans Naval Hospital was spread over what was once a golf course at one end of Queens, in a neighborhood filled with Catholics whose outward faith was stronger than a bank vault. Then a few blacks from South Jamaica, lawyers and shopkeepers, moved into frame houses sold to them by white Catholics. They were followed by Basie, the orchestra leader, Robinson, the baseball player, and Davis, the entertainer, who moved into the larger houses. The St. Albans neighborhood turned out to be, however, perhaps the only place in North America where people preferred not to live alongside Lena Horne. The white Catholics, their bank vaults of faith already on the moving trucks, started to flee, and the place was drained of whites in months.

Catechism question:

Q. Where is the dislike of blacks always the highest?

A. In any decent Catholic neighborhood.

"I see the sisters walkin' their dogs," Robards said, his forehead against the window. "I waves to them."

He raised his left arm and waved it back and forth. There were bandages piled at the end of his right arm.

"Are you left-handed?" Owney said to Robards.

"I am now."

By this time, it was an old line between them.

Glancing out the window, Owney saw a workman on the circular plot at the hospital entrance, a rake in his left hand, the right scratching the small of his back. Now he whipped the hand out from behind the back and scratched a bite on the back of his neck. The left hand jiggled the rake.

Two hands. And Robards here had one. Contrast, Owney had decided in bed one day, was one of the main implements of the Devil. It has to be luring Robards into a sin of envy, he thought. He also had figured out, during his months in bed, how it helped wars. Because bishops and priests of his church performed so much of what were generally regarded as women's duties—comforting a widow, or visiting the sick—they were disturbed by the contrast of them holding some old lady's hand in a funeral chapel, and a military man, with a blue jaw and sunglasses and looking good and tough, and became jealous of the hard guy and really wanted to be with him.

As Owney passed the nurses' station, the woman at the desk, who was so heavy that her white uniform buttons couldn't keep the front closed, said, "You won't be back?"

"Bet on it," Owney said.

"That's what it say." She held the folder.

"All right."

"Tell the girl I was askin' for her."

"What girl?"

"She come here all the time holdin' your hand and you ask me what one."

"Dolores," Owney said. "I'll see her this afternoon."

"You say hello."

He was depressed that she had mentioned Dolores because he had been walking along thinking about getting his prick sucked and you could get that done from one end of Myrtle Avenue to the other and he was stuck with somebody he made into a Madonna when his best move right now was to find a whore. He wondered why he was even worried about it. You get a woman trying to run with her baby so that from a distance it looked like she was carrying something bad and she gets everybody mixed up and crazy and they blow her and the baby away. Who the fuck cares about anything?

He walked past the pay phones in the lobby. For the first time since he had been in these hospitals, he was leaving without being picked up by relatives or by some army officer. He just wanted to do everything himself today. He didn't want to be picked up in the driveway in front of the hospital. He wanted to go out in the street and get wherever he was going on his own.

He passed the workman in the grass plot and went through the gate and then turned right. The hospital grounds ended at the driveway to the J. Foster Phillips Funeral Home, which got more than its share of losers from the hospital. He walked under a railroad trestle and then past a bootblack, a Chinese laundry, a florist, a hair cutters, and then on the other side of the street was a two-story building decorated with imitation wood beams and a sign over the door that said it was the Tower Inn. Owney walked in and found three men and a woman at the bar. He put a dollar on the bar.

"Give us change for a call, will you?"

The bartender reached into the till. Owney suddenly felt a gladness about being in a bar. He had gone all the way, from the bus ride to Fort Bragg right through until today, without even smoking a joint. Not one. And he knew plenty of others who did the same. Raised on alcohol, they stayed with it. Others, who were from states where the drinking age was too high for them and who therefore never had been allowed in a bar, went to dope. The division was most prominent in the field, when the drinkers waited for their two cans of beer to be sent in iced bags, and the heads called for Coke. Everyplace you looked, they were using drugs like table salt. The throat working deliberately to cause a pill to slide down. That was a sin that covered the soul with slime. He felt great that he never used dope. He decided to have a beer before he made a phone call to get home.

The bartender was bald and wore a blue sweater. The color of the sweater was pleasing to Owney.

"Give us a shot of rye, too."

He took the shot first; it was bar rye, and it burned like it was poison and brought water to his eyes. He held his breath so he wouldn't have to taste it, and then he swallowed half the glass of beer. But the beer was closer to lukewarm than cold and it brought the taste of cheap whiskey full into his mouth. He wouldn't touch that again. He pulled a pack of Pall Malls out of his breast pocket and lit one. He inhaled deeply to overcome the whiskey.

"Give us another," he said.

"Beer," the bartender said.

"And a shot," Owney said.

The second dose of rye went down like velvet. As Owney exhaled, he looked at himself in the mirror. He had his chin raised and saw the start of the scar, which began with a pink knot at the base of his throat and ran down to his stomach inside his shirt. He closed the top button of his shirt. I look like a fucking baseball. Now, with his throat covered, he felt comfortable. He took a deep drag. The doctor over at the hospital had told him, Don't smoke, it'll ruin your throat. And Owney had told the doctor, Tell them don't shoot me in the fucking throat and I'll be all right. Cigarettes? What about shrapnel?

He went to the phone.

"Four One's Car Service."

"Fats."

"Owney baby. Where are you, baby? I'm busy."

"St. Albans. I'm at Linden Boulevard and 177th Street. Get me out of here."

"You're out?"

"On the street."

"Where are you going to?"

"Someplace good."

"You'll see me first. Stay there. Give me, let me see, about twenty minutes, Owney. I'm sending my best man, Rocket Man, after you."

When Owney hung up, he looked at an old picture that hung on the wall by the phone. It was a small young white basketball player in a uniform that said "St. Pascal Baylon." The picture was from a thousand years ago, and was the only decoration in the bar.

"Who's that?" Owney said.

"Cousy. Used to play basketball," the bartender said.

"I saw him announcing on television, I think," Owney said.

"Somebody say he used to live 'round here. Used to come in here or somethin'. It was here when we come here. So we leave the picture up."

The woman at the bar with the two men slid off the stool and walked over to the picture. She had on a gray sweat shirt with the sleeves rolled up and cut-off dungarees. She held her drink in one hand and the cigarette in the other and she looked at the picture.

"What's 'St. Pascal Baylon'?"

"That's the church around here," the bartender said.

"And he was a famous basketball player?" the woman said.

"He was with the Celtics," the bartender said.

"This little shrimp here was with them?"

"Long time ago," the bartender said.

"Sheeeet. He ain't big enough to sniff Walt Frazier." The woman and the men with her roared.

Owney had had three more beers and a shot by the time he heard the horn sounding outside. He picked up his change and went out to the car. The driver, Rocket Man, was slouched at the wheel with his left arm hanging out the window, the fingers drumming on the sign painted on the door, "Four Ones." The apostrophe is a word that people in Ridgewood have heard of, but, as with the Pantheon, are unsure of its proper location.

As Owney got in, Rocket Man had the cab rolling while the door was still open. The damaged muffler was too loud to allow conversation, so Owney watched himself exhale smoke as a couple of miles of black neighborhoods went by. After which they climbed a hill and went on the parkway toward Ridgewood. Along one winding stretch, cemetery headstones sprouted from the ground on either side. Rocket Man called out over his muffler, "You goin' home?"

"I'm going to see Fats."

While Owney was away, his father had met a hearse driver at barside, Putnam Inn, and through the driver discovered what he felt was the finest living arrangement in the history of the world: for being gatekeeper at one of the Jewish cemeteries along the parkway, he received not only a small fee but a rent-free family apartment on the second floor of the cemetery house, the bottom floor serving as offices. Owney didn't look at the cemeteries as Rocket Man had the car racing noisily past them.

Rocket Man went down Fresh Pond Road, which was Sunday afternoon empty except for saloons on every corner whose windows were filled with heads in baseball caps and the backs of colored softball shirts. He made a U-turn in front of a storefront that stood at the edge of a parking lot. The store window advertised the Four One's. Fats sat inside at a desk with a microphone in front of him.

"Yo, Owney! Give us a kiss, baby."

He kept looking down at the slips in his hand. Fats had light brown hair slicked straight back. He wore round glasses over a face that had the shape of a fat owl. When Owney bent down to kiss Fats on the cheek, his nose crinkled at the smell of old-time hair tonic. Fats's hair was as stiff as a book cover.

Then he spoke into the microphone.

"Stumpy, when are you going to be light, Stumpy?"

Fats kept looking at the slips in his hand.

A voice came over the loudspeaker on Fats's desk. "About three minutes at Halsey and Irving."

"Stump, keep right on and get the Half Moon for a deuce."

Stumpy called back. "Half Moon for a deuce."

Fats looked through the slips again. "Owney, they got me killed here. Killed."

At a second desk a short man with a crew cut answered a push-button phone, said little, wrote on a slip, and passed the slip to Fats. The crew cut then punched the next button. The private car service was a most radical change in Ridgewood, where for years the Germans had walked miles rather than pay an extra fare and ride the bus to the subway. The bones of cab drivers who had starved to death were buried somewhere. But the advent of blacks, the most feared people ever to walk the face of the earth, changed all this. At night at this time, the police of the 104th Precinct stopped an average of four hundred cars driven by blacks a month and refused to allow them to cross the border from black Bushwick into white Ridgewood. The people regarded this as self-defense rather than a transgression against the Constitution. No matter how strict the policing, the Ridgewood Germans thought it inadequate. Therefore, people who once walked miles to save a half dollar now called for a two-dollar door-to-door car in order to go a block.

"Eddie, where are you, Eddie?"

"On the expressway."

"Turn around and go back to the city. Pick up Kimmie at Gordon's. Thirty-fifth and Eighth."

"Pick up who?"

"Kimmie. The Chinese whore. She's waitin' in Gordon's, Thirty-fifth and Eighth Avenue. Eight dollars. Got that?"

"Kimmie the Chinese whore for eight dollars."

"Beauty." Fats looked and saw he had still more slips in front of him. "I can't get out of here. Give me like a half hour. I'll meet you across in Jimmy's."

Owney walked across Fresh Pond Road toward the bar with his head down and his hands in his pockets and when he looked up, here was little girl Cindy dancing out of the doorway of Borchert's Paint Store. She wore the first psychedelic skirt in Ridgewood, orange and short. Owney then noticed Jackie Kranz huddled in the next doorway. A good place for Jackie, as this hallway went straight back and into an alley behind the building. Most policemen, built like canned hams, would have no chance to run down Jackie Kranz, whose pockets were full of the best dope and smack.

"Got four dollars, Owney?" little girl Cindy said.

"I'm gone over a year. That's the best you could say hello to me?"

Her bitten fingernails dug into a small wad of money in her palm. "Owney, I want to cop, Owney."

"What have you got there?" He pointed to her hand.

"I need four dollars more, Owney. I have to get three bags."

"How much is it?"

"Seven dollars."

"Fuck him. Seven dollars."

Jackie Kranz's square, acned face stared from the doorway.

"You're robbing this girl," Owney said to him.

"I got to get seven." Kranz's gray eyes looked up and down the street. "I got to meet a guy in Bickford's pretty soon."

"Owney." Little bitten fingernails pressed into his arm.

Owney took her by the arm. "Fuck you," he said to Jackie Kranz.

"Owney," Cindy said.

"Come on, I'll step you up," Owney said. He guided her through the door and into the Idle Hour bar, where they were met with dimness and a Crosby, Stills & Nash record blowing out of the juke box. The bartender was in his middle thirties, but he had seams under his eyes that seemed to put him in his late forties.

"Give us two martinis," Owney said. He had an arm around Cindy.

The bartender opened his mouth to roar over the juke box. He had a front tooth missing.

"I wouldn't know what a martini looked like," he said.

"Give us two shots of rye and two beers," Owney said.

Cindy shook her head. "I don't want this," she said.

"It's the best." The door opened, but instead of Fats walking in, there were two guys in warm-up jackets. They were in their fifties, but both the jackets and the bar were essential to them. The jackets, with a team name written on the back, were a cloak of youth. Without the bar, on a Sunday afternoon, the men would stay home and screw and since none of them used contraceptives, half the women in Ridgewood would get pregnant before dinner was cooked.

When the bartender put the shot glasses down, Owney put a twenty on the bar. He held up the shot glass.

"It beats dope," he said to Cindy.

Hesitantly, she picked up the shot glass.

"I never had one of these in my life," she said.

"Never? What the hell have you had?"

"Acid."

"Are you nuts? Here you go!"

Owney threw the shot down. Next to him, Cindy choked and put the shot down, with half the whiskey still in it. She grabbed the beer and took two huge gulps. She made another face.

"I don't like this, either. Can I have a Coke?"

"Drink the whiskey."

"Never."

"It'll step you up."

"Give me a Coke."

"Will you drink the whiskey?"

"Owney, I want four dollars to smoke dope and have fun. And you want me to puke on the floor. That's not being nice."

He took five dollars off the bar and gave it to her. "I tried."

"Oh, wow. Thanks, Owney. I'll give it back to you, Owney."

Her orange skirt burned in the dimness of the bar. Then the skirt halted.

"Owney, you want to come, too, Owney?"

"That's not my game." Then suddenly his prick came into his mind from nowhere. "Are you coming back?"

"You want me to?" she said.

"Yes."

"Where?"

"Right here."

"I'm going to be a while."

"What time?" he said.

"Seven o'clock?"

"I'm here," Owney said.

She was gone and he sat at the bar and had a couple of shots and beer, he wasn't keeping track, and he kept waiting for Fats, and when he didn't come, Owney walked across the street to the cab office. Fats held up his hands in surrender.

"I can't move, Owney. I don't know what to tell you."

Rocket Man was standing in the window.

"Get Old Jack, Irving and DeKalb," Fats said.

"I stop here for a second to piss," Rocket Man said.

"Then do it fast. We don't have any time. Pick up Old Jack. Two-fifty. You know who Old Jack is, don't you?"

"I know," Rocket Man said.

"You better," Fats said. He looked at Owney. "You know who he is, don't you?"

"Fuck him," Owney said. "Come buy us a drink."

"Own, I'm jammed here an hour at least. I'm sorry I made you come here like this. I'm such a fucking liar. I thought I could get out."

"That's all right. I got to meet somebody there seven o'clock. I'll be around."

"Meet who?"

"Cindy."

"Cindy girl! Oh, I love her!"

Owney felt his eyelids droop with whiskey. When he walked out into the air he saw Rocket Man's car pulling out of the driveway. He waved and got in the front seat. "I need to hang my head out the window like a dog so I can straighten out," he told Rocket Man.

At the corner of Irving and DeKalb, Rocket Man honked the horn. Old Jack sat at a window table in an espresso shop. Three younger men stood at the table as if praying at a grotto. Old Jack didn't move. He said something to one of the young men, who dived for the counter and brought back a sugar bowl. Old Jack carefully spooned out sugar. He then held the cup of espresso high, to indicate that a man of his stature, a gangster, proceeds only at his own pleasure.

"Fucking guinea," Rocket Man said.

Owney lit a cigarette. He and Rocket Man sat in silence for almost ten minutes. Then Owney grabbed the radio.

"Fats, this man is making a fool of us."

"Owney, baby, what can I tell you? You know who the man is."

Owney sat in silence for another five minutes. He was going to put his hand on the horn and keep it there. Now Old Jack came out of the place. Three strands of white hair were arranged over the skin of his head. The dark blue suit seemed to have been ironed onto his little body. He stood on high Cuban heels. One of the young guys, who wore a mustache, black bell-bottoms, and lavender patent leather shoes, came out of the espresso shop and took Old Jack's hand. The diamond pinkie ring on Old Jack's hand became a silver fire in the sun, glaring off the espresso shop window. The young guy kissed Old Jack's hand. Old Jack beamed. He walked up to the car, took out a cigar, and elaborately bit off the end and lit it. Now Old Jack motioned with his hand that he wanted the back door to the cab opened for him.

Owney realized that Old Jack was looking at him, and he expected the door to be opened for him. Owney stared straight ahead.

"Be nice," Old Jack said.

Owney said nothing.

"My back. I can't get in and get out so good because the back hurts."

He stepped up to the car and reached in and pinched Owney on the right cheek.

"Nice kid."

He pinched the cheek just a little too long for affection and when Owney pulled his head away, Old Jack's dark eyes became lifeless. The man gets mad inside in a hurry, Owney thought. Rocket Man slid from behind the wheel and walked around and opened the door. Old Jack smiled and stood in front of the open door for several moments in order to let everybody in the espresso shop see that the door was being held out of respect for him. Then he put a hand onto Rocket Man's arm, as if his back were bad, and climbed into the car.

"Where to?" Owney said. He had the car rolling. In the mirror he could see Rocket Man standing back on the curb.

"Just a little way," Old Jack said.

"Where?"

"Roosevelt Avenue and Fifty-eighth Street. Then we come back to my house."

"Where?"

"Troutman Street."

"Is that for two-fifty?" Owney said. "I heard them say two-fifty. This trip costs way more than that. You're going to Fifty-eighth Street. That's all the way over in Woodside."

"They only charge me two-fifty. I go to California they charge me two-fifty."

As he drove, Owney said, "How come a big guy like you uses private car service?"

"Chauffeurs no good," Old Jack said. "Everybody who has a car and a chauffeur gets killed by the chauffeur."

When Owney got to Roosevelt Avenue, which sat under brooding el tracks, Old Jack remained still. A Peruvian restaurant was on the corner, and a young guy in a yellow shirt, gold chains, and bushy jet-black hair walked out, bent over to speak to Jack.

"You stand outside like a good kid," Old Jack said to Owney.

Owney got out of the car for a moment, then Old Jack said, "All right, kid," and Owney got back behind the wheel. The other guy walked quickly back to the restaurant.

Owney made a slow U-turn. A city bus was bouncing along quickly under the el. The red light was against Owney, and the bus, which had a green light, was almost at the intersection when Owney pressed the gas pedal. The car tires squealed and the muffler roared and in the back seat, Old Jack made an involuntary sound. "Doo-doo." He saw his life in a photo finish with a silver and green city bus, which by now filled the car window.

The car just made it past the bus, whose horn blared. The street ahead was empty of cars and Owney went through a stop sign without bothering to look and that gave him a good idea and he pushed the car as it approached Queens Boulevard, which at this point has twelve lanes that are always heavy with traffic. On the far side of the boulevard, on the right corner, was a high fieldstone cemetery wall, and atop a sharp grass incline there was a large statue of the crucifixion.

"Hey, Jack."

"You stop."

"See up there, Jack? You think the nails hurt?"

The lights in the boulevard were yellow and Owney rushed toward them, and as Old Jack realized that they were going to shoot the boulevard he let out a high-pitched sound.

The yellow light turned red as Owney was crossing the boulevard. Horns blared and grillwork shot at them. A gold Lincoln whipped out in the far lane and the driver saw Owney and got stubborn. He wasn't going to stop. The distance grew smaller and Old Jack was whimpering and now the Lincoln stopped and Owney was across the boulevard and heading down a slope. He threw his hand out in a wave at the Cross in the cemetery.

"What do you think he just said to us?" Owney called out.

There were two cars in the street ahead of them and Owney went into the wrong lane to pass them and now Old Jack had spit at the corners of his mouth.

"Please, kid."

"Kid? Me? I'm no kid, mister. I'm old enough to have a driver's license. Want to see it?"

He turned around and looked at Old Jack.

Owney went under the expressway without looking and he was bouncing across a pock-marked street and had the car doing ninety when he came onto Troutman Street, which is Old Jack's block. It starts on an empty factory street and goes for a mile up to Old Jack's house, which was in a row of brownstones.

"We better hurry up. I don't want you to be late," Owney said.

The buildings danced as they shot past them. He shot the first red light without looking. One block up, a car was turning onto the street and Owney went to the horn. The car lurched to the curb and now all along the street there were cars and crowded sidewalks in front of houses and the muffler roared so loud that people looked out the windows. At Irving, pennants hung over the street and they moved at Owney so quickly he felt the onset of vertigo. A bus was lumbering across Knickerbocker Avenue. It paused in the middle of the street, completely blocking the way. Owney had the car at its limit, somewhere over ninety, and the level of thrill was rising and he wondered which way he was going around the bus, and then he saw more room to the left and he smiled at the red light staring at him and he burst out onto Knickerbocker and there was the green Plymouth on the right side of Owney's car. The green Plymouth was death.

Old Jack screamed.

Owney braked the car, which howled and skidded. His shoulders rose as the front of the car made it past the Plymouth and then Owney was in a dynamite explosion and he was thrown forward and his stomach was instantly sick. Owney's car spun halfway around. The green Plymouth stopped dead in its own glass.

"Are you all right, guy?"

A kid from the neighborhood, muscular arms sticking out of a black

T-shirt, was a couple of paces away from them. The kid was properly afraid of blood. Owney moved his arms. He shifted his feet. His chest pained him as he breathed, but when he touched the chest nothing seemed broken. All that really bothered him was the nausea and a pain at the base of his neck. He rotated his neck against the pain. Then he looked at Old Jack.

He was alive but motionless, somewhere between mortal terror and deep shock.

"That'll be two-fifty," Owney said.

"You dead," Old Jack said.

"Two-fifty."

"You die."

"You already told me that. Where's the two-fifty?"

"You cockasuck."

"If you don't pay me the two-fifty, that's what I'm going to have you doing."

Old Jack's fingers crept to his shirt pocket and he brought out three dollars.

Owney took out a half dollar, which he gave to Jack as he took the three dollars out of Jack's other hand. In doing this, Owney had his face into the odor coming from Old Jack.

"Hey, Jack."

Old Jack tried to shift his body.

"Jack, you shit your pants. What are you, a gangster or a fag?"

"I kill your fuckin' head."

"And I'm going to tell the whole world you shit your pants."

Owney started walking for the Idle Hour bar.

In the middle of the night or the start of the morning, or whenever it was, he sat on a wicker hamper in the bathroom of Fats's apartment. He knew it was Fats's apartment and he knew his throat throbbed. She stepped out of the shower and stood directly in front of him with the towel held up under her chin. Damp seaweed neared his face. He put a hand flat against her stomach.

"Irish," she said.

"Leave me alone."

"You don't mind going near it when you're drunk," she said. "I did it to you sober. You had to be drunk to go near me."

Personal shame rose through the nausea.

The towel still under her chin, little girl Cindy smiled at him. "Irish."

"I've got to go," Owney muttered.

"It's Monday. I got to go to school take my last Regents'," Cindy said.

The first time Owney used the cemetery as an address was the day in Washington when a colonel took him by the arm and led him into a circle of microphones.

"In Pleiku Province, Specialist Morrison's unit encountered intense fire from well-fortified enemy bunker positions. Specialist Morrison jumped across a canal, moved through heavy enemy fire to within a few feet of the position, and with disregard for his own safety, assaulted the bunkers with hand grenades and rifle fire. Two soldiers were seriously wounded. Specialist Morrison ran through heavy fire from another bunker to assist his fallen comrades. He was hit by a burst of fire from the bunker. In spite of his own painful wounds, Specialist Morrison unhesitatingly attacked the bunker in order to shield the wounded men from enemy fire. While wounded, he again used hand grenades and rifle fire to destroy the enemy position. The sustained, extraordinary courage and selflessness exhibited by this soldier over an extended period of time are in keeping with the highest traditions of the United States Army."

Suddenly there was this toneless California voice. Owney found himself looking first at all the rosebushes and then his eyes fell on the lawn. Sun striking a blade of grass sent a lonely feeling through him. When somebody called out that Owney was another one from Brooklyn, Owney corrected him. He gave the street address of the cemetery, 1176 Taylor Avenue, Queens, New York.

That night, when the colonel flew up from Washington with Owney and, going up the driveway between the headstones, saw what the address meant, he slapped Owney's knee. "Damn, but you got the smarts. If you told them where you actually lived, they would've gone into all sorts of things, drive us crazy. Man comes from a cemetery, likes dead bodies so much, the man goes out and makes a whole batch of new ones. Mister Original Body Count, Mister Macabre. I tell you, you're some quick-thinking character."

Owney didn't answer. If he had told the guy the truth, that they lived there because his family would sleep in graves to beat the rent, the guy would have jumped out of the car, Owney felt.

Owney put his head into the kitchen sink and let cold water pour on the back of his neck. The inside of his head was still a dance hall. A few months ago, he had only needed to splash his face in the morning and the day became his friend. Now, he had washed his face in the bathroom and by the time he got in the kitchen, the dance hall was throbbing again. He mopped his wet auburn hair with a dishrag and went to the kitchen table. His hand shook as he put a cigarette to his lips. The big flame lighter also wavered in his hand as he brought it up. His mother kept telling him on mornings like this that he was too young to shiver. And now she sat across the table from him and wore a prosecutor's stare.

"You shake like you just got out of an auto accident," she said.

"I'm still jumpy from the thing," he said.

"Something at work?"

"No. The other thing."

"I don't see you shake when you don't take a drink. I'll say it again. You're too young to get like this."

He became silent. His answer, that he still was unnerved from being shot at in Vietnam, was not a direct lie, he thought. Of course, it was; whiskey was more dangerous than Verdun.

Owney focused his eyes by sighting across the top of the toaster on the windowsill alongside the kitchen table. Across the top of the toaster on this morning, jiggling a bit in his vision but polished by a fresh spring sky, were the tips of many spires. When the toast popped up, Owney stood up to grab it and now through the window he was looking at a field of tombstones, many of them topped with spires, spreading as far as he could see. The graves began under Altman's gray spire, which was almost directly under the kitchen window, so close that Owney, standing with his toast, could read the inscription on the base of Altman's spire.

WE LIVE IN ILLUSION
AND WE DIE IN DESPAIR

Alongside Altman was the square white headstone for dead Zucker. Owney remembered back in the winter, probably on an anniversary of his death, when Zucker's two wives came at separate times and stood on the tan-yellow grass and regarded the headstone with equal disdain. As the old cars in which they arrived and common coats indicated, Zucker's love might have been enough to go around, but not his estate. Owney had been walking by when the second wife stood with a hand running through a pile of white hair as she told the headstone, "You said you'd take care of me. You certainly did. You put me in a hole deeper than the one you're in."

Next to Zucker was a light gray mausoleum in which a half dozen

Roths were stuffed. Then came monuments, spires, mausoleums with stained-glass windows, narrow headstones, curved headstones, all in irregular rows and uneven heights and spread across the grass like chess pieces. Thousands of gravestones, the stone all of the violet register, all the finest granite, Rock of Ages granite, for marble cannot be used in cemeteries in Queens because the moisture in the air coming from the sea eats at a mother's headstone just as surely as the chipmunks devour her eyes. The graves climbed hills, spilled over the tops, and ran down the far sides. Almost everything in this part of Queens's earth was made prosperous by the dead, with over a dozen cemeteries running into each other: from the Jewish Machpelah and Beth-El to the Cypress Hills National Cemetery to the nondenominational Cemetery of the Evergreens to the other side of the low hills, over on Queens Boulevard, the true power of a Catholic bishop, Calvary Cemetery, some 315 acres, for which Catholics humble themselves for plots so small that the deceased would be more comfortable if inserted vertically. All this melancholy earth was essential to Queens, for at this time, in the spring of 1970, there were two million reportedly alive and four and a half million dead, the deceased therefore outnumbering the living in Queens by more than two to one. Where Owney now stood, in the center of this deadness, was the caretaker's apartment of Mount Sinai Cemetery, five rooms atop an archway whose gloom demanded the sound of horse carriages clopping through the mist.

By now Owney's father regarded the apartment and the land on which it sat as a Sutter's Mill with headstones. As the job called for a Christian who was available on Saturdays and Jewish holy days, when Jews were not allowed to lift a finger, Owney's father wore a Miraculous medal large enough to thrill a Puerto Rican, and prominently, outside rather than inside his T-shirt, with the street shirt over it unbuttoned in order to remind the cemetery manager that his caretaker was of the correct persuasion. For opening the gates at six each morning and closing them at five each night, three hundred sixty-five days a year, and doing exactly nothing else, the Morrisons lived rent-free, and in an apartment that was a level above anyplace before this that had served to keep their heads dry. Nor did the munificence end there; for simply swinging a gate twice a day, Owney's father also received two hundred a month, which was money dropping from the sky. Furthermore, out of the sandhog's pay, the father needed to extract no rent, which permitted him almost always to have something on the bar besides his elbow. He then could take this extra two hundred a month from the cemetery, from a side job that required no work, and throw the two hundred on the kitchen table as a sign that he truly loved his wife. (The fact that his wife had to close the gates at night because he was in the bar didn't bother him.) If he had to take back forty or fifty dollars for something important, that was fine, that was a personal loan, and it did nothing to detract from the original grand gesture of throwing the whole two hundred on the kitchen table.

Psychologically, the cemetery was a smashing arrangement, as it freed the Morrison family of the sandhog's first fear, inability to pay the rent during the long periods of unemployment that went with the trade. In the first months in the caretaker's apartment, though, Owney's mother kept the shades drawn during the day in order to keep her from glancing out a window at death.

Taking the toast out of the toaster now, Owney gagged at the thought of pale butter on it. He opened the window and threw out the toast. Starlings dived for it.

"You can't eat," his mother said.

"I feel sorry for the birds," Owney said. He opened the refrigerator and brought out a twelve-ounce can of Piels, pulled the tab off, and took the first swallow with the tab still in his hand. The beer was cold and high and he swallowed more.

"I'm sorry for the birds, I'm sorry for you, all that drinking," his mother said.

Owney extended his left arm and placed the can of beer atop his head. The hand was that of a statue. The can did not move.

"I told you what it was from," he said. "I just made myself stop thinking about it. Now look at me."

The mother indicated the beer. "Have some more and you'll be singing me a song," she said. "What time did you get in last night?"

"I didn't look."

Owney worked in tunnels under the implied agreement that his past gave him personal power, and also that respect was best offered in silence; the fawning need not apply.

By age, he was one of those who split the union down the middle: the young who banked by check and went from the job to home, and considered the raw work of the job as something that would lead to a business above ground. Several even used the job to support their habit of learning. One, George Carroll, worked nights at the High Bridge job, finished college in the Bronx, and wanted to attend law school, but his aptitude test score caused every New York school to relegate him to night classes only. Leaving work one night, he drove past Yeshiva University, a few blocks away from the job. Inspired suddenly, he went there the next day and applied at Yeshiva College Law School as a minority, an Irish Catholic. The admissions man at Yeshiva allowed nothing to cross his face. "We don't embarrass easily," the admissions man said finally, and Carroll said, "Well, I do. So why don't you embarrass me by letting me in so I can become a lawyer?" In the mail a month later, Carroll received a letter saying he had been accepted. He showed early on the first day and never left. Another young guy on the night shift at Roosevelt Island attended City College and became a candidate for a Rhodes scholarship. "It's a pain in the ass," he said to Owney one day. "I have to go up there while this old guy buffs me up for the interview. I say, 'Look at my marks. I have all A's.' He says that I have 'an inner anger' that sometimes comes out. He wants me to subdue it. I told him, 'Hey, my name is Finnegan.' You know what he said? 'I know. It shows that we'll never truly understand why brains end up where they are.' "

The other half of the union was of the past, of men who threw their pay on the bar and then took the remainder and threw it on the kitchen table when they got home. Owney, fresh from the war, a hero to both young and old, had his choice of going either way.

One day after work, Owney went into Brendan's on Katonah Avenue in the Bronx, four blocks from the job. The inside of Brendan's was a fog bank. Owney's father and four others from the job, all older men, sat in the smoke with their packs of cigarettes on the left hand, bills in the center, and shot glasses at the right hand. The only sound in the place came from the men sucking on cigarettes and exhaling. Then his father started talking about the job. "You know the only trouble with what we do? The bad atmosphere we got to breathe all day." He raised his glass in the smoke and threw it down. Then they got into a discussion over how much money the President should be paid.

"Only one of them ever buys a drink with his own money—Harry Truman, I know that," Owney's father said.

"He put it right up there," Turk, one of the men, said.

"Bet a horse, buy a drink right at the bar. Good man," Owney's father said.

"Then drop a bomb in the fuckin' morning," Turk said.

"He did that."

"I wish he was around now. You'd know he was around by the noise. Boom! That was the end of Russia you just heard."

"And we get a little leukemia," Owney said.

"They just say that," Turk said.

"Guys got it in Vietnam just from a spray they used to kill trees," Owney said.

"Well, what could you do?" Turk said. "I'll take a little leukemia if it means the end of the fuckin' Russians."

In the midst of this it began raining outside and Turk stared out the window at the rain beating on the street. He cocked his head and said to Owney, "See them across the street?"

In a doorway were two black kids of about fourteen, faces peering up from under rain hats, measuring the rain before running for the el stairs at the corner.

"What does that make you think of?" Turk said.

"What?" Owney said.

"I think the mother ought to lock them in a closet, prepare them for goin' to jail. All nigger kids their age is goin' to jail inside of two, three years. Mother might as well get them used to it, lock them in a closet."

"Unless they grow a couple of feet and get rich at basketball," Owney said.

"Did you see those fuckin' Knicks last night?" Turk said.

"No." He had been at the Arena Disco with Dolores, dancing with a bottle of beer in his hand, and he could see that she loved him for doing it. He liked that better than this bar full of old men, but if he went out at this hour of the day he probably wouldn't be able to find anybody he knew to drink with.

"Knicks lost bad," Turk said.

"How bad?"

"Eighteen."

"What did Frazier do?"

"Thirteen."

"Off night."

"Off night, my prick," Turk said. "Frazier goes around thinks he's God. He's just another nigger who can shoot a basket. To think of the money they give him."

"What about this Sojourner?" Jerry Malone, in a red cap, said. "Sixth, seventh man on the Nets. What do you think Sojourner gets? Eighty-five thousand. How do you like that? Big nigger cocksucker can't spell his own name, gets eighty-five thousand dollars."

"That's why hockey's the best game," Turk said. "White man's game. Go see a hockey game, you at least got twelve white guys playin'. No niggers. Not a nigger in the whole of hockey. No wonder nobody watches basketball anymore. People sick and tired of watchin' niggers show off how high they can fuckin' jump."

"They're not jumpin'," Malone said. "They're falling out of the trees they were born in."

"And people think they're jumpin'," Owney's father said.

"They're falling out of the trees, the nigger bastards."

"I want to see them ice-skate," Turk said.

"They'll shiver to death," Malone said.

"They'll be skating all over the place soon," Owney said.

"You think so?" Turk said.

"Sure. They'll hump us all. They'll build indoor ice rinks in Africa."

They laughed and Owney laughed with them, which was a manifestation of the wavering that always went on inside him with this subject. With the others at the bar, skin color was fairly simple. It was fine to work with blacks—even better than fine, for it enraged the men in the other construction unions. Nor was pity ever offered as a form of courtesy to a black working in a cave. This behavior was altered by the clock's crawl to the end of an eight-hour shift, for upon leaving the "hog house" each day, the blacks went their way, nobody knew where, and the white sandhogs went into the bars and made derision of blacks a relentless part of conversation, as it is with nearly all American whites wherever they gather. This daily parting of black and white was done in the manner of Southern whites who, at age eleven or twelve, used to leave forever the black friends with whom they had been playing since each was able to walk.

For the white sandhogs, each day was one of halved feelings, respect for blacks underneath the earth and utter contempt for them above it. And always, in the pits of their stomachs, as immutable as the rock they faced each day, was the flat acceptance that the blacks would work at the same rate of pay as the whites, and that in a union of fathers and sons, the black son was a son first and he could be called a nigger kid later, after he had his union card. Causing the sandhogs to become the very thing they hated: liberals.

As this fact is never raised in conversation—although as a contrary point it would do something to relieve the boredom of bar talk: niggers are bad, the reason for this being that they are niggers—the conversations were persistently mindless. On this one topic, Owney had been through so much more than they had that his interest in what they had to say was annihilated. They sat with him in a bar and talked about blacks, and here Owney had wound up in and out of a war because of them.

In the laughter, Owney thought for a moment about the time in Duc Co, with the sand sifting through an opening in the tin roof and this Daniels, an old black sergeant, he had to be as old as thirty or thirty-one, was saying: "I caught it so bad off this 'ho in Germany that they had to keep me in the hospital down by Wiesbaden. Same time, I couldn't get this one 'ho off my mind. They let me out of Wiesbaden and I go to see this same 'ho again. What do you think happen? Here is this same big old 'ho an—"

"What's a 'ho?" Owney asked.

" 'Ho," Daniels said.

"What?"

"I said, 'Ho!"

"I don't know what's a 'ho," Owney said.

"A 'ho. A great big 'ho. So I go to see this same 'ho again, right the—"

"I still don't know what a 'ho is."

Daniels's face contorted. "Man, stop that. Stop fucking with my *sequence*."

A few nights later, some rural white from North Dakota was asleep when shots were fired and he threw a grenade out of the bunker that hit something on the top and dropped back in and blew off some of Daniels's leg and almost all of his organs. As they carried Daniels off, he probably still qualified as a nigger in white barroom conversation, but Owney and everyone else in the bunker knew that Daniels was no nigger. Afterward, Owney might sit in a white bar and seem to listen intently to conversations about niggers, but he heard little, and when he spoke himself on the subject his phrases were simply a style of speech. When these others talked—people who hadn't been in Vietnam and who didn't work as sandhogs, and therefore in Owney's mind didn't do enough to qualify for saying anything—he pretended to listen but he resented them. For when Owney first came home, he became one of the few white American males who semiconsciously, perhaps gracelessly, but nevertheless steadily moved toward a state of soul that permitted the love of somebody different.

Ahead of him, he had all the chances to work out his life as he kept his trade: the third water tunnel would take fifteen to twenty years to build. It began at a reservoir at the Bronx-Yonkers line, a place where the water that flows all the way down the sloping land from upstate New York comes out of a reservoir that is 295 feet above ground and rushes under the reservoir gatehouse with such force that the stone gatehouse whines like an old factory. The flow must be kept slow or the water would race through the old water tunnel for the length of the city and at the last street, at the Battery, the water would attempt to rise to the level of the reservoir, 295 feet above ground. Finding cast-iron pipes attempting to prevent this, the water would simply blow up the tunnel and the sidewalk over it and screech foamy white into the sky.

Announced by a morning cough, Owney's father walked into the kitchen. All parts of him were dressed for labor, except the face, which looked out the kitchen window and measured the start of the day as if it were a wall to be climbed by a fingernail. A fist went to his mouth and he coughed again, this time hard enough to send a wobble into his knees. "They got people out there already," he said.

"For what?" Owney asked.

"Your friend."

"What friend?"

"Oh, a real friend. The kid got killed so nobody has to fight anymore. He probably was in college so he wouldn't get shot at."

"Oh, that guy," Owney said. He had seen one mention of it in the paper, some guy from some college somewhere who got himself killed. He had read no more of it because the subject bothered him. They had made an issue of telling Owney not to say anything about war resisters. "You act like a man and let the public see for themselves how despicable the others are," the colonel had told him. Still, Owney thought, the kid could go and fuck himself.

"They got a big funeral for him in New York," his father said. "I'd like to see how many would show up for you or for me."

"They're getting real good notoriety," his mother said.

"Why didn't he worry about the poor woman walks out of St. Fortunata's," Owney's father said, "gets hit right on the head, doesn't even have the holy water dry on her forehead?"

"I don't want to hear about it anymore," Owney said.

"He should of got killed twice," the father said. "Once out there and once here. They should of let people torture him to death. The fuck."

"Don't curse, that sounds terrible," the mother said. "You want something?"

"Something cold," the father said.

"Take a glass of milk."

"Milk is no good. It puts sludge on your heart."

"Then have a cup of coffee."

"Got no time."

"You got time for coffee. How long do you need to get to work? One cup of coffee. Where do you have to go to, anyway?"

"Somewhere between Westchester County and Long Island," the father said, which was the answer he gave anytime she asked even an offhand question about the details of his employment.

"Is it nearer to where we're going to live?" his mother said, sarcastically.

"I don't know that. I know that we're going. Out on Long Island. Near the water and near the parkway."

"You told me that after we lived here three weeks," she said. "Now we're here two years. We move around less than the people in the ground."

The father's neck became red. "Yeah, well, I don't mind it here at all, lot of Jews so dead they don't even try to sell you anything."

"I heard that when we first moved in here," the mother said. "Where do you think you can move to at this stage?"

"I see this ad the other day. Exit sixty-eight, Long Island Expressway. A house they call a mother-daughter house. That means you could fit two families in, doesn't it?"

"How much will that cost?" the mother said.

"Not that much. You'd be surprised."

"Surprise me then."

"It was nothing. Eighty-five thousand."

"I see. How much of this do you have to put down?"

"That's the problem. They want a whole third. But we'll get it."

The father turned to Owney. "All right. Let's go. I'm not going to get a house sitting around here."

"When did the house business start?" Owney said.

"When she told me that I never would be able to get one," his father said. "Get your shirt and let's go."

Owney watched the smoke streaming in the light over the top of the can of beer. "Not today."

"What's the matter?"

"Can't make it."

"I never heard of a thing like this. Guy your age. Once you're up, who misses work?"

"I do," Owney said.

"I never did anything like this. I always made work in the morning."

"I have something to do today," Owney said.

The father shrugged and walked out. Owney stared out the window.

At ten-thirty, he tried the day again. His mother was in the kitchen this time, and when Owney went to the refrigerator, she said to him, "What are you doing?"

"Taking some beer. I might go to the beach. I get thirsty down there."

The mother said, "You don't want beer at the beach. I'll give you some nice ginger ale. Krasdale's ginger ale from the store."

She stood up and went to the refrigerator and held a hand to protect the beer.

"Maybe I don't want anything," Owney said.

"That's good," the mother said.

"Let me get out of here," Owney said.

He found her in the middle of the afternoon on a street at the bottom of a hill in the Forest Hills Gardens neighborhood, which is arranged into an English village of Tudor houses with red tile roofs and lawns with no fences. Dolores sat sideways in her Frosted Bar ice cream truck, with her feet hanging out so she could kick pink snowdrifts of cherry blossoms from trees whose branches brushed the truck roof. On the other side of the truck was a gully with trees and the first flowers of the year showing at the top of the gully.

He stood alongside the truck in silence and beauty and looked at the sun on her hair and did not talk.

"Why didn't you call me since Sunday?" she said.

"I don't know."

"I can't believe you didn't call me. I waited all day Sunday. And then two more days?"

Owney said nothing.

"That's the first time in four months that you didn't call me."

He didn't answer. Somewhere in him there was a soundless groan. A young girl with a young heart suddenly issuing commands with the manner of an old housewife. Yet any annoyance was drowned in a fear that what he wanted would escape him. If she was this cool over unanswered questions, what would happen if he gave her a fresh answer? Maybe she drives away in the truck, he told himself. The thing that surprised him was that he never thought of walking away from her first. In the sunlight, she had him afraid.

"What are you thinking about?" she said.

"You."

"What are you thinking about me?"

"That you look pretty here. Beautiful girl in a beautiful place."

"I only go to pretty places like this," she said. "I'm the first woman they ever hired for this job. They told me they knew I wasn't going to be selling ice cream at some factory." She laughed. "Besides, I'm the only ice cream truck in Queens that isn't selling drugs."

He liked the laugh. That got him out of talking about Sunday. "You're too pretty for that," he said.

"You think that?"

"All the time."

He bent down and he nuzzled her neck. "I always heard your voice, saw your face, and could feel your neck."

"I know that's what you wrote me."

"I meant it."

"That's good."

"I'm thinking about us getting married."

"When did you decide this?"

"This morning. Now. I don't know. I just decided."

"You said it before this."

"Said it when?"

"In your letters. You just told me you meant them. Now you don't even know what you said."

"Yes, I do."

"So why do you say that you just made up your mind now?"

"Because that's what I said. What do you have to say about it?"

"Oh, I have to think," she said.

"Why?"

"Because I have to think. This is a very serious thing. Now let me think."

She looked at her feet as they moved through the pink snowdrifts. Then she slid out of the truck and stood up and put her face to his and kissed him lightly. He took her in his arms in the sunlight and pressed his mouth against hers.

She pulled her head back slightly and looked in his eyes. "I'm not leaving school."

"Who said that?"

"What does that mean?"

"I'll work. You go to school."

He put his hand on the small of her back and pulled her against him in a long kiss. He was getting hard against her leg.

A woman in a long green robe who was inspecting the rosebushes on her lawn called to them. "You two behave."

"Why?"

"You could get married."

4

BILLY KAUFHOLD had died a few years earlier, and so, that September, her uncle, Matty Kearns, Sr., an operating engineer, his face and hands wet from nervousness, and also from the colossal amount of weight he carried, gave the bride away. The ceremony was at St. Pancras Church, with the vows as read aloud by the Reverend Edward M. Pfister containing so many phrases such as "I will" and "I will not" that it was a question whether this was a wedding ceremony or a sentencing to prison. Still, the rigidity only increased the power of the moment: a few Latin phrases transformed Dolores from a young neighborhood girl into a woman with the appearance and demeanor of a Queens housewife. Standing in the vestibule of the church after the ceremony, Dolores greeted older women with the ease of an equal.

The wedding reception was held at the Elmhurst–Jackson Heights American Legion Post, and as most people omit the church service and arrive at the reception in high thirst, the crowd in the vestibule of the Legion hall had the doorways blocked as they waited for the affair to begin. When the bridal party arrived, there was pushing to get them inside the hall. Immediately, Matty Kearns, Sr., forced himself and a party of four men, all nearly as large as Matty, into the barroom, where they immediately made a bartender out of the Colombian kid who was supposed to be polishing the bottles. By the time the regular bartender came on duty, the bar was packed with free-swallowing men, most of whom were built like overstuffed chairs. As a member of the wedding party, Matty Kearns, Sr., was the central figure at the bar, waving a hand and ordering drinks and speaking loudly to a cousin, Jimmy O'Mara, who answered with difficulty; in honor of the formal occasion, O'Mara kept his top lip folded down to conceal three missing teeth on the right side. Kearns himself, when laughing, revealed a missing incisor. Construction workers are weak in enamel.

There was a particularly loud noise in the doorway and Fats came into the vestibule, immediately grabbing Owney by the arm and pulling him to the bar. Fats was wearing a brilliant powder-blue jacket and gray slacks. Trailing him was little girl Cindy, who had not been invited to the wedding and was not dressed for it. She wore jeans and a yellow blouse.

"Look who I brought," Fats said.

"Hi, Owney," Cindy said.

Fats got them both white wine, and a VO for Owney. He put an arm around Cindy and drew her close to his wide body. "Cindy wants to pay you back what she owes you," Fats said.

"Forget about it," Owney said.

"What's the matter with you?" Fats said. "Cindy, tell him how you're going to pay him back."

"Suck cock."

"My man!" Fats held his palm out.

A hand grabbed Owney's arm and without looking at who was tugging him, he allowed himself to be brought up to the bar, where a man with a pork face and neck of a blowfish stood in a semicircle of admiring faces. He wore pressed light brown. His eyes widened as he saw Owney. He waved with one hand, and with the other, he poked a man next to him, a bell buoy in a shapeless blue suit who was swallowing beer with his eyes closed. Dark curly hair, with the first gray in it, drooped onto a lightly sweating forehead. Upon feeling the arm poke him, the bell buoy opened his eyes.

The pork face now held out a hand that was large enough to be menacing, but when Owney shook it, he found the skin as soft as pastry. On the thick wrist was a watch that told time with dots. "I'm Connie Heaney, the city councilman, yeah?" the man said.

Owney murmured a hello.

"You're something, yeah?" Heaney said. Heaney introduced the bell buoy as "my associate."

"You have a drink?" the bell buoy said.

"Give us some vodka, yeah?" Heaney said, not bothering to ask if

Owney wanted anything different. Quickly, glasses were passed, and Heaney held his up in a toast. Owney drank his fast. Cold and cloudy. The bell buoy poured a bottle of Piels into a glass so quickly that it spilled down the sides. He took a big swallow and put the glass down.

"Sandhog?" he said to Owney.

"You got it," Owney said.

"We got to get you out of the sandhogging," Heaney said.

"If you know a better way I could make money," Owney said. "I'm married now. I better make up my mind now."

"What would you like?" Heaney said.

"A safety deposit box you can't fit any more in."

Heaney laughed. His hand went out, holding an empty glass. The bell buoy took it, then took Owney's empty glass and began rocking his head to summon the bartender.

"You thought of anything, yeah?" Heaney said.

Owney gulped the drink. Up to this point, the Morrisons had been a family that remained sheltered from the possibilities of American lightning. There was no poet, painter, doctor, lawyer, business success who rose from generations of work with bended back. Jack Morrison, who had worked for the lawyer Quinn, found that combining jobs with futures and a dry throat was irreconcilable. He died a bartender in Queens Village. The Morrison family history was one of loyalty to church, union, country. Beyond that, there was an interest only in those things that require no more thought than boarding a bus. There was an understanding that most American success originates in an obstetrician's hands: if he pulls you out of a woman who is in the right marriage, your future is assured.

Owney now put the glass down and said to Heaney, "All my family ever did was work. Someday maybe I'll try running for office in the union. But I first got to show the men how good I can work. Men in my union won't vote for anybody who doesn't show them how good he works."

"You should get the world," Heaney said loudly. "Hero like you. You deserve anything you want."

"The world," the bell buoy said.

"Man's a hero," Heaney said. He finished his drink and Owney raised his, but now the ice came against his lips and right away he had the glass on the bar for more.

It was in the middle of the next drink, with the cigarette smoke streaming in the air, that Heaney said, "I know what this kid should be. He should be a deputy commissioner of Ferries, under Ports and Terminals."

"Good job!" the bell buoy said. Cigarette ashes fell on the suitfront.

"You know that's the job for him," Heaney said.

"Beauty," the bell buoy said.

The bartender handed out more vodka, which Owney found wonderful. Then Dolores walked in and Owney introduced her to Heaney, who kissed her cheek. "What about this guy?" he said.

"I love him," she said.

"What are we going to do with his life?"

"It's up to him," she said. "He has to live it."

"Then I know what to do," Heaney said.

A man in a Legion cap gave Heaney and the man with him roast beef sandwiches, with dripping cole slaw sticking out from under the bread. Heaney held the sandwich far out and craned his neck as he took a bite. His brown suit was clear of the juice as it dripped on the bar. The bell buoy ate with cole slaw dotting his suit.

Heaney got up to leave. "I just wanted to show my face and give you congratulations. And I got to tell you, I won't forget a word I said."

He and the bell buoy left. Dolores took Owney's hand and led him back to the vestibule. Owney stepped away from her to talk to an aunt. In the middle of the vestibule, Dolores swung around and noticed a thin guy in his early thirties. His name was Robert Hale, and he had been her favorite teacher, of biology. He had obvious difficulty with his own gender, something the wedding party noticed immediately. Dolores's cousin, Virginia, was supposed to ease the day for him, but she was lost in the crowd. A hand went nervously to light brown hair. He relaxed when he saw that Dolores was paying him immediate attention. He kissed Dolores on the cheek and then held up a finger and said, "No matter what happens, I'm going to see you finish school. Remember that."

Owney's uncle on his mother's side, Jerry Hayes, standing directly behind them, said loudly, "What school? She got no time for school. She's going to be raising a whole school of her own."

Hale said, "I'm sure she's capable of doing both."

Hayes growled. When Dolores stared at him, Jerry Hayes gave a false laugh and started to push her toward the bar.

"I'm right," Hale said to her.

"We'll see what happens," Dolores said.

"Make sure that it happens," Hale said.

"I'll try," Dolores said.

Hale stepped out of the way as Queens women advanced on the bride.

At this point, the high, soft sound of a saxophone warming up came from inside the Legion hall. At the reed's sound, the bartender ducked out from his station and left the barroom, which was a direct way of announcing that the cocktail hour was over. The transition caught Owney's uncle Jerry with an empty glass.

"This is a fuckin' disgrace," he yelled at the bartender. His head, a cement block, swiveled until he caught sight of Matty Kearns, Sr., who, as the man who gave the bride away, was the official host. "Hey, Matty, be a good fellow and have the guy give us another drink."

Kearns laughed. "Come on, Jerry, this is a party for the kids." Alongside Kearns, his wife, Winifred, said, "I'm so dry I barely could talk. We'll all have a drink inside." Winifred, who was called Winnie by everyone, was five foot three and weighed more than two hundred pounds, most of which was stuffed inside a gold evening dress that had a cape arrangement at the shoulders so as to cover her great fleshy upper arms. Her girdle was so tight that she took steps like a penguin. A great pile of taffy-colored hair did nothing for her jowly face.

"Be a good girl and tell your husband to get us a drink," Hayes said.

"We'll have one inside," she said.

"They make us wait too long at a table," Hayes said.

"You're an asshole," Matty Kearns, Sr., said to Hayes.

"Were you talking to me?" Hayes said.

"Right to your face," Kearns said.

"Then you're going to get a bellyful of me before we're through here today," Hayes said.

His attention was taken away by the appearance of the Colombian boy, who was tugging an ash can full of ice to the bar.

"Give us a round," Jerry Hayes said. He held out a big hairy hand. The South American kid took the bill, stuffed it into his shirt pocket, and went back to moving the ash can of ice across the floor. Jerry reached into the kid's breast pocket and took the money back. Everybody in the room was saying, You see, there is no way you can trust a fuckin' South American spic. They all then began reaching behind the bar to grab bottles of beer. Drinking beer from the bottle, they went into the hall. All walked as stiffly as hospital patients. This was the result of many hours through many years of standing at bars. Also because their thighs were so fat that in order to move without chafing them they were forced to walk with their legs quite wide apart.

Inside the hall, the formalities of a Queens sit-down wedding reception were handled expertly by bandleader Bobby Duffy. For thirty-five years Bobby Duffy had played at every Irish occasion worth attending in New York. Bobby Duffy was dressed in a red plaid dinner jacket and had hair that could be viewed as modish by the young or merely acceptably short by those older in age. Very early in his life Bobby Duffy learned that antagonism does not feed.

"Here goes, ladies and gentlemen," Bobby Duffy announced. "Here goes for the first time, dancing as husband and wife, Mr. and Mrs. Owen Morrison."

Bobby Duffy's saxophone led his musicians into "Prisoner of Love." The bride and groom stepped into a yellow spotlight. All the people stood applauding at the long bingo tables that had been covered with red table linen and set for dinner, ten at a table, thirty tables about the room. Lowered lights kept the electric basketball scoreboard and the Fire Department's occupancy limit sign from intruding on the regal atmosphere. Overhead, flattened against the ceiling, were the baskets and backboards that could be lowered in case there was a basketball game, although a sparsity of white kids able to jump high enough to play the game even for amusement made the baskets obsolete.

Playing his music, Bobby Duffy came to the end of the stanza: "I can't *excape,* for it's too late now. I'm just a pris'ner of love."

He had the wedding off to a good start. He played "Danny Boy" and then he asked everyone who was seated facing the band to place an arm around the person to his right, and everyone seated with his back to the band to place an arm around the person to his left. Bobby Duffy told the crowd that when he started playing the next song, those with right arms out should sway to the right on the first note and those with left arms out should sway to the left first. Bobby Duffy then played "East Side, West Side" and the mirror effect of one line of people swaying one way and the next line the other made everybody dizzy. Immediately, the first whiskey appeared on tables, followed by thin soup and dried banquet roast beef slices.

The room turned into crumpled napkins, spilled drinks, and rising egos. When Dolores arrived at the table where Robert Hale was sitting, she found him being lectured to by one of the sandhogs—she had trouble with the names—who kept poking a thick finger into Hale's chest.

"Puttin' in kitchens, that's the work," the guy was saying. "It's better than plumbin'. Or what I do. You know why?"

"I don't think I do," Hale said.

"Ha! I knew you didn't. I could tell by lookin' at you. I come into your house, and say even if I only put in new doors, cabinet doors, new countertops, it's still like fifteen hundred. I take fifteen hundred off you. But now every time you come in the kitchen for a drink of water, you see that countertop, you see them new doors. But if I put in plumbin', if I put in fifteen hundred dollars of new plumbin', it's buried. You never see nothin' of your money. You know? And then when you *ast* the public to pay millions for where I work, a water tunnel they can't never see, then, forget it. You know? You know what I'm talk——?"

From a table, she heard a growl. "Look at this little hump!" Jerry Hayes glared at Hale. Dolores stepped back from Hale and then walked up to Hayes.

"What *is* the matter with you?"

Which of course did it. Matty Kearns, Sr., and Jimmy Morrison, Owney's father, stepped quickly through tables toward Hayes, and Kearns was there first. The sense that keeps most people from stepping off mountains told Jerry Hayes to get up, which he did, exactly in time to see Matty Kearns, Sr.'s right hand, a sloppy right hand, thrown from too far back. Jerry Hayes ducked and the right hand skidded across the top of his head, rippling the slicked-back hair. Jerry Hayes half punched and half shoved Matty Kearns, Sr., back. Immediately, both Dolores's mother and Winnie Kearns were out in front of the wedding cake, which sat on the edge of the dance floor, for all to admire while gliding by. Winnie Kearns, being wider than Dolores's mother, stood in front of the cake, as if a hockey goalie.

In the scuffling, Jimmy Morrison suddenly pushed Kearns out of the way and punched Jerry Hayes hard. Ducking, Hayes took the punch on the back of the neck, and went down on his face in a rage. He grabbed a chair alongside him and, rising from his knees, folded the chair—a folded chair being a far better weapon than an open one. Jerry Hayes swung the chair like a baseball bat. Jimmy Morrison ducked. Matty Kearns, Sr., swayed backward. The chair whirred through the air and whacked the side of Winnie Kearns's pile of taffy hair. Winnie Kearns's elbow went into the cake as she fell, gold tips of her shoes straight up, oblivious to the riot occurring over her. There were at least four people fighting now.

From his seat at the head table, Owney slipped under the table, crawled out the other side onto the dance floor, and went to help Winnie Kearns, who now stirred. Eyes rolling, attempting to focus, she rolled in her beautiful gold dress onto her right shoulder. Seeing Owney, she smiled. "You're a good boy." Seeing the smear of white cake frosting on the elbow of her dress, she looked up with fear at the cake. When Winnie

Kearns saw the gash in the side of the cake, she came off the floor rapidly, her bison's behind pushing her erect, and Owney tried holding her but she yanked her arm free. And with all the anger of all the years of Queens womanhood and the sanctity of wedding cakes rushing through her, she found Jerry Hayes in the fight, brought back her gold foot, and then sent it forward into Jerry Hayes's testicles.

Bobby Duffy was running from the vestibule to the bandstand, with his musicians after him, and Bobby Duffy, with thirty-five years of working in jungles such as this, grabbed the microphone and without waiting for the music, began to wail: "Oh-ho, say, you can see . . ."

By "what so proudly we hail'd" the other musicians were coming onto the stand. Matty Kearns, Sr., gasping for air, pulled himself together. Solemnly, he saluted. The sounds of the other musicians picking up knocked-over chairs and music stands distracted Bobby Duffy. He stopped singing for a moment. This moment of silence was used by Jerry Hayes, testicles shriveled in pain, who threw a right-hand punch that caught Matty Kearns, Sr., under the salute. Matty Kearns, Sr., went down like an air raid victim. His fat wife, fingernails flashing, went for Jerry Hayes's face.

On the bandstand, Bobby Duffy's mouth was numb as his mind refused to hand him more words to "The Star-spangled Banner." Without this patrio-religious music, brush fires burst out all over the auditorium.

"Play something!" Bobby Duffy said to his musicians.

Without thought or hesitation, the group swung into "Tiger Rag." This caused the heavy-equipment union people to roar against each other, the women's handbags flying, and as the music drove everybody wilder, Owney grabbed for Dolores. He moved quickly to the side exit, as he knew he was only instants away from the point when somebody got the great idea of taking on the war hero groom and knocking him dead.

Outside in the alley he lit a cigarette and they listened to the noise inside. Owney and Dolores laughed.

They went on a two-week honeymoon to Fort Lauderdale in Florida. They came home and moved into the first-floor apartment of a semi-attached two-family house on 74th Street in Glendale, a half block down from Myrtle Avenue. Dolores had quit the ice cream truck. She went back to school and Owney went to the tunnel. They were home for three days when Heaney, the councilman, called Owney and said that an appointment had been made for him with a man named Mortarano of the Department of Ferries, under Ports and Terminals. Owney wrote the name down on the inside of a wide matchbook, and when Heaney had further instructions, Owney had to go to a second matchbook to put the time and location of the meeting, noon on the following Thursday at City Hall.

"I deliver, yeah?" Heaney said.

"I guess so," Owney said.

"Well, you're a hero and you deserve the world, yeah?"

Owney met Dolores later in the back yard of Caffee Licata. They had Italian sodas at a table along a brick wall that was thick with ivy. Through a black grille gate at the end of the yard they could see a tomato garden that was being tended by an old man in a white shirt and baggy pants who had a short black cigar between his teeth.

"Heaney called today. He said I have a job with the Ferries Department."

"They're just going to give you the job?" Dolores said.

"Because of the medal."

"Really?"

"Why not?"

She pursed her lips and thought for a moment. "All right. Why not? Is it for you? What do you have to do?"

"If it's a job, I can do it."

"I don't mean that. I'm not worried about you doing a job. But will you like a job where you have to sit all day in a building? That's important, isn't it?"

"I'll take it," Owney said.

The next Wednesday, the night before the meeting, they went out for a while and of course Owney wanted to tarry wherever he was and the time in the night outpaced them and at four in the morning Owney was in the bedroom, the door open, looking at his new brown job suit that was on a wooden hanger hooked to the top of the bedroom door. Actually, he saw one brown suit and half of another, so he closed one eye to consolidate the clothes and in doing this he saw that the lapel hole was still sewn. He took the blue rosette for his medal and said to himself, Let me see what this looks like in my new suit. As long as I'm going, put on a show. He went into the bathroom for a razor blade, then took the brown suitjacket off the hanger. Actually, he yanked the suitjacket off and in doing so lost his balance and fell onto his back on the bed. Keeping one eye closed, he aimed the razor blade at the sewn lapel hole and his hand darted at the material, causing the razor blade to cut completely through the edge of the lapel, miss the hole entirely, and slice his thumb. Blood smudged the lapel. Owney swore and began cutting at the lapel as if it were tough beef until he had the rosette in place.

"How's it look?" he said, flat on his back, holding the jacket up with both hands. The blue rosette for the medal had a nest of brown tufts sprinkled with dark blood spots.

Dolores, watching from the doorway, said, "Fine."

"You bet it's fine."

In the morning they took the M train, which ran on a ribbon of rust between apartment houses where Puerto Rican women in housedresses leaned out top-floor windows of rooms in which there were mattresses with no sheets. The train then climbed the Williamsburg Bridge, and squealing, scraping, passing windows with more Puerto Rican women staring out, it dove into a tunnel in lower Manhattan.

In front of City Hall, limousines were parked with their rear tires against the sidewalk. Owney and Dolores went up many wide steps with grooves worn in them from seventy-five years of people running up them and trying to leap through the doors and make a huge splash in the gravy. At the top of the steps was a line of French doors, with only one of them open. The policeman on duty inside felt comfortable only when the usual municipal thieves walked by. As Owney approached, the policeman inspected him, saw with satisfaction that Owney had short hair, and allowed him to pass. In the lobby, standing on a marble staircase leading to the second floor, were lacquered men with starved eyes.

"I think I'll wait here," Dolores said in the lobby.

"You come with me," Owney said.

"No."

"Hey, this has got to do with you, too."

"No, it doesn't."

"If I get it, then you get it."

"In a way."

"What's that supposed to mean?"

"That I'm staying here."

She put her purse on a radiator top. With a shrug, Owney walked up the stairs, reading his matchbook cover, which said his appointment with Mortarano, the Ports and Terminals Department man, was outside a hearing room on the second floor. Owney asked a cop, who pointed to a thin man with hooded eyes who stood in an open doorway that looked into a large room where a woman with a clipboard was screaming into a microphone at a circle of men seated at a high desk.

When Owney introduced himself, Mortarano's hand came out solemnly, as if at the entrance to a funeral chapel. "It is my honor to meet you."

"Heaney told me," Owney said.

"I know. How can I assist you?"

"I'm supposed to get a job."

"You're not working now?"

"I'm in the sandhogs."

"What's wrong with that?"

"Nothing, I guess."

"I think that's a very good job."

"In a way. Heaney said I ought to be here."

"Of course you're a very hard man to turn down. A record like yours. The trouble with my department is, you've got to take the civil service test."

"Heaney told me you were supposed to see me about a job has no test," Owney said.

"What job did he tell you?"

"Deputy for ferries."

"That's my job!"

"I didn't know," Owney said.

The hooded eyes were wide in alarm and the soft voice now ran up the scale. "Who told you ask for my job? Did Heaney tell you this?"

"I told you what he told me."

"Did you speak to your county leader before you came here? Are you coming here to push me out of work?"

He whirled and looked into the big room. The woman shrieking into the microphone was waving her clipboard. Mortarano said, "Now look what you've done to me. This is my hearing. A new slip for Staten Island. I'm supposed to be running it. Excuse me now." Brisk steps took him into the big room.

Owney went to bed early that night in order to be fit for work in the morning. As he stretched out in bed, the anger kept his eyes wide open. It was hours before he fell asleep. He wanted to be someplace where the rock overhead, no matter how dangerous, still protected him from the disorder above ground.

He walked in his boots through the mud puddle that ran the length of the wooden floor between the rows of lockers, the sudden flopping sound causing men to look up, for at this time of the morning—six-fifteen—it was the loudest noise in the long hut, even though there were already more than fifty men dressing for their day's work in the mine. Their fingers moved across shirt fronts like tired crabs. Low coughs formed their most coherent sounds. Always, these men boast loudly of the great money to be made in the mine; money for them at this time was marvelous, six and seven hundred dollars a week, depending on overtime, but all of this talk is done at a distance from the job, out in a bar someplace where they talk through their glasses. Here, in a wet hut and approaching the moment when they must put up their bodies in order to finally realize this money of which they talk so much, tongues stick to the teeth.

Overhead, dry street clothes hung on chains from low rafters. The hut was called the hog house by workers who would use it for the length of the job, probably fifteen years. It looked like the dressing room of an old fight club, and gave the same feeling that somewhere outside the door, waiting for each arrival, was some sort of a calamity. Of the couple of hundred who used the hut each day, there would be, before the job was finished and the hut torn down, deaths and feet crushed and bones rotted by dampness and livers rotted by drink and babies born and daughters married and fathers crying at graduations. And, always, in the darkness of a morning, the fresh face of somebody's son, in grammar school when the job first started and now presenting his own body for a man's hardest labor. No matter what the occasion of the moment, whoever was in the hut each morning through all the years would sit without words.

At the end of the rows of lockers was a picnic table, at which five men, the first dressed for work that day, sat in plaid wool shirts, yellow rain pants, and boots with metal tips. They played cards silently. One of them, James, a black with a close-cropped beard, was a member of Owney's work gang. He had his lunch bag on the table, and next to it a Bible. When James opened the Bible each day to read it at lunch in the tunnel, inside the cover he had pictures of his house in St. Croix, a squat cinder-block hut that had a tin roof and a dirt path from the door that led out to a road where people waited in the dust for two and three hours at a time for rides. James found four rooms in the Bronx, with heatless days and cold water in the winter, with extra locks on the doors and guns in pockets of people on the street, a vast improvement over the stillness of St. Croix.

On the bulletin board behind the picnic table was a sign reading: ANYBODY CAUGHT STEALING WILL BE KILLED.

Owney stood in the doorway and looked out at equipment sheds and, beyond them, trucks and bulldozers. Then a slick hill rose from the mud, and atop the hill, dominating the area and placing a curse in the sky that caused the eye seeing it to look away, was the high tower of red steel, and the great, angry wheel hanging from its top, that marked the presence of a mine. The wheel spins and metal lifts loaded with human flesh drop into the deep hard cold folds of the earth.

In the mist in the morning in Wales, in Merthyr Tydfil, men step from their mean row houses and walk with their heads bowed toward the black tower and great ugly wheel suspended at the top. And at Newcastle-upon-Tyne, where the wheel is also black, and men work deep and far out under the bed of the North Sea, hunched over in tunnels four feet high, and at Cabin Creek, West Virginia, where men step out of trailers dug into the side of the hill and wearily go toward the tower and the wheel, at all the places all over the earth where men give up their dreams and their bodies for the money of mining, the wheel dominates. As he looked at it, regarding it as an enemy of his youth, he heard from somewhere in the air the squeak of a boxing shoe on canvas, and somewhere in him he knew what this was, but he paid attention only to the ugliness of the wheel.

Owney stepped out of the hog house and into the moist air and then walked behind the shack and up to a chain link fence, on the other side of which was a street of two-family houses, good houses of the upper Bronx, frame houses with aluminum siding and storm doors that had family initials. Owney faced the side of the nearest house, which had butter-yellow aluminum siding. He grasped the chain link fence and rattled it, causing a loose section of the chain link to slap loudly against the metal post holding it. Right away, in the butter-yellow house, at the ground-floor window, a small face appeared. The window opened.

"Rock Man!"

"Bang bang!" Owney answered.

The face was gone and now there was a sound at the side storm door. A boy of about four came running out in a yellow pajama top and the rest of him bare. Ran to the fence through the mud with a hand out. "Rock Man!" Owney took a piece of rock out of his shirt pocket, rock from the mine, a rock maybe five hundred million years old. He pushed the piece of rock through the fence and the kid grabbed it.

"You're the second boy in the whole world ever to touch this rock," Owney said.

"Hi, Rock Man," the kid said.

Owney pointed at the house directly across the street from the boy's. Pale green aluminum siding all sleeping in the morning light.

"That one!" Owney said.

The bare bottom raced away. Tiptoed across the street, hopping once when he stepped on a pebble, ran up the front stoop to the top where he held up the rock and twisted his body around, the lips pursed in mighty effort, and let the rock go at the front door. The rock struck one of the glass panes under the mailbox and bounced back. Nothing was broken but the rock had made noise enough in the stillness. The kid started to hop down the stoop.

"Chris boy!" A mother's voice.

Bare bottom teetered on the stoop as he looked over at Owney.

"Bang bang!" Owney's finger pointed at the milk box on the stoop. The bare bottom spun around, saw nothing, and looked back at Owney. "Bang bang!" Owney called again, finger remaining at the milk box. Bare bottom spinning, he saw the milk box and Owney yelled, "Yeah!" and then the kid picked it up, high, empty metal, an off day, which was too bad, for a full milk box would have been more fun for both the kid and Owney. The kid held the milk box to his chest and then heaved it against the door. Heaved it only a couple of inches, because after all, he was a small boy, but heaved it enough to make a loud noise as the milk box struck the storm door. In the clattering, the bare ass came down the stoop and went across the street, giving a great leap when the foot hit another thing, a stone or a stick, that hurt.

And behind him at the green house, the storm door opened and a man looked out sleepily.

"Yo!" Owney called to the kid. Who stopped in midstride, a jumble of bare legs and bottom turning around to face the man in the green house and recite lines that had been learned perfectly over the months of mornings.

"Fucko!" he yelled at the man.

"Give it to him good," Owney hissed.

"You fucko!" the kid yelled.

Now he turned again and came bounding toward Owney at the fence. There was a sound at the side of the butter-yellow house, the boy's house, and the side door opened and she leaned out, her long black hair asleep on her shoulders, her eyes squinting, and the lace of the top of the white nightgown looped across her breasts.

She heard her son cry again, "Fucko!" and her voice carried along the side of the house: "Chris!"

The boy started scurrying along the side of his yellow house to the woman in the doorway.

"Rock Man!" Owney called out.

Again, bare legs and bottom jumbled around and the boy came flying to the fence. Owney went into his pocket for another rock. Slow, go slow. Take your time. He had some of his vision on the shirt pocket with the rocks in it and the rest of it on the woman just inside the doorway. Slow, go slow, then maybe she will come out and stand in the morning light in her white nightgown.

"Chris-to-PHER!"

The kid turned around without his rock and ran to the side door. The mother had a hand out for him. She looked across at Owney with feigned exasperation on her face. "Lunatic!" she called to Owney.

I want to see you, Owney said to himself.

The woman looked down as her son slipped through the door. Which then closed.

Tomorrow morning, Owney thought.

He wanted his life to be on the other side of the fence, dancing in the air like a kite, trying for that one moment when the kite, caught full by the breeze, shimmers in excitement. Bare bottom causing the heart to leap with a rock banging against a window so loud the whole house jumps up. And a woman outside the door with the light streaming through her nightgown and over her body. All fun. Kite in the sun.

Once, at the start, he enjoyed things inside the fence. There was the day when he came into the hog house after a shift and here was one of the men, McSweeney, who sat on a wooden bench and scratched the side of a bare foot that was stained gray from the day's mud. McSweeney looked up with eyes that had been stabbed by a lively night.

"No showers," he said, pulling back on an old blue worksock and leaving as dirty as the earth could make him.

Outside, Owney's father, as shop steward, was talking to the contractor, Deutscher. Owney walked out and stood alongside him.

"That's a crime we got no showers," his father said.

"I'm just hearing about it now," Deutscher said.

"We told your office yesterday," Owney's father said.

"That's just what we did," Owney said. The contractor seemed irritated that Owney cut in. But Owney's father was comfortable with it.

"This is the first I heard of it," the contractor said.

"What are you going to do about it?" Owney's father said.

"Get it fixed now?" Owney said.

The contractor exhaled. "You'll have showers tomorrow."

"We'll hold you to that," Owney said. His father nodded.

"So hold me. Then take a shower."

The next morning, Owney stepped noiselessly toward the bedroom door. A bundle stirred in bed. "You have to leave me the car," she said.

"I know. You told me last night."

"I got to go to the doctor's. You can't forget."

"What do I forget? My father's picking me up outside."

"I'll come for you at three-thirty," she said.

Later, when Owney came out of the hole and into the cold afternoon, there was thick mud clinging to his hands and his face and inside his shirt, on his chest and stomach. At the hog house, there was a crowd at the entrance to the shower room. "It don't even drip," one of them said.

Owney's father stood outside the hog house. "I've got to make up my mind," he said.

"To do what?" Owney said.

"To strike the place right now, have no night shift, or to wait until we come back tomorrow. Have this shift start the walkout."

"Fuck. Nobody'll get paid," Owney said.

"What's that got to do with it? Are you supposed to be yellow, sit there do nothing when the guy gives you no water," the father said.

"No, I know what to do with the bastard," Owney said.

"Do you?" the father said.

"I'll fix him and maybe we don't have to go out and lose money," Owney said. "Give me like two hours. I'll call you."

The father shrugged and Owney walked over to the contractor's trailer. One of the bosses on the job, Podhoretz, sat at the desk.

"Deutscher just left," Podhoretz said.

"He told me come for dinner. Me and my wife. Now I lose the address."

"He told you dinner?"

"He's got a nephew going to get drafted. He wants me to talk to the kid."

"Deutscher didn't mention that to me."

"What's he going to do, talk about something personal? His nephew is scared to death. I'm going to give him some real draft counseling."

"How could you do that?" Podhoretz said. "You went all through the thing. How can you tell somebody else how to cheat?"

"I'm not. I'm going to teach him how to make the war go fast. I'm going to teach him how to kill a lot of guys at once."

"Oh," Podhoretz said. He began going through a folder.

"I also want to teach him to make sure and listen to them as they go. The blood gurgles like a bitch. It's great."

"Oh," the man said again. Hurriedly, he wrote an address on a slip of paper. Seventy-five View Lane in Dobbs Ferry, which is in Westchester. Owney took the slip and got his clothes and walked down to the car in his work clothes.

"What did the doctor say?" Owney asked Dolores.

"I'm pregnant, all right."

"That's what he said last month."

"He'll say it next month, too."

"Do you feel like taking a ride?" he said.

"With you? Like that? Yes."

She moved over in the front seat and he got in, wearing rain pants and coat, hard hat tipped back so that a smudged forehead showed. He took the parkway to Westchester and then drove through streets of lawns for a half-hour before he found the contractor's house, a ranch house that reached everywhere and had a flagstone walk. Behind the house, there was a line of leafless trees through which, in the near distance, the Hudson River could be seen. The contractor's wife, upon opening the door and seeing Owney, was apprehensive. She tried to smile as her eyes first flicked over the muddy forehead and then ran down the caked rain clothes. When she looked at Dolores, the woman put some life into her smile.

"Let me leave these here," Owney said. He bent down and pulled off his boots. "You two go right in."

Dolores walked into the house and the woman, puzzled, stepped in, too. Owney, his clothes over his arm, his street shoes in his hand, walked in barefoot. The woman saw his muddy feet walk across the foyer tiles and then she sucked in her breath as he stepped onto the living room carpet.

"Abe!"

Inside the house, on the far end of the living room, the contractor stirred in the den. He looked out and saw Owney. He stood in the doorway waiting for him.

"Nice place," Owney said. He walked past the contractor and went down a hallway. He looked in one door that was a closet and then disappeared into the next.

In the living room, the wife, a blonde with a few too many years in her face, concentrated on the known, Dolores. "Well, and how are you?"

"Fine."

"Take her coat, Roz," the contractor said.

"No, thanks. We'll only be a minute."

The contractor stood uncertainly. Then from down the hall he heard the faint sound of water running.

"I'm glad somebody has hot water," Dolores said.

The contractor's grin showed a mouthful of yellow teeth. "What do you mean?"

"Hot water for the shower my husband is taking."

"You don't have a shower at home?" Deutscher asked.

"No, we only have a bathtub. When my husband wants a shower, he goes to work. He loves a shower."

The three sat in silence and listened to the faint rain of water coming from down the hallway. Fifteen minutes later, Owney stepped out of the bathroom, a cloud of steam billowing behind him, and walked into the living room smiling. He was dressed in street clothes.

"Let's go, Dolores. I feel great."

She stood up and he took her by the arm and they walked out. At the door, Owney called in to the contractor, "Thanks a lot. I'll see you tomorrow."

All the way to Queens, he and Dolores laughed. When they got to Myrtle Avenue, Owney said he wanted to stop for cigarettes and he pulled in front of Gibby's.

"Come on in," he said to her.

"I'm too tired," she said.

"Have one Coke or something."

"Get your cigarettes and we'll go home."

"Just one. Don't I deserve something for what I did?"

"Only one," she said.

"That's all. I just want to laugh once."

"We just did in the car."

"This is different. Come on."

When he walked into Gibby's, Fats was there. He shook his head. "I was just trying to leave."

"I'll drive a car for you tonight," Owney said.

He laughed and made a motion with his hand and the bartender brought two big cold beers that caught the light from the neons and looked so pleasant that Owney's hand couldn't wait to hold one of them.

"A Coke," Dolores said.

"Oh, yeah, I forgot her," Owney said.

He swallowed beer and Fats threw most of his down. Then Owney raised his glass again, finished it, and put it out on the bar.

"You said one," Dolores said.

"I didn't even buy the cigarettes yet," Owney said. He was halfway through his second beer when the door opened and a guy Owney knew from the neighborhood, Jackie Collins, walked in.

"I don't want nothing to drink," Collins said. "You can torture me and I won't drink."

The bartender put a beer on the bar in front of him.

Collins stood still.

The bartender put a shot glass on the bar and filled it with Fleischmann's.

Collins picked it up, threw it down, and stood waiting for another.

Fats clapped.

"Owney," Dolores said, "my back hurts sitting here."

He handed her the car keys.

"I just want one more. I'll walk it."

She took the car keys and as she walked out the door, Owney said, "Get dinner ready and I'll be right home for it."

He wound up with Jackie Collins in McLoughlin's on Bailey Avenue in the Bronx, and from McLoughlin's Owney went straight to work. He was the first man into the hog house that morning, and he found plumbers packing their tools to go home. Owney walked inside and saw steaming water dripping from one showerhead. He turned them all on. Soon the room was filled with steam

Owney stood proudly in the hog house as the men came in for work and immediately noticed the showers. When his father arrived, Owney nodded.

"Good boy," the father said. "That's how you do union work."

Alongside the hog house, in the lunch wagon, Owney said, "Ham and Swiss."

A man who had been sitting asleep atop a stack of soda cases on one side of the doorway stirred. In his hands was a container of coffee that was nearly empty.

"Want more coffee?" Owney asked him.

The man was offended. "I don't drink coffee. I'm a sandhog." He leaned out the door, poured the last of the coffee onto the ground, and then held the cup out. "Put in something good," he said.

"What?" the woman behind the counter said.

"Something from a brown bottle."

"I got no liquor, Slattery."

Owney said to the woman, "Give us a beer."

Slattery took the can of beer from Owney and poured it into his coffee container until the beer, slightly discolored with coffee, spilled down the sides. Slattery tried to swallow the beer all at once; his idea was to drink beer, not taste it. As Slattery poured more of the beer into his container, Owney decided that he wanted one, too, and he was about to say this to the woman. But he knew that this was wrong and that he shouldn't drink before work. In the lunch wagon now he heard this small squeaking sound. Then the opponent, alcohol, was there in front of him, moving easily, one hand beckoning. The opponent looked like Jack McAuliffe, scarred and bony, a couple of hundred fights on his face, and right now his hair matted with blood from a cut on the top of his head, put there by a bite during a clinch. The beckoning hand called on Owney to come in and mix it up.

Owney put his feet flat and threw a punch at the vision and made Jack McAuliffe go away.

"Give us another beer for Slattery," Owney said to the woman. When she gave him the beer, he turned around to hand it to Slattery, but Slattery was too busy swallowing his first beer, so Owney looked at the can in his hand, thought for a moment about drinking it himself, and now he heard the small squeaking sound and had the can up high, with his middle unprotected, and in the excitement of the fight, as he suddenly swallowed, he never felt the kick as the beer went into his empty belly; Jack McAuliffe grunted as he hooked with his left into Owney's middle.

The beer went down so quickly that he barely tasted it, which was a shame, he thought, and he also thought it would be better if it was tap beer in a bar and he thought of that for a moment. Then he ordered two more cans of beer from the woman.

As they walked through the mud toward the tower and the angry wheel, Slattery began to babble just a little bit. "The freedom. One thing about being Irish. You learn about freedom. You know enough to get yourself a job like we got. Say as you want, do as you please. A man got his freedom." Now they started up the hill toward the tower and Slattery's legs became uncertain. "I don't know," he said, stopping.

"What do you need?" Owney said.

"I wonder where the hell they got a bottle. I need one to keep me going."

Owney kept walking.

Slattery did not move. "I don't think I can make it unless I get a starter in me."

A man in a red shirt and white hard hat was standing at the low wire gate in front of the entrance to the shaft. A face gray from the ruined nights of his own life inspected the men walking up from the hog house. The man was in charge of the union alcoholism program. Unlike politics, where fat, bald, disagreeable men, unable to be candidates themselves, teach a President how to act on a public stage, or the sports world, where a first baseman who cannot hit a curve ball goes on to become a great manager, alcoholism programs are run by retired champions. Seeing Slattery, the old ruined face broke into a gentle smile.

"Slats, you're going the wrong way for a drink."

"I'm going to work, Navy," Slattery said.

"You know you don't want to go down there," Navy said.

"I'm a good Irishman," Slattery said.

"Oh, I know that."

"I'm a good Irishman. I can take a drink."

"You sure can."

"I'm a good American, too. I go to work in the morning."

Navy walked up to Slattery and rested his hands on his shoulders. "You show up on time, anyway."

"Then get out of my way. I'm going to work like a man."

"You don't want somebody getting hurt around you," Navy said.

"How could I hurt anybody?"

Navy laughed. "Not while Slattery spends the day at the bar." He tried to walk Slattery away from the shack, but Slattery's face, as red as a stoplight to begin with, became more flushed, and his boots, responding to the anger in his head, dug into the earth as if he'd been called upon to defend his faith.

"Do you want a drink of whiskey?" Navy said.

"Never. Where is it at?"

"You take a walk with me and you'll get yourself one of the best drinks you'll ever have in your life," Navy said. Now Slattery willingly walked with him. And Navy glanced at the beer can in Owney's hand and then at Owney's face. Owney resented the look. Take care of your fucking old drunks. I'm a young guy having a good time. Slowly, with a flourish, Owney drained the beer. Then he walked up the mud hill.

When he was dressed, he walked outside and saw Danny Murphy, the numbers runner, who stood in the mud and accepted money from the men who kept walking past him.

"What are you doing out here?" Owney said, and Murphy glanced at the shed alongside the shaft, his usual place of operation, and answered, "They got a small conference going on."

Owney took out a ten and a clump of singles. He handed the ten to Murphy. "I don't have enough for the bar, so I might as well use it to win a yacht." He stabbed at a number in his mind.

"Seven thirty-four."

"Where's it come from?" Murphy asked.

"Oh, it's a good one," Owney said.

"I asked you, from where?"

"From the priest at my church. He told me the number came to him in a dream."

"Go on."

"No, you go on. The man told me he had a dream about seven thirty-four. He wouldn't know where to go, play a number."

"Should I play it?" Danny said.

"That's up to you," Owney said, and he walked away. He knew that leaving Murphy in indecision, and forced to make his own judgment, would cost Murphy most of his salary as a numbers runner for the week, for with nobody looking at him, he would bet his living room on even the report of a priest's dream.

As Owney walked up to the shaft, there was the sound of his father's voice inside the shed. Glancing in the doorway, Owney saw the father standing with his blue hard hat tipped back and his arms folded. The father stared at a large man in his early sixties who had silver hair brushed straight back, wide shoulders, and a red muffin face, which was Irish and made the clothes—black suit, white shirt, white tie—visually wrong. They required a swarthy face and a different setting, Cicero in the 1930s. Yet the Irish guy wore his attire so proudly that he seemed ready to pose for a mug shot.

"Now don't get so excited," the silver-haired man said to Owney's father.

"I'm not excited," Owney's father said.

There was a door to the men's room and somebody inside called out, "Be nice."

"I'm not such a nice guy," Owney's father called through the door.

The silver-haired guy stood up. A manicured hand reached out for the father's shirt. Owney's father slapped the hand down.

Owney stepped into the shack. His father signaled him to get out.

"Who are you?" Owney said to the silver-haired guy. The silver-haired guy's eyes became pale blue stones in boiling water. Owney kept staring at him. "I asked you who you are," Owney said.

Owney's father snapped, "I'll let you know if I need you." Owney did not move. "I said, that's it," the father said again.

The toilet flushed inside the bathroom and a voice could be heard saying, "I don' want no fuckin' trouble."

Owney's father stared at Owney and caused him to leave the place reluctantly. He was walking through the mud and did not see the inside of the equipment shack, where the toilet door opened and Old Jack stepped out.

"So what have we got?" Old Jack said.

"We got a guy with no word," the silver-haired man said.

Outside, an engine coughed and then sent fumes into the morning air.

"Wait a minute," Owney's father said. He walked outside and began calling out directions to the men gathered around a motor that was pulling a powder wagon up to the lift.

Old Jack sat down grumpily. Nice, why don't guys do the right thing and keep everything nice? He stared at the shack wall and remembered when it all started. What was it, seven weeks ago? Look what happened to the thing already. Old Jack was offended. He remembered Charlie O'Sullivan, face flushed with excitement, running a hand over his silver hair, saying to him one day, "I see a guy last night," which Old Jack accepted as an introduction to a scheme, which it was. O'Sullivan said the guy was a messenger for Jimmy Morrison of the Bronx tunnel workers, who wanted to make a private deal that would result in three or, better yet, four ghost jobs.

In all of the labor movement, there are two jobs most prized. One is a job that requires almost no work. This is good, but not as good as the greatest job on earth, one in which nobody comes to work and they give you the check for the nonexistent worker.

The Bronx larceny was simple. The union sent gangs down a man short here and there, and guaranteed there would be no complaints. Old Jack was needed to tell contractors that if no objections were raised about this little thing, these three or four ghost jobs, there would be true labor peace, particularly with concrete drivers, whose allegiance was to the Mafia, of which Old Jack was a member most proud. It wouldn't cost the contractors any extra money, for they would merely be sending the same number of checks to the job. They would only give up the right to ask questions. On the other side, this particular corner of the union would work a little short-handed here and there, and in matching silence.

Both sides were needed for a maneuver that would produce as much as eight or nine hundred a week for Old Jack and O'Sullivan, with the other seventeen hundred for Morrison. Old Jack, who pushed drugs for tens of thousands with the same fervor as he filched a newspaper from a candy store, loved the idea. Steal anything and steal always. He knew O'Sullivan would kill for any figure; O'Sullivan took twenty-five a month off theatre usherettes and said they should be overjoyed that he didn't want thirty. As the arrangement involved no wildcat strikes by truck drivers, which would need the sanction of many big Mafia bosses, Old Jack felt he could keep all the money for himself. This meant he was stealing not only from the tunnel job but from the Mafia, too, and if there was one thing he liked better than stealing once, it was stealing twice at the same time.

Before agreeing to the plan, Old Jack asked O'Sullivan one nagging question. "Why doesn't this Morrison come to see us himself?"

"Morrison don't deal with guineas direct."

"Why don't he talk to you, then?"

"Because I'm with you, he makes me a half a guinea."

"I don't see enough of honor here," Old Jack said.

"He could give us nearly five hundred apiece every week. He only says you were a guinea."

Old Jack thought that O'Sullivan passed on the insult too easily, and he also loathed the idea of anything that didn't involve getting even with Morrison's kid. He even wondered if somehow this was going to produce another assault on him by the kid. He was so overwhelmed by the instinct to steal, however, that he plunged into the scheme, although with suspicions that made him uncomfortable and were merited.

One payday a couple of weeks later, Jimmy Morrison sat at the bar alone and exhaled smoke over the four checks he had picked up earlier, in his capacity as shop steward. "It's a shame guineas have to get money from decent Irishmen," Jimmy Morrison said to himself.

The checks on the bar, the first ghost checks, were in the names of Chris McCafferty, at ease in the Bronx; Georgie O'Neill, doing not too much in Windsor Park, Brooklyn; Willie Cunningham, enjoying the Bronx; George Tully, taking it slow in Amagansett, Long Island. Not one would question anything; all would rush in if anything went wrong. There was no charge for using their names. I done enough for them guys, Jimmy Morrison assured himself. Lots of times, he thought, guys went down in the tunnel and did fuck-all and nobody ever complained. He remembered one of his ghosts, Tully, sleeping in a tool trunk during a shot. The trunk and Tully got blown halfway down the tunnel. So nobody misses four guys on a big job.

Jimmy Morrison swallowed some of his drink. For all that I done for this union I deserve something nice. He looked down at the checks again. The four checks on the bar totaled $1,974.82. The only trouble was, in a half-hour, he had to meet a guy and hand out $985, to go to Old Jack and O'Sullivan.

He pushed the four checks at Sharon the barmaid. For cashing services, Jimmy gave her fifty dollars. "I got to meet somebody right away," he told Sharon. Reluctantly, he left to make the payoff.

He did this for several placid weeks. And then there was a day when he again sat at the bar, with Sharon across from him, and this time, rather than mutter to himself, he sat up straight and said aloud, "Why should a guinea get money from a good Irishman?"

When Sharon cashed the four checks, Jimmy Morrison put the money into his pocket and remained on the barstool.

"You goin'?" Sharon said.

"No."

"I thought you hadda meet a guy."

"Not this time."

Warmth flowed from his pocket and through his body. "I don't want to go hurting my back hanging storm windows on hooks," he told Sharon.

"What is this storm windows?"

"The storm windows I'm going to have on Long Island. I want the kind that you just slide in."

"What Long Island?"

"I'm buying a house there."

"With that?" she said, indicating the money in his pocket.

"Absolutely."

Two drinks later, he told her, "I'm goin' to live in a house at Exit Sixty-three. I give the guineas fuck-all."

He kept all the money that week. He liked that so much that he kept all the money the following week, too.

When Morrison reneged for the third week in a row, O'Sullivan reported to Old Jack, "He says he's buying a house and then he thinks maybe he can send us something."

"I told you he got dishonor," Old Jack said.

Old Jack at first thought he had to keep his fury in secret. If he went back and told subcontractors to stop paying Morrison for ghosts, this would be so astounding that the Mafia would hear of it and convict Old

Jack of cheating, punishable by ice pick. After two more weeks went by, however, the thought of Morrison collecting all that money had flames crackling inside Old Jack's head. Soon, Old Jack's caution deserted him and now in his fury he appeared personally at the Bronx tunnel job.

Where, as he sat in the shack, listening to Jimmy Morrison's shouting outside, Old Jack became livid.

"When he comes back in, you let me talk to him," Old Jack said to O'Sullivan.

"How are you going to talk to this man? He thinks you're from the sewer."

Now Owney's father walked back in and stood with his arms folded. "All right."

Old Jack smiled. He reached out and tried to pinch Jimmy Morrison's cheek.

"Hey, keep your hands away," Jimmy Morrison said, pulling his head away.

Old Jack shrugged and sat down. "What do we do here?"

Jimmy Morrison didn't answer.

"Two, three, four weeks, you collect all this money on account of us."

"That's thousands of fucking dollars," O'Sullivan said.

"You don't do the right thing," Old Jack said.

"We'll have to see," Owney's father said.

"See what?"

"See if we really need you. I never made the deal with you myself."

"Your man did," O'Sullivan said.

"So now I got to see him. I think he made a bad deal. I don't think you deserve anything. Especially."

"What especcially?" Old Jack said.

"Especially that you're a fuckin' guinea," Jimmy Morrison said. "We never had a guinea near a sandhog job in the Bronx and I think we ought to keep it that way."

He turned around and walked out on them.

O'Sullivan kicked the wall of the shack.

"Be nice," Old Jack said.

"What do you want me to do?"

"We go," Old Jack said.

As they were walking to the car, Old Jack said, "His kid, he was good and fucking fresh to me, too. They think I forget."

5

THE CAGE came to the surface and somebody pulled apart the two wire gates in front of the lift. There were about forty men who got on, with Owney pushing aboard last. The cage had no sides; it was just a metal floor that rose and fell on the cable from the angry wheel overhead. Somebody closed the gates and the cage groaned and the cable whined as the men looked in silence at the sky for the last time. The first shadows started on the metal floor and the cage dropped into the metal shaft and the faces all looking up at the sun now were covered with shadows and then the men stood in darkness as the elevator took them down to their cave, which was nine hundred feet under the streets of the Bronx.

The lift broke into light and bounced at the bottom of the shaft, and the two gates were opened and the men walked out into a temple of stone that ran the length of two football fields and had a curved ceiling that went as high as a cathedral. Seven stories high, it was forty-five feet wide. The temple had been blasted out of the core of the earth and some day would be filled with huge pipes and two-hundred-ton switches that would route enough water at manageable speed to supply tens of millions living in twelve counties. This switching chamber was designed to last as long as people managed to remain on earth.

Owney got off the lift and walked through mud water under floodlights that bathed the sullen gray rock walls. Smaller lights were strung along the walls like Christmas decorations, and as the lights ran up the walls, the line of lights became smaller and smaller until at the top, far away from the eye, up along the cathedral ceiling, the light looked like stars at dusk.

Halfway up the walls on both sides there were ledges that ran the length of the chamber. Standing on the ledges now were large and loud men who became insignificant as they stepped through shadows in this great stone cathedral; no pharaoh, explorer, or conqueror ever had seen or imagined such a sight. Running off the ledges on each side of the chamber were the entrances to seventeen separate tunnels—noisy catacombs, thirty-four of them, enough crevices to hide a great religion from those who would end it by sword—catacombs that were thirty feet high, with rail tracks and flatcars and men standing around waiting to ride the cars along the tracks into the darkness.

For this moment in the morning, as men stepped off the lift, Owney wanted to stand here on the wet bottom and look up at the stone cathedral ceiling, stand here in his white hard hat, khaki jacket, and yellow rain pants, and lean on his coalminer's shovel. Breathing air that was dark and flat, he thought of himself as a miner in Kentucky someplace. *How you?* In New York, nobody even knew that there was this stone cathedral under their feet, or that there were men working in such a place. He found the solitude of being this far underground pleasant for a few moments; no hand or thought from the confusion of life above ground could reach him. If there was no order to the day on the ground above, there certainly was here. All of which faded as he climbed a ladder in the lifeless air to the ledge and then walked to his catacomb. Overhead, in the shadows of the cathedral ceiling, there were many metal straps, Band-Aids, eight and ten feet long, fastened to the rock by one-inch bolts that went ten feet into the rock and were meant to prevent rock from falling. When a piece does happen to fall, it is rarely small: a chip can weigh a ton. At the entrance to his catacomb, Owney walked over to the motor, a squat yellow diesel locomotive, grabbed a handrail, and rode to work hanging on to the motor as it ran down the tracks through a tunnel of gray-black bumpy rock that looked like a shark's gullet. The mind was numbed by the sameness and shadows and silence of the rock as it passed over him. When Owney looked straight ahead down the tunnel, the rock began to revolve. Cellar air blowing into his face was not enough for a complete breath.

"The air's bad," Owney said.

"The money's good," the man next to him, Delaney, the foreman, said. A cigarette hung from his mouth.

The motor ran through darkness and then out into areas bathed in bright light, where sandhogs stood in puddles in the lights and smoked cigarettes.

"Oh, the money's wonderful," Delaney said again.

Now water dripped from the rock roof, which was supported by iron arches placed only a couple of feet apart. In the spaces between the arches, Owney could see the rock that everybody despised, rock with white streaks that had been shot into it millions of years ago, like soda water, weakening it to the point that like any formation or populace without strength, it is eternally dangerous; let the whitened rock shrug just once.

For one stretch, the rock was so threatening to the eye that in places where the top of the metal arch was not flush against the white rock, the spaces were packed with wooden planks. Someday, when the miners were finished hollowing, the caves would be lined with six feet of concrete, which would support the rock for centuries. Until then, the miners would labor under a roof they suspected of being a murderer.

The motor slowed and the tracks ended in rubble and mud water. The miners from an earlier train ride stood at a wooden table that had a coffee urn and cans of evaporated milk. A few yards down from them, exposed by a mean light, weeping in anger, with the water forming a large dark pool at the bottom, was the face of a mountain from a half billion years ago, a mountain that once stood high in a sky afire and then, pulsating with the same pressure that first caused the earth to form, shook all the land around it, creating valleys and fields. Then the mountain dropped, roaring hot, toward the middle of the earth.

Here it now stood, a mountain underground with part of its side exposed in the mean light, revealing a striped rock, the light stripes of quartz and feldspar, the dark stripes of biotite mica, rock known to man as Fordham gneiss, which is the way of dealing with anything beyond the feeble limits of logic and imagination—affix a label consisting of a familiar name, thus denying mystery—and all the while deep inside this rock there was a woman who had died young and who now walked tormented at dusk down a road between empty fields as she called for the children she had left at her bedside. Her call was muted, a woman whispering the names of children so softly that the names cannot be heard, but there are times when the woman, engulfed by her sorrow, moans with such an intensity that crows in the field take startled to the air, cawing loudly, and it is at this moment, crows crying, mother moaning, that the rock parts and allows the woman to search further for her children.

Once, when they blasted into the rock and began one of these cata-combs running from the giant chamber, they must have opened on to the edge of one of the fields where the woman walked, for that day, Owney saw her moving about nervously, her shoulder brushing the first layer of rock, a woman in a shawl and a long brown skirt that kicked as she walked. A hand kept tugging on strands of damp tangled brown hair as she looked about.

"Where are my children now?" she moaned. "Perhaps I must walk all the way to the sea to find them playing on the shore. Their father wouldn't know. He is a man. He lays in bed and cries for his own loneli-ness."

Her moan rose in intensity as the crows rose excitedly into the freezing sky. *Caw, caw.*

But on this morning in the cave, the woman in the rock was silent and Owney stuck his ham and Swiss into a cubbyhole on a wooden bench against the cave wall. Owney saw that there were two empty spaces alongside his sandwich, which meant that he was down in the hole with only a seven-man gang. In the row underneath, there was another space, which meant one of the other gangs was a man short.

"We're all short," he said to Delaney, the foreman.

Delaney threw a cigarette away and fumbled in his shirt pocket for another. "Slattery got drunk."

"What about the second man? And they're one short in one of the other gangs. You should have hired a shaper."

"See your father."

"What's he got to do with me working on a short gang?"

Delaney turned away and called out, "All right, lads, let's get at it. One, two, three, lads."

Owney walked to the face of the tunnel. Burning along the left side of the cave was the devil's tongue, a red laser beam that did not diffuse or distort as it silently blazed through the darkness, six feet above the floor and only a few inches from the side of the cave. If the laser was aimed down the center of the tunnel, trains and equipment would stop its beam. Placed along the wall, the laser each day struck the rock at the same spot; a ray from a stopped sun. A lanky surveyor, who had a brown hard hat pulled down over a clean college face, stood at the face of the tunnel, held a ruler into the laser beam, then measured three feet out onto the rock face from the beam, and one foot down. A man with him marked the point with yellow paint. The surveyor looked at a chart. Then he touched another spot. Again, the man dabbed it with paint. The surveyor touched another spot. More paint. Owney stood to the side and waited as the surveyor kept going to the chart, tapping a spot on the wall as the paintbrush dabbed. The painted dots went in a circle around the thirty-foot circumference of the wall. Now the surveyor started a circle of dots inside the perimeter circle. As he consulted his chart more rapidly, there were more dots of yellow paint, forming circles within circles, and a dozen paint spots became half a hundred and then a hundred and finally at the center of the rock face, the dots went into a different pattern, a diamond and, inside the diamond, a large square with four dots inside it. When the surveyor and painter were finished, the rock was speckled with one hundred fifty dots. The miners were to drill a hole sixteen feet deep at each of the painted spots.

The diagram had been drawn months before by another surveyor, a man so painfully shy that he looked down when others spoke to him and who was so uncertain of his words that he kept a pipe between his teeth, causing the sandhogs to suggest that he was a complete homosexual. Standing outside the surveyors' trailer, the sandhogs boasted of the damage they could do to each other with their heavy fists; inside, the surveyor they thought was a fag sat at a desk, excitedly biting his pipestem as he worked out a method of blowing up tens of tons of rock with a pattern of explosions whose image caused his heart to shriek with joy: one hundred fifty holes drilled into the rock in a pattern, then stuffed with eighteen hundred tons of explosives timed to go off sequentially. On paper, the surveyor's diagram resembled a page from a children's connect-the-dots book.

When the surveyor in the tunnel was through marking his dots, the miners took over, stepping over the hoses and wires running along each side of the tunnel, walking in the noise of the engine parked on the tracks and the sound of a second motor that pushed a double-decked white metal platform over the tunnel bottom and up to the face of the rock. On the decks sat eight two-hundred-pound hydraulic drills. With a splash, the metal platform stopped in the water at the face of the rock, and foremen throughout the tunnel began calling out Delaney's "One, two, three, lads."

Owney climbed the steps to the top platform of the rig and slapped a hand on his drill, which stood on a Jackleg. Mickey Doherty, the chuck tender, came up and began to inspect the hoses that ran from the drill to the motor on the back of the decks. Doherty worried about the drill, a new model that had been perfected by the Russians. It used high-speed bursts into the rock, relying on cumulative effect rather than the old

American industrial style of banging into the rock with a single arm-ripping blow, as if it were the face of a personal enemy.

For a week, as they grew accustomed to the new drills, Doherty had been worrying that if the Russians were this far ahead in mining equipment, then their bombs might be designed along the same lines: quick bursts everywhere. Doherty's view of the world always had been that there would be one huge bomb falling into Manhattan, killing the heathens instantly, while his street, just off Katonah Avenue in the upper Bronx, would be touched only by unseen and painless fallout that would produce a slow death for Mickey Doherty, with him sinking a bit each day but never with pain, and with time for the Pope of Rome to transmit through the local parish, St. Brendan's, a plenary indulgence, which would leave Mickey in peaceful, sainted weakness, able to say only his rosary, and then, bursting with grace, rise one morning into Heaven. That was his old dream.

His new fear was that the Russian nuclear attack, small, speedy, numerous, patterned after the mining drill, could mean a spray of small nuclear bombs all over the town, including one that would crash onto Katonah Avenue and blow up Mickey Doherty at the precise moment when his soul was covered with the slime of an hour with Marge Ryan, of 239th Street, a woman known to Mickey's wife as a lonely widow and to Mickey as a girlfriend who would keep a secret. Mickey Doherty saw himself dropping into Hell like a broken elevator.

Standing on the platform alongside Owney, Doherty looked sourly at the drill. "The fucking Communists."

Owney slowly put on heavy ear protectors, which would keep him from going deaf, but also left him uneasy, as there would be no way ever to hear the dead mother moaning louder and causing the crows to shriek —caw, caw, caw—as the rock roof opened up while he stood in the last instant of his life.

Owney was almost at the cave wall on the right, and he had to maneuver the drill on an angle into his first yellow spots. Doherty, standing alongside the tip of the drill, held a light on the yellow spot. Owney adjusted his protective goggles, switched the drill on, and pushed it against the rock. On the tip of his drill was a one-and-seven-eighths drill bit, with water spraying out of a hole in the bit to wet down the rock dust. A groove on the side of the drill bit allowed water heavy with sediment to run back out of the hole as it was being drilled. This hole on the perimeter was the first of twenty that Owney had to drill this morning, holes an inch and seven-eighths in circumference going sixteen feet into the rock.

A tunnel thirty feet in diameter running for miles under a city is built by shaving off the face of the rock in fifteen-foot sections. Drill sixteen feet, blast away fifteen, and then start drilling again. Driving tunnel, forty-five feet a day, explosions on two shifts, two hundred twenty-five feet a week, is the order on paper in offices up on the ground. Under the earth, in the flat, dark air, the wet, gloomy rock gave quarter grudgingly, and after each shot, its white-streaked roof caused the miners to take hours throwing up iron arches, packing the tops with wood, losing time so that the tunnel had moved ahead only one hundred nine feet the previous week.

Now on the top and bottom decks of the drilling platform, all the drillers had whirling fangs cutting into the striped rock. One driller, with a large bit, chewed at the four spots that had been painted inside the square in the center of the circle. These holes were to be nine inches in circumference. As the drilling went on, the rest of the tunnel was taken up by the ceaseless work of mining: railroad track being put down, steel arches being brought up, air and electric lines being tugged by men in the dimness. Fuming cherry pickers and payloaders bounced over the wet, rocky floor and soured more of the air.

Sometimes, while Owney drilled, he sang Rolling Stones songs. Or he imagined he was surfing. He stopped a couple of times to change drills as he went deeper into the rock and needed a longer piece of steel. The lengths went up to eighteen feet. Then, with his arms and back feeling the effort of the drilling, he began to think what it was going to be like mucking out after the explosion, with two men missing from his gang and at least one other gang working down here short. See your father, Delaney had said. Owney was surprised at his own docility in accepting evasion as a reply. Meanwhile, you work two hands short. By code and custom, sandhogs always count heads in front of the shaft and if they find a gang does not have a full line-up, the short gang does not go into the hole until one of the bosses goes over to the hog house and hires a shape-up man and brings him back. Promises of sending somebody down to the hole in a few minutes are as acceptable as personal checks. Get us the man we're short or we sit here and drink beer for the whole shift. That his father would countenance anything like that today was an interference with family lore: miners give the sacrament of work in return for which they are to receive certain small honors of life, and these are to be delivered promptly and undamaged. One of the best moments he ever had in the place was yesterday, when they were going to strike over the showers. Work with a short gang? He better tell his father to count heads. Maybe he's getting careless. On the rock face in front of Owney, there were only four painted spots left. His drill went into each, stopping to put on extensions so that at the finish he had the longest drill in his kit. When he finished at last, at the end of an hour and forty-five minutes of steady drilling, he put the big hydraulic drill down and waited for the other drills to cease. When Owney saw the last one, somewhere along the bottom, pull away from the rock, he took off his earmuffs and went down the platform steps and walked along the wall until he came to a length of rock that formed a ledge wide enough to sit on. In a small crevice over the ledge, covered by a piece of wood, was a bag of beers that Owney's father kept hidden there. The beer was warm and it sprayed when the tab came off, but Owney covered the can with his mouth and sucked quickly. Then he started to swallow the can of beer and tasted it only after it was finished, and then he used the taste as a reason for opening another can quickly.

He was almost through with this second can when his father and a surveyor walked past.

"We're short today," Owney said to his father.

"Why do you think I'm on the run all morning?" the father said.

When his father kept walking, Owney finished the second can, grabbed another, and walked up the face, where his father stood, reading from a diagram. The father reached into a cardboard box that contained long, yellow electrical wires that had white-numbered tags on each of them.

"What do you think?" Owney said to his father.

"I think you better leave us alone."

The father held a yellow wire that had the number 18 on it. The father checked this with the diagram, and then stuck the wire into a hole on the perimeter of the rock face. The hole directly above it, the diagram said, was another 18. Owney's father took another wire with an 18 tag and stuffed it into the hole. He was following the script that would run an explosion just as a playwright moves characters about a stage. Following the diagram, Owney's father went around the top and bottom arcs of the circle and stuck 18s into most of the holes. He then worked around the outside—or contour—holes and stuck them with 18s and then 17s and down to 16s. After this Owney's father began to work the maze of holes, placing high numbers on the outer ring and then using lower-numbered wire as he worked toward the center. The diagram called for no wires to be placed in the four nine-inch holes at the center. The numbered wire stood for the sequence in which the explosives would detonate, fractions of seconds apart, with the low numbers on the inside—the 1s, 2s, and 3s —going off first and the others blowing up in numerical order, the explosion rippling across the rock face in a series that actually forms one long explosion that lasts for fully ten seconds. Detonated all at once, the eighteen hundred pounds of explosives could cause the face of the wall to fracture, in large broken ribs, but it would not drive the rock back and create more tunnel. Cumulatively set off, the eighteen hundred pounds of explosives cause the rock to peel like an onion, and the final explosions in the series, the number 18s along the top and bottom parts, cause the rock to lift from the top and be pushed up from the bottom simultaneously and turn into a pile of thick muck and boulders while the rest of the rock disintegrates and fills the tunnel with thick dust.

When Owney's father was finished wiring the holes, he climbed off the platform, looked at the beer can in Owney's hand, and muttered, "Where's mine?"

"What about getting us a man?" Owney said. "We're two down. Are we going to have to do all this mucking out short-ganged?"

The father looked at the other men crowded in the tunnel and, eyebrows raised, looked back at Owney. Are you trying to make me look bad? his stare said. "I'm going for a beer," he said, walking away.

Now another squat yellow engine came out of the darkness, horn sounding, and behind it on a flatcar was a red locker plastered with warning signs of explosives. The powder monkey, a white-haired man, opened the locker and began handing out sticks of explosives called Tovex, which is dynamite without the nitroglycerin that has made so many miners so sick over the decades.

Owney went up onto the drilling platform and shoved two sticks into one of the holes he had drilled. Then he took the yellow wire in the hole, the tip of which carried a silver blasting cap, and stuffed the blasting cap into the second stick of Tovex. Owney then took a long wooden pole and shoved it into the hole, crushing the Tovex sticks against each other, sending them deep into the hole until they reached the end. The long yellow cord hung out of the hole like a rat's tail. Owney then put in two more sticks, pounded them in with the pole, and went into his pockets for two more sticks. Each hole took sixteen sticks of the Tovex.

When they were all packed, the surveyor grabbed the yellow cords dangling from the holes and attached them to a long coil of yellow-and-blue-striped wire that ran into the darkness of the tunnel and up to the spot where the explosion was to be touched off.

As they were short-handed, it took nearly two hours for the holes to have their throats stuffed. The powder monkey and a surveyor handed out lighter charges, a water-jelly composition for the contour holes, which had to blow up, but not crack, the outside rock walls.

In the center, the four large holes were not loaded. The holes directly around them, the ones with number 1 and 2 and 3 wire in them, were filled with heavier charges than those used anywhere else in the rock. As each hole was stuffed, a surveyor grabbed the yellow cord sticking out and attached it to the long coil of yellow-and-blue-striped wire.

When all the holes were stuffed and the wires connected, the miners stepped off the platform. A motor coughed and the platform was drawn away from the rock face, leaving it with yellow cords hanging from its striped mouth. A victim about to be executed. But then Owney's eyes went upward and here was the same striped rock, with a slash of ugly white running through it, and he knew that somewhere deep in the rock, the woman strolled on the road through the fields and whimpered for her children.

The blaster, who had learned his trade in the mines, stood at the face, and his eyes counted the yellow wires connected to the coils of yellow-and-blue-striped wire. When he saw that nothing was loose, he stood for one long moment, pondered the rock face, and then started walking up the tunnel, with everyone ahead of him. The blaster connected the yellow-and-blue line to a short blue wire, the shooting line. The blue wire was attached to a small metal object that looked like a doorknob. When the blaster was a thousand feet away from the wall, he unscrewed the metal doorknob. He put a .22 cartridge into a bracket inside the doorknob. Horns sounded. Then he clapped the two halves of the doorknob together. The .22 cartridge inside the doorknob popped. And down the tunnel there were flashes in the darkness as the characters rushed about the stage. The first low numbers exploded in their holes and the dynamite headed for the weakest point in the rock face and found it in the nine-inch holes left unloaded in the center of the face. Rock from these initial charges blew to the center, relieving itself of pressure by collapsing into the empty holes. Rapid-fire, the holes blew up in their pattern, headed out, three-four-five-six, but they headed out only in time, for the explosions were caving to the center and the center was opening, opening, opening, as the holes exploded, and finally, there was a pinwheel of 18s along the perimeter, the contour line, top and bottom arcs, explosion going into explosion and the rock in the darkness suddenly became thick gravel in the air.

Now rolling up the tunnel toward the men one thousand feet away there came a dark rush of air, air carrying concussion: dark, heavy air that at first was like the rush of wind when a subway train pulls into a station, but in the subway, when the train stops the wind ceases. Here in the tunnel the wind rolled on its own, uncontrolled, and the concussion rolled along the rock walls of the cave and for a moment there was the thought that the air never would be controlled again. Owney's hard hat blew off his head.

The day she knew she was pregnant, when she stayed in bed unable to move from nerves and an upset stomach, she also felt guilty that she had not made dinner for him. When he did not arrive home until nine-thirty, with his breath carrying the smell of a suddenly thrown open cellar, she accepted his "I'm sorry" and allowed the lost hours to pass into the small history of their marriage.

She completed her second year in college exactly four days before she entered the maternity wing of St. John's Hospital and gave birth to a baby girl, whom they named Christine. When the baby arrived, there were long nights with an infant who shrieked endlessly for food because of stomach muscles that were not yet formed enough to provide the sensation of fullness. Fed until the stomach was overfull, the baby simply threw up and, upon stopping this, immediately began screaming for more food. As this kept Dolores awake through the nights, through long hours when she took the baby into the living room so that Owney could sleep, she found that she had only one part of a day, at the start of the afternoon, when she could try to live for herself. She thought of going to the library for a book, but found she could concentrate only on soap operas. She watched a succession of husbands suddenly disappear and leave their wives alone forever on *The Guiding Light*, and she believed in the stories so much that the disappearances pained her. She made fun of herself for this. One day, you're going to be like one of these women doctors, and the next you're another housewife on the block afraid of your husband, she told herself. Yet often, when Owney came home late and was annoyed to hear the baby crying as he walked in, Dolores knew she should be angry, but here with the baby she suddenly was too susceptible to her past, to her own story of a mother and father who had left her. Except for a magnificent coincidence, she would have been raised in the bare walls of an orphanage. She knew the fear was unreasonable and that it was changing her, but it was her baby and her fear.

* * *

After blasting, there usually are ten minutes of waiting for the heavy rock dust to leave the air, and also for any delayed explosions. But this time, right after the shot, a boss somewhere called out, "Let's go." And another voice followed and soon Delaney, the foreman, would be telling them to hustle the big jumbo drilling platform back up to the face of the tunnel.

For some reason, they were using up old dynamite instead of the Tovex. A few men had long poles, which they poked as a precaution at the rock roof and Delaney made them work quickly and he suddenly pronounced it safe and had crews and machines up to the face to move the piles of rubble. Owney noticed that nobody had washed the rock face. Usually, after each shot, a man hoses down the tunnel face in order to wash out any explosives that failed to go off on the previous shot. A hole might be stuffed with explosives. He noticed that there had been no washing, but he had enough whiskey in him from the night before on Katonah Avenue to drown the sense of danger.

When Owney got up on the platform and placed his drill bit onto the first spot, he tried to watch the water pour out of the bit; if the water stopped, then his move was to shut off the drill before it burned itself out in dry heat. Drilling, drilling, with the water from his drill bit spilling down the face of the rock, taking rock dust with it. His eyes closed for a moment and he forced them to open and saw, three inches below the drill at the most, the water splash rock dust off the wall, and there, shining in the water and light from the chuck tender's flashlight, the hot drill head chewing rock only inches over it, the yellow-and-blue wire attached to a blasting cap and a stick of dynamite stuck in the last traces of an old drilled hole.

Owney turned the drill off. He signaled for a plastic water pipe. He aimed a stream of water at the hole and the blasting cap and dynamite washed away. All harmless now. A few moments before, he had been drilling three inches away from the end of his life.

He put the drill down, walked off the platform, and went up to the tracks to wait for a motor.

"Owney!"

Hearing Delaney's voice made Owney walk faster. While he waited for the motor, he picked up a piece of pink rock, feldspar, prehistoric pink untouched by any other hand except perhaps God's. He put the rock in his pocket and climbed aboard the motor.

In the hog house, he dressed alone. He let his body give one shake as he thought of the explosives left in the hole. Then he walked up the wet floor from his locker and he was going directly home, with the pink rock in the pocket of his yellow shirt, and then his father was standing at the picnic table in the hog house. The father had a bottle of Jim Beam in one hand and a paper cup in the other. He raised the cup. "That tastes good. Want one?"

"I have to go home. I can't get in trouble."

"What's trouble? What can happen to you with a drink?"

"I near got killed," Owney said.

"The fact is, you didn't."

"I said I nearly got killed."

"So say you. And so you walk off."

"I might stay off."

"What for?"

"Until we stop working short-handed."

"I don't know that you are."

"You're telling me I can't count?"

"I didn't say that."

"You're telling me that I don't know what I'm doing?"

"I'm telling you that I don't know what you're saying. What I'm going to do is go over this whole thing tonight. I'll do it without walking off the job, either."

As the father and Owney left the hog house, an engineer came out of a trailer and waved to the father. Noticing Owney, the engineer said, "Family conference?"

"He claims we got ghosts working," the father said.

The engineer smiled and he and Owney's father walked to the lift.

When Owney was on the Bronx-Whitestone Bridge, with the sun high in a hot sky over the buildings of Manhattan off to the right, and splashing on the water below and sending sunstreaks across the surface from shore to shore, he thought for the first time about his father's remark. Who the fuck mentioned ghosts?

He was going right home, of course, and he stopped at Fritz's on Myrtle Avenue only because the place was just a few blocks from his house. Inside the barroom, which was a place that begged for a broom and dreamed of soap, a woman sitting in a wheelchair in the dimness reached up to the bar for her glass of whiskey and ice. She drank it quickly and looked at the empty glass in her hand and then looked at Owney. As she was in a wheelchair, she expected people to buy drinks for her.

Owney ordered a beer for himself and told the bartender to include the woman in. She cackled as she got the drink. "This is how I do it every day," she said. "I start out here, I'm history after that."

Owney found the first taste of beer bitter, then he swallowed it all, ordered a shot of Fleischmann's, and threw the shot down and had another beer. He took that in two swallows and wiped his mouth and stepped away from the bar. He went to the juke box and let his eyes run down the rows of homemade cards: "Kevin Barry"/The Clancy Brothers. And then, "Sean South of Garryowen/The Dubliners." There was no Rolling Stones song to make the walls pound and his body throb. Most bars in Queens are run with the idea that all customers are over fifty. As the hand reaches for the first drink, youth is supposed to slip out the door.

It was late in the afternoon when he decided to drive home. He went up Myrtle Avenue but passed 74th Street without looking, and when he got over to Queens Boulevard he put his car in the parking lot of the Hamburg Savings Bank. The rear door to Pep McGuire's was at one end of the parking lot. Inside, there was only one other person at the bar, a court clerk from across the street who drank beer and mumbled to himself.

Owney had a shot and a beer and listened to the mumbling, which mixed in with the sound of water dripping in a tub under the bar. He wondered why he was alone. Then he began to think of Dolores. He saw her standing in a golden light that picked her out of the darkness. She held their baby and he stepped up to her and kissed her on the neck. She raised her chin and nuzzled flesh that was as soft as sky. He kissed the baby on the soft hair atop her head. He held the image as he drank cold beer. Sitting at the bar, he imagined the smell of Dolores's neck and the baby's hair. He now felt enormously satisfied with himself because he had shown great love for his wife and baby and so, of course, this made him a good father.

"You give us one, will you?" he said to the bartender. With the flick of a finger, Owney indicated he wanted to buy the mumbling man a drink, too.

Now there were a few more people, much younger, in the place and a band came in and the first sounds of an electric guitar came over the loudspeaker system. A drum rolled and the first people were dancing. As Owney looked to see if there were girls at the bar, his foot slipped from the railing and he decided to go home rather than try dancing. Then he decided to have another drink. He had the drink and it made him sleepy.

He put his head down on the bar for a moment, and the saloon manager came over and tapped him. "I wish it was the men's shelter because I'm tired, too, but it isn't," the manager said. "Here, come with me. I'll show you something."

He took Owney into an office where there was a high-backed red leather chair. Owney sat in it and closed his eyes. When he woke up, the manager was at a desk, adding up checks, and four men smoked and played cards at a table along the wall.

The manager spoke to Owney without looking up. "Feeling better?"

"I don't know how I feel. I better go home."

"Home? You'd better go for coffee and get to work."

"What time is it?"

"Quarter after five."

He went to a diner on Queens Boulevard where whipped-cream cakes spun on a turntable inside a glass case. The Greek behind the counter did not move.

"Coffee," Owney said.

The Greek kept staring out at the last of the night traffic on the boulevard. Reluctantly, he turned to the coffee urn. The whine of truck tires outside told Owney that the morning had started. He thought about calling Dolores. Too early.

At six o'clock, he found himself on Katonah Avenue, nearly asleep at a red light, and when he stirred he saw a telephone booth next to the light stanchion. He decided that the baby was up by now, and it was all right to call. He parked the car and began dialing. Something told him to stop, to get his story put together, but his finger kept going and Dolores answered on the first ring. She must be in the kitchen, he thought.

"I got hit on the head by a piece of rock and this kid doctor got afraid and made me stay in overnight. I wouldn't let anybody call you because I didn't want you worried."

She hung up without saying a word to him, which was fine with him because if she had asked the name of the hospital, he would have had considerable trouble.

In front of Brendan's, a man appeared with a broom. He had the suggestion of gray hair covering an old red scalp. He began sweeping the sidewalk. Now he changed. He became younger, and uglier, and he was standing on the sidewalk in boxing trunks, with his bare chest heaving with effort. His face was smeared with Vaseline and his eight-ounce gloves were dark and old from sweat over many rounds. Now the gloves came up and they beckoned to Owney. He looked clearly at the opponent, alcohol, and he parked the car and got out to mix it up.

"Oh, we're not open yet," the old man said.

"You can be open for me," Owney said.

"I'm only the porter."

"Then I'll serve myself."

"You can't do that."

"I sure can."

He walked past the man and into the dimness of the place, where two men older than the porter, wearing rain jackets and coughs, sat with shot glasses.

The porter, following Owney in, said, "Friends of mine."

"So am I. Shot of Fleischmann's and a beer."

Owney put up three dollars, which the porter first pocketed and then poured the drink. Owney swallowed the shot and drank half the beer.

"Change?" he said to the porter.

"Oh, I can't give you change. I'm only the porter. I can't go near the cash register."

"Then you can give me another drink," Owney said.

"Not without money I can't," the porter said.

"Use the change from the money I gave you," Owney said.

"I said I've no change," the porter said.

"Then just pour me a drink. Who'll know what you're doing."

"I'll know."

The porter was motionless until Owney put three more dollars on the bar, which caused the old man's hand to move as swiftly as a fox's foot. The money was gone and the drink appeared. The price was a bit high, Owney thought, but he also was paying for privacy: no one in the hog house could see him taking whiskey before going into the hole. He had a third drink and when he finished that, he felt like another.

He woke up at dusk. His eyes ran over the wall of his bedroom in the cemetery house. When he picked up his head, he saw the rows of tombstones in the shadows.

Then dusk turned to dawn—or had it been dawn all along?—and he went to work.

When Danny Murphy noticed Dolores walking toward the hog house, he regarded her as the first plane over Diamond Head. He assumed that she was there to collect Owney's paycheck, and this was intolerable, for a man only has one liver and one paycheck. "They're not even here yet," he said.

"My husband isn't here?" Her mouth was open in alarm.

"Oh, he's here. I mean the mahosker isn't here. It don't come until later."

"The what?"

"The checks. The company don't bring them here until after two."

"I'm looking for my husband, not his check."

"He's inside."

"Would you get him, please?"

Murphy hurried inside and then as quickly, embarrassed, Owney came out. He walked past Dolores and made her follow him until they couldn't be seen from the hog house.

"I'm up two straight nights," she said.

He didn't answer.

"I called the police to see if anyone was killed."

He looked at the ground. "How did you get here?"

"I took a cab. For twenty-five dollars. Wasn't that nice?"

He ran a hand over his face.

"I want to ask one question," she said.

"So ask."

"Do you think something is the matter with you?"

"Me?"

"Let me rephrase it. Is there anything the matter with me?"

"You?"

"Can't you please look at me and just say something?"

"What?"

"All I want is for you to hug me and tell me you love me. Everything would be so easy after that."

"I do that."

"In the morning with a hangover. Then all you want to do is screw me and go to work."

"I work. You see me here."

"When you're at a bar, do you ever think of me?"

"Sure."

"Then why do you stay there? How could you still stay there?"

He didn't answer.

"Did you ever think that I could get lonely? I am lonely. Do you realize that I'm a young woman and I'm sitting alone all night? That I can't even go to bed? I'm terrified that you're dead someplace. I certainly didn't have a child so I could live like this."

"I know."

"What did you think of when you married me? What did you think it would be like?"

"I thought I'd get ahead in a hurry and we'd go live someplace nice and be in love with each other."

"Fine. So what's happening?"

"I'm going to get there."

"Like this? Do you ever ask yourself what you're doing?"

"I just keep going."

"Do you think something is the matter with you?"

"No."

"Why didn't you come home last night?"

"I got stewed."

"That's no answer."

"Everybody on this job drinks. What am I going to do at the end of the day, walk out on them?"

"Everybody drinks? Every young guy is a drunk? Should I go inside and ask them?"

"They go for a drink."

"They do?"

"Sure."

"I can't believe that. I can't believe all these people here are drunk. Let me go in there and ask them."

"Come on."

"Or is it that you only know the drunks?"

"I go with my family."

"Well?"

"What did you say about them?"

"That they drink too much. I think your father wants you drunk. He feels like a hero with you next to him. Why aren't you looking at me?"

"I am."

"No, you're not. You're looking at the ground. Are you afraid to talk to me?"

Now his eyes came up and looked right at her. "I'm not afraid of anything on earth."

"Oh, I'm sorry. I think you are."

"Afraid?"

"Yes."

"Me?"

"Yes, you're afraid."

"Of who?"

"You're afraid to face yourself."

He made a face and turned and walked away. After a few steps he spun around and said, "From now on, stay away from this job. This is where I work."

"If they have a mirror inside, why don't you take a look?" she said.

He walked away, and she did not cry until she was outside the gate and back in the cab.

Back in the hog house on the bench next to Owney's locker was a sleeping man who had a face covered with hair and a mouth with no teeth.

The man's eyes opened slightly. "What have you got?" he muttered.

"Hot coffee," Owney said.

The eyes under the hair closed. The derelict's name was Eddie Meagher, and he was there purportedly to shape, but he hadn't worked in weeks and was using the place as a bedroom. But when Owney was dressed, Meagher got up and followed him outside.

"Where are you going?" Owney asked him.

"To work."

Owney walked fast to get away from him. Delaney stood up at the top of the hill, talking to Owney's father.

Meagher, walking with the loosest feet, called out, "You go down one short."

"Be off with you," Delaney said. "The only thing we're short of here is people who can work."

"Hey, Jimmy Morrison. What do you say? The gang's one short. I fuckin' know it," Meagher said.

Owney's father threw a hand at him in the air and walked off toward the equipment shed.

"Bullshit," Meagher said as he approached Delaney. "I counted two gangs going down one short."

"Counted what? What you drank?"

"I counted heads. I'm claimin' one of these fucking jobs."

Owney and Delaney walked slowly and Meagher brushed past them and went up the hill, and as he got closer to the shaft his stride improved and he walked up to the low gate and unhooked a length of wire holding the gates together and the click of this caused the gateman's head to pop out of the shaft. "The lift's not up," he called.

Meagher pushed the gate open and strode in for the lift, which was not there. He was about to step off into the air when he noticed this. He paused on the lip of the elevator shaft, standing on wood that looked like a floor but was actually jutting out over the shaft. He had no balance and he held his hands out to steady himself. The wood under his feet shifted. Meagher's head was turning in alarm when now the wood tilted. Owney, walking up with Delaney, walking quickly now, could see Meagher paw the air as he dropped into the black hole that went deep into the ground.

When they brought the lift up, Meagher's body was covered with a blanket, the indentations of which showed that he was in wet pieces. The lift sat in the shadows and the men stood in the sun and waited for the ambulance to arrive and remove the body.

"Does this mean we take the day off?" one of the blacks asked Delaney.

"Out of respect for him—the man died," Delaney said.

"He never worked here. He just an old drunken *mon.*"

Delaney used a cigarette to disguise his fury. "Eddie Meagher worked here for years."

"I here five years, I never see him do anything but get all drunk up."

"He worked. I say we take the day off just like we would if one of us went down," Delaney said.

"I never walk up to the shaft drunk," another voice said.

Delaney concentrated on his cigarette. Owney, looking around, saw that a few whites, while shaken by the body in pieces in front of them, were thinking through the emotion of the moment and reaching the point on the other side where they could see themselves receiving checks with one day taken out for their honoring of Eddie Meagher, who died a drunk. Then, this instant passed and they all accepted gloom.

Now the crowd parted and an ambulance rocked its way up to the shaft. Three uniforms jumped out and then became motionless as they saw the blanket over the pieces of body, the blanket, green, now black from the blood beneath it. They brought out black rubber body bags and a wire cage to carry them. The driver got back in behind the wheel, leaving the two medics to pick up the body.

"Let's go, lads, we'll give him a hand. One, two, three."

"They'll do it," the driver said through the window.

"We're just giving them a hand," Delaney said.

"It's their job. Are you trying to take their job from them?"

"I'd never do that. I'm for the workingman."

"Then let them do their job and you do yours."

Delaney called out, "Nobody touch their work. We got our job, they got theirs."

They stood still and waited while the medics shoveled the parts of Meagher's body into the bags and then carried them to the ambulance. When the ambulance backed away, the men stood hesitantly in front of the shaft.

"Do we go down or not?" somebody said.

Delaney seemed confused. "Where the hell is your father?" he said to Owney.

"I'll go down and see what the guys in the hole think," Owney said. "Why doesn't everybody stay here until I find out."

Delaney nodded and Owney stepped onto the lift alone, standing clear of the blood slick atop the mud in the middle of the floor. Owney stared at the sky and then the elevator started down and the sky disappeared and he rode down through the darkness. He wondered if any parts of Meagher's body were still stuck to the sides of the shaft. He tucked his chin inside his slicker, to make the target all the smaller in case one of Meagher's old feet came flying off the side of the shaft.

There was no noise at the bottom of the shaft, as no one was working. A gang was standing along the sullen rock. Before Owney could ask them what they wanted to do, they began walking onto the elevator. At the edge of a puddle, glistening in the light, was a piece of rock that seemed to be a crystal. It was a small piece, and the only one that Owney could name on sight: muscovite. The geologist in the contractor's trailer once had told Owney that the rock was as old as the earth but was named muscovite because in some centuries in the past, the churches in Russia had used this rock for windowpanes.

Owney's thumbnail peeled a wafer off the rock. He held it up so he could see the light coming through. It was stained glass made by the earth a billion years ago. As he looked through it, standing deep under the streets of the city of New York, the glass was first green and then almost pale yellow. He thought about an old woman in Russia someplace staring at the light coming through the window of her church. Russian praying to God. He started to say the Our Father for Eddie Meagher, but then somebody on the elevator called and Owney went over and stepped on and put the rock into his shirt pocket. He forgot to resume the prayer and when the lift brought him back up to the ground, he merely indicated the men around him and Delaney called out, "No work today, lads. We've a man dead."

Passing the picnic table to leave the place, the men took up the bottle of Jim Beam as if they were receiving bus transfers. Some drank from the bottle and left with a hand wiping the mouth; others poured the whiskey into paper cups and walked out gulping. All had a mixture of anguish and excitement and need of a forum in which to stand and make their grief public and at the same time share in the shock and glory, for they, too, work in the place of death.

Now his father was in the hog house, reaching for the bottle. Without looking at Owney, he poured Jim Beam into a paper cup and held it out. Owney took it.

"What was he saying about short gangs?" Owney said.

"Who could listen to the poor bastard?"

"Maybe I could."

"What are you saying?"

"I been down here short twice when I nearly got hurt," Owney said. His father walked away.

Owney was about to follow him, to begin bringing up everything that he had noticed lately, but then he thought of Dolores and he decided that he had to call her first, to use the excitement of Meagher's death as a reason to talk to her. Of course he couldn't use Meagher as an excuse, and indeed shouldn't even mention his name. There are rules against frightening somebody out of their anger. But he would allow the energy of the moment to recommend something as he talked; he would come up with something good, he knew that.

When she answered, he did not say hello and thus give her the chance to shoot anger at him. He said: "A guy just went right out of my hands into the shaft. I don't know what to do. It brought back the whole freaking Nam to me."

"Oh, Owney. Who?"

"Eddie Meagher. The nicest guy in the world. He just stood in the shaft and the boards fell out from under his feet. I just got my hand on him. Then, poof, he's gone."

"Are you all right?"

"I'm throwing up."

"Come right home."

"If I can. I swear. I was over the shaft myself."

"Just come home. Please don't drink."

"Right away."

He hung up and grabbed for the bottle. He was elated that he was out of trouble with her. As he drank the Jim Beam, he thought of Eddie Meagher. I'm sorry, but I needed you.

She opened the door with wide, worried eyes. He went into his shirt pocket for the piece of muscovite and handed it to her.

"That's beautiful," she said.

"Hold it up."

She murmured as she looked through it.

"That's stone," Owney said.

"It's the same as stained glass."

"That's exactly what they used to do in Moscow. They put it in the church windows. While I was driving here, I was thinking of how you'd look standing in light from a window like that. You'd look beautiful."

"Thank you."

"Standing in church in faint light."

"What was I doing in church?" she asked.

"Praying. You looked beautiful."

"And what was the occasion?"

"You were getting married to me."

When he got out of the shower, she said to him, "Are you all right?"

"Unnerved."

There was something about the way he said the word that caused her eyes to change from open sympathy to inquisitive. She looked at the pouchiness of his eyes. The shower had not taken the weight out of his eyelids.

When he fell asleep, she took the baby over to her mother's.

6

"I JUST HEARD THEM talking about it by the wallpaper store," Aunt Grace said.

"Oh, it was on the television last night," Dolores's mother said.

"Imagine putting a subway station in this neighborhood?" Aunt Grace said. "I said to myself, I swear on God, I don't believe this."

"You didn't see any of it on the news?"

"I never watch the news. I just told you, I heard them talking in the wallpaper store."

"You should keep up with the news."

"All they got on television is a big black man telling you about car accidents."

Dolores fidgeted with the usual mixture of embarrassment, resignation, and guilt. She sat in her aunt's kitchen and looked through its open door and through the open door of her mother's apartment across the hall and saw her baby, who was asleep in a playpen on the kitchen floor. Among those things with which she had been forced to live, and which she swore to her soul that her child never would know, was the amount of inexperience that caused this sort of conversation.

Because now her mother said, adding to the discomfort, "I guess they got a lot of them on television."

"I'm looking this one night," Aunt Grace said, "and here they have this Black Muslim or something talking to this pretty girl that does the

Channel Five news. You should have seen him leering at her like she was stark bare naked. I said to myself, I swear on God, somebody should be there, put handcuffs on this big Muslim because any second, he's going to molest her. Really molest her right on television. Then you know what he does? He turns around and starts to give the weather."

"I bet you he said a storm was coming," Dolores's mother said.

"Ma!" Dolores said. "Now that sounds really stupid."

"I guess you're right," the mother said. "I was trying to be funny."

"You sounded about as dumb as you can get."

"Any dumber than putting a subway stop in Glendale?" Aunt Grace said.

Dolores stood up and went to the stove. "Putting a subway stop out here wouldn't help us? Want coffee?"

"I do, but don't give me so much milk this time. I don't want any subway in my Glendale," the mother said.

"Give me, too," Aunt Grace said. "Nice cup of coffee. Course, no subway is going to do anything but ruin the lives of the people living around here."

"Putting a subway here wouldn't help us?" Dolores repeated.

"It would help me get to Boynton Beach, Florida," Aunt Grace said. "I'd go live there by Jewel Feeney. She says in the supermarket in the shopping center they let you push the cart all the way out to the car. You just leave it there in the parking lot and a boy comes running out of the store and takes it back into the supermarket. They don't let you do that in the Pathmark on Myrtle Avenue. They got concentration camp poles sticking up so you can't push the basket outside. I don't have to tell you, that's all I need to put me in Boynton Beach, Florida. A subway stop to Glendale. You'll see my shopping cart sitting out there in the sun, all right."

"Where does that leave me?" Dolores said. "I have to take two buses to get to the Eighth Avenue line."

"Well, you can just imagine what comes up the subway steps if we ever got a station here," Aunt Grace said.

"You don't have to tell me," Dolores's mother said.

"You're waiting at the top of the stairs for your husband and all of a sudd——"

"The two of us wish we had husbands. See what I'm saying, Dolores?" Her mother's chin stuck out smugly.

"I'm going to go out buy a husband when I go to the store," Aunt Grace said.

"You'll find the shelf empty," Dolores's mother said.

"So I'll come home with Clorox again. I'm saying that you're standing there looking down the steps, the whole thing at the bottom as dark as the ace of spades, and you hear somebody coming up and you're waiting to see the husband and here it comes. The ace of spades himself!"

As this form of conversation had been a part of Glendale life since Dolores was old enough to understand what she was hearing, she attempted to change neither direction nor focus. In the life surrounding Dolores, the language of Glendale women as they ruminated in front of the television set usually approximated that of cave women before an afternoon fire. It was only when the talk of the feared and frightful blacks came up that the women of Glendale demonstrated that they were so consumed by the subject that their vocabulary bristled rather than bored. Beyond the streets of Glendale, Dolores knew, her mother thought that Martin Luther King was fine and so was Muhammad Ali, although Aunt Grace never would call the fighter anything but Cassius Clay. The two women, her mother and aunt, also liked Sammy Davis, Jr., on the *Tonight Show* and Harry Belafonte, as long as he just sang. Dolores's mother did not like Autherine Lucy because she showed up to integrate the University of Alabama while wearing a fur coat.

Dolores always felt guilty while she listened to them, as she was of the younger years, although she was not ready to depart from the white centuries of her past and move in next door to an apartment house full of them, with the men in undershirts sitting on car fenders and the women leaning out the windows and the young boys walking around in unlaced sneakers, the idleness in their faces more prominent than their nose widths; that was the thing to fear, their not working. Perhaps if they all had jobs it would be a horse of a different color—aha, that sounds like my aunt Grace—but they don't and I can't fix that for everyone. The sandhogs give them jobs; I don't know what else I can do. Still, out of some duty to her age and the future, she told these two women at the table, whose vision had extended to what they thought was the fullest upon their respective thirtieth birthdays, all that she felt she could pack together at the moment:

"Ma." She said it in a firm, sour voice.

"Oh, no," her mother said. "What's right is right. If they put a subway car out here in our neighborhood, all they have to do in Harlem is get on it like it's a train to Heaven and ride until the station says Glendale. Walk right up the stairs."

"Put the station right by Sacred Heart," Aunt Grace said.

"That's right."

"At least you could look at the church, remind yourself to pray for your life," Aunt Grace said.

Dolores stood up and decided to walk across the hall to her mother's apartment to check on the baby as a pretext for leaving the table when there was the sound of slippers shuffling in the hallway and Aunt Grace's daughter, Virginia, walked in. A cigarette hung from her thin lips. She bent over the stove and lit the cigarette on a burner. Then she poured a cup of coffee.

"What's it like out?"

"Going to be warm," Dolores said.

"You leaving the baby here?"

"For a while."

"Maybe I'll help mind her. I got the week off. Got nothing to do today, really."

Aunt Grace said, "My daughter could use a rest. She made out a cable the other day for you know how much? A hundred million dollars. It was a loan to Argentina. She knew that because that's what she had to type."

Dolores's mother blessed herself. "Jesus, Mary, and Joseph, to think of that kind of money."

The aunt said, "You know what else they got? They got a good cafeteria."

"You could meet a lot of people there?" Dolores's mother said.

"She better," Aunt Grace said.

"Four of us sitting here in a kitchen with nobody," Dolores's mother said.

"Not Dolores," Virginia said.

"She's trying," Dolores's mother said. "She got a husband, now she says she don't like him anymore."

"Ma!"

"That's what you tell me," the mother said.

"You and Owney fighting?" Virginia said.

"Oh, I don't know," Dolores said. "I'd rather talk about the subway."

"Owney didn't even come home for two straight nights," her mother said.

"Whose fault is that?" Dolores said.

"He didn't come home."

"I kept him out of the house?"

"You tell me he didn't come. The wife's responsibility, keep a nice house, have the man there."

"That's insanity."

"I don't call it that."

"I'd rather work in a knitting mill than live like you say."

"You could get a job in my place," Virginia said.

"As what?"

"In my section. Federal funds section."

"Sounds all right to me," Dolores said.

"Bite your tongue," her mother said.

"What's the matter with where I work?" Virginia said.

"Nothing. But she don't work anymore. She got a husband and a baby to take care of. You better go to your cafeteria at work and get yourself the same thing."

"I'll say," Aunt Grace said.

"Get yourself what, a husband doesn't come at night?" Dolores said.

"All I know," her mother said, "was I went away on a honeymoon and all I did was cry I missed my family. My sister-in-law heard about it, she said, 'You must hate my brother. I'm going to tell him to leave you.' That stopped my crying."

Virginia watched the smoke she exhaled as it lazed in the sunlight coming through the kitchen windows. "You're probably right," she said.

"You bet I'm right," Dolores's mother said.

"Cafeteria," Virginia said as much to herself as to anyone in the room.

"It's on the same floor where she works," Aunt Grace said. "Doesn't even have to go on the elevator."

"It's great," Virginia said slowly.

"Rains, don't even get her clothes wet."

"One guy in the cafeteria since I've been there," Virginia said, "he sat with me at lunch a couple of times. I made sure he wasn't married. That's all we got around the rest of the place, married men looking to take you out. Well, this one wasn't married. He sat with me at lunch a couple of times. One day he said, 'Aren't you tired of eating here?' I wanted to say, 'Not as long as you keep showing up.' Then I thought about it and I told myself, Go ahead, Virginia, and I said to him, 'It's no fun with every day the same. Why don't you do something about it?' So he says, 'Tomorrow, we'll go out for Chinese.' I was up six o'clock in the morning getting dressed. I tried on five tops until I felt good in my new blue top from Ohrbach's. I got to work and I'm at my desk, right in my federal funds section, and I don't see him all morning. I go looking for him when the coffee wagon comes around; they don't have the cafeteria open until lunchtime and they send a wagon around with the coffee. Well, I look for him by the coffee wagon. Nothing. By lunchtime, I'm so aggravated, the papers are rattling in my hands. He doesn't come. What do I do? I go out for a walk at lunch, instead of eating in. Like a klutz, I go right past the China Song on Nassau Street. Here he is sitting right inside the door with this girl from the trust division, up on the thirty-second floor. They're lookin' at menus so they can order. If you want to know why I took this week off from work, that's why."

"You hear that?" her mother said to Dolores.

"What's that supposed to mean to me?"

"Of all people, you should know that a baby needs a mother and father. I don't know what would have happened to you if your father didn't come along and pick you up when the people that really had you, the real parents if that's what you call them, whatever kind of people they were, walked off on you."

"I never thought of that," Dolores said dryly.

Her mother walked her downstairs. On the stoop, as Dolores was about to leave, the mother turned around and inspected the front door. The two glass panels, polished furiously with vinegar, blazed in the sunlight. The twin window shades were drawn evenly; a difference of half an inch would have sent the mother into the vestibule with a ruler.

The yellow brick six-family house, three stories high, was attached to identical yellow brick houses that ran the length of the Queens street. The opposite side of the street was the same: the same stoops, with the same black railings leading up to the same polished glass doors. The houses were old, but had been built with buttered bricks—the mortar slapped on each brick as if it were toast being buttered—and with the bricks baked to order on the street in front of the houses as they were being built. Brickwork now is done with premixed mortar that is slapped into a common ditch, three-eighths of an inch thick, between rows of unbuttered bricks; a driving rainstorm hitting new houses leaves the sidewalks covered with pieces of mortar washed out from between the bricks. Watching the houses as she walked past them, Dolores wondered if her life would take on the sameness of the houses.

He stood in the doorway and smiled as he watched the baby. A Glendale housewife's eye knew that a man who gazes away from his baby, or if he does watch, does so with the body fidgeting, is someone who feels deprived and jealous. Owney looked steadily at the baby. Smiling, he seemed unaware of anything else.

"Owney." Dolores stood next to him.

"Yeah." He kept looking at his daughter.

"How could you go out and forget her two whole nights?"

"I won't do it again."

"You don't feel the need to run around drinking like that, do you?"

"No."

"There isn't something making you do it?"

"Not me."

"I keep thinking of the night we had dinner with your father. The waiter brought a drink and when he started to go away your father was positively terrified. He thought the waiter wasn't coming back."

"My father wasn't serious."

"I think he was. You're not like that, are you?"

"Nope."

"I don't remember my father ever drinking at home. But I told you what my mother says about her family. The Kearnses always had so many rings on the dining room table that it looked like a design. Never any people sitting there. They were all in bed before the dinner even came. Just rings from glasses on the table."

"I had trouble once. It won't happen again."

She walked into the kitchen and took a can of asparagus down from the shelf. She held it and thought for a moment. "Owney, look at this."

He stepped into the kitchen. "Look at what?"

She held up the can of asparagus. "Could you give this up for two months?"

"Easy."

"For six months?"

"I could go without it forever."

"Could you give up beer for two months?"

He tried not to swallow. "Yes."

"Then we don't need this," she said. She opened the refrigerator and with each hand took out a bottle of Piels. She dropped them in the garbage and was about to reach into the refrigerator again when his arm blocked her.

"They cost money."

"But you don't need them. And I certainly don't." She patted her stomach.

He reached into the garbage for the two bottles. "Stop wasting money like this. I got to work too hard to throw it away like this. What do you prove?"

"That you don't have to drink them all."

"All right," Owney said. "You want to test me? You want to test a guy can do anything, we'll put them in there and see how long they stay there." He put back the two bottles.

"They'll be gone by ten o'clock," Dolores said, half smiling.

"If I say it, that means they'll be here forever." As he spoke, he swung his shoulders cockily.

She gave a full smile. "I know what you'll do. You'll have twenty bottles of beer on the way home and come in here so filled up that you won't be able to look in the refrigerator without becoming ill."

"Forget about it. See those bottles? Look at them. They'll be in this family for centuries. We're leaving them for Christine and her children and the children that come after that. We'll put a note on every bottle. 'Don't ever drink this. Not ever.' The bottles will turn to rock. They'll have to get a miner to come in and drill them out."

He leaned over and kissed her on the neck. For part of an instant, her chin began to rise. All she really wanted was to hug him and have him put his arms around her and curl his legs around her and fit his body close to hers so she could feel him get hard. Then maybe he would slowly caress her, holding her face in his hands and then slowly run his hands all over her body, slowly and lightly, telling her all the time how much he loved her.

Instead, she moved away from him and turned her back and said she had to take care of the baby.

They had steak and asparagus for dinner and Owney grabbed the glass and was about to drain it when he realized that the glass held ice water.

After dinner, they turned on the television, but there was a special on Vietnam and Owney turned the set off without gambling on another channel. Dolores looked at a news magazine, then a fashion magazine. Owney smoked.

"What time is it?" he said.

"Eight-fifteen."

He closed his eyes and inhaled. The night doesn't want to move, he thought.

He got up and went out on the stoop. Dolores followed him. "There's a movie on at nine," she said. Owney nodded. The guy three doors down, Bruce Cataldo, came out for a minute. He was a fireman, and Owney didn't want to talk to him. Cataldo always talked about how the Fire Department didn't want anybody working a second job as a sandhog. Owney's sense was that Dolores would get right in the conversation tonight and begin asking why he didn't take the fire test. Then Emily

Schweitzer, Owney and Dolores's landlady, came out. She had a sweater over her shoulders and carried a small bag of garbage. The proper Glendale housewife keeps such a small garbage can in the kitchen that it must be emptied four and five times a day. The sweater tossed over the shoulders goes with the chore.

"Now I'm finished," she said. "I can go back upstairs and have a nice, good mouthful of cold beer. I deserve my beer at the end of the day."

"Don't take too much of it," Owney said.

"Oh, you never catch me taking too much cold beer. George and I sit there watching television and I have a nice, good mouthful of cold beer. That's all. You won't catch me doing more than taking a mouthful of good cold beer. You care to stop up, have a nice, good mouthful of cold beer?"

"No, thanks," Owney said. "We're going to watch a movie."

He walked inside the house and sat down and turned on the television.

"It isn't time yet," Dolores said. "It's only twenty to nine."

Owney grabbed a pack of cigarettes.

When the movie finally appeared, he couldn't concentrate. It was still before ten o'clock when he was in bed and Dolores was in the bathroom, scrubbing the make-up from her face. She was humming. Owney thought of the bottles in the refrigerator. Brown and beaded. No good. Then he began thinking of the table by the door in the hog house. At the end of the day, they would be sitting there playing cards and right in the middle of the table, where you had to reach through the card game and nobody ever minded, there would be a square bottle of Jim Beam whiskey. Take what you want.

That was at the end of the day. Now, he wanted to think of the morning, of the lunch wagon and the woman in the clean white apron reaching into the refrigerator and taking out a can of beer, a can covered with cold dew.

At midnight, damp, his eyes wide open, he imagined he saw the form of the Holy Ghost at the end of the bed.

He slipped out of bed and went into the living room and watched the *Tonight Show* and then an old British movie about a woman who cheated on her husband and kept meeting a man in a train station. At one point, the woman ran out on the platform and was about to jump in front of an express train, but then stopped.

"Fuck. You should have jumped," Owney said.

He thought of the refrigerator, and his body was damp and his mouth dry, but then he made two fists and he stayed in the chair. He watched a half-hour life history of Mussolini and at the end, when Mussolini was hanging by his heels with his broad next to him, Owney's body jumped and he realized that he had been asleep for a moment. He went back to bed and immediately was asleep. It was only a couple of hours, but it was enough for him to go to work with enough guts to dress and walk directly to the cage without stopping for the beer he so desperately wanted.

He went for two days and then realized that he could do it no more without something else to do. He and Dolores drove to Jamaica after dinner and Owney enrolled in the school for labor relations that was established for union members, the Delahanty Institute, on Sutphin Boulevard. The school, housed in a red brick building, was first established to prepare young men for the Police and Fire Department exams. The founder, Michael Delahanty, was a New York City bureaucrat who was famous for taking twenty-three civil service exams and finishing in the top two percent each time. Once, at a New Year's office party in the offices of the city comptroller, the all-male staff brought in a prostitute to entertain in the workmen's compensation claims section. Delahanty spent the day locked in a tiny office, where he pored over pamphlets pertaining to his next test, for senior chief clerk, grade 17. He refused to open the door when other workers pounded on it and declared that he had to say hello, at least, to the young prostitute. Delahanty remained locked inside with his test booklets. Thereafter, municipal workers said, "Delahanty is so sick that he would rather take a test than have his prick sucked."

When he founded the police and fire school, he had a greater effect on the city than all of the city's colleges. In the 1960s, when competition cut his police and fire business, Delahanty introduced labor relations courses and installed Harry Kellerman, an old publicist for the Transport Workers Union, as dean of labor studies.

On Owney's first night in the course, Kellerman appeared with white hair uncombed and shot an arm forward, bent his knees, in the speaking form of the old Communists from the transit unions, and then bellowed to the class: "Letters to the editor! The basic protest of the union man. Whenever you see an anti-union story in a newspaper, sit down and write a letter to the editor. Let no insult go unanswered. We will read and discuss Eugene Debs after you have mastered the letter to the editor."

Kellerman then gave his rules for a letter: refer immediately to the article, say immediately that the article was unjust, and then in two short paragraphs prove that it was wrong by using a fusillade of facts.

"If you don't have a fact, then reach into your heart and find one,"

Kellerman said. "Don't worry about a detail being out of line. Truth is what counts. And a labor union is truth. Oh, yes. I do assume that you understand that basic English grammar is to be used."

Owney sat alongside a forty-year-old man named Claffey, of Ironworkers Local 40. As Claffey listened to this, his attitude was that of a prisoner hearing the warden explain that as long as they were in a penitentiary, they might as well wear leg irons.

Riding home on the bus that night, Owney read the *Long Island Press* and saw nothing against labor. When he got home, he spoke to Dolores about Kellerman's assignment.

"We'll just have to read every paper closely."

"I'll get them on the way home," he said.

"I'll get them," Dolores said. "Just in case they'll be gone by the time you start home."

"What's that supposed to mean?"

"That a candy store owner sends the papers back the next day."

She said it with a smile, but a small one. She saw that Owney was irritated even by this, and she said no more.

The next day, Dolores bought the papers, went over them, and found nothing essentially anti-labor. The day after that, she went up to the big newsstand on Myrtle and Wyckoff and bought the New York City dailies, along with the *Wall Street Journal,* which upon inspection at the kitchen table carried an article on page twelve with a headline saying: "Fewer Ride New York's Subways as Union Indifference Rises." The story blamed maintenance practices in the repair shops as the reason for loss of ridership. Dolores circled it and had it ready for Owney when he came home.

"So I'll answer it," he said.

"What are you going to say?" Dolores said.

"That you shouldn't blame a workingman," Owney said.

"That's no answer."

"Then what is?"

"You can think," Dolores said. "Why do people you know complain about the subways?"

"Only one reason. But you can't put that in."

"I don't see why you don't put the truth in," Dolores said.

"All right," Owney said.

"I know what you mean. So say it. You know more than almost anybody. Put it down." She left him at the table with a legal pad and pen and went into the living room to watch the news. The news hadn't been on five minutes, through scenery shots of Paris that included foreign politicians at a meeting, one of those stories that are the heart of network news, that give importance to a travelogue, when Owney called for her. He ripped a sheet off the legal pad and gave it to her.

"In your story in yesterday's paper, you said people don't ride the subways because of union mechanics in Brooklyn. As a member of organized labor in this city, I say that your wrong. If you rode a subway in this city you would see that the true reason is color fear. Every time two blacks get on a subway car, three whites jump off. I could count. That gives the subway car a minus one. So don't blame a poor union worker for all the trouble out in the world."

"The 'you're,' " Dolores said, reading it.

"What 'your'?"

"Here, you say that 'your wrong.' That's a contraction. You and are. Come on."

Her tone changed as she saw desperation ripple through his eyes, which went right to the refrigerator. His hand grabbed for the cigarette pack, even though he had one smoking in the ashtray.

"Owney, you just wrote it quickly so you could make me laugh. You happened to skip an apostrophe. Take your time. You wrote me beautiful letters from Vietnam. That's why I married you. Now get going. But go slow."

He wrote on the pad for several minutes and then the phone rang.

"I'll get it," she said.

"No, no, you sit. I'll get it."

"Channel Two right away," Ralphie Schmidt roared.

Owney hung up and went into the living room and changed the channel. The picture on the screen was of fighting in Vietnam. Some young kid with an old man's stare carrying a gun. Now the phone rang again and this time Dolores went to answer it.

"Yes, Ralphie," Dolores called out. "Ralphie, don't do that. I said, Ralphie . . . Keerist!"

"What?" Owney said.

"He shot at his television set. I could hear the noise."

Owney grabbed the extension. Ralphie's voice was raving over the phone.

"Ralphie."

"Yeah, boy!"

"Did you knock anybody down?"

"I blew the gook prisoner sky fucking high. I take no prisoners. Did you see him go?"

"Sure I did," Owney said.

"Beauty," Ralphie said. "I got one problem."

"What?"

"How do I watch *The Dating Game* tomorrow?"

Owney immediately turned off the set.

They hung up and Dolores said, "That's sick. How can you lead him on like that?"

"It's good. Ralphie likes that."

Owney was so elated that he had Ralphie crazy that this time he had his hand on the refrigerator door before he realized what he was doing. He licked his lips and sat down and worked hard on his contractions and then he decided that he'd had enough and he put the pad atop the refrigerator.

"Let me see it," Dolores said.

"It isn't finished yet. I have until Thursday."

"I thought the way you were going was all right," she said.

"Come on. The three white guys getting off when the spade gets on? I was doing it to make you laugh. That's all right to talk about."

"No, it was taking some license, but it was essentially based on the truth. You certainly were using more of the truth than they were in blaming the maintenance men."

"You can't go around sending in to the newspapers something like that."

"Owney, if you live on Seventy-fourth Street, what are you supposed to call it?"

He thought about that. "Do you know you're smarter than I am?"

"Smart enough to keep you away from there," she said, pointing to the refrigerator. "Let's go for a nice walk. Only on streets with all houses. No avenues."

Outside, she rang the upstairs bell and asked Emily Schweitzer to watch the baby, and then, holding his hand, she led Owney through a network of streets that had no bars on them.

As they were walking up 78th Avenue, they saw the brown bus coming from Woodside. Right away, Owney had a vision of the place where the bus began its trip, around the corner and all the way up 80th Street, next to Durow's, with the side door opening and the gold light from the inside of the bar spilling over the sidewalk.

"Take a run?" he said.

"Don't overdo it. This is just fine."

"No, I want to do some running. Come on."

He took off and she kept walking. He ran as quickly as he could to the corner and then he went around it, onto 80th Street, and now he heard her yelp.

"You bastard!"

He ran down 80th Street, hearing her flat shoes pounding after him. He looked back once and she had the sweater off her shoulders and held in one hand like a baton, and for a girl, a woman, she was flying.

"Owney."

He kept running because he had it figured out. This had to be fun for her, and at the end she would be out of breath and laughing and they could have one nice beer together. He had to get to Durow's. They had red leather barstools in the gold light. And a helluva guy, the blond German guy with the hair slicked straight back, tending bar. Owney ran for the corner and as he was on the opposite side of the street, under the trees in front of the houses, he decided to stay here and right at the last moment cut across the street and into Durow's without losing a step.

He put his head down and he ran and he heard her shout again and he took a look back and saw that she had her head down and her arms pumping. For some reason, the determination took the thirst out of his mouth and he stopped dead and stood laughing as she ran up to him.

"A child," she said.

"I was having fun with you."

"You were a little boy running away from his mother. Bastard." She took his hand. "Home."

As he walked with her, he threw one glance to his left and looked at the side door to Durow's. The gold light came through the curtains stretched over the door. His legs froze.

Dolores held his hand tighter and at the corner she guided him into a turn and now they were walking up Myrtle Avenue, with a closed bakery and an espresso shop as the best the place could offer. The old Rodgers, a place with an ugly brick front, was in the middle of the next block, but she had him turn onto 79th Street, with its trees and houses on both sides all the way down to the cross street, which was made up of more trees and houses.

She patted his back. "I'm burping you."

The next night, the two sat and worked on the letter, and when he was getting confused and fidgety, she seemed to notice right away.

"Go in and watch a game on television. I'll finish it for you."

In the morning a feeling of confidence ran through him as he picked up the letter, all done neatly so he could read the parts she had done, most of it, he admitted, and he went in and kissed her on the neck and she smiled in her half sleep.

He went directly from work to Delahanty's and sat in the classroom in the late afternoon and copied the letter in his own handwriting. The letter was longer than Kellerman had proposed, but Dolores's language was tight and connected and he found it too difficult to save any words. In one section, she had written, "The fundamental problem facing the transit system is that each time two blacks step aboard a car, it seems as if three whites leave. This assumption, which might seem to be mere hyperbole, enters the realm of proven fact when the ridership totals are inspected." She had placed some tone into the subject, but now, late of an afternoon, and with a surprising amount of indecision, he was concerned about using race as a topic. Then he went out to the luncheonette on the corner and found the place empty and the owner cleaning the coffee urns.

"I can give you a meat loaf sandwich, but I only got Coke to go with it," he said. "You got me right as I'm closing, as you could see. I can't stay open past dark." The owner muttered as he picked up a knife, "These shines."

Owney felt this made his letter even more credible, and he went back to the classroom and confidently handed the letter to Kellerman, who was incredulous and overjoyed as he looked at it.

"There! You've got it! You have put your finger not only on the transportation system, but on the entire urban plight. The masses have allowed themselves to be split by the rich. Blacks and whites belong together on the subways. Then they must rush up the subway stairs and together . . . destroy the rich!" Excitement caused his hands to fumble as he dug through a briefcase and produced an envelope and a stamp, which he handed to Owney. "After class tonight, we shall post this letter immediately!"

In his lecture that night, Kellerman expounded on his theories of letter writing: anything to the *Daily News* should be kept to two paragraphs, the first of which was to contain a personal insult to the paper or to the subject of an anti-labor story. A letter to the *Times* newspaper should begin with a mention of the offending article, a factual presentation and not a personal insult, for Kellerman said that the *Times* was a Jewish newspaper and the editors were so ego-ridden that they needed to be told that even their obvious misdeeds were intellectually sound. After the class, he walked Owney to the mailbox on the corner of Jamaica Avenue.

When Owney dropped the letter in the box, the slot door's metallic sound filled him with the sense of a completed task, and the desire for immediate reward. This he was able to suppress and he was quite pleased with himself for doing so.

Standing under the el, looking about, Kellerman said, "Let's get a drink."

"I got to get home."

"Have one."

"I think she made something to eat."

"If the food waited this long it can sit there for another twenty minutes. Besides, I want to tell you just how quickly you can advance yourself in this business. Moreover, just how much this business needs you. Lord, we haven't had a young union guy with your class in ten years."

A few yards up from the mailbox was the green awning of the Capri, an old Italian restaurant that was now a saloon. Owney saw himself with a Coke in his hand, a Coke in a large glass with ice. He wondered if Kellerman would get mad when he ordered a Coke. He took a step toward the Capri and then felt Kellerman's hand on his bicep. "Across the street is better," Kellerman said. With his briefcase under one arm and his other clutching Owney's, Kellerman led Owney through the traffic and toward a place across the street that had a front door with as much grace as a plant gate. The sign said, "O'Looney's and Burke's." Kellerman shouted in the noise of an el train, "Ah, the Capri tends to get a bit dark. This is a railroad conductor's place. All white, of course. Much more comfortable."

In the harsh light in the doorway, Owney saw the spotted hands of an old fight second leaning through the ropes and yanking up the gloves of the opponent, alcohol, who stood waiting for the bell. The opponent's face was smeared with Vaseline so the punches would slide off. Owney walked straight at the opponent, who jabbed and then went back through the door and into the bar and Owney went in after him. Inside, in the smoke and noise and harsh ring lights, the opponent danced and beckoned to Owney to come in and mix it up.

Now Kellerman, making his entrance, stood just inside the doorway and bellowed, "Ja-mayy-ca. Change here for trains to . . . Hunting-ton . . . Far-ming-dale, and Port-Jeffer-son."

The railroad conductors cheered and Kellerman stomped to the bar. "Libation!"

Owney, in the middle of a desperate first minute of the first round of this fight, pushed alongside Kellerman and had his hand out. "Beer."

The bar was long and barren, with railroad conductors in uniform sitting at the bar with mounds of wet money in front of them. They were fresh from the Long Island Rail Road terminal down the street. The money was also fresh; conductors who sell tickets on the train have to account for the money exactly once a week, and usually store it on the bar. The tragedy of facing an accounting once a week often is suddenly relieved by a group of twelve purchasing costly round-trip tickets on the very train that the conductor is taking to his accounting appointment. This system causes railroad bars, such as O'Looney's and Burke's on Jamaica Avenue, to be somewhat lively.

Kellerman had two drinks and then began to cackle. Owney played pool with a trainman while Kellerman got into a discussion with a conductor who proudly kept his gold-braided hat on.

At eleven, Kellerman said to Owney, "You've got to take a ride with this guy and see the conditions he has to work in."

The conductor was tall and wide and had a great black mustache. He was proud of himself in his shiny suit and with a nearly complete load of whiskey inside him.

"This is Mikey Mastrangelo," Kellerman said.

"Pleased," Mastrangelo said.

"We're going with him," Kellerman said.

"Where to?" Owney said.

"What do you care? We'll perform a service for labor. And we're going in the bar car," Kellerman said.

Owney thought about going home. Then he heard the high squeak of boxing shoes. He decided to mix it up.

They walked down Sutphin Boulevard to the five-story railroad station and went through a lobby where a couple of blacks drank wine. Up one flight, there was a counter that sold hot dogs, whose normally pleasant smell was overwhelmed by the odor of hot grease. Up another flight was the outdoor platform and a train of battleship-gray cars, many of whose windows had spider-web cracking from rocks being thrown at them.

The big conductor led them into the second car, which was half filled. At one end, the old smudged imitation leather seats had been pulled out and there was a metal bar cart set up. A young girl with long light hair and a round face shining with sweat stood at the bar cart.

"Vodka and ice," Kellerman said. He looked at Owney.

"What the hell." Owney said, "Same."

She served them drinks in plastic glasses and collected the cash and they drank standing as the train left the station.

"Where does this go?" Owney said.

"To the fishing grounds," Kellerman said.

"To where?"

"Montauk. We're on the last train to Montauk, young man. It is the male fishing capital of the world. Key West gets written up, but that's fags with reels. This is where the men go. Say, young lady, how much do they pay you for this job?"

"I'm only summer help," she said.

"I don't care when you work. It must be paid for."

"I get four dollars an hour."

"A trainman gets ten! You ride the same train!"

"I get good tips," she said.

"How do they tip you?" Kellerman said.

"Usually, they tip me right when they buy a round. You forgot to do it."

"I didn't forget," Kellerman said. "I refuse to demean the American worker by making him beg for tips."

"I'm not begging, mister. I just take whatever I get. From you, I got nothing."

Kellerman lurched away and went to a seat. "Fresh punk," he muttered to Owney. "She's exactly the kind of person that gives the American labor movement a bad name."

"I don't care about her," Owney said. "I can tell you that I'm never going to last to Montauk. We'll have two more and get off."

"How will we get home?"

"If there's no train, we'll go for a cab," Owney said. The car was suffocating in the night heat. Owney, running a hand over his face, looked around and saw that everyone else was hot. He put his hands on the window, but there was no way to open it.

"Say!" Kellerman called out. Mastrangelo was swaying down the aisle toward them.

"Yessir, professor," Mastrangelo said.

"Who handles your grievance about a lack of air conditioning?" Kellerman said.

"We tell the shop steward," Mastrangelo said. "Lot of good it does. We have so many cars without air conditioning that the shop steward hardly listens to complaints anymore. We just pray for winter."

"Ah, I see. Well, you can figure a way to open a window for us somewhere and we'll come sit by it."

"Professor, there's not a window on the train you can open."

"You should take this to the Central Labor Trades Council tonight," Kellerman said. "It must be a hundred in here."

Kellerman stood up and took off his jacket. The yellow shirt had a button missing and through the opening could be seen a soaked T-shirt.

"We'll have one more drink," he announced. "Then we're getting off."

Owney stood up. "Forget the drink now. I'll buy you one when we get off. Let's just get off now."

Mastrangelo smiled. "You guys got a bit of a wait."

Owney looked out the window to see where they were. Below on the right was Sunrise Highway in the middle of Nassau County. "Anyplace is fine," Owney said. "Are we up to Freeport yet?"

"This train doesn't make a stop until we get to Westhampton Beach," Mastrangelo said.

"That's way the hell out in the Hamptons," Kellerman said.

"That's right."

"Just make one quick stop at the first place you see and we'll be gone," Owney said.

"I thought you wanted to go fishing," Mastrangelo said.

Kellerman smiled. "That thought seemed nice back in the bar. But, good Lord man, we've got three hours more on the train before we get to Montauk."

"Three hours and twenty-nine minutes," Mastrangelo said.

Kellerman smiled. "No, Brother Mastrangelo. I think we best get off."

"You said you wanted to go fishing."

"That was back in the bar."

"You better start wanting to fish again. I can't let you off until Westhampton."

Kellerman smiled. "Just stop the train, brother."

Mastrangelo shook his head.

"I'll do everything I can to get you fired if you don't stop this train," Kellerman snapped.

"Hey, Brother Professor."

"Don't brother me. I'll be at the Public Service Commission tomorrow morning with evidence that you're a fucking drunk and a menace to passengers and should be fired."

"Is that how a good labor man talks?"

"That's how a man talks, you ignorant guinea slob."

The two of them went onto the floor with a crash. The light-haired girl with the bar cart let out a yelp. Owney sat in his seat and stared at the vodka glass. He was tired of stupid-ass fights. Finally, he decided to get up. As he reached for the two, each with a hand clawing the other's face, the train came into a lighted station. Owney got up on the seat and yanked the red emergency cord. The train squealed and jerked. Bottles flew off the bar cart. Owney put his foot in the aisle, got it over one of Mastrangelo's hands, and then stood up with all his weight on the hand. There was a grunt and then the start of a howl. Kellerman, wisps of hair in his face, climbed up. Owney pushed him toward the doors. Kellerman was past the bar cart when he saw the small individual whiskey bottles rolling around the floor. He stopped and grabbed several, which momentarily blocked Owney and gave Mastrangelo a chance to follow. Growling, he rushed for them, but Owney was out the door and onto the platform. Heads popped out of the open train doors up and down the length of the train. Owney could hear Kellerman on the staircase going down to the street. Now Owney turned and looked for the conductor, who was lurching out the door, hands out to grab somebody. And then the conductor saw Owney's eyes. The conductor's hands grabbed the doorway and he stayed just inside the door. Now he looked closely at Owney's eyes. The conductor saw a darkness to them, unblinking, hurtful, that caused him to step back, one hand reaching for the button to close the door. Owney turned and walked down the stairs.

Downstairs, Kellerman stood in the street light and held up a miniature bottle of Red Label Scotch. He tore the stamp, opened the bottle, and took a swig. He handed it to Owney.

"Guineas like that should not be allowed to work in any setting where there are real human beings," he said.

Upstairs, the train was moving. Owney looked around him. The sign said Amityville. There was a cabstand with no cabs.

"We'll go broke getting home," he said.

"I don't care. I wouldn't ride a train with one of these slobs again," Kellerman said.

The cab to work cost sixty dollars. Owney went right to the hog house, where he slept on a bench. When he woke up at five-thirty, two people looked at him intently.

The opponent was the first. He was asleep on a cot with an army blanket over his bare body. He raised his head slightly, saw that there was nothing for him to do, that it was happening by itself to the other guy, and he rolled over onto his stomach and fell asleep on his face. He began snoring through a nose that had been broken so many times in so many winning fights.

Navy was the other to notice Owney.

"Morning," he said.

"Is that what it is?" Owney said.

Navy smiled. "What time did you get home?"

"I believe I missed doing that."

"How are things at home for you?"

"All right."

"For sure?"

"Absolutely."

Navy smiled. "I was just thinking about myself. I came home one night and my wife had her head in her hands. She needed a washing machine and I was walking in broke. In the middle of the night. Some guy in the bar said he needed fifty bucks for table money and I whipped it out for him. Like a millionaire. Then I go home broke. I see she's feeling bad and I want to say something to make her feel better. So I put my arms around her. I'm stewed and I say to her, 'Don't worry, dear, no matter what happens, I'll never leave you.' She breaks into tears. Bawling. I thought I was saying something nice to her. She thought it was the end of the world. I wasn't leaving. That meant she was going to have to kill herself."

Navy laughed. Then his blue eyes became serious and he said softly, "It shows you, you don't understand what you're doing when you're screwed up drinking."

"With me, it's fun," Owney said.

"Oh, it can be some fun," Navy said.

"The only fun in the whole world," Owney said.

It took until the middle of the morning, when Owney was trying to think up an excuse to give Dolores, before he realized that the story about Navy's wife had not made him laugh.

7

FOUR DAYS LATER, Dolores Morrison stopped for cigarettes at Prine's candy store on Myrtle Avenue, picked up one of the two *Wall Street Journals* from the newsstand, and went immediately to the editorial page. The signature under the last letter to the editor said, Owen Morrison, Local 147, Tunnel Workers Union. She raced through the letter, noticing that it had been cut and that the paper had done some slight word changing: instead of printing Owney's "three *blacks* getting on," the *Journal* made it read, "three *thugs* getting on." Synonym.

Finding one phrase that was solely hers—"you cannot commingle an opinion issued from a carpeted office with the experiences of a working-man riding the transit system"—she exulted. Embarrassment rose as she thought of her anger at Owney for his absences and drinking, an ire clearly out of proportion to what had happened: a few mistakes by a young guy who obviously had so much in his past that he was having difficulty pushing aside, yet at the same time there clearly was so much in front of him that mature behavior simply would occur. She bought the paper and read it twice on the way home.

She even tolerated his being three hours late and groggy from brew upon arrival. He was surprised at her amiability, and also at the pleasant feeling generated by the sight of his printed letter. Owney wondered what he had to do to get letters like this in the paper again.

By the time Dolores had her nightgown on, he was asleep with his arms spread and his hands open, a sports page picture of a fighter who just got knocked out. She smiled at the thought. Nobody knocks him out, she told herself, he just has to change this least bit.

That was Tuesday. Owney went the rest of the week without a drink. On Saturday, he congratulated himself on this, and at the same time reduced in size the notion that something in a glass was dominating the life he was living. Oh, that wasn't his idea to say the drinking was a problem. It was something he had seen in the looks of others. Navy.

That night, he and Dolores went to the Mets–Atlanta game with his father and mother. The father ordered big beers from the vendors, but Owney shook his head and Dolores had a Coke. In the ninth inning, with the Mets ahead by a run, the Braves got two on with nobody out and Gil Hodges, the Mets' manager, walked to the mound and signaled for the left-hander. Owney's father began yelling.

"He's bringing in McGraw. Up the Irish!"

The father now turned frantically, looking for the beer man. Sound was everywhere in the park as out of the bullpen came McGraw. He got to the mound just as the beer man got to Owney's father, who bought four beers. Owney and Dolores shook their heads. "That's fine with me," the father said. He put the two extra beers between his feet.

McGraw struck out the first man, got the second on a pop fly, and now the place was delirious with tension as Aaron came up for the Braves. Owney's father had one beer gone and was operating on the first of his extras when McGraw blew one past Aaron. Owney came out of his seat clapping. Up the Irish! McGraw blew another past Aaron. Owney looked quickly at his father, who offered the extra beer. Now McGraw threw with his body down to his toes behind the pitch and Aaron swung the bat an entire instant early. The scroogie. McGraw gave a little leap and the catcher ran out to him with the ball held out for McGraw. Owney felt the beer placed into his hand at a moment so delicious that drink was required. Rain for the turf. From somewhere inside him he summoned a strange resolve. The beer became alien in his hands. Back to the father went the beer. Owney used both hands to applaud McGraw.

Later, at Lum's Restaurant over in Flushing, Owney drank ice water.

"That was some game," the father said.

"Sure was."

"Take a drink."

"No."

"You got the flu?"

"Cooling out."

"That's what a beer's for."

Dolores said quietly, "He isn't drinking tonight."

"What does that mean?" the father said.

His loudness intimidated her and she looked at her food. She could feel the tension coming from Owney.

"I just want water," he said, firmly.

Dolores relaxed.

During the meal Owney said he was going to the union meeting the next morning.

"I don't think I can make it this time," the father said.

"We're going to look at a house," the mother said.

"You are? Where?"

"Selden."

"Exit Sixty-three," the father said.

"A big ranch house with a lawn in front and a back yard that goes through to the next street, where there's nobody even living."

"We got to see the real estate man, ten o'clock," the father said.

"I'm having trouble believing this," the mother said.

"What made you decide on a house?" Dolores said to the father.

"Because I got to have something," the father said. "I work all my life and I don't have a thing to show for it. Clothes on my back, that's all. I got to have something. A house."

"I hope you know what you're doing with the money," the mother said.

"I know what to do. You get a mortgage. They got all kinds of forms you fill out, then they give you the house."

"With our credit rating?" the mother said. "We have to put the phone in my maiden name, all the years they shut us off."

"I'll get the mortgage with my cash rating, don't worry about it," the father said.

On Sunday morning Owney woke with his limbs covered with nerves. In attempting to deal with the confusion inside him, he thought of Vietnam, but discounted that, unless it was coming from someplace so deep in him that he wouldn't know how to find it anyway.

He could taste a beer as he got dressed.

At the nine o'clock Mass at St. Pancras, he held the baby and his mind wandered too much to permit effective prayer. He thought of the union meeting, which was scheduled for eleven that morning, and became elated at the idea that he could be out of the house on official business on the day belonging to the Lord in the morning and children in the afternoon.

When Owney stopped in front of the house after church, Dolores didn't move.

"I'll go with you," she said.

"Go where?"

"I want to watch."

"That's ridiculous."

"No, it isn't. We did the letter together. Look what happened. Let's try the same thing again."

"There's no place there for a woman."

"I'll go upstairs. Nobody'll know I'm there."

They drove to Manhattan and parked in the silent morning on the empty business streets around the Polish Hall. There was nothing open on either side of the hall, and the closest distraction was the White Rose bar on 14th Street, which did not open until noon; therefore those arriving for the meeting had no place to go except where they were supposed to be, at the meeting.

"Brother Morrison!" Harry Kellerman stood in the old lobby with so many newspapers under his arm that he looked like an old packhorse.

Owney didn't answer. Kellerman suddenly dropped the papers on the floor and pulled a folded paper out of his suit jacket, a gray pinstripe with a dark patch on the underside of the left sleeve, the result of misreaching for a glass and consigning the cuff to constantly flopping onto bars wet with beer and whiskey.

"Magnificent!" He unfolded the *Wall Street Journal* and waved the editorial page.

"Isn't that great?" Dolores said.

"Magnificent," Kellerman said. "May I introduce myself? I'm Professor Harry Kellerman."

"I'm Dolores Morrison. Of course I've heard of you. And this is our daughter, Christine. Who is right now sort of asleep."

"Saving her strength for the battles ahead!"

"I guess so."

"And there shall be many."

Dolores made a face. "You can forget about us in battles."

"Oh, no. We're going right into the trenches."

"Not with my husband you're not."

"The front lines, then."

"Put him down for the Peace Corps."

"It's just language," Kellerman said.

"I could do without it."

"But make no mistake, there shall be a struggle throughout all of labor." His voice rose to intimidate her.

"I'm for that," Owney said.

"And I take it you're ready to help," Kellerman said to Dolores.

"I'm here," she said.

"I must tell you a story, little lady. At the time the Pennsylvania and the New York Central railroads were talking merger, I was hired by Mike Quill of the Transport Workers. He had twelve thousand trackworkers involved with the merger. Well, anyway, I was hired by him to go to Washington to the ICC and attempt to protect his interests. You can't believe the ICC. It's set up like a French courtroom. When I walked in, the man pretending to be a judge was sitting up there on the highest bench I've ever seen. A French court! I had to look to the ceiling to see the tip of his nose. I start presenting my matter to him. He treated me like I was scum. For four days I fought for those twelve thousand workers while the big sharks sent their lawyers in and out as if they owned the place. Of course they did. While I was there, looking up until I got a neckache, what do you think was happening in New York?"

"The union pulled something," Owney said.

Kellerman waved a hand at him and looked directly at Dolores. "This is for you, little lady. What do you think was happening here in New York?"

"I'm sure I don't know."

"Then let me tell you, little lady. The head of the railroads came to Quill's house himself. Up on Seventy-second Street. And here was Quill's lovely wife, smiling, bringing big drinks filled with ice out of the kitchen. Then, smiling, always smiling, and never listening, she wouldn't dare presume—dare presume!—to listen to the men, she slipped out. But those drinks settled that labor dispute. I was in the French king's court in Washington. With all my brains and all my energy and persistence I could not get done at the ICC what this woman accomplished in her kitchen."

He rocked back. His eyes sparkled. When Dolores did not answer, his eyes narrowed for an instant. Then he said cheerfully, "Well, that's my story about good union wives. I guess we can let you get home now."

"Oh, I'm not going home. I'm staying."

"You're staying here?"

"Sure."

"Where?"

"I'll sit up in the balcony with the baby. I can't wait to see what's going on."

"Oh, your husband can tell you when he gets home."

"I'd prefer to be here myself."

"Aren't you afraid of being in the way?"

"No, I'm not afraid."

"Not at all?"

"No."

"Well, I am." Kellerman snorted.

"She'll be fine," Owney said.

Kellerman put his face so close to Owney's that their foreheads almost touched. "Brother Morrison, this is a serious business. You have shown aptitude for this business. I am here to see that you go to the top. I shall brook no interference."

He touched the baby under the chin. Then he put a hand gently on each of Dolores's arms. His eyes were riveted on hers. "Now, little lady, I must explai——"

"I think there's a bit more to my life than me being a little lady."

His eyes rolled and then returned to hers. "You must realize that I think your husband is on the verge of something. The entire union movement is wide open. As a good union wife it is your duty to assist him in every way you can. The main way is never to force yourself on the union men."

"Is sitting in a seat forcing myself?"

"Inhibit! That is the word. You inhibit and then you impede. A girl like you belon——"

"She stays," Owney said suddenly.

Kellerman shut up.

"I don't mean to intrude," Dolores said, "but I do think I have my life kind of tied up with his. Uhm, the two of us have this baby, not just me, you know, and I really think I'd like to at least see some things for myself. See you." She walked up the staircase to the balcony.

Kellerman fell silent. Finally he said, "We'll discuss this at another time."

"I don't know what's so bad about it," Owney said.

"If I am to manage you, I must have freedom of decision," Kellerman said.

He bent down and picked up the piles of newspapers. Watching him,

Owney tried to remember when he had agreed that Kellerman would run his union endeavors.

Kellerman now walked with Owney into the back of the old hall. Kellerman took a great breath of air.

"I smell union. Take a breath. Some men walk in here see a hall. I see a temple. Magnificent, brother! Look at this place. See the windows?" The windows along one side of the hall began at a point higher than anybody's reach and went almost to the ceiling. "They make a joke out of these windows. They say they're placed high out of reach in order to protect the usual denizens of this hall, the Polish people, from themselves during their most joyous moments. The windows are too high for anybody to be thrown through them. Slander at its most despicable. I stood in this very hall and attacked this story. The Polish might be my favorite people. Great union men. Housewreckers Local Two Thirty-seven. And what culture streams through their blood. Chopin! Paderewski! Incredible people, these Polish. Let someone tell a Polish joke in my presence!"

Abruptly, he dropped the papers and slipped out of a large wooden door, which he shut after him. Owney stood for a few moments. When Kellerman came back, he was reeking of whiskey.

"You got a bottle," Owney said.

"I don't use a bottle," Kellerman said. "What do you think I am, some degenerate bum in the gutter? I carry a flask."

Owney nudged him and Kellerman went through the door with Owney following. In the shadows at the head of the stairs, Kellerman pulled from his jacket pocket a flask as big as a canteen. He tapped a large dent on the side.

"From the Crimea campaign."

The whiskey rushed like bad medicine into Owney's mouth. He gagged and bent over in case he threw up.

"Rugged in the mornings," Kellerman said.

Owney held his breath and took a large swallow. It barely got down.

"What ails you?" Kellerman said.

"I'm all right."

"Of course you are. Have another before we go."

Owney took a swallow and handed the flask back to Kellerman. Kellerman had it to his mouth as Owney tried to choke without sound.

Kellerman put the flask back in his pocket and looked around. "See how they keep the ceiling lights off out here? No windows here, either. That's by design, brother. They wanted these Polacks to fight in the dusk. They might miss a couple of punches, the ignorant bastards."

On the stage, there was a table with four men in business suits that were wrinkled from trying to stretch across too much belly. One of the men, Billy Callahan, the business agent for the union, stood up and took off his suitjacket, loosened his tie, and rolled up the sleeves of his white shirt.

"I got dressed up for church this morning, but I don't need no tie on for you people," he said.

The crowd of about one hundred fifty laughed. Most of them smoked cigarettes.

Kellerman whispered to Owney, "We'll take seats in the back and play this cool. Today, we'll just watch. They know about the *Wall Street Journal*. Don't worry, I made sure of that. We're taking care of your career."

Owney found the pronoun "we" strange, but said nothing. "I want to sit further up," he said. "I got something to say."

"Say what, brother?"

"I don't know."

He walked up the middle aisle and grabbed a seat. Looking back, he saw Kellerman alone on a chair in the back. Owney threw a glance up at the balcony, but Dolores had made certain to sit away from the railing and therefore remain out of the line of sight. Owney regarded this as a retreat from her earlier boldness. She was a girl having her moment. The next meeting she won't even come.

On the stage, Billy Callahan gripped a microphone and called out, "Now let's get on with it. Meeting come to order. The first thing we got is a letter from the Safety and Health Committee concerning safety and health."

At the table, a vice-president, Hennehan, tugged at a shirt collar that was barely making it around a neck the size of a truck tire, adjusted a pair of half glasses so that they covered his fat eyes, and began reading a long report about men failing to attend Monday morning safety meetings. As the speaker droned on, Owney thought about his father. He should be here to talk about these short gangs. Then his eyes glanced at Jackie Donnelly, who wore a shirt and tie, had his dark brown hair brushed neatly, and was leaning forward, his face reacting eagerly to each monotonous word. He was an ass kisser in school. Oh, bet your life on it. And then he walks around like a tough guy, Owney thought. He is so tough that he's exactly my age, and he didn't go near the service. Plenty of heart.

When the report was finished, Callahan said, "I want to say one thing about Brother Danny Murphy. He got picked up by the cops on account of he was walking with his shopping bag and they said there was numbers in it and of course he don't admit there were even slips in the shopping bag, much less slips with numbers on them. He didn't say nothing to the cops, but he wants to say something here in this room."

Danny Murphy stood up. He, too, was dressed for church, in a light brown suit and a white shirt and flowered red tie. He clearly was not used to this attire. He hooked a finger into his shirt collar and gazed at the ceiling.

"Brother Murphy."

The finger kept tugging at the collar and the eyes remained on a point overhead.

"He's afraid," somebody said.

This shook Danny out of his reverie. "I'm not afraid to put my foot in your face."

"Brother Danny Murphy, now that you have broken the ice, will you tell us what's bothering you?"

"We got a lot of guys here who have cops for friends," Danny said. "I'm not calling a good union man a rat. But you could meet a cop friend in the hardware store or in the bar on the way home and you mention somethin' to them about the job. Maybe you say you play a number. It's all by accident, you don't mean nothin' by it, but then the cop goes right out like the rat that he is and they come after me. What I mean is that we all should keep our fucking mouths shut when we talk."

Callahan now roared, "All right. That takes care of that. Remember what you just heard. Now I want to discuss with you the three-cents-an-hour donation to the Political Action Committee. I want to tell you that the three-cent PAC is pride in your union. Look at the Veterans Day we put on. We give out our T-shirts to the kids and Chris Doyle give out hot dogs to the members. If we didn't have the three-cent PAC, we would've been assholes at the parade. Brother McNamara, you got something to say?"

McNamara had a shock of white hair and he wore a blue knit shirt that was tight around a body that still was hard. He stepped into the aisle and spread his feet and rocked back and forth.

"I want to ask you, Brother Callahan, as our business agent, do those men that don't put up the three cents an hour still get an official union T-shirt for their kids and then get hot dogs free at our official union affairs?"

Callahan made a face. "What am I, a business agent or a fucking cashier at a lunch counter? How do I know who eats what? We got twenty guys in the whole union who don't put up for our PAC. What am I supposed to do, check a dues book before I let them put mustard on a fucking hot dog for somebody?"

Callahan started to say something else, but Crawford, a black man, fat and his hair gray, stood up without raising his hand. He took a cigar out of his mouth and looked down at it. "What about dis *mon* Eddie Meagher?"

Callahan shook his head. "May the Lord help the poor fuck. Now we better not start talkin' about this matter in public, either. These insurance lawyers hear anything, they're worse than cops."

"I agree wit' you on dat. But de *mon* die because somebody tell him to go to de shaft on account of de gang was down dere shorthonded and dis *mon* Meagher, he could get on and work."

Callahan's eyebrows went up and his lips pursed to show doubt.

"I look around on my job," Crawford said. "Sometimes de gangs are short."

Owney felt his feet move involuntarily, the left forward and the right backward. The man seated next to him glanced at Owney.

On the other side of the room, a hand was raised. On the stage, Callahan called out, "Brother Donnelly."

Jackie Donnelly looked around the room, his face pleasant and relaxed, and then began talking. "Brothers. We are bonded together in a union that would not permit one brother to work harder than a human should, or to risk his body any more than we all risk ours every time we go down into the hole. Now there are times when the deployment of personnel makes it seem as if somebody is missing from a gang assigned to, well, to give an example, assigned to helping run in an air line. Perhaps when you are on the platform drilling the face, there appears to be a man short or something, but there surely is not. I can't believe that anybody would send union men down in short gangs."

Crawford still had not sat down. He examined his cigar and then his head rose again. "Dey say on de ot'er gangs a *mon* is missing here, a *mon* is missing dere. When dey check up, to see if dey is on some duty like you say, dey find de *mon* simply is not dere."

Donnelly smiled. "Perhaps Brother Morrison . . ."

Owney looked up, startled. Donnelly in his white shirt and dark tie, a smile doused with olive oil. A mutt, Owney said to himself.

"What?" Owney said.

Donnelly began talking, his head turning to all corners of the room, regularly and mechanically. He stopped and looked directly at Crawford.

"I can understand your anger about a man, any man, being lost on a job. Naturally, we hope there is something or somebody to blame. So that we can prevent it from happening next time. But I just can't help but feel that we should see if the men simply aren't exercising the necessary precautions. Well. Here. Brother Morrison's father is the shop steward for the job of which you are pointing these things out. Unfortunately, his father isn't in attendance today. But Brother Morrison here, Brother Owney Morrison, can certainly tell us that it is a lie about gangs going down there short-handed. I can't imagine such a thing happening if there is one Morrison alive. Isn't that right, Brother Morrison?"

Donnelly, eyebrows up and smile slick. Owney stood up. "I can't speak for any other Morrison because I'm the only one here," he said. "I don't know what to say about short gangs on our job except that if they are short it is a mistake that can be explained. But while we're waiting for the explanation, we're going to see to it that there are no short gangs tomorrow morning. About Brother Meagher, I can tell you that I was there when he got killed. I dogged it."

Still on his feet, looking at Owney, Donnelly cut in: "I don't know of any man in this room, or in this whole country, who can use that word in your presence. I also would like to point out to the members that like a good union man, Brother Morrison wrote a personal letter to the *Wall Street Journal.* They printed it nice. I'm sure you all saw his nice letter in the *Wall Street Journal.*"

"What paper is that?" somebody said.

Donnelly seemed surprised. "The *Wall Street Journal.* It's the management paper they print on Wall Street."

"Wait a minute," Owney said. "That letter was attacking them for what they said about the subway workers."

"Anyway," Donnelly said, "it was printed in the *Wall Street Journal* and I congratulate you. Not many union men got access to a management paper."

"I dis——" Owney stopped his tongue as he was about to slur. He found it amazing that a half drink like he just had out in the hall could put weight on his tongue this quickly. He took a breath.

"The letter took a shot at them."

"Anyway," Donnelly said quickly, "it was printed in the *Wall Street Journal* and I do congratulate you."

Owney decided that he had this one speech about Meagher in his mind and he wanted to concentrate on it. He was afraid if he started in on the newspaper he would get mixed up with the thing about Meagher. To prevent slurring, he began talking slowly.

"As for doggin' it on Brother Meagher, I say I did. I complained about short gangs. Then I let it go at that. So I damn near got killed drilling into a hot hole. The hole was hot because nobody washes the thing down. You ask Larry Delaney. I put in a beef."

"Did Delaney tell the shop steward about it?" Donnelly said.

"I don't know," Owney said.

"Isn't your father the shop steward?"

"Yes."

"Perhaps you ought to ask him."

From the stage, Callahan's voice boomed, "Look, this is a meeting for the whole union. Not just for you two guys. Tomorrow being Monday, we'll take care of these disputes over short gangs on the Van Cortlandt job run by Brother Morrison. Jimmy Morrison."

Owney and Donnelly sat down. Now Callahan said, "We can't have guys standing around here snarling at each other like fuckin' dogs. All right. Now let's get back to the reading of the letter from the Safety and Health Committee concerning safety and health."

Suddenly, Donnelly's arm shot up.

"Brother Donnelly."

Donnelly again looked around the room to catch as much attention as possible. "Brothers, we've been told that the health and safety aspects of this job are costing us money personally. Can somebody please tell me why our union, and therefore the union members, the workers, have to pay for their own safety?"

On the stage, Callahan, obviously pleased, bellowed: "Brother Donnelly, thank you for bringing that there subject up. Because I want to tell you people once again that the federal Occupational Safety and Health Administration, that is OSHA, of which we all hear so much about it, well, I just want to say again today that OSHA is nothin' more than a jerkoff. You know it and I know it. They pull our pricks. We got eleven men dead on this job since we got started. Eleven men. It's a fuckin', fuckin', sad, sad situation. And how many of you ever saw a federal health and safety inspector? Let me see the hands. Let me see one fucking hand go up. You bet, not one. You know why there's no hands up? Because they got no inspector to see us on the job. We do it ourselves. Thank you, Brother Donnelly, for pointing this out. All right now. The next order of business is to announce to you that we are going to honor

Eddie Coffey, from the Central Labor Trades Council, with a pin from this union for his twenty years of service on the council."

A hand went up.

"Brother Reilly."

An older man stood up, pulling the cigarette out of his mouth. "Are we honoring Eddie Coffey senior or junior?"

"Senior."

"Good. I got deep *detest* for junior."

Now that the meeting was about to examine the personal aspects of all not present, and soon would turn to those actually in the hall, with the predictable results, Owney got up and walked down the aisle and looked up at the balcony, where he saw Dolores's face, ready to pull back like a turtle if somebody happened to glance up and see her. Owney gestured toward the door. As he went through the high wooden door, Kellerman was right behind him.

"Cheeky bastard," Kellerman said.

"Donnelly?" Owney said.

"Who else?" Kellerman said.

"Tried to make me look bad."

"Jealousy," Kellerman said.

"I got no time for it," Owney said.

"Good boy."

"He's nothing," Owney said.

On the way home, Dolores said to Owney, "Who was the guy who stood up and talked?"

"I don't know. Who?"

"You know very well. The fellow our age."

"He asked me about my father?"

"Yes."

"Donnelly."

"What does he do?"

"Just another guy working. Works the Roosevelt Island job."

"The way he got up indicated to me that everything was on some sort of a schedule. Don't you think they must have gone over everything before they walked in there?"

Which immediately drew up the picture of Donnelly, sitting erect, the coffee in his hands, the hands afraid to raise the coffee to his mouth because he was too busy saying yes, and laughing at the most minor of remarks as he tried to please the business agent and his staff in the coffee shop before the meeting. Owney muttered a profanity under his breath.

* * *

On Monday morning, Callahan, as business agent, stood with a clipboard, with Owney's father alongside him, and they counted heads together as each crew went down. Owney said nothing. The father appeared either too busy or too wounded, Owney felt the latter, to talk to him. The reason for the wounding bothered Owney. When Callahan was off to the side talking to someone for a moment, Owney said to his father, "Did you see any houses you liked yesterday?"

"You asked me that on the way here this morning," the father said. "I told you. We looked."

The father's head turned away quickly. Owney, disturbed, went to the lift.

His father didn't talk to him for the rest of the day. Owney had left the car with Dolores and driven to work with his father. After work, his father got as far as the turnoff to Glendale and then he went another exit and turned in the wrong direction.

"I told her I'd be home. It's her birthday and we're going into the city. She likes that."

"Have one."

Owney failed to argue. The father drove down the hill to Jamaica Avenue, a street of low, weary buildings with a late afternoon sun coming through el tracks and falling in pale oblongs on the cracked, empty sidewalks. The father stopped in front of a bar that had no name. The door was held open in the warm air by a barstool that had a ripped leather covering.

When they walked in, the barmaid did not move. She sat motionless on a stool by the window with a cigarette in her left hand. A lion's mane was dyed black and the thin lips were penciled white, a statue with hard lines.

"Dead," Sharon said.

"Tough day," Owney's father said.

"I had to move last night," she said. "My boyfriend come around with a U-Haul truck. We couldn't move till late. The landlord goes to Gotscheer Hall every Sunday night. That's when I moved out."

"You owe the rent?" Owney's father said.

"What do you think? What do you think I'm movin' for at night, to save the couch from the sun?"

Slowly, she slid off the stool. "I made a real big move in my life. I moved from nowhere to nowhere."

She put small beers in front of them and then shot glasses of bar rye. Owney threw down the shot, which burned, and took the beer in two swallows. It had that first heavy malt taste, but the second beer she gave him went down cold and quick. He lit a cigarette and stared at himself in the mirror behind the bar. The place was the worst. You got to be eighty to like it in here, Owney thought. He wanted some place with loud, fast noise.

Owney took out his wallet and went through it. One hundred and forty dollars. The bills gave him an empty feeling. When he cashed his check the other day, he remembered putting up forty on the bar and telling himself that was all he was going to spend.

His father, seeing him puzzled by the money, said, "What are you worrying about? I got it."

"I need some to take home."

The father went into his pocket for money that was folded in half. He put it on the bar, where it seemed inches high. "Take what you need." There were fifties and hundreds, easily the most money Owney had ever seen his father carrying.

Looking at it, Owney whistled. Which caused the father's eyes to flicker nervously.

"She's putting all this away for a house," he said.

"But where did this come from, an armored truck?" Owney said.

"I heisted a shipment of bullion," his father said, attempting to laugh.

"Where did it come from?" Owney said.

"Don't worry about it. She goes right to the bank with this in the morning. I can't short her."

"What are you talking about, short her?" Owney said, fingering the money. "She never saw money like this in her life."

"Forget about it," the father said.

"How can I forget about it when it's jumping up at me?"

"What do you need?"

"I need to know where the money's coming from?"

"Someplace."

"What's that supposed to mean?"

"Just what I said. Here, what do you need?"

"I need table money, but not from there."

"What's the matter with you?"

His father drained a drink and tried to make himself quite busy calling for another.

"The money," Owney said.

"Let me get my drink."

"The money comes out of the job and you're in some swindle with those guys I saw you with at work."

The father kept his head turned. "You're daft."

"You're taking money for ghost jobs."

The father now turned and looked directly at Owney. Made the mistake of looking directly at his son. For as he mumbled a reply there was an uncertainty in the eyes that caused Owney not to hear what his father was saying.

"You're taking it right out of somebody's body," Owney said.

The father's eyes became slits. "Don't worry about it. It'll all be all right."

"What are you doing with those two guys?"

"It'll be all right. I'll give them what they want and then it's over. Don't talk about it anymore."

"Don't talk. What the fuck am I supp——?"

There were footsteps and Owney glanced at the woman walking in. His father's hand went over the money. A little too much weight was on her face. She carried a paper bag with a package wrapped in meat paper sticking out. She put the bag on the bar and sat on the stool two places away from Owney's father. She went into her pocket for cigarettes. She said nothing, and the barmaid put a Scotch and water in front of her.

Owney's father had stuffed the fat roll of bills back into his pocket. He left a few wet bills on the bar, and the barmaid took the money for the woman's drink out of this. Owney's father sat looking straight ahead and sucking on a cigarette. He put the beer to his mouth.

Owney picked up his beer and then put it down. "I'm going."

His father handed him the car keys. "I'm not."

Owney went past the woman sitting two stools away from his father and he didn't look at the woman and she didn't look at him.

"Don't you want money?" his father called.

"I'll fucking die first," Owney said.

Outside, as Owney got into the car, he saw his father turn sideways on his stool and talk to the woman.

He drove toward Woodhaven Boulevard, instead of home, for his stomach was churning and he knew he had to sit alone on the boardwalk at Rockaway and think, or go crazy.

Halfway up the street, sitting at the top of the el steps to the end of a station that was closed, O'Sullivan pulled his silver head back from between the iron spokes of the banister as he saw Owney walk out of the bar alone. His large hands twisted on the taped handle of the baseball bat between his legs. "Just the kid by himself," he said.

Behind him, leaning against the locked door to the el station, was a young guy in a leather jacket who chewed gum furiously. Standing next to the young guy was Old Jack.

"We do it here," the silver-haired guy said.

"That's what I want. I don't wait no more for these guys. I get them right today," Old Jack said.

O'Sullivan's lips compressed. He never took orders well from anyplace, a wop most of all. What can you do, he told himself, take your piece and shut your mouth. They got all the strength.

He peered through the banister spokes and saw Owney drive off.

"There goes the kid," O'Sullivan said.

"The kid?" Old Jack said.

"Just drove off."

"Why didn't you tell me?"

"I did. You didn't hear me."

"That fuck. I want his blood."

"That's nice. Who are you going to send, Junior here, down after him? This kid is liable to send Junior back wrapped in a newspaper."

Junior, chewing gum, muttered.

"Relax, Junior," O'Sullivan said. Then he looked at Old Jack. "I thought we were here for business. What's the kid got to do with the money?"

"Nothing," Old Jack said.

"Then we wait for the father. Put the kid on the shelf for tonight."

O'Sullivan's manicured fingers kept squeezing the handle of the base-ball bat. He didn't care that the steps were making his suit dirty. He stared down the metal el steps leading to the street and he remembered the day when he went down another flight of stairs—metal, just like these —with a bat in his hand.

The steps were at the Polo Grounds and they went from the dressing room to the center-field grass. One game in his life, they let him play.

They pitched me outside, O'Sullivan muttered to himself on the el steps.

He didn't play the next day. After the game, they had the newspaper on the dented tin shelf of the locker, next to his bottles of cologne. He had thrown the paper away in the morning, but they dug it out and left it for him. Remembering this now, he told himself: I brought class to the joint, I showed hillbillies how to smell good; the only thing they ever had on was witch hazel. Let them use my bottles. What do they do for me? They ride me. The story in the paper said that the first baseman just up with the Giants, O'Sullivan, wore more perfume than a labor racketeer, but he was still smelling up the joint. Labor racketeer.

Now O'Sullivan's hands tightened on the bat. He was as furious about the story in the paper right now as he had been the day it was printed.

"O'Sullivan." Oh, he remembered how the manager yelled from the office as he saw him, newspaper in one hand, bat in the other, walk out the door and start down the metal steps to the field. O'Sullivan went down the steps and through the outfield shadows and onto the infield dirt. He kept looking up at the press box, which hung from the upper tier. A green tin roof: he remembered that. By the time he was at the pitcher's mound, he could hear the clacking of the telegraphers sending the stories into the newspaper offices. Labor racketeer. He had on a white Giants home uniform and he walked off the field and through the lower tier and up the ramp, the spikes sounding on the cement in the empty ballpark.

"If you want Woods, he left," a Morse code operator said when O'Sullivan stepped into the press box.

"When?" O'Sullivan asked.

"Just now. He left on the dead run."

The next morning, O'Sullivan was gone from the major leagues forever. When his father went to prison, O'Sullivan replaced him in the lineup—as a labor racketeer.

Now, over thirty-five years later, on a late afternoon in 1971, O'Sullivan sat on the Jamaica Avenue el steps with his hair silver and his face jowly and a baseball bat between his hands. He picked up the bat and waved it. He wanted to do something to somebody right here in broad daylight.

He peered down at the bar where Owney's father sat. "I hope this guy comes out before it's dark," O'Sullivan said. "I don't feel like playing a night game."

At nine o'clock she sat at the kitchen table, folding clothes. When her mother had arrived in the morning, they had used the washer in the basement, which was a concession on her mother's part. Her mother used to live in Ridgewood, which is the home of German machinists, but she liked her clothes touched only by nature.

Dolores opened the dryer, but her mother acted as though the machine was contaminated. Her mother carried the wash up in a basket and hung it on the line running from the window of the small bedroom out to the telephone pole at the rear of the garage. Her mother sat at the window with a cup of coffee and watched the wash as it lifted, curled, and flapped in the breeze running through the small yard behind the house.

When the mother pulled the wash in, she placed the basket in front of her daughter and said, in triumph over the dryer downstairs, "See how good it smells now? Smells sweet. You can't get that out of a machine with no fresh air circulating inside."

Dolores was going to ask her mother to examine the air, which had on its lower levels a mixture of natural blue and Maspeth factory smoke, and explain how that could be better for the clothes than a dryer, but raising this would only produce more silent determination. The mother would trudge through the house looking for more things to wash and hang out on the line.

She said nothing and her mother went home happy.

Now, as her husband stood in the kitchen doorway, she was grateful to have the wash, as it gave her something to do with her hands. The notion of throwing something was in her mind an act performed in another time, one done by people with gray hair and sour mouths. Yet at the same time her hands wanted to get something firm and heavy and hurl it at his face.

"What do *you* want?" she said.

"I'm messed up," Owney said. "I've been driving around for three hours trying to get my head straight."

"Really. What am I supposed to do about it?"

"I don't know what to tell you. Except I'm messed up."

"And now you're back in time for me to cook my own birthday dinner." She folded a towel.

He started to say something, but she said, "For me it was a relief. I only had one baby on my hands."

His eyes went to Christine, who was in an infant seat on the floor. He made a sound for the baby.

"She's three months old," Dolores said. "I estimate that for one third of her life, so far, she hasn't had a father. Congratulations."

He picked up the baby and talked to her. Dolores sat with the wash. A black nylon headband pushed her light brown hair off her face as she bent over the wash basket. She was cold and humiliated and she told herself that she didn't know whether she wanted him or not.

"I'm not going to drink for a while," Owney told her.

She concentrated on the wash.

"In fact, I might not take a drink for the rest of my life."

Her answer was a deep breath.

"I figured out something. That I don't notice what I'm doing to myself. From now on, I know that I have to look out."

When she didn't answer, he said, "Well, at least I did that. I'm messed up."

He kept talking and her mind drifted. She thought of the bedroom window, which her mother had done with cold water and vinegar and then had rubbed so clear with chamois cloths that ordinary daylight became blinding when it reflected off the glass. It became just another square of sky to a bird, a cardinal, which flew into the window with a thump that startled Dolores. The cardinal flew out into the back yard, turned, and came straight back at the window, slamming into it beak first. The cardinal dropped like a stone, but quickly worked his wings and was gone. Fifteen minutes later, the bird crashed back into the window.

Her husband made her think of that sound. He starts flying, she thought, and doesn't look where he's going, either. Am I supposed to sit here and listen until I hear him hitting himself against a wall?

Owney was saying, "I can't figure out what I did."

"Well, I did some thinking," she said.

"If I talk to you, maybe I can figure out what I did."

Talk, she thought. Whenever he has anything personal to say, he waits until the third paragraph before he even gives you a hint. And he's better than his father. The father hasn't talked to the mother in twenty-five years. Dolores thought of Owney's mother, who had spent three hours with her earlier in the day and couldn't talk about anything except supermarket prices.

Now Owney put the baby back and went into his pocket and brought out a pink rock.

"I want to give you this before we get into a war here and I forget about it. I got it for you on the job today. The engineer told me that it's at least a billion years old."

She looked at it and said nothing.

"See the black lines running through it? The bands. Now, this is what the engineer told me. The bands came from pressure and heat when something happened a billion years ago. Continents collided with each other. I'm the first person to touch this piece of rock since the earth had an explosion or something a billion years ago. Go ahead. Touch it. That makes you the second."

She touched the rock with her right hand. Her fingers felt the rough surface and ran along the black banding. A primitive feeling ran up her arm. She gripped the rock, which was the size of an ashtray, with her thumb and forefinger, the way you hold something you want to scale into the water at Rockaway.

Since Dolores was seated when she scaled the rock at his face, it did not have the force she wanted. But it caught him, all right, even with his reflexes, and he always had the quickest body movements of anybody she had ever seen. Caught him on the left side of the forehead and caused his eyes to explode.

"What do you call that?" Owney yelled.

"The best I can do instead of a gun."

"Now what am I supposed to do?"

"I'm sure I don't know," she said, her hands going back to the wash.

He spun and went out of the kitchen, but turned and walked to the bedroom. She stayed at the kitchen table and heard him take off his work clothes and then pad out to the bathroom. The shower went on.

Twenty minutes, she said to herself. You made yourself feel better for a second and he gets twenty minutes to hide.

She looked at the baby. Where am I going to be next year with you? Am I going to be sitting here like this? She shook her head quickly.

Later, she put on a pale yellow Christian Dior nightgown, from Loehmann's in Lefrak City, and got into bed with her back to him. The space between them, over which no foot would slip, was insignificant in width, but as a boundary was as effective as a desert.

Most of her thoughts were on getting back at Owney. She thought of going to work on a job that would get her home at six at night, in time to bathe the baby and put her to bed. Her mother could mind Christine while she was gone. Meals, she thought, would consist of anything that could be eaten by hand. She liked that idea. Give away the knives and forks, and just keep paper napkins for pizza.

She felt his hand on her side. She moved her body further to the edge of the bed. The hand now slid under her arm and was about to touch her breasts when she shifted her entire body and went onto her back. The hand withdrew.

"Where do you get the nerve?" she said.

"I like you when you're mad," he said.

"I never heard of such bullshit."

He put his right arm across her body and now his chest was atop hers and his mouth reached for hers. Her head turned to the left and she held a hand up.

"Stop."

More of his body weight began to spread onto hers. Now her voice was sharp.

"If you don't stop."

He hesitated and then the weight was gone from her. She rolled onto her side and kept her eyes open, a sentry in the night, until she heard him asleep.

8

I'M HERE TOO LONG NOW," Sharon the barmaid said. She shook her dyed-black lion's-mane hair. "Just because I got here late today, they don't send no one in to relieve me. Look at it. Nine-thirty and Sharon is still here. Sharon got better places to be."

"You have a date, someplace to go?" Owney's father said.

"To some other bar."

The woman who had been sitting all evening with Owney's father said to the barmaid, "You meeting somebody?"

"Oh, I have a date," the barmaid said. "Sharon is going to stand at the bottom of the el steps and wait for her date to come off the train. He's coming from the Sherry Netherland Hotel in the city. He's got five thousand bucks in his pocket, and he's riding out here to spend it on Sharon on Jamaica Avenue."

"He's only got five thousand?" Owney's father said.

"I didn't tell him to bring any more."

Her arm reached out, and she picked up a bottle of Scotch and poured herself a shot. She looked around the old bar, which had six listless customers. In front of her, Owney's father sat sideways on his stool, facing the woman who, since late afternoon, had sat two places away from him. Her grocery bag, with its packages wrapped in meat-market paper sticking from the top, remained on the bar, alongside the ashtray.

"Are we just going to sit here all night?" the woman said to Owney's father.

"I don't know."

"You've had enough time here to decide something."

"All I know is that I needed to relax today. I work in a cramped-up place all day. I needed to take it easy."

The woman said, "Ever since I come in, you've sat here with your feet hooked onto the rung of your stool. I don't know what you consider being cramped up."

"Saloons are the best as long as you're not working in them," the barmaid said. "At least in another place I could have somebody serve me a drink," she sighed. "That's the only place I'd be, another bar. I might as well face it. I was born to live in a bar. I had no chance. Not the way I was brought up."

"Where are you from?" the woman with Owney's father said.

"A nice place," Sharon said.

"What nice place?"

"East New York nice place. I was in love with the boy next door. I even went to his funeral when he got killed."

"Then you went into a bar after the cemetery," Owney's father said.

"And I never came out."

"Good a place as any to spend your life."

"I guess so. I got myself three husbands out of it. I guess that's a couple more than most girls get."

"That's three more than what I got," the woman said.

"Well, I sure got three," Sharon said.

"How?" the woman with the packages said.

"I picked out weak guys and I told every one of them that I was in love with them before they said anything to me. They didn't want to hurt my feelings so they said they were in love with me, too. Then we got married."

"Then the trouble started."

"Because the three of them were so weak that you couldn't live with them. The last one was supposed to be out stealing for me and he's so gutless he was dryin' dishes. You ready for another?"

The woman put a hand over her glass. "I got to go home."

"I'll have one," Owney's father said.

"You're not coming with me?" she asked him.

"Are you going?"

"Yes."

"I'm not," Jimmy Morrison said.

The woman looked at the packages wrapped in paper from the butcher shop. "You're not hungry?" she said.

"No."

"You're just going to stay here?"

"I need to relax."

"Oh. Terrific."

She looked at him as he sat across from her in the smoky air. Then she stood up, said, "See you around," picked up her bag, gave Sharon a nod, and walked out.

Outside, at the top of the el steps, O'Sullivan gave a start as he heard the barroom door swing open. He peered through the metal banister spokes.

"Here's his broad," O'Sullivan said. The baseball bat was in his hands.

Behind him, Old Jack said, "Put on the mask. Here, get the hat on, too. Junior, go start the car."

O'Sullivan pulled a ski mask from his jacket pocket and wiggled his head into it. He reached back and the old man put a leather machinist's hat into his hand.

"Why do I need these things?" O'Sullivan said. "I want the bum to know where it came from."

"Who wants somebody else in the street to see a face?"

O'Sullivan grunted. He pulled the hat down over his silver hair. He resented the mask and cap, but he reminded himself that he was wearing the same black suit he had worn the last two times he had been to the tunnel job to see Jimmy Morrison. The guy better recognize the suit, let him know exactly where this is coming from, O'Sullivan said to himself.

Then he saw the woman carry her paper bag down the street and nobody was following her out of the bar.

"Alone," O'Sullivan said.

The old man said, "This does it. I can't wait here no more like this."

"We'll wait five minutes more, Old Jack," O'Sullivan said.

"We go now," Old Jack said.

Rather than give O'Sullivan the chance to argue, Old Jack walked down the el steps. O'Sullivan followed, using the baseball bat as a walking stick. "I'll wait one minute here," O'Sullivan said. He eased up to a doorway next to the bar entrance.

The old man made a face. "We're going to come around with the car and that's it. Then we go."

Inside the bar, Owney's father sipped his drink.

"She's mad at you again," Sharon said.

Owney's father stared into the mirror, swallowed the rest of his drink, and began to pack for the trip home. He carefully put his cigarettes into his shirt pocket, assembled his money, pushed a couple of bills and a pile of change across the bar at Sharon. He was surprised to see how late it was. Makes it hard to find a cab, he told himself.

He stood up. "I got to get home," he said.

Sharon nodded. Somebody down at the end of the bar needed a drink and she walked slowly down to the man. Owney's father walked to the door.

"Yo!" Sharon called to him.

Owney's father didn't turn around. He held his arm up in a farewell wave and pushed the door open and stepped out onto the sidewalk into the spring night. He was looking to his right, down the empty avenue, for a cab, which he didn't expect to see, but he was looking for one anyway. Looking to the right. As the barroom door he had pushed open swung shut, here was O'Sullivan, the old hat and ski mask covering his silver hair, furious from hours on the el steps. He swung the baseball bat left-handed, swung it with his wrists, shoulders, and hips all moving in one piece.

Owney's father felt something and started to look into the bat, which hit him across the mouth and on the chin. Two of his front teeth went out and a third down his throat; his eyes went up into his head as he pitched forward onto his face. Blood bubbled onto the sidewalk.

Now O'Sullivan swung as if chopping wood, bringing the bat whizzing down from his left shoulder. He cursed to himself as the first swing landed low on the back of the head and didn't cause the head to split open. O'Sullivan pulled the bat back and now the door swung open and Sharon stood with Owney's father's cigarette lighter. O'Sullivan swung the bat in her face. For an instant, the barroom door was in his way, or at least was distracting, but he caught her on the forehead and she went straight back against the now-closed door and then fell to the sidewalk like a wet towel.

He was about to bring the bat up again, and this time he was going to put his whole life into a swing that would split Owney's father's head open forever, but then he thought for an instant about the two of them being on the sidewalk and for sure somebody else walking out from inside the bar to look for the barmaid. Quickly, he bent down and went through Morrison's pockets until he found the wad of money. At least I get paid.

Carrying the baseball bat like a walking stick, O'Sullivan went to the car idling at the curb, got in, and pulled the ski mask off his flushed face as Junior drove the car away.

After the phone rang that night at 11:30, and an unmodulated voice said that his father was in the Wyckoff Heights emergency room, Owney went first into the drawer with his shirts and pulled out a blue turtleneck to cover the long scar, still bright red. The shirts were on one side of the drawer. Alone on the other side was a cardboard box that had stenciled on it "Medal of Honor and Holder One."

He was still pulling on the shirt when his legs began to run down the hallway to the front door. Dolores looked out from the kitchen, where she had the baby squalling in one arm. She had the phone in her other hand.

"I'm coming," she said. He didn't answer and was out the door and down the alley to the car. As he backed the car out, he scraped the side of the house. His wife was at the curb in a robe. She jiggled the baby. As she slid into the front seat, the baby's wail caused Owney to stiffen.

"What do we do with her?" he said.

"Don't worry about her."

Owney made the run down Central Avenue with his hand on the horn. When they reached Wyckoff Heights Hospital, he double-parked and ran through the waiting room past Dolores's mother, who stood with her hands out for the baby. Owney's mother sat like a statue. Owney heard Dolores running after him.

In the emergency room there were a policeman and a nurse and Owney called out, "Morrison?"

"He's up in X-ray," the nurse said.

"Where?"

"Upstairs. You can't go up there. Why don't you just sit and be comfortable. It'll be a few minutes."

Owney was through a doorway and up the stairs to a dim hallway that had gray walls. His father was on a cart with his mouth and chin distorted by swelling. Blood covered the lower half of his face. His eyes opened, looked at Owney, showed no recognition, and then closed.

"You're all right," Owney said. "I can see from here that you're all right."

A doctor stood in a small room that had banks of lights on the wall. He stared at X-rays. Owney stood in the doorway and Dolores pushed alongside him. "What is it?" Owney said to the doctor.

"She's a strong girl. She'll be all right," the doctor said.

"No, I mean my father, Morrison."

"He's a pretty strong fella, too. I didn't see any fracture. I can't tell about the bleeding, but his reflexes are good. The pupils are not dilated. Of course, we'll have to run some tests. But I'm not uncomfortable about him now."

"What do we do with him now?" Owney said.

"Take him upstairs to a ward and watch him. Why don't you wait downstairs?"

Owney went outside and stood with one hand on the cart. Dolores bent over the father and whispered to him: "We're here and you're going to be fine."

Now the door to the X-ray room opened and they wheeled out Sharon, the barmaid, whose bare feet stuck out from under the sheets. Owney stepped over to her. "You're fine," he said. Her black hair was matted and the swollen forehead was an angry welt.

"It must've been a baseball bat," the attendant said. "If it were metal, the skin would have split. No, this was a baseball bat. You got a big welt, but the skin didn't break."

He kept one hand on the cart, alongside his father's shoulder, until they were upstairs. The attendant didn't want Owney touching the father, but Owney put his arms under his father and helped lift him into bed.

The nurse looked at Dolores, who stood in a gray plaid robe with the yellow Christian Dior nightgown showing under it.

"Are you a patient?" the nurse said.

"She's my wife," Owney said. His hand went out and touched Dolores.

They stayed in the doorway, while doctors walked in and out and nurses peered, until there were footsteps and then voices and approaching them were two detectives.

"Could I see you for a moment?" one of the detectives, short and squat and with light hair, said quietly. Owney followed them down to a room off the nurses' station. Dolores walked with them.

"I'm sorry to have to do this to you, but we think we got a real good chance with this thing," the squat detective said. "Your father got mugged about ten o'clock. Now there have been a few muggings in that area and we brought along a couple of pictures we'd like you to look at."

"I wasn't there when it happened," Owney said.

"They said you were in the bar with him," the detective said.

"I left way earlier. How you know it was a mugging?"

"That's what we think. Maybe you ought to take a look at these pictures, anyway."

"I didn't see anybody when I left."

"Right now, you might think you didn't. But maybe you happened to notice someone who was hanging around on the street, and the face might come back to you now, if you see it again."

The second detective, whose stomach pushed against the button of a blue blazer, had five photos spread out on the table.

"Why do you say he was mugged?" Owney said.

"He had no money on him," the squat detective said.

"He had a lot of money when I left him there," Owney said.

"That's it," the detective said.

"How do we know somebody else didn't take his money?" Owney said.

"Who?" the detective said.

"A cop. Or somebody in the ambulance. They hit his wallet, and we could be here looking for a mugger who never was."

The squat detective closed his eyes and blew out air. "In case you don't know it," he said with irritation, "we got a war going on out there. It's as bad as any war you ever heard of."

"Oh," Owney said.

"And I'm out there on the firing line. Right in the front. And you're not helping me fight the war with that attitude you got."

"There's only one good thing to come out of the whole night," Owney said. "That I know I'm not as dumb as you."

"I don't have to take that," the detective said.

"Do what you want," Owney said.

The second detective smiled. "We know you're upset. Why don't you just take one look at these pictures for us."

Owney leaned over the desk and glanced at photos of five black Hispanics, who had mustaches or scraggly beards.

"They don't mean anything to me," Owney said. He took Dolores's hand and started out of the room.

"Don't you care who hit your father?" the detective in the blazer asked.

"Yeah, that's why I don't have any time to waste with you," Owney said.

They went back to the room and when another doctor came up at six o'clock, Dolores spoke to him and listened as the doctor mentioned types of bleeding—subdural, epidural—and then spoke again about the father's reflexes being fine. Dolores listened intently and Owney let her run the conversation. At six-thirty in the morning, when he saw his father's leg move in the bed, Owney looked at Dolores, who smiled, and now he suddenly felt tired.

On the other side of the hallway, the two detectives were looking into a room where, in the bed nearest the door, Sharon the barmaid was muttering, "Sharon has nothing to say. Except that they shouldn't have hit Sharon. They shouldn't have done that to Sharon."

It took two days for the father to come out of it. When he did, he sat propped up in bed and stared with eyes that were filled with blood.

"Well?" Owney said.

"Baseball," the father muttered.

"Is that what it was?" Owney said.

"O'Sullivan," the father said.

The silver hair was in Owney's mind now. The next thing he thought of was a gun.

The father's eyes tried to follow Owney as he left. "Hey!"

"Coffee," Owney said. He was out the door and into the hall. He paused for a moment and looked into the room where Sharon now sat up in bed. Her discolored forehead hung like a ledge over her eyes.

"See what they did to Sharon?" she said of herself.

Owney went to the elevator banks.

He turned onto Forest Avenue and stopped at a two-story frame house that had gray aluminum siding and a front door with new black paint. Ralphie Schmidt sat on the edge of the flat roof, his legs dangling, the sunbathed right arm raised over his head and waving a hammer.

"Up here," he said.

"I see you," Owney said.

"You got to take care of roofs," Ralphie said. "You don't take care of the roof, then you won't have a roof over your head, you know?"

"I want to talk to you," Owney said.

"So talk."

"No, I want to see you."

"You need something?"

"Absolutely."

Schmidt brought the hammer down on the roof. "My man!" He pulled himself from the edge of the roof and disappeared. Owney went up the stoop and was about to press the bell when a woman with heavy bare arms and wearing a housedress pulled the door open.

"He's yelling at me to let you in," she said.

"Hello, Mrs. Schmidt."

"Come in, Owney. How's the baby?"

"She's fine. You look good, Mrs. Schmidt," he said.

"I'll tell you, it's an accident, living with him."

There was a staircase as they entered and Ralphie Schmidt stood at the top, his teeth showing in a great smile. Ralphie led Owney into his bedroom, where he had draped across the headboard a belt of .50 caliber bullets, the brass dull in the bedroom shadows. On the night table was a large framed photo of a dead Vietnamese. He had been naked in order to keep loose clothing from tripping any detectors. Ralphie always insisted that the body was missing a leg when he first saw it, and so he picked up a loose leg from another body and fitted it onto the one he photographed. As evidence of this, Ralphie always pointed to the feet and then at the caption he had printed with a marking pen: "Two left feet. Photo by Ralphie."

Schmidt now stood in the closet and held a heavy black pistol with a short barrel. "Three fifty-seven. Beautiful."

Owney took it and stuffed it into the right pocket of his fatigue jacket.

"Ralphie, you take care of my car."

"What do I have to do with it?"

"Make sure nobody steals it."

Ralphie went to the window. "I shoot from here if they try."

Owney stepped toward the door.

"Are you sick?" Ralphie said. He held out a box of bullets.

"Good man," Owney said, taking them.

"I'm not even asking you what it's for," Schmidt said.

"Thanks, Ralphie."

Owney walked down to Fresh Pond Road and used a phone in the bar across the street from the Four One's car service. He asked Danny Murphy, the numbers guy from work, about O'Sullivan. Murphy, who knew the bars men attended as others know the colleges people went to, said that O'Sullivan hung around a place called the Green Fields bar on Eleventh Avenue, on the West Side of Manhattan. "I think he might even own the joint," Danny said.

On the way to the city, he had the driver play the radio as loud as it would go; the Grateful Dead filled the car. Owney wanted the Rolling Stones. He did not think of where he was going or what he was going to do there. He knew only one thing: the man had hit his father.

He got out of the cab at 48th and Eleventh and looked for the bar. He walked two blocks and then came to an appliance store that had Spanish music howling from a loudspeaker over the entrance and next door to it was the Green Fields bar. When Owney walked in, everything suddenly was heightened: the bartender's face, wrinkled from alcohol, the two men in olive-drab work shirts at the end of the bar, the young guy in the sweat shirt on the wall phone, the man sitting at a black Formica table and reading a newspaper that was wreathed in his cigarette smoke. No silver-haired man. No O'Sullivan. Owney walked to the men's room, opened the door, saw it was empty, and came back and sat in the middle of the bar, at the aluminum drain under the taps. The smell of wood soaked with last night's beer filled the room.

"Beer," Owney said.

The bartender put a cigarette in a red tin ashtray and pulled a beer. Cold new smell in last night's air.

"I'm supposed to see a guy here," Owney said.

The bartender stared at the beer. His neck showed he preferred no such conversation. "Who was it you were looking for?" he said finally.

"O'Sullivan."

"He went by his sister. She works usher today."

"Where's that?"

"You don't know the sister?" His voice had a new coat of apprehension.

"I only know O'Sullivan," Owney said.

The bartender called to the men in the work shirts down at the end. "Which one does Sissy work at?"

"The one on Forty-sixth Street. The Lyceum."

"That's tonight," Owney said.

"Matinee today. Two o'clock show, she gets there one o'clock. Gets her programs together and everything, goes to work."

Owney finished the beer, pushed change at the bartender, and then held his fingers on the change. "Give us one more."

Owney drank it in two gulps, threw a dollar onto the change, and left. He put his hands in his pockets, the left one gripping the gun, and walked back to 46th Street and then started crosstown, toward the theatre district, first going past old West Side buildings with fire escapes on the fronts and women with sparse gray hair and arms as thin as wire, smoking cigarettes at windows that had old flowered curtains. The next street was lined with restaurant awnings that stuck out of the bottoms of brownstones. He was under the third awning when he heard another sound, a steady squeaking, although there was no breeze coming up from the river to cause the canvas to pull on the brass poles holding it up.

Owney stopped in the squeaking. "What's the time?" he asked the doorman.

"Five a twelve."

Owney glanced into the restaurant. There was a polished bar that had curved brass decorations that caught subdued light, and a bartender's fresh white linens formed a background for the brass. The apron in particular seemed so white and stiff that the hands would have to wring it to cause any wrinkling. A waiter in stiff white linens carried a silver plate of oysters on a bed of ice that glistened in the lights. The bartender picked up a clear bottle, vodka, and began to pour a drink.

Owney saw a clear, cold brook on a hot day. The squeaking was louder. And now Jack McAuliffe stood in the air over a cement sidewalk that was supposed to be in Manhattan but was really the alley behind Herbridge's pool hall in Terre Haute, Indiana. The part of the alley right by the garbage cans, the exact same spot where he started his American career by fighting a cop with a fresh mouth. Jack McAuliffe hit the cop in the mouth with two of the five punches he threw. He was a kid, then, and he was wild with the left hook. The cop still was on his feet. Jack McAuliffe took care of that with a butt. He split open both the cop's eyes and left him sitting atop the garbage cans. Then Jack ran out of town and became a scarred old champion. Now, over the sidewalk and under the awning, Jack McAuliffe rocked his head back and brought it forward, right into Owney's face.

"How are you today?" the bartender in the fresh white linens asked Owney as he sat down.

"I don't know if I'm dressed for here," Owney said, moving his shoulders inside the fatigue jacket.

There were two women having an early lunch at a table a step away from the bar and one of them, in her late forties, with large round glasses perched on her nose, looked up at Owney. "I think the jacket is cute. This is the theatre district. You're supposed to dress like that."

"If you say so," Owney said.

"Absolutely."

The woman smiled and went back to her conversation with a light-haired woman who leaned across the table and said, hungrily, "Now continue."

Owney looked at the bottles behind the bar and pointed to the pale one. "Vodka martini."

The bartender nodded and poured. Owney couldn't remember the last mixed drink he had ordered, but he knew he had to do something in a place like this—he couldn't tell the guy a beer and Fleischmann's—but as he held the drink, he decided that there was something the matter with it. There was something the matter with taking a drink that had almost no odor; it was somehow mixed up with the secrecy of drug taking. Vodka. The least you ought to be able to do is smell the poison you're taking. Then Owney drank the martini like it was a beer and it sure didn't taste bad and he had the glass out for another. Owney tasted the cigarette smoke and at the table near him, the woman with round glasses laughed.

". . . I get to Bergdorf's and on the lingerie floor they have everything on sale. They have it all out on racks. These lovely, filmy things. Delicious. I went through a couple of racks and then I found this one nightgown I absolutely adored, loose and long. You were wearing mist. I was thinking that I could take this gold chain I have and use it as a belt on it."

"Exciting," the light-haired woman said.

"Absolutely. Then up she comes. Just walked up to me out of nowhere."

"What did she say?"

"She said to me, 'Well, I hope you have somebody special to wear that for!' "

"She really caught you."

"That was before I knew what kind of a life *she* was leading."

The two women laughed and began to pick at the oysters on the plates of ice and Owney took a sip and then a large swallow of his second martini. The conversation he had heard caused the blood to rush between his legs. He thought of the woman in the Bronx in her nightgown looking out the side door in the morning. He saw himself finding a hole in the fence up there and following the little kid right up to the door and talking to her, with her moist breasts hanging out of the nightgown in the morning. He was astonished at how quickly his mind could succumb to the temptation of a woman. Walking along neat mowed grass, breathing clean bright air, and suddenly there is a woman and the grass turns into an ugly grave with gray dirt rising to cover you. The Devil is a fearsome enemy, he thought.

Quickly, casting the vision out of his mind, he picked up the martini and drained it. He paid, and then, his hand gripping the gun in the jacket pocket, he walked past the women whose talk provoked his prick, and into the street to find a real enemy, O'Sullivan. He never noticed Jack McAuliffe outside the bar, for McAuliffe now was asleep on a rubbing table. His old boxing shoes were soundless. He had won for the day.

Smoking a cigarette, Owney wandered through the lunchtime crowds. He stopped at an outdoor stand on Broadway for coffee and a hot dog. The head had to be cleared, for he had to plan what he was going to do to O'Sullivan. Owney saw himself jabbing the gun into O'Sullivan and forcing him into an alley someplace, or down into the back of a parking garage, and then he would give this dirty old bastard the beating of his life. Open his head with the gun butt. If the fucking thing went off, that would be too bad, too. Just make sure to get the guy alone someplace.

It was twenty after one when he finally got to the Lyceum; the marquee told him *Borstal Boy* was playing. One of the polished brass doors swung open and Owney went in.

"Yessir," the ticket taker said. "Sir?"

Owney was through the door and into the rear of the orchestra. A short, heavy woman in a black dress stood in his way. She held out a *Playbill.*

"I'm not going to sit," Owney said. "I'm looking for Sissy O'Sullivan."

The woman turned and pointed to the white-haired woman usher who stood at the last aisle of the orchestra.

Owney walked up to her. She pulled out a *Playbill.*

"Is your brother around?" Owney said.

"He was just here," she said. "He just come over to see me and he was . . ."

Owney looked at the fat head with the silver hair slicked straight back. A fat crimson neck at the bottom of the silver hair. He was seated halfway down on the right side of the aisle. He was one of the first ones seated. Look at him. Empty seats all around him. Now Owney saw the red exit lights on the wall. Bright red light. He saw the silver hair, shining in the red light. He saw the size of the silver head and the distance from the wall, two red seats with black armrests. Owney walked down the aisle. He could feel the breath as it came through his nose and down his throat and into his lungs. He could feel the floor under him, as if he were walking barefooted. He could smell the dust from the curtain and the old wood of the stage and his left hand went into the fatigue pocket and took out the gun. He switched it to his right hand and held it against his pants leg. He had no trouble doing this, for his hands were still and his nerves were suddenly coming down, down, down, and no part of him moved unless he wanted it to and he saw and thought more clearly than he had in a couple of years. He walked up to the row and leaned in and the gun was coming up. Put it right into his ear. And then the silver-haired man turned and Owney looked into a red face and Roman collar.

"Yes?"

"Excuse me, Father," Owney said.

The silver-haired man stared for a second, shrugged, and turned back to his *Playbill.*

Owney smuggled the gun into his jacket and walked back up the aisle.

"You thought that was my brother," O'Sullivan's sister said. "I tried to tell you, he left for Florida. You get him down there tonight."

Owney pushed open one of the polished brass doors and went into the sun on the sidewalk. His scalp tingled. His forehead and hands were wet. He sat on the curb. His body quivered.

The theatre doorman walked up to him. "You ought to pull in your feet. Cab'll come along and run right over them. I don't want nobody hurt here."

"You're right," Owney said.

The next drink was a Fleischmann's, which turned into formaldehyde in his mouth. He sucked in cigarette smoke against the taste. The diesel engine of a bus outside on Metropolitan Avenue in Ridgewood shook the windows and outthrobbed the juke box. He had the loaded gun in his pocket and a mind aching from his walk on the lip of the earth. Danny Costello, who had gone to high school with Owney, was at the bowling machine, grinding the weight back and forth. When the bus outside pulled away, the juke box again filled the room.

At the bowling machine, Danny Costello said, "I just seen Shady over at the A. and J."

The bartender said, "Havin' an early supper."

"Yeah," Costello said. "He was at the A. and J. He was havin' an early supper."

Owney threw the shot down and kept looking at the glass. He threw his head to the side. The bartender poured another.

"How's it going?" Owney said.

"Same as always. You know what it is," the bartender said. "We just stay here and give people a service."

There was a grinding sound and then bells ringing as Danny Costello played the bowling machine. The bartender started to say something and Owney grabbed his money and left before he could hear any more of the place. He walked up to the Old Forest, which had a washed tile floor and a bar filled with men too old for Owney. He knew the bartender, Jimmy Breckenridge, who once had fought for money and now had a face that was a worked-out mine.

Breckenridge gave Owney a shot and a beer and then poured one for himself. The bartender held his shot high in a salute. Eyes rolling, he swallowed the shot. He spun sideways and his fists rose.

"I'm boxin' Ernie Durando."

Head bobbing, body snaky, Breckenridge began shadowboxing down the length of the bar. "Aaaahhhh! Left hook to the belly. Boom! Same hand to the head. Oh! Pow! I just got nailed." He came backward with his arms folded over his face. "I'm hurt."

He stopped at the bottle of rye and poured himself another drink. Then he hit himself on the chin with his right fist. He fell backward onto the duckboards behind the bar.

"One! . . . Two! . . ."

Breckenridge waited to hear Owney laugh, the way the old men in the neighborhood always laugh when he does this. This time he heard Owney push the change into the gutter of the bar as he left.

The third bar was on Cypress Avenue, a wounded old place sitting in a row of empty storefronts. When Owney walked in, the barmaid held out a quarter.

"Go play this song, 'Yakety Yak.' It reminds me of myself."

Owney played the song and sat down in the music and had another shot and beer. Looking at the two empty glasses, Owney decided he did not like the place and that it was time to go home. He could either pick up his change and get out, or he could have another one. He decided to go home. He started to pull himself off the barstool.

"Give us another," he said to the barmaid.

The barmaid had long, stiff blond hair and a cigarette hanging from a small mouth. First, she poured vodka into a glass of Bitter Lemon for herself. Then she picked up a bottle and filled Owney's shot glass. Behind her, alongside the cash register, an outsized fish tank, an octagon, bubbled. Inside was a black fish, large enough to live in a bay. The fish had its nose against a corner of the glass.

"Here's to you," the barmaid said. She took no money from Owney.

"Good girl," Owney said. He wanted to think about something that would make him smile. The barmaid stood in front of him and wanted to talk.

"You got a name?" she said.

"Owney."

"Good. My name's Patti. You got a Social Security number?"

"Sure."

"That's good. Least you're legitimate."

The barmaid swallowed half the drink. "Going to be a chop breaker next week."

"Yeah?"

"You bet. Going to break my chops all next week. My boyfriend got his kid coming. I need this."

By now the whiskey was warm sugar as it went down. He picked up the full glass of beer and drained it.

"Do something for me," Patti said. "Feed this fuckin' fish."

"Why don't you?"

"I'm scared of him. He's a piranha." She held up some plastic bags of goldfish.

"That's all he eats. Goldfish. He's a piranha."

She tapped a small cutout from a book that was pasted on the tank. The duckboards creaked as Owney stepped behind the bar.

He swayed for a moment and was surprised at the unsteadiness. I used to drink all day and didn't feel a thing, he said to himself. The fish in the tank was the same as the drawing: stubby, taut, about a pound and a half. Up close, the fish was charcoal. The underlip jutted out. The eyes almost contained a fleck of expression.

The barmaid held out the plastic bags of goldfish. "This is all I ever seen him eat." She tapped a fingernail on the glass in front of the dozing piranha. Something tiny, a single crystal in one eye, responded to the tapping fingernail. The barmaid moved her finger a couple of inches to the right. The left eye of the fish rolled until it showed white. The under-lip bumped along the glass until the mouth of the piranha was even with the finger.

"How do you like this?" she said.

"He's just a fat tropical fish," Owney said.

"Eat you alive."

"Your ass."

"You say. They brought a guy in here the other day, he owed some money to Buster. You know Buster? Buster grabs the guy by the wrist and says he's gonna put his hand into the water with the piranha. You should of heard the guy yell. I said to myself, I don't believe this. I ran into the ladies' room."

Owney pushed his fatigue jacket up his arm. He hooked his armpit over the tip of the tank and sent his fingers reaching through warm water for the piranha, which was near the bottom. Lacy gills moved the fish backward. Owney had an index finger crooked and he made a pass at the piranha, trying to get the finger into a gill. The fish slid under the finger and went along the bottom of the tank.

"The piranha is yellow," Owney said. This time his index finger went into the bony side. The piranha's tail flicked, left to right, and the fish ran away from the finger and into a corner of the fish tank.

"See?" he said.

"Yeah? You should of heard the guy screaming the other day."

"I bet he doesn't even eat the goldfish," Owney said.

"Oh, no. This I've seen. Here you are." She took the plastic bags, four of them, with two and three goldfish in each bag, and emptied them into the tank. The water splashed as the goldfish went wriggling in.

The piranha's mouth was open wide enough to be on hinges when it hit the first goldfish from behind.

"See?" Patti shrieked. "Now watch what he does. Watch!"

The piranha worked his mouth around so that the goldfish first was sideways in his mouth, then head first. The piranha began to chew on the goldfish with the mouth motions of a human.

The barmaid said, "He always eats the head first. See? Look at him chew. He eats just like a mailman."

Laughing, Owney put his arms around the barmaid. She laughed with him and he pulled her body full against his and brought his head down to kiss her. She buried her face in his chest and he could not get at her mouth.

Her hand brushed the pocket of his jacket and she stiffened. She looked up at him with alarmed eyes. "You got two bad habits," she said. "Molestin' nice girls. And comin' in here with a gun. I thought you told me you were legitimate." She pushed hard and got away.

Owney walked out from behind the bar and reached for his change. "I got to give it back to somebody," he said.

"Please do," the barmaid said. "Make sure it don't go off on the way."

Just walking along, looking into the windows of the Idle Hour bar, Fresh Pond Chop Suey, and on down past Grande's bar and the Everglades bar, and then he turned up Grove Street, walking along and looking at the doorways as he passed them, just walking and looking. He did not notice the police car, which was half a block behind him, rolling slowly. He continued up Grove Street, where at the first corner the music was blowing out of the Swallow's Nest bar and into the start of the night. Ralphie Schmidt suddenly appeared in the doorway with his sweat shirt arms rolled up to show his tattoos. He was smoking a joint.

"I finished the roof," he said.

"I finished using your machinery," Owney said. "I was just bringing it up to your house."

"I just come down here an hour ago," Schmidt said. "I look out the window and here you are."

Owney put his hand into his fatigue jacket for Ralphie's gun.

"Is it cleaned?" Schmidt said.

"It didn't get dirty," Owney said.

"That's too bad," Ralphie said. "Let's have a beer." He pulled open the door to a saloon that was a civic disturbance. Young girls shrieked in the music. Young men sat at the bar, on the nod.

"I'll pass," Owney said, pushing the door shut.

Schmidt looked at him. "You look cuckoo."

"I have been all day," Owney said.

"Then you belong here inside."

"I don't need any more," Owney said. He handed the gun to Schmidt, who stuffed it into his belt. Schmidt brought out two bags of pot and stuck them into Owney's breast pocket.

"Slow you down," Schmidt said.

Now the door opened and small bitten fingernails pressed into Schmidt's arm.

"I need ten dollars, Ralphie."

Schmidt shook his head. "I gave you before."

"I need, Ralphie. Oh, Owney, you got ten dollars, Owney?"

"Don't give it to her," Schmidt said.

"Oh, Owney." She said it in a little girl voice. Owney's hand went into his pocket.

"Here," Schmidt said quickly. He handed Cindy a ten.

"I'll give it back to you, Ralphie, you know I will."

"Cindy, why didn't you tell me you had a baby?" Ralphie said.

"You had a baby?" Owney said.

Cindy nodded.

"Why didn't you tell us?"

"Sometimes I forget," she said. With a twirl she went back into the bar.

"What year are we in?" Schmidt asked Owney.

"Nineteen seventy-one."

"We won't make nineteen eighty," Schmidt said. "Ridgewood doesn't have a chance. What do we need a bomb for? We got people worse than bombs." Schmidt started to laugh, but stopped as he saw the patrol car pulling to the curb.

"All right, fellas, everybody stay right there." A fat cop with eyes like a trout walked across the sidewalk as if it were coated with oil. Owney pushed Schmidt through the doorway and into the bar. He wanted Ralphie, the gun in his belt, out of this.

In the light from the streetlight that touched the cop's face, Owney could see that the guy had been drinking.

"Where's he going?" the cop said, waving a hand at the disappearing Ralphie Schmidt.

Owney thought fast and held the two bags of pot out to the cop. "Happy birthday, officer."

"Look at this," the cop called out. The other cop, a sergeant, got out of the car.

The fat patrolman took the bags of pot from Owney and held them under a flashlight for the sergeant.

"Let's go, hump." The sergeant stepped behind Owney and took Owney's right hand.

"Hey, it's nothing, I just did you a favor," Owney said.

Whiskey stink from the sergeant's pores was the answer. Now the saloon door opened and Ralphie Schmidt stepped out.

"Officer, could I say something?"

"Say nothing," the patrolman said.

"This guy is a hero from Vietnam."

"You say."

"It's the truth. Ah, fuck it. You don't want to listen. Here, let me show you the man's wallet. He got his discharge papers."

Ralphie stepped toward them. The sergeant held Owney's right hand and Owney put the left out to stop Ralphie. The fat patrolman had his nightstick out, however, and he jabbed it. Ralphie Schmidt stepped back and then came forward again. The nightstick jabbed. The tip of it went into Ralphie's sweat shirt, just above where the gun handle stuck out of the belt and was covered by the sweat shirt. Owney couldn't believe he'd come back out without stashing the gun. Ralphie blew out breath. Owney's voice rose, for he was sure that the next jab would hit the gun and then there would be real trouble.

"Ralphie, will you get out of here!"

The urgency reached Schmidt and he went back inside the bar. Owney felt a handcuff close on his right wrist; a loud ZZZZZ into the evening air. The handcuff bit into his wrist. Now that it was real, Owney could not believe that they were doing this to him and he started to turn and talk to the sergeant, but the sergeant had Owney's left hand now and here was this ugly metallic sound.

"Hey!" Owney said.

"Too tight?" the sergeant said.

"Yeah. Come on now."

"You'll remember this the next time, you hump."

He shoved Owney toward the patrol car. The hands manacled behind him, the stumble as he was shoved, caused him to feel naked. The sergeant pushed Owney up to the patrol car and opened the back door and now that it was being done for sure, now that they were trying to take him away, Owney put his left shoulder against the post between the front and back doors, set his feet, and looked up at the dark sky.

The sergeant put a hand on Owney's hand and tried to push him into the car. Owney set himself for the second push. He heard the sergeant's feet shifting and then there was this great sniffing sound as the sergeant, seething, fed his rage with a gulp of air.

Owney never felt the right hand crash against the side of his face.

The precinct, only a few blocks away, had its doors open, with the light streaming through them as Owney was pushed up the two worn cement steps and onto the dusty, cracked cement floor and municipal green walls. Behind the high brown desk, a pinch-faced man with sparse gray hair neatly combed sat in a short-sleeved white shirt with a gold lieutenant's badge on the breast.

"Two twenty oh three," the cop said. "And resistin' arrest. Two oh five thirty."

The lieutenant picked up a big record book and a pen.

The sergeant stepped behind Owney and unlocked the handcuffs. Owney brought his wrists up to rub them. They were angry red and each had a white line branded into it by the pinching steel.

"On the rail," the patrolman said.

Owney put his left hand on the rail. He brought the right hand up to feel the side of his face. Fingertips touched a lump that seemed many inches out from his face.

"I said on the rail," the patrolman said. He grabbed Owney's hand and slapped it onto the rail.

"I better stay here with this hump for a minute," the sergeant, behind Owney, said.

"Put your personal belongings up here," the lieutenant said, patting the top of the desk.

"One hand at a time," the patrolman said.

Owney reached for the wallet in his back pocket. His fingers slipped off it and he had to make them go back again. When he had the wallet on the desk he went into his right pants pocket and took out the house keys.

"Money," the patrolman said.

When Owney took the silver out of his other pocket, it fumbled out of his hand. He started to stoop down to pick up the change but the patrolman slapped his arm. "Keep your hand up. Let it go."

The sergeant's shoe scraped as he kicked the change toward the doorway.

"He said *money.*" the sergeant said.

"In the wallet," Owney said.

"All right," the lieutenant said, taking the money, twenty-seven dollars, out of the wallet.

"Shirt pocket," the patrolman said.

"My cigarettes," Owney said.

"Let's see them," the lieutenant said.

Owney put the cigarettes and the lighter on top of the desk. The lieutenant looked at the cigarettes, Salems, and said, "We ought to have these looked at too."

"All right," the patrolman said.

"They're cigarettes," Owney said.

"Shut up," the patrolman said.

Now the first anger came through the numbness.

"Name," the lieutenant said.

Owney didn't answer.

"Name!"

The sergeant brought his hand down on top of Owney's head. Owney saw black for a moment, then pain shot from the right side of his face and made his hair stand up.

"Tell the lieutenant your name."

Owney stamped back with his right foot. He didn't get the sergeant cleanly on top of the foot, but he got a piece of it, a good piece, and now Owney came around, with his right elbow trying to get the sergeant's belly.

With a shout, the fat patrolman fell on Owney with arms that were surprisingly strong. There was shouting and here was another cop, big white teeth and olive skin, who reached in and grabbed Owney by the hair and yanked his head up. Hard and high. "Come on now, you ain't a fucking nigger."

Owney felt a handcuff bite into his right wrist. He slipped his left hand inside his shirt so they couldn't get at that.

"Come on, now," the olive-skinned cop said.

Fucking guinea, Owney said to himself.

"Take it easy now. We don't want to treat you like some nigger."

The Italian cop began leading Owney by the hair to a doorway in the back of the room. The sergeant and the fat cop with him each had Owney by an arm.

The Italian cop pulled Owney into a narrow toilet. "I'm going to stuff you down the shitter," he said.

"That's it, Viglietta," the sergeant said.

Viglietta pushed Owney's head down. Owney pulled his head away as it was about to go inside the rim of the toilet bowl. His hair came free of the Italian cop's hands. He was on the floor, on his knees and his hands in the wet piss where the last cop to use the place had missed. A fist thudded against Owney's back. He folded his arms over his face as fists and feet pounded into his back and shoulders. The three cops, jammed into a narrow area, could not get the leverage they needed to deliver heavy blows. Owney put his right hand into his mouth and took out the bridge. He made a gagging sound. Mouth open, holding his throat, seemingly gagging, he turned his face to the cops.

"Tooth . . ."

"What tooth? The fuck."

"No, no. Look. It's out." Owney kept his tongue away from the gap in his teeth so they could see it.

Owney put both hands to his throat and made one long choking sound.

"Jesus!" Viglietta had his eyes wide with fear. He put a hand on Owney's shoulder. "Easy, kid." Then he said to the other two cops, "What should I do?"

"Put your hand down his throat."

"No. I'll get a doctor."

The sergeant shrieked. "No doctor. Get him something."

Owney made a gagging sound. He felt the Italian cop leave. The fat patrolman leaned over Owney and said, "Put your head down. You'll be all right."

Owney made a better choking sound.

"Hurry the fuck up!" the sergeant yelled.

There was the sound of running feet and now Viglietta dropped to the floor and held out a piece of white bread covered with thick peanut butter.

"It's good, it's good. Coats the throat. Push the tooth right down. It won't be blockin'. Here, here. Eat it."

Viglietta's eyes were excited and pleading as he held out the bread. Owney gasped. Olive drained out of the cop's face. Owney took his right hand from his throat—the left was at his side, the bridge clenched in the fist—and grabbed the peanut butter sandwich.

The three cops, heads bunched together in fear, watched as Owney put the peanut butter to his mouth. Then took it out and slapped it, peanut butter first, into the fat cop's face.

Outside at the big high desk, the lieutenant heard all the screaming as he was pushing Owney's belongings, the cigarette lighter and house keys, into a manila envelope. Then the lieutenant started to close the wallet so he could shove this in, too. The lieutenant's face became rigid as he saw the card in the wallet with the picture of the medal on it.

Right away, when the door to the courtroom was pushed open, Owney saw his wife sitting in the bright light with a blue bankbook in her hands.

He ducked back into the space between the detention pens and the door. "I'm not going out there," he said.

"It'll only take a couple of seconds," said the lieutenant from the police station of the night before. "It's a shame somebody didn't tell her that she didn't have to bring anything. There's no bail needed for this thing."

"Whoever got her here can send her back," Owney said. He sat on a wooden chair and folded his arms. The lieutenant walked to the back of the detention pens and went through a door.

Outside in the courtroom, Dolores sat with the bankbook in her hands and her eyes nervously following the courtroom workers, who kept walking about with stacks of papers. A judge walked to the bench for a moment, but then turned around and went back through a door.

"These places take time," a woman with red hair, thirty maybe, said to Dolores. The woman's eyes were tired from a sleepless night. It was nine A.M.

"How do you know when your case gets called?" Dolores asked.

"You don't," the woman said. "You just wait."

"You been here before?" Dolores asked.

The red-haired woman nodded. "Too many times."

"Who for?"

"Husband. That's what you call him when he's home, anyway, a husband." She spread her hands. "What can you do?"

"Get out," Dolores said.

The woman laughed. "With two kids? Can't go nowhere with two kids. You're stuck till they grow up. I'm stuck in Broad Channel until my kids grow up. I guess everybody is."

"I don't think so," Dolores said.

"Who are you here for?" the woman asked.

"Right now, I'm not sure," Dolores said.

Inside, there were ten people in the detention pen, eight of them black. The lieutenant brightened when a door at the end of the pen opened and somebody called to him. The lieutenant made a motion and Owney followed him down to the door, out into a hallway, and into a small office.

"Have a seat, boys, I'll be right with you," the judge said. His hand trembled and his neck bobbed as he swallowed water. He shook his head and ran more water. "Oh, boy." He came over from the sink and sat at the desk in his small, bare office. He had steel-gray hair that was slicked straight back, and a square, blue jaw. His eyes brimmed with morning tears. Painful sunlight came through dusty Venetian blinds. "Do me a favor, fella, close those blinds, will you like a good fella?" He nodded at the lieutenant, who got up and closed the blinds.

"A little more. Yeah. Now we're all right." The judge looked at Owney. "How's the eye?"

Owney took the towel from it. The ice cubes had melted and he had been holding the towel against the eye out of habit. When they had taken him to the hospital on Queens Boulevard, St. John's Hospital, the night nurse in the emergency room had given them a couple of towels filled with ice, which for the next three hours the lieutenant kept getting re-filled at the diner across the street from the courthouse. They sat there waiting for the morning, and the court to open.

"It's all right, eh?" the judge said.

When Owney remained silent, the judge cleared his throat and spread the court papers in front of him.

"Now you understand how this came about," the judge said.

"No," Owney said. "Maybe this fuck can tell you." He nodded at the lieutenant.

"No, I mean why we're here in this room. You call this a robing room. Now we want to do something for you. You're just back from a war, you've been honored by the President of the United States. But we can't just ignore the matter. We're stuck. You see, once it's entered in the book."

"This fuck told me that twenty times last night." He glared at the lieutenant, who accepted the language as part of his overhead.

The judge ignored Owney's anger. "Let me tell you why you're here, son. We don't want anybody out there gawking at you. You know, the press. And, Lord, in Queens the word of mouth alone could kill you. Guy sees you in here today, he goes over to the Pastrami King and he tells a waiter who he saw and then he goes home to a gin mill in Rego Park and he says, 'Geez, who do you think I saw in court today?' You know how it is. So what we're going to do is dispose of this case perfectly legal. Right now, we're waiting for the assistant district attorney and your lawyer. Well, here's one of them, anyway. Hello, fella. Sit down, fella."

A young man with dark eyebrows bunched over dull eyes sat down.

"This is the assistant district attorney. Now we're waiting for your lawyer. Where the hell is he, anyway? I called him twice."

"I don't want a lawyer," Owney said.

The judge smiled. "If there is one thing you should carry away from this disheartening experience, it is the one great rule of law: a person who acts as his own lawyer has a fool for a client. You ever hear of that?"

"Yes. But this fool isn't going to go for five hundred dollars for a lawyer."

"Listen to what I'm telling you," the judge said. "Forget the money."

The judge went back to his desk and the room fell silent. A few minutes later, an immense belly came into the room. On top of the belly was a nose the size of a trombone. Large brown eyes rolled around. The man wore a raincoat that was buttoned to the collar. Owney could see pajama sleeves inside the raincoat. Brown leather slippers on bare feet made a flopping sound. The hair was uncombed. Black sleep shades were pushed up onto the hair.

"Hello, hello, good morning," the man said in a voice twice as loud as needed. "I was asleep, I was asleep. You woke me, I was asleep."

"At least you could have dressed yourself," the judge said.

"You told me it was going to be in your robing room so I came here disrobed. I came here disrobed."

The judge said to Owney, "Before you get worried, just trust in me that this man will protect your interest. This is Philip McNiff and he's one of the best lawyers we have on Queens Boulevard."

The belly put his hand out. "Let me introduce myself. My name is Philip McNiff and I'm really a very good lawyer, but I usually don't get up in the daytime. I've gotten very lazy lately." The outsized brown eyes stopped rolling and now they were fixed intently on Owney. "I like to sleep all day. I'm so overweight that I need a lot of sleep. I'm overweight because, you see, my wife left me. She walked right out on me. My wife. She left me! And it's horrible. I live right across the street. I eat ice cream all night long. I wouldn't eat so much ice cream if I could get any sex. So anyway, I'm terribly pleased to meet you. You're a hero. A great hero. A hero! I'd like to be your lawyer for two reasons. One, because the judge asked me. And two, because you deserve a good lawyer for nothing. You're a hero. After that, all I can tell you is that I need to get laid. Nobody will have me. And I don't get any vegetables now that my wife doesn't cook for me anymore. You know what I need? I need broccoli and a blow job."

"Phil."

"Excuse me. Yes, judge."

"Maybe if you won't talk for a moment, we can get your client out of here. It's nine-fifteen and I have to start court at nine-thirty. You wouldn't know about that, I realize, but others are here today," the judge said. "All right. We'll make this an ACD. For your information," he said, turning to Owney, "that's an adjournment in contemplation of dismissal."

"Fine, your honor," the assistant district attorney said.

"Dismissal right now. We might want to sue for false arrest," McNiff said.

The judge smiled. "Phil . . ."

"Your honor, I am his lawyer." McNiff looked at Owney. "I'm your lawyer, am I not? I realize we never even asked you. Would you care to have me keep acting on your behalf?"

"Yes," Owney said.

"Fine, fine, I'm his lawyer, I'm his lawyer," McNiff said. "And I want a dismissal."

The judge shook his head. McNiff pointed at the lieutenant. "These people made such a big deal out of two lousy bags of pot that they are in here with this other charge. Resisting arrest. I mean, really. Two crummy bags of pot."

"Wait a minute," the judge said. "Let's not start with *this two lousy bags.*" He pointed at Owney. "You're still getting your legs back around here, son, but I sit here every day and see marijuana leading kids on to other things. Heroin, cocaine, pills. Christ, everything. Breaks your heart having to sit here and see these kids, nice kids, come from goddamn respectable homes, Christ, come in here on the worst charges of possession. These aren't niggers I'm talking about. These are the *neighbors' children.* So you know, as unpleasant as this is for you, and I imagine it's as unpleasant a thing as ever happened to you in your life, it might save you from getting in trouble in the future with something stronger."

"You'd be surprised," the assistant district attorney said. "We see it. We know. These drugs are insidious."

"Who says he had anything to do with drugs?" McNiff said.

"Didn't he have the drugs in his possession? Didn't he hand them to a police officer?"

"Who says they were his?" McNiff said. "This man, a bona fide national hero, saw drugs and picked them up and was trying to hand them to a policeman, who then arrested him and had him beaten up. I'd like to let a jury consider this."

"Go home and get dressed," the judge said. "This case is over. Morrison, we have some obligations to you. But you have some obligations to the people. You have to set an example for them. You can't be going around like the rest of these creeps using drugs. Come on. Jesus, you're Irish. Do what you're supposed to do. Get up to the bar like a man and take a drink."

"They use a lot of pot in Vietnam," Owney said.

"Come on! Don't tell me our kids are over there fighting for their lives, fighting for our liberty—hell!—fighting for the right to use this very courtroom every day! Don't tell me they're on marijuana. Keerist! That's all the Communists want. Having our GIs on dope."

McNiff touched Owney's arm. "We're holding everything up now. Thanks, judge."

"Am I going to see you for lunch?" the judge said.

"I guess so," McNiff said.

"Are you going to be with us?" he said to Owney.

"I don't think so."

"Just as well. McNiff and I get together. What am I talking about? I get in enough trouble on my own. Took the wife to Joe Abbraciamento's for dinner last night. Then we stopped around at this affair at the Astoria Manor and I'm sitting there trying to take it easy and here's Jimmy Musto—you know Jimmy, guy got a restaurant on Hillside Avenue—he's sending over one drink, then two drinks. The next thing you know, I'm a blind beggar. Wife hadda drive me home. Geeeeezusss!" The judge's laugh turned into a wet, rolling cough. He turned and headed for the sink with his mouth full of phlegm.

The lieutenant told McNiff that he would go into the courtroom and get Dolores.

"We'll be out front," McNiff said. He led Owney through the hall and out a door in the back of the courthouse and into a parking lot alongside the block glass windows and white brick of the detention house. In the middle of each of the windows there was a small pane of glass that was pushed open to reveal thick green bars and to allow prison sounds to rub harshly on the ears. Behind the bars now, voices called out in military cadence, "Hup . . . tut . . . thrip . . ."

"Muslims doing their exercises," McNiff said. "They're well organized. They run the prisons."

"I wonder how many of them I know," Owney said.

"There's a guy up there with one leg who killed a cabbie. He lost the leg in Vietnam. Marvin Kleinberg has the case. You know what the guy said when they asked him why he shot the cabbie? He said, 'Because he tried to fight me.' How do you like that for an answer?"

"He told the truth," Owney said.

"Hello, hello," McNiff said when introduced to Dolores out in front of the courthouse. "We'll have a drink, we'll have a drink."

Dolores started to say something but McNiff was already halfway across Queens Boulevard with his feet nearly coming out of his slippers. As the boulevard here is six lanes wide and the traffic was morning heavy, walking with McNiff was hazardous.

When McNiff came into the bar across Queens Boulevard from the courthouse, the Part One bar, he took off his raincoat and sat at the bar in his flannel pajamas, which had a blue-striped top that came to his knees.

"I want three Manhattans," he told the bartender. "And a beer chaser. Three Manhattans, three Manhattans. And a beer chaser. A beer chaser."

Owney ordered a shot of Fleischmann's and a beer. The bartender looked at Owney as he took the order, but he did not seem to notice the lumped eye.

"Nothing for me," Dolores said, sharply. Her look was meant to wither, but they were too busy with their glasses to notice.

"Now let me tell you something about dru—— Hey! I said *three* Manhattans, not a triple Manhattan. Three separate ones. Thanks. Now let me tell you something about drugs that even *you* don't know. Incidentally, I'm quite proud of you that you didn't throw up when he started telling you about drugs. They're quite dumb over there, quite dumb. Anyway, what I wanted to tell you was the way society positions itself on matters. There has been information developed over the years as to what is good and what is bad. Drugs just happens to be one of the things listed as bad. Nobody knows why really. Nobody knows where they got the information from. But they have the information and it says that drugs are bad and that's all there is to—ahhh! Thank you very much. That's fine. Now I want the other two right behind it here on the bar. One, two, three. Very good. Now what I'm saying is that drugs are against public policy, whatever that means. Yes, whatever that means. But unfortunately it means if you do drugs you are going to be in continual trouble. Excuse me."

Eyes rolling, he took the first Manhattan, cherry too, in a gulp. His head came down long enough for his hand to exchange the empty glass for a full one. The eyes rolled and the second Manhattan was gone. As was the third.

McNiff tapped the final empty glass on the bar. "Bartender, bartender, remove these glasses. Remove these glasses. Anyway, to get back to drugs. I think alcoholism is more dangerous than drugs. But drugs are worse to use right now. The reason drugs are so bad is the cruel way society treats addicts. We shouldn't allow people to use drugs because if they get in trouble on drugs we persecute them. Alcohol. If a person develops into an alcoholic he becomes a comic figure and then ultimately a tragic figure. But at no stage does society throw him into a cage and beat him up and let some big spade stick it to him. But we do that with an addict. So because we treat addicts so bad, we shouldn't have any addicts until we learn to be nicer to them. I mean, look what they did to you. Threw you in a cage. Punched you. Punched you! A true military hero and they punched you. A national hero!"

"What about the cop that hit me? Does he get away with a thing like that? You wouldn't even let me—"

"I stopped you, I stopped you because then they would have remembered to make us sign a waiver saying we wouldn't sue. They shouldn't have given the dismissal. They're supposed to get a waiver first. They forgot. We kept our mouths shut. Now we can sue. The city won't have the balls to go to court against you. The city'll settle. Call me about that tomorrow. Tomorrow night. Not daytime. I can't get up. I wish I could get laid."

When McNiff stopped talking, Dolores said to Owney, "I hated it there."

"What could I do?" Owney asked. "I'll explain it to you home."

"I don't want to hear about it. All I know is that I hated it."

"I'll explain it home," Owney said.

"I'm explaining to you now that I'm better than this," she said.

Dolores stood up. I'm going out to get the car," she said. "If you're not there when I pull around, I'm just gonna keep going."

McNiff's eyes followed her as she walked out the door.

"She's mad," he said.

"She gets over it," Owney said.

"I think you're overlooking some difficulties," McNiff said. "I don't like what I see so much that I think I'm going to have three more Manhattans. Three more Manhattans, not a triple Manhattan. I want to drink them one right after the other."

Owney put the beer down and started to walk out so he would be in front of the bar when his wife pulled up. At the doorway, he stepped aside to let a woman pass. The woman went to the pay phone.

"Excuse me, I'm a little drunk," McNiff called to her. "Would you care to have sex with me? My wife left me and I haven't had sex in a long time." The woman walked out of the bar. McNiff's blue-striped arm waved. "I read that you can send to Poland for a slave girl. A slave girl! You can beat her up and make her give you blow jobs. Then she has to cook dinner." He called to Owney, "Here, you better take another drink. Get drunk. Public policy states that you cannot be around with people your own age. You must sit in a saloon with an old man like me and drink until you get sick. You're not allowed to be young and use drugs. Excuse me now, I have to leave. I'm getting drunk. Oh, it's probably so much easier using drugs. I wish I could be a drug addict instead of a drunk."

"Why don't you?" Owney said.

"Because I can't afford a lawyer. Neither can you."

9

O N T H O S E   D A Y S that followed, days that ran into weeks and then became part of weeks that turned into months, on each of those days, he started across a slippery deck, with one hand clutching a taut rope, and always there was the temptation to let go and be carried away with the water and over the side into the heavy seas. Resisting, he would trip the rope with both hands. He simply would raise his arms and feel the water smack him on the chest and sweep him off. He was returning home less and less frequently. Often he would wake up in the hog house, or in his old room in the cemetery, and stare out at the headstones and flinch at the depression that shook him to the legs.

In the house on 74th Street, Dolores Morrison felt the first shadows of every evening were aimed directly at her life. There was one night when Gladys Farrell, who lived four doors up, stopped in. A white top covered a midsection that embarrassed her. Unbrushed brown-gray hair made her seem older than her fifty years.

"Waiting," Gladys said.

"Looks like it."

Gladys Farrell sat down heavily. "For a change, Eddie's home. Home dead. He was out so late last night he was a zombie today. He was going to take me out last night. A movie. Huh. At eight o'clock, no word from him. At nine o'clock, he calls me from up the avenue. He said he couldn't look at a movie. You know why? 'My eyes hurt too much.' "

"You didn't believe him," Dolores said.

"Who knows what I believe anymore. I went up to meet him for a drink at Fritz's. He was saving my life inviting me out. When I walked in, and I say walk because we don't have a car, you know that, well, when I walked in and saw him with all this money spread over the bar, I felt sick."

Dolores nodded. "Owney brings me money like he found it in the street."

"I'm married thirty-two years; I can't do much now. If I was your age, I'd know how to handle it."

"How?"

"Stop protecting him. If he lies when he gets home, I wouldn't believe him. If he doesn't get home when he says he's coming, then I wouldn't let it pass."

Dolores said nothing.

"I'd find the saloon he goes into and I'd walk right in while he's there and have a drink while he's there."

"That's not me," Dolores said.

"Why?"

"Because I'm better than that."

Gladys Farrell shook her head. "Confront the man! That's the only way to change things. After all, you loved him enough to marry him. You can't just turn off an emotion. You love him."

"He ought to remember he loves me."

"It takes these men time to realize."

"What do you call time?"

"Thirty-two years and I'm still trying. But I'm hoping. That's love, I guess."

"Whose love?"

Gladys said nothing, finished her cigarette, and left. Dolores sat as the shadows came down the alley outside her kitchen window and reminded her of the hours that kept passing. That night, Owney was late. How late, she never knew. She slept on the couch.

In the morning, he did not stir and she walked about the kitchen and tended to the baby.

"Dolores."

"What?"

"Come here."

"Why?"

"I want to talk to you."

His voice, equal parts plea and command, created one of those humili-
ating instances that she had been raised by gender and landscape to
accept. She now thought of how many times she had answered that call,
walking to bed like a servant girl in bare feet. Even with this, when he
called again she found herself reluctantly considering the idea of going in
under the fiction of asking what he wanted. But once in the room she
walked right past the bed and toward the bathroom.

"What's the matter with you?"

"Nothing. It's all terrific."

"Then come here."

She slammed the bathroom door behind her. Inside, as she reached for
the shower handles, her bare feet on the cold morning tiles caused her to
remember the night when she knew she was pregnant with Christine. The
oil burner had been shorted all during a chill, dark day, which had the
house as cold as the street outdoors by late evening, when the burner
finally was fixed. Stepping into the shower at that time, Dolores had
found the bathroom floor still so cold that she had to stand on the rug.
She had waited for several hours for this chance to be alone in front of
the long mirror on the inside of the door to see if there would be any
reflection of what she knew was happening in her body. She had no idea
how long she had been pregnant; her period wasn't due for another week.
Nor that day was her body signifying anything specific: the breasts had
gathered no heaviness and while she was a little bit queasy and quite tired
at the moment, she at first attributed that to staying out too late with
Owney the night before. "One more," he kept saying. Upon thinking, she
decided that her fatigue was not something caused by the hours of the
day or night. She knew that she had become one in the highest order of
women. Not that she had been part of an underprivileged group to begin
with, for she believed out of her education that Catholic married women,
under normal living conditions, without even being pregnant, were the
only complete women, for theirs were the only bodies nurtured by sperm.
How can these other women be whole, she had been taught, if while
avoiding God's clear wish that they have children, they so clog their
canals that sperm cannot seep into their bodies, thus leaving these
women walking around with parched insides? While the pill did not
prevent sperm from entering the recesses of a woman's body, it caused
the blood in the womb to turn sour.

The distinction was made between a married body and one virginal
and thus in need of nothing more from a male beyond a bouquet of roses.

Her husband, she remembered now, entered fatherhood with the same level of consciousness exhibited by all Morrisons at those slender moments when emotions were raised by beauty and sinew was useless: on the night in which she stood in this bathroom and first examined her face and torso for any signs of added life within her, Owney was in the living room, where he shouted and stamped his feet as he watched the Monday night football game with Artie Brooks, who lived three houses up the block in those days.

"God owed me one!" Owney called out that night.

As her husband reveled in the simplicity of a game, she stood with all the mists of the unknown gathering inside her body.

Now, here at another time, in the morning so long after that first pregnancy, as she picked her feet off the cold tiles and stepped into the shower, the idea of another pregnancy caused a small, blank anger. How did you ever do it in the first place? she snarled at herself. Immediately, she thought of the baby and said a small prayer in penance. This did not diminish the hostility to the mention of the word in her mind. She felt slightly bloated from taking the pill. Better than the other, she thought, stepping under the water.

The first time she used the pill was when the baby was two months old and cried through too much of the night and of course her husband failed to come home on one of these nights. He called from the job at six A.M. and said that he had worked overtime and fell asleep. On another night that week, he arrived home at midnight, with a scrape over one eye and the knuckles of his right hand dotted with fresh scabs. He said the marks were from work; she thought a barroom fight. When he reached out to hold her, she went into the next room. She slept on the couch that night, and went to a doctor the next afternoon and got a prescription for birth control pills.

After several months of using them she went to confession at St. Pancras on Ash Wednesday, the start of Lent. Kneeling alone in a pew in the late afternoon, she prayed and examined her conscience. From years of teaching by the sisters at St. Matthias on weekdays, and by priests of the diocese on Sundays, she believed that birth control by any other means than rhythm was a mortal sin that could send the soul to Hell. There was to be neither deviation nor hope for change in policy. This was a matter dealing with life itself, not some grubby ecclesiastical mistake buried in a subclause such as the taking of meat on Friday, which once was termed a mortal sin. If, after sufficient reflection and full consent of the will, a pot roast was chewed up on a Friday, it was a sin of such magnitude that if the person did not confess it before death, the soul was immediately consigned to the ceaseless fires of Hell. At the same time, so many dispensations were being given out around the globe that more Catholics ate meat on Friday than ever heard of mackerel. Finally, meat on Friday was thrown out as a sin, and presumably the billions of souls burning in Hell for the sin of pot roast on Friday simply saw their sentence sheets changed from eating meat on Friday to being brazen in the face of God. The crackling fires went on.

Birth control was different; the Church was so adamant that women took to contraceptives with the dull understanding that henceforth they were living in terrible sin. Dolores, however, had decided to differentiate between the received opinion that birth control interfered with life and her own feelings that these church rulings were made by whim and hearsay of the same sort as the backward old Italians who once excommunicated any Catholic who did not believe that the world was flat. She began to think that the old men in Rome were jealous of life in a place like America and that they attempted to pull this life back into lines set out by their dusty thinking. All Catholic theology, as she read and listened, seemed based on ensuring that nothing hinders the movement of male sperm. Nowhere did it set down any obligation attendant to the male discharge, yet there were so many rules for women that one became distracted. So the man could shut his eyes and sleep and the woman suddenly could have a changed body and mind for the next nine months and undoubtedly forever.

She understood the religion's hatred of abortion. Dolores never questioned the idea that life begins at conception, at the very instant, and that life came with a soul placed there by God. Abortion, therefore, was unthinkable. Always, she remembered the sermon in church on the Sunday following John F. Kennedy's assassination. The priest at Dolores's Mass pointed out that although it had taken a priest in Dallas some time to reach Kennedy's body at the hospital and give the last rites, it still was considered a valid sacrament, for the soul remains in the body for about two hours after the signs of life have departed. And this very same soul, the priest pointed out that morning, takes up its residence at the very moment that the sperm and egg are joined in the womb.

Once, she attempted to go past this belief. The baby was eight months old and suddenly midday of the twenty-eighth day of her cycle passed and Dolores had no sign of her period, though her body usually was as orderly as a parade. By the next morning, her mind was cold with worry. She thought of the word *abortion*. It could not be a killing of the same magnitude as that of a human being who could be seen and spoken to.

All through that day she thought of her husband and pregnancy and each time the word *abortion* sounded loud in her mind. She theorized that the soul remained in Kennedy's body for two hours after his death because there was no exact way to identify the moment that physical life finally slipped out of the body, thus signaling to the soul that its time on earth was gone and that it must now head for preliminary judgment; final judgment comes on the day the world ends. There was, as Kennedy's death illustrated, a reason for the soul to linger at the end: the last sacrament, extreme unction. What would be the reason, however, for a soul to be placed into some collection of cells that were just starting to grow inside a woman? Much too early for a soul, Dolores thought. Perhaps, then, an abortion was not the hideous crime she once felt. Immediately, she prayed for forgiveness, as it was clearly the Devil who was tempting her and what she felt was logic really was his dark influence. That afternoon, however, she was in the Glendale library reading an article about abortion. She became furious that while sitting there in anxiety, the magazine in her hands told of how the civil interpretation of abortion might wind up being based on an old court case involving bakers who were overworked by their owner. The first court ruled against the baker not because he took advantage of needy human beings and he misused them, but because the bakery workers, once they had worked past sixty hours in a week, would in their fatigue bake bread that would make the public sick. Then a second court, the Supreme Court, said that this deprived the bakery worker of his freedom and he certainly could work on. So when an abortion case got to the Supreme Court, the justices might well use the bakery case to determine that a woman had the freedom to get rid of her fetus.

A bun in the oven, Dolores thought. That's precisely how they see the whole thing.

I fit no category, she told herself. I haven't been raped and I'm not somebody whose boyfriend got her in trouble. Nor am I some bored woman who doesn't want any more children. I have one baby and a husband who drinks too much and I'm trying to think of a way to get him to stop. If I am pregnant now, it will be a disaster. I am an individual with my own conscience and soul and I will be judged by God for what I am, not for what some old man in Rome, or in a court reading bakery cases, says I am.

At noon two days later, she found her pantyhose stained, and she never thought of the word *abortion* again, nor did she remember how involved she had become with the word and its meaning. At a distance from it again, she allowed it to remain in its category of capital sin.

Birth control was different. On that Ash Wednesday afternoon as she knelt in the pew of St. Pancras, she went over it in her mind once more, then got up and stood in line behind a young grammar school girl at the confessional booth of Father McMahon. The schoolgirl skipped in and out and then Dolores pushed the dusty velvet curtain aside and stepped into the box and immediately the small panel behind the screen window slid open and there appeared the faint outline of a priest whose head seemed heavy. With no preliminaries, Dolores went immediately to the only problem. She said that she had been practicing birth control.

The priest sighed. "You'll have to stop."

Dolores shook her head. "I don't think so."

"You'll have to. You cannot receive absolution unless you promise to your God that you will cease and desist from committing this grave sin."

"I don't know if I feel it's such a sin," she said.

"It is a very grave sin."

"How can it be? It's not stopping a child by abortion. It is nothing. It's stopping the male sperm."

"I can't give you absolution."

"Then I'm sorry," Dolores said.

She blessed herself and walked out of the confessional and into the pale light of a neighborhood church in the afternoon. She glanced across the pews and standing in front of the confessional on the opposite wall was an unfamiliar priest, a small, thin man with a dark face. A woman came out of the pews and up to the confessional and the dark priest went inside. Dolores went over and looked at his name, which was printed on a sign over the priest's door. "Father D. Jhabvala."

Dolores went into a pew and knelt and looked up at the light coming through the top of the stained-glass window over the altar and she became so intense in her prayer, so in awe of a priest from India suddenly appearing at this moment, that she felt it was the Lord helping her alone.

When she went in and told the priest from India that she was practicing birth control, the priest said in a soft voice, "I understand that this is considered a serious sin here and as I am visiting this country only for a short time, I must try to speak in the same voice as that of the others in this diocese. So let me say that it is a sin, your birth control, but that it is a sin that you must measure against your own conscience. I say that you must do this. I shall grant you absolution, but you must pray for guidance and examine your own conscience."

He blessed her and, free of sin, she walked out. She threw a glance at the box where the old Irishman sat and then she left the church.

Her memories and thoughts now were interrupted by sharp knocking on the bathroom door.

"Yes?" she called out.

"I can't wait for you," Owney called. "I'm going to work."

"Don't you want a shower?" Dolores said.

There was grumbling and he was gone.

Dolores held her face up to the warm water and tried to think of something hopeful, of another priest from India walking into her life in some new form, perhaps as a saint who could stop her husband's drinking.

Later in the morning, she left the baby with her mother and walked resolutely up to Myrtle Avenue, through the peace of houses from which only small, pleasant noises sounded—water running in the sink, a window being opened, a wash line being pulled—and got on the bus to Jamaica. The ride was long and bumpy and required her to change in Richmond Hill and ride along under the el into the fading old shopping center in Jamaica. Dolores pushed her face against the window and watched the construction of a new building growing in the middle of the old cemeteries and ancient-looking boarded-up churches that sat under the el. She remembered walking with her mother on these sidewalks, when they were crowded, and shopping in the Gertz store for an Easter outfit.

One of the closed churches, a red stone building with severe Protestant lines and a spire so high that even people riding on the el trains had to look directly up to see its tip, was so old that the front was designed to receive worshipers arriving by horse cart. A long railing for tethering horses ran on one side of the church, a leftover from the times when Jamaica was a proper German farm town. On the other side of the church was its concession to the new, a cinder driveway that ran in the gloom alongside the church and under a great old maple tree and then out to the street behind the church, Archer Avenue, where an old wooden bar called the Boar's Head sat in the fumes from trailer trucks and the noise from another set of elevated tracks, those of the Long Island Rail Road commuter lines. It was in this cinder driveway, right under the tree, Dolores remembered, that a man one night had strangled a woman, a waitress from the Loft's candy store on Jamaica Avenue. The man left the woman on the cinder drive under the tree and went to the Boar's Head and sat on a barstool and did not leave until a patrolman walked in the next day to use the men's room. The guy at the bar said to him, "She shouldn't have yelled."

"What's that?" the patrolman said.

"I said that she shouldn't have yelled. I don't know why, but it set me off."

"What do you mean set you off?"

"I never would've put a hand on her, really, but then she started screaming and look what I wound up doing to her. I got that scarf in my hands, I wouldn't let go."

The policeman was brought over to City Hall and given an award for dogged investigation. That was when murder was remembered for years —no, more than years, sometimes full lifetimes—after the crime. Someone would point at the spot and say that it was here, a long time ago, that a famous murder took place. All murders were famous. But then, Dolores remembered, the life of the city's neighborhoods changed, and in Jamaica there was a druggist dead on the floor behind his counter, or a jeweler being carried out of his store with blood dripping from the sheets on the emergency cart and coloring the sidewalk. Only the families of the victims remembered where the crime took place. Murder no longer was rare enough to be famous.

A block from the church was the bus stop, on the side of a corner greeting card shop, where everybody waited for the orange buses that went up the hill to Queens College. For Dolores, it had been one more bus ride after the long one in from Glendale. Most afternoons, she had been able to get a ride home, but she had always used this bus to reach school. When the crime began to change the streets under the el in Jamaica, her mother worried about her taking the bus to school.

"Ma, what could happen to anybody at eight o'clock in the morning?" Dolores asked her.

"If one of them is up, anything can happen," the mother said.

By the phrase "one of them," the mother was not referring to Croatians. In order to soothe her mother, Dolores promised that from then on she would take the bus from Glendale to Flushing, although it went on such a circuitous route that the trip to college took at least twenty-five minutes longer. Still, her mother remained wary of the idea of Dolores's going to college. "You take biology?" her mother said with a sniff. "You get all the biology you need just by living. You get married, you'll see what I mean."

One day, when Dolores had gone to school by her unannounced Jamaica route, she stood on the street corner by the card shop and reread one of Owney's letters. It was the letter in which he sent her a picture of two Vietnamese children, with almond eyes and short faces looking severely at the camera, as if a ceremony were being performed. He wrote that he had found the picture on a body and that there was no one else he could speak to about his pain. He asked Dolores to pray for the children and their mother, wherever they were, and then to beg God that he, Owney, never would have to go through something like this again. Even though she had read the letter many times, she was still shaken by it. Looking around her at the young people waiting for the bus, she found herself in disdain of what they were speaking about: the social impact of a rock concert. She was in love with Owney Morrison, who dealt in life and death and needed her help. His face was so clear in Dolores's mind that her hand rose for an instant and started to touch him. When the orange bus pulled in and they all got on for the ride to school, Dolores got on, but was concentrating on things other than a class.

Thinking of this now, with her face pressed to the window, she suddenly decided to get off. The bus stopped two blocks up, and she walked back and stood on the corner by the card shop. A couple of older people waited for the orange bus, their eyes looking up a street that reflected the years. A building that once had been a nightclub now was a storefront church. A saloon had its windows soaped. A rock hole was in one window. And here at the corner, the racks of gay cards, with inscriptions to loved ones and children making First Communion, all were under the care of a man with folded arms who stood grimly by a buzzer that unlocked the front door for any customer who appeared not likely to stab him.

She stood on this sidewalk, where she could see her roots by glancing in any direction, and she thought for the first time of being alone in a library again, thinking for sure that everyone around her was so much better, and then simply staying longer and, the next day, or a couple of days later, finding out that she was better than almost all of them. She reminded herself that she had a baby and a husband. For the first time, standing on this familiar sidewalk, she thought about fitting her own life around her home.

"I can do any *fucking* thing."

A woman turned and looked at Dolores in surprise.

Dolores, more amused than embarrassed, walked along under the el tracks to New York Boulevard. Gertz's department store was on the corner. She walked along the side of the store, heading south on the boulevard, which was only a two-lane local street and hardly could be called even an avenue. She walked along the length of the Gertz store, whose windows, once the showpieces of the Jamaica shopping center, were desolate. At the side entrance to Gertz's, a few people were going in and out. A few doors down the street, hanging out over the sidewalk, with the Long Island Rail Road tracks serving as a backdrop, was the sign for the Sea Grill bar.

A black woman, a bit heavy, stood in the doorway. She smoked a cigarette furiously.

"Dog," she said.

A voice inside the bar called out, "You say I'm a dog?"

"Dog," she said again.

"Then you nothin' but a motherfuckin' leash!"

She pulled the cigarette from her mouth. The other hand dug into her already mussed frosted-tip hair. She walked back into the bar with the cigarette held up in the air, as if entering a drawing room.

There were, of course, two doors to the bar. Dolores had heard the story many times as she was growing up, particularly when she was of high school age and could listen without becoming visibly upset. When her real parents had fought in the bar, the wife went out one door and the husband went out the other. Billy Kaufhold stayed at the bar and drank his whiskey.

Inside the Sea Grill now there was an eruption and several voices hollering and out of one door, the one closer to the railroad tracks, came a man with a round face contorted with fury. He had on a white knit shirt and he wheeled to the right and headed for the underpass to the Long Island Rail Road tracks.

And stumbling in haste out the door nearer to Dolores—in fact, almost knocking Dolores down—came the woman. Had she been close enough to the guy, she would have used the cigarette on him. This was apparent, for she threw it after him like a baseball. The cigarette dropped yards short, of course, but it was the act that counted. She went after him, her flat shoes pounding on the sidewalk. Along the street the man went, the woman after him. Something made Dolores follow. At the corner, Archer Avenue, the light was red and the man kept going, dodging a bus and a meat truck. The woman broke into a trot, her wide hips going side to side, and there was a splash as her foot went into a puddle. Infuriated, she began to run. They went through the underpass and out onto the street where the old rooming houses sat atop the grass embankments. When Dolores walked through the underpass, she found the place where the houses had been was now flattened into a parking lot for the Gertz store. The lot was nearly empty. By now, up the street, the woman was back to a walk and the man was outdistancing her with each step. Dolores stood by herself and a loneliness went through her. It was more than twenty years ago that her own mother had stood here, or maybe a few yards from here, and said that whoever wanted the baby upstairs on the bed could have her. Then the mother walked out. Dolores looked down on the sidewalk. The cement had been there a long time. Probably, her real mother had stepped right on this same flagstone as she walked away.

Up on the railroad tracks, a train headed noisily out to Long Island, causing Dolores to turn around and head back to Jamaica Avenue. On the green bus going back to Glendale, she glanced out the window at the card shop on the corner and saw the orange bus sitting at the curb with the route sign saying "Kissena Boulevard–Queens College." Small white lettering on a black background, so small that the only ones who could read it were those young enough to go to the school. She rode home thinking of her mother walking away from her, just walking down the sidewalk and leaving her, a baby, in the middle of a rooming house bed. She became impatient with the bus and instead of transferring at Lefferts Boulevard, she waved to a cab, for she suddenly wanted to hold her daughter.

Two days later, on an evening when he was home on time and his insides chilled with the glasses of water and tomato juice at dinner, Owney turned on the television, saw the start of the news report on Vietnam casualties, then turned to a local channel, which carried a rerun of *Gilligan's Island.* He turned the set off and looked out the window.

"Owney."

He was silent.

"Owney, look at me."

She was sitting at the end of the couch with a cigarette.

"What?" He didn't turn around.

"Owney, I must have been madly in love with you. I used to think of you all day. I can remember walking up the street and not seeing anybody else because I was so busy thinking about you."

Now he turned. "You don't do that anymore?"

"I'd like to."

"You mean you don't do it anymore? I still love you."

"I don't love what you're doing."

"I stopped."

"When was this?"

His hand moved impatiently.

"I stopped and I'll get you your own car. That's all I hear from you, anyway, a car."

"When cornered, attack."

"I'm answering you, that's all."

"Don't you think it would be better if you thought about it?"

"About what?"

"That you drink so much."

"I told you, I stopped." He snapped the words.

"You can't run away all the time," she said.

"I never ran in my life."

"Yes, you do. Whenever I bring this up, you either go out and don't come back or you hide behind some wall you put up. 'I stopped.' That's your wall tonight. You hide. That's your way of handling it."

"How can you say I hide?"

"Because you do."

"When they were fucking trying to kill me, I didn't hide. I was right there for them to see." He put his hand so that it covered the cheeks under his eyes. "They could see my eyes. They tried to put them out. I was standing right there. I walked away and they didn't. Here I am and here they are." He pointed to the floor.

"When cornered, attack."

"What am I supposed to do?"

She kept her voice level. "I would think it would be better to try anything except what we're doing. If something is malfunctioning and it keeps shaking, don't you take it someplace and have it fixed? So it works smooth?"

"Go someplace? Where?"

"I would try somebody who counsels people like you. Like us, really. I'm in it with you."

"We got Navy at work."

"Do you speak to him?"

"No."

"Why not?"

"Because I got nothing the matter with me."

"Just talk to him."

"Never. Let all these guys at work see me like I'm weak? Have to talk to Navy?"

"Then try somebody nobody will know about."

"Like who?"

"There are psychologists who might be able to help."

"Psychologists? You mean some shrink?"

She nodded.

"You'd tell me to do that?"

"Don't you think it would be better than living with this tension?"

"You'd tell me to do that?"

She nodded.

"You'd tell me go to a Jew?"

"Go to a Catholic, then."

"There aren't any Catholics doing that."

"Owney."

"That's all Jews, that business. Both sides. The psychiatrists are Jews and the patients are Jews. When you walk in there the first thing the guy says, he doesn't even say hello, he says, 'You're not happy with your sex!' "

"Don't be ridiculous."

"Huh. You say. I see things in my sleep at night that I don't even tell you about."

"I know you do. That's why I'm saying that you should tell somebody about it."

"Who? Some Jew doesn't know what a fistfight is? I'm going to walk in and tell him about how you got to break somebody's arm—*break* the fucking thing!—to make it fit into a body bag. They're all around the place with their arms stuck up in the air so stiff. I got that on my mind, all your guy wants to hear about is what I'm doing with my prick."

Dolores shrugged. "When cornered, attack."

"What do you mean?"

"Because you sound so stupid, and you know that you're being stupid. But you'll hide behind anything, even stupidity, instead of correcting something shaking inside of you."

He turned to the window.

"Owney."

"I don't want to talk about it anymore. I stopped drinking and that's it."

He turned around and walked out of the living room, throwing her a glance as he left.

"I got to get some sleep."

She did not look at him. Slowly, she picked up the television guide from the coffee table and began to look for movies that were on late.

In the morning she felt her feet pushing against the arm of the couch, and this woke her up.

The phone rang that day in the middle of those hours she resented the most, when the freshness was gone and the energy was out of the sounds on the streets, leaving her with no sense of accomplishment and with the only challenge in front of her the balancing of her life with that of her husband and with his second person, the one whose life dripped out of him as he sat on a barstool.

"Yeah." Ralphie Schmidt was on the phone.

"He's not home yet. This is you, Ralphie, isn't it?"

"Yeah," Ralphie Schmidt said. "You wouldn't believe what's happening here."

"Such as."

"I got, let me see now, I count four patrol cars outside and two trucks. One big one and one little one."

"What about?"

"Me," Ralphie said.

"What is it you're talking about?"

"It's over a domestic dispute. Owney could tell them for me. They're crazy."

"Ralphie, what dispute?"

"It began when the woman from the phone company called. I just got home yesterday. I been away. You know little girl Cindy? I been away to Keansburg with her last two weeks. I just get in the house and the woman calls me up and says they're removing my phone right away on account of I haven't paid. I said, hey, I just got home. The woman, a nigger woman, says, that is no concern of hers. I said, hey, bitch! Nigger bitch. She hangs up. So today, I look out and what do I see? The phone company man going up the pole outside. He's going to rip my wires right out of the box. Well, I don't have to tell you. I fucking let him know. Put two under his fucking nose."

"You did what?"

"I fucking put two under his nose. You heard me."

"You shot at him?"

"Shot near him. Not at him. If I shot at him, he'd be dogmeat."

"And the police came?"

"Yeah, they came. Then this Cindy goes fucking nuts. I try to calm her down. She's a complete moron, you know. Messed up on mescaline. She goes jumpin' out the window, probably out telling them now that I tried to kill her."

"Ralphie, do you have a gun now?"

"You know it."

"And what are the police doing?"

"They're nosing around. I got the place all barricaded up. I'm ready to go shot for shot with them."

"Ralphie. I'm going to call Owney and get him over there as soon as I can."

"That's good. They'll respect him. He can straighten it out."

"But while I'm getting him, let me at least try to talk to the police myself."

"When you're talking to them, you better tell them to remain down. Specialist First Class Ralphie Schmidt got no trouble with weaponry."

"Ralphie. You sit still. What if your mother comes home in the middle of all this?"

"There won't be a middle. She won't be back until tonight late. Nobody gets in before her. You should see how I got the front door and windows all barricaded up."

"Sit there. I'll call you back."

"I'll sit as long as they don't move."

"Do that now."

"Okay."

She hung up and dialed 911 immediately. The phone rang once.

"Police operator fourteen. What is your emergency?" The West Indian voice, rising and falling on the last word, made it sound as e-mer-gen . . . cee.

"There is an armed man barricaded in a house at Sixty-two–thirty-five Sixtieth Street in Ridgewood, Queens. The man just called me. Police are outside his house. His name is Ralphie Schmidt. My name is Dol——"

"You are talking too fast to me."

"My name is Dolores Morrison and I am at VA one seven five six two. If you have a pol——"

"You live at One seven five six two what street?"

"That was my phone number. Have someone call me right away."

"This *mon* cannot call your house. He got to know de number of de telephone."

"I gave it to you."

"I am sorry but you did not give me de telephone number. You gave me de number of your house, but you didn't give me the street de house was on. So you did not give me de phone number or de house number. If I tell the *mon* to get you, he could not call you up on de telephone because he do not know your number and he could not drive to your house because he do not know. You did not give me de number to de telephone."

"Yes, I did."

"You only gave de number to de house. You didn't give me de name of de street you got your house on."

"The phone number is VA one seven five six two."

"Stop yelling at me. I hear you. What is your house address? De house can't tell me where it is. You must do dat t'ing."

"I am at Seventy-eight–twenty-eight Seventy-fourth Street in Glendale, Queens."

"And de *mon* is barricaded in your house?"

"Give me a supervisor, please."

"One moment."

Dolores waited for about a minute and then a fast voice came on. "Sergeant Duddy, shield number three five seven four."

"Ralphie Schmidt of number Sixty-two–thirty-five Sixtieth Street in Ridgewood, Queens, just called me to say he is barricaded inside his house and that police are surrounding it. My name is Dolores Morrison and I can spe——"

"Just hold for a moment."

There was about a twenty-second wait and then another white male voice said, "Detective Cleary. Shield two three eight five."

"A man named Ralph—"

"I have that on the screen. You are Dolores Morrison at VA one seven five six two."

"Yes."

"Hang up and keep the line clear and I'll have an officer from the scene contact you. Just hang up and remain off the line."

She hung up. The Irish, they're born for police work, she said to herself. She followed the second hand as it went around the kitchen clock. At one minute and twenty-two seconds, the phone rang.

"Yeah. Lieutenant Regan, emergency service squad, here. I'm told you have been in contact with Mr. Schmidt?"

"I have. My name is Dolores Morrison. My husband is Owen Morrison. He was in Vietnam with Mr. Schmidt. He has Mr. Schmidt's respect. I am going to call my husband at work now and he can get right over to help you. In the meantime, I've asked Mr. Schmidt to please not hurt anybody, or himself."

"He's armed, you know," Regan said.

"Yes, he told me."

"He fired a couple of shots inside the house."

"He didn't tell me that."

"The girl who was inside the house with him said that he did."

"Cindy?"

"That's her name."

"I wouldn't believe her in church."

"I'm afraid we have to take her word for it."

"Do as you like. I'll call my husband right now."

"Then call me back. I'm at a neighbor's house. I'm at VA one six three eight seven. Got that now?"

Dolores repeated the number as she wrote it on the pad alongside the phone.

She then called the hog house, where a voice answered gruffly and then let the phone dangle. Then the voice came back and said that Owney was gone. Dolores began dialing.

"Yeah?"

"Brendan's? Is Owen Morrison there?"

"Wait a minute."

She could see the smoke over the phone and could see the bar crowded as the man called for her husband.

"Not in."

"If he does come in, could you please have him call his home. It's an emergency."

"Sure. Wait just one second while I write this down on my pad."

There was a silence. Then the guy said, "Fine. I got it written up for him."

"Mayo Inn."

"Owen Morrison?"

"Not in. I can see by looking."

"If he does come in, would yo——"

"Have him call his home. Sure."

"It's an emergency."

"Somebody sick?"

"No."

"Nobody hurt or dying or nothing?"

"No. It's jus——"

"Then let me tell you what an emergency is if you got nobody sick or hurt. An emergency is when I don't have enough money to buy a drink!"

"A friend of Owney's is inside his house with guns. The police are all around the house."

"Where?"

"In Ridgewood."

"Then what do we care? We're in the Mayo Inn, Katonah Avenue in the Bronx. Fuck them. Let them blaze away in Queens. We're drinking in the Bronx."

She made three more calls. Then she sat and waited for Owney to call. It was three-fifteen. At three twenty-five the phone rang and she grabbed it.

"Lieutenant Regan. Emergency service squad. Were you able to contact your husband?"

"I'm waiting for him to call me now."

"I'll get off the line. You've got our number. We'll send a patrol car for him if you locate him."

By four o'clock she had heard from nobody. She called every bar back and then called the number for the lieutenant and it was busy. She called Ralphie Schmidt.

"Yeah."

"Ralphie, I'm just waiting for Owney to call me and then I'll have him right over."

"That's good. I was just lookin' down from the attic again. Those fucks all crouched down. They think they're out of the line of fire. I ought to let them know. I ought to send them a fucking message. Dust 'em off."

She could only think of saying his name, but then suddenly she found the words streaming from her. "I love your mother and you love her too and we simply *can't* have her hurt anymore, Ralphie. I know that woman was on her knees in church every morning. When the sidewalk was a sheet of ice outside she was there. She walked there. So she could pray for you every day. Ralphie, you *can't* hurt that woman. Listen to me. I'll tell you exactly what to—"

"I don't want to hurt my mother."

"Then you'll listen to me."

"What do you thin——"

Ralphie's voice went off the line. Dolores quickly dialed his number. The call didn't go through. She tried again. Nothing happened. She called the police lieutenant's number and the line was still busy.

At four-thirty, she wrote a note to Owney and put it on the front door. Then she took the baby to her mother's house.

"Why so late?" the mother said.

"I'll be right back. I just have to go to Ralphie Schmidt's house. He has a lot of trouble. If Owney calls, make sure to tell him that he better get to Ralphie Schmidt's house right away."

On 60th Street, the sidewalk in front of the Swallow's Nest was packed, full glasses clutched and necks craning to see up the block. On the far side of the street, two policemen in flak jackets and wearing baseball caps were screaming at a black in a compact telephone company repair truck.

"Right away," one of the cops said.

"I just do what the orders say," the black repairman said.

"I'm a police officer. I'm ordering you to fix the lines."

"I take my orders from my foreman."

"You'll take them from us. You're interfering with police work."

"I'll drive away, then. Give you all the room you need."

"I'll arrest you and throw you in jail."

"Go ahead," the telephone man said.

"Fix the lines."

"Go ahead and arrest me. False arrest."

The other cop tried to talk to him, but the guy shook his head. Finally, face reddening, he yelled, "You fuck!"

"My orders say disconnect the phone and I disconnect the phone. I got no order says to me, put it back on because a policeman says so. You got to go to my foreman before I move."

The cops sounded as if they were being strangled and the phone company guy was glancing down, obviously at forms in his lap. Dolores walked past them and up to a rope barricade a couple of doors down the block. She explained who she was to a patrolman and he took her by the elbow and walked along the sidewalk to the back of a large truck that was parked half on the sidewalk and half in the gutter. On folding chairs in the back were several cops in baseball caps, all leaning around little girl Cindy, who had a large sheet of paper in her lap.

"You done this good," she said.

"That's his job, doing diagrams of things like banks when they got a hostage situation."

"You sure got Ralphie's bedroom down good."

"I'd be surprised if she knew anything about the rest of the house," Dolores said.

Cindy looked up with the face of one who was caught. Then she gained confidence from the cops around her and sneered. "Why don't you go in there and get him if you're so smart?"

"We're going to have to do something," a man with captain's bars on his shirt collar said.

"Can't you talk to him?" Dolores said.

"Not on the phone. We use the bullhorn but he won't answer."

"Why can't you just wait until he falls asleep?"

"Because we're going to have to keep a whole block full of people coming from work away from their houses. We'll go crazy trying to handle that."

"Isn't that easier than having someone shot? My husband will be here by then."

"We'll see," the captain said.

"You know so much," Cindy said, "why don't you get out there and take care of this thing?"

Dolores stepped away from the truck and peered down the street. There were policemen on their bellies in the gutter, and others crouched behind stoops. She thought she saw someone up on a roof, but whoever it was withdrew his head quickly. She stepped a little farther away from the truck to see.

"You'll get killed!" a voice hissed.

By Ralphie Schmidt, she thought. She looked at the policemen ducking down, like kids playing war. Behind her, she heard the infuriating voice of little girl Cindy. Playing cops and robbers. Dolores ignored the shouts as she walked across the sidewalk and went up the stoop to the open door of a frame house two doors down from Ralphie's. She called out as she stepped through the open vestibule door.

In the living room, a cop was standing with a pained face and a phone to his ear.

"The whole block is knocked out," he said.

Dolores spoke to the woman, who was seated at the dining room table. "You got any wash?"

The woman seemed surprised. "In the washing machine in the cellar."

"Do you mind?" Dolores said.

"Go ahead," the woman said. "I don't know what you're doing, but go ahead."

Dolores went down to the cellar and took the wicker wash basket and filled it with wet towels, bedspreads, T-shirts, and sweaters. The wash came to her chest. She put in sheets and several pairs of pajamas to bring the pile nose high. She walked out of the house and onto the empty sidewalk with the top piece of wash, a pair of blue pajamas, and directly underneath them a white bedsheet. She walked along the sidewalk and she now was in full view of Ralphie Schmidt's windows.

"Get back!" a voice called through the bullhorn.

Dolores did not look up or answer. She just walked straight for Ralphie Schmidt's stoop. As she reached it, she could feel the tension; she now was in his flight circle.

"Ralphie, you'll open up. I got my arms full of wash," Dolores said. "I got to use your wash line."

In Ridgewood, where the streets and houses are so clean that people feel the wearing of shoes is a filthy habit, the presence of wash in any form is as important as a religious ceremony.

As Dolores stood on the stoop, conscious of the guns behind her, but with the wash in front of her, wash that a safety pin could go through, not to mention a bullet, she felt as if she were standing behind something as impenetrable as a mountain. She felt the power radiate from the wash and go through the front door of Ralphie Schmidt's house.

Behind which there now was the noise of something being moved. Then more things being shoved. The locks sounded and the door opened partly.

"Well? I can't fit through *that* space."

Ralphie Schmidt now pulled the door so open that he was in view of the street.

"Drop the gun!"

Dolores placed her body directly between Ralphie and the street outside; she regarded herself as the right color that stills the hand of the hunter. Here was Ralphie, however, gun clutched as if it were sacramental, head held erect as if receiving high religious honors, and for part of an instant Dolores thought of the police at her back being equally proud. Rather than controlling a situation, she would simply be somebody in the way. Shot front and back. As she stepped past Ralphie and he shut the door, she felt easier. A clicking came from Ralphie's body; she noticed that he had gun belts wrapped around him. Brass in the light. As she walked with the wash basket into the living room, she saw that the couch was badly torn. No, slashed. Insides were all over the floor. Look at them. Glancing up, she saw that there was a long slash through the wallpaper over the couch. Then the back of a stuffed chair was laid open. At the entrance to the dining area she had to step over a chair. There was no table, and the floor was covered with broken china. The dining room table was in the kitchen, pushed against the back door as a barricade.

"I'm ready for them," Ralphie said.

"You can be ready for them, but I've got to get my wash done," Dolores said.

"I want them to come in on me," Ralphie said.

"I want my wash done," Dolores said.

She put the wicker basket on the floor and then reached for the window.

"You got to stay back from the window. Don't put yourself in the frame."

"Ralphie, I've wash to hang."

She stood full in the window so that whoever was out in the garages at the other end of the narrow back yard could see who it was. Then she pushed up the window and took a handful of clothespins from the cloth bag hanging outside the window.

"Ralphie, you'll hand me my wash," she said. She put three clothespins in her mouth.

She held her hand out and Ralphie gave her the blue pajamas. She pinned them to the line and then moved them out, boldly, the pulleys on the far end of the line, on the telephone pole flush against the garage, squeaking loudly and comfortingly, sending out her pennants for all to see up and down the line. She hung a bedsheet next. Then she mumbled through the clothespins, "Give me the blue bedspread."

She felt the fabric on her hand and she clutched it and pulled it up and onto the line. Her body motions were familiar and the sound of the voice coming out from around clothespins was something that both Dolores and Ralphie had heard as babies, and the wash line squeaked and the wash was fresh to the hand.

"Next. Give me another sheet, Ralphie."

Same sound, same body motion, same squeak. The hand went out to him again.

"Now give me the rifle."

She felt it in her hand, metal on top, wood on the bottom. She never thought about whether she had a proper grip on it or not; she just raised it up, keeping the barrel pointing up at the ceiling and then at the sky and then she dropped it out the window into the back yard. As she pulled the wash line so that the pulley squeaked and her hand reached back inside the kitchen so Ralphie could give her more wash, the cops crashed through the front door.

* * *

In bed that night, she was more surprised that the police had not been able to talk their way in than she was at her own powers. She wondered if any of the police understood how to put the violence into the recesses and keep it there by performing an act so familiar and serene that physical danger could be removed without bringing around even more force. I know one thing, Dolores told herself. I can handle things better than the police.

She was still awake in her excitement when she heard Owney open the door. It had to be about one A.M. She threw herself on her side and closed her eyes; she was too disappointed in him to bother looking at him.

The first thing she felt in the morning was his hand on her side, a touch so soft that of course it was only a dream he was having, or the involuntary twitch of a muscle coated with thick sleep. She shifted away from the hand, which simply returned and slipped persistently under her arm until the fingers touched the rise of her breast. As she sat up and swung her legs on the floor, the hand refused to desist. It was now on her back.

"Where do you get the nerve?" she said, standing up.

"I'm trying to make it up to you."

"By doing this?"

"Come here." He said it with a whine.

She took her gray plaid robe off the hook on the door and walked out without looking back at him.

"Come here," he said again.

When she kept going, she heard the covers sound. Kicking his feet like a child. He wants to make it up to me. Once, she had reluctantly gone along with the fiction that despite his awakening in a state of hangover, filled with a craving that set fire to his system, he still wanted sex with her for his love of her. It had taken some time for her to admit to herself that his passion was made of alcohol and that his deep admiration for her on these mornings was centered on the great assistance she gave as he satisfied himself.

She tied the robe in front of her with angry motions.

On the kitchen table, in morning sunlight coming through the windows over the sink, she saw a wad of money folded in half. The sunlight only reminded her of where he would be in the late afternoon and she accepted the money on the table as an insult.

"Why don't you bring your money in a check like everybody else?" she said.

"Because I cashed it," he said from the bedroom.

"Where? At some bar?"

He didn't answer.

"Terrific. We start out with most of the money gone over the bar."

"Not most."

"I thought you said you stopped drinking."

Again, he was silent.

"I'm your wife and I'm sitting home with your daughter. And you're at the bar with our money, I said our money, all over the place. Buying drinks for strangers. Talking away."

When he still said nothing, her level of annoyance rose.

"Speaking of talking to somebody, did you think about who you intend to talk to? Did you get the names of some decent Catholic therapists?"

She was standing with her back to the doorway, seeing nothing in front of her but her anger.

"No? You can't find a Catholic. Well, then, you just better get yourself to a nice Jewish therapist. Because you need one."

"I'm going nowhere," he said, finally.

She happened to glance up at the top of the refrigerator, where the brown window envelope containing his check for the Medal of Honor was unopened. She took it, folded it, and stuck it into her bathrobe pocket, then went into the shower.

When she stepped out of the bathroom, she looked at the clock.

"Owney."

"What?" The voice was drowsy.

"Six-fifteen."

"I can't make it today."

"Just get up."

"Call the job."

"Me?"

"You got to call for me. I can't move."

"And say what?"

"Tell them I got the flu."

"The *flu?* This is like calling grammar school."

"You got to do it."

She stood in the bedroom doorway and looked at him. He had the cover up over the cheek on one side of his face, but not so much that a small snaking red line on his cheek couldn't be seen. The eye above it was closed, but there was a suggestion of gray under it.

"Call," he murmured.

"I thought you hated weak people," she said.

He didn't answer.

"That's just what you're turning into."

He kept his eyes shut.

In the kitchen, she dialed the number pasted under the phone and asked for the foreman, Delaney. When he came on, she said, "This is Owen Morrison's wife."

"She don't work here."

"I'm calling for my husband."

"Then put him on. He's the one that works."

"He can't make it today."

"What happened?"

"He just isn't up to it."

"Then the man must have cholera. This is his third day out in the last ten. Tell him I said so."

She strode into the bedroom and hit his leg. "You don't even go to work? What do you do when you leave here?"

His hand came out from under the blankets. "Come here," he murmured.

"What are you saying to me?"

"You talk too much," he said. "Come to bed like you're supposed to."

"You never talked like that to me in your life."

"I am now. Come here."

She clutched at clothes and left the room, slamming the door. She got dressed, made coffee, and at nine-thirty she put the baby in the stroller and walked up Myrtle Avenue to the Ridgewood Savings Bank. His government check was in her purse. At the bank, she stood at a glass counter in the somber light that came through cathedral windows that were on either side of the centerpiece of the bank, a mural that reached the ceiling, two stories high. The mural consisted of a deity bathed in light and looking down upon a pot of gold surrounded by baled wheat. The title of the mural called out to the German women of Ridgewood, and their machinist husbands: "Savings Is the Secret of Wealth." Dolores signed Owney's name on the back of his Medal of Honor check and made out a deposit slip for her checking account. Ahead of her on line, a woman with long, worn fingers nervously touched the deposit slips and bills that she kept inside her book. She turned her head and looked at Dolores. The woman was in her late sixties, with a long, scrubbed face that was framed by a somber kerchief.

"I don't know whether to put this all in or keep some out," the woman said.

"If you save it, you won't spend it," Dolores said.

"Oh, I know that, dear," the woman said.

"Then save it," Dolores said.

"I don't leave myself anything to eat," the woman said.

"Well, you keep out enough money to live on, don't you?" Dolores said.

The woman answered with an uncertain look.

"You must have food in the house," Dolores said.

"I know. That's why I'm so mixed up all morning. I'm all alone. I lived through having nothing once. Then I had a husband. Now I got no husband. You got a husband, dear? Me, if anything happens to me, all I'll have is what I got here in the bank. Who knows what could happen ten years from now?"

"You better worry about dinner tonight," Dolores said.

"You go to the store, dear, buy chuck chopped. Three dollars eighty cents a package. I swear on God, three dollars eighty cents. You bring it home, it cooks down to the size of a half dollar. I can't afford to buy."

"It's ridiculous you don't," Dolores said.

The nervous fingers made a scratching sound against the deposit slips. "I got no husband no more," the woman said. "I'm all alone. I got to worry."

Dolores went off the line. She pushed her stroller over to a low partition and spoke to a bank officer, who was unsurprised. "We had a woman two months ago who was living with no heat in her house," he said, "and she got pneumonia. They put her in Wyckoff Heights. She had eleven thousand on deposit here. It's no fortune, but she could have spent two hundred dollars on oil. What was she saving for? Unfortunately, it's very common. Always the widows. Here, let me see this woman. Thank you very much."

Dolores walked onto another line and watched as the bank officer took the woman back to his desk and began talking to her. When Dolores saw the officer reach for new deposit slips, she stopped looking. She deposited her check. The amount, $250, was her first deposit since she had taken his last check to the bank. She pushed the baby home, where she walked into the house with feet striking the floor firmly, to awaken Owney, and found the bedroom empty and the sheets and blankets on the floor.

Glancing at the money on the kitchen table, she guessed that Owney had taken about half of what he had left the night before. She did not touch the money.

She gave Christine a couple of crackers and then sat at the table in the discomfort of an anger that came through her on a bitter, freezing wind. In front of her, Christine turned a cracker into crumbs on the highchair tray, then ran a hand back and forth and swept the crumbs onto the floor. Dolores thought for a moment about the woman in the bank: spent her life in a box of a room like this, and now at the end she's afraid to buy food. Dolores walked out into the hallway again and looked into the bedroom, at the sheets and blankets on the floor. She stepped back into the kitchen and absently tried to guide the baby into putting the cracker into her mouth, instead of breaking it up. As Dolores did this, the baby's soft blue eyes became angry stones. The lips pouted and the hand threw the cracker onto the floor.

You said it, Dolores said to herself. She went out to the front door, opened it, and looked out onto the street, as if its familiarity would have an influence on her. Then a gust, which rattled the dried leaves of the maple tree at the curb, caused her to shut the door.

Walking back through the house, she glanced into the living room, which had the stillness and gloom of a place unused. Anybody I know here is gone, she told herself.

In the bedroom, she took her gray plaid bathrobe from the hook behind the door. Might forget it later. She took a canvas tote bag from the closet and inspected the dresser. The hair dryer, its presence on the dresser signifying the size of the bathroom, was in front of the framed wedding picture. Holding hands with Owney and walking back up the aisle at St. Pancras, eyes very wide, smiling, walking at a time when wisdom consisted of commenting on the quality of the sunlight. She regarded the picture now as she did the wallpaper. She dropped the hair dryer into the tote bag, then pulled open her top drawer. She took out her underwear and put it on the bed, went into the other top drawer for her pantyhose. Costume jewelry from a tray and then into the bottom drawers for blouses and sweaters. She thought for a moment. The large blue suitcase was in the basement. Might as well get that now, she told herself.

Downstairs, which was free of dust and clutter—the landlady, Mrs. Schweitzer, would scrub the foundation walls if she could get through the floor—she picked up the blue suitcase from a table. Her coats hung from hangers on hooks and she threw her dark blue winter coat, a corduroy car coat, and a lined raincoat over her arm. Upstairs, she looked in at the baby's room. She decided that the crib was too big for her to take today.

The portable one in the dining room would do for a while. She went into the bedroom, put the suitcase on the bed, opened it, then stepped over to the closet, got one arm behind her dresses and pants, and took the hangers off the rail until her arm was full and she barely could see over it.

She thought of him once. That was when she had the baby in her arm and she was watching the driver from Four One's Car Service struggle with plastic garbage bags that were filled with boxes of disposable diapers. Her thought was basic: if he had lived another kind of life, then I would have my own car now instead of this cab. The rest of her life with him produced only emptiness as far as she could see in her mind, a prairie with nothing growing on it, and dust rising with each move of the air.

"You going on a trip?" the driver, who had a body of mashed potatoes, said.

"Twenty blocks," Dolores said.

"Looks to me like this is a walkout," the driver said. "A complete walkout."

"Any walking out around here was done by somebody else," Dolores said.

She walked through the house, and then came back to the kitchen and thought about whether to leave a note or not. Yes, I'll do that, she told herself. She sat with the baby twisting in her arm and took a sheet of paper from the pad atop the refrigerator and wrote, "Went to my mother's." She put it on the refrigerator handle. Then she opened the refrigerator, whose insides were dominated by six bottles of beer, which he had brought home deep in one of the last couple of nights, but had obviously been in no condition to get one of them open. She stuffed the six bottles into the tote bag that was over the same arm holding the baby. She left the house, shutting the front door without feeling anything. On her way to the cab, a battered station wagon, she dropped the bottles into the garbage can in the alley.

"What do you call that?" the cab driver said.

She said nothing and slammed the top back on the garbage can.

"You can't do that around me," the cab driver said. He went to the can and took out the six bottles.

"They're filthy," she said. "They have coffee grounds all over them."

He stood with his arms folded around the six bottles. "So I'll wash them off," he said.

Dolores made a face.

"I'll take them to the Board of Health and ask if it's all right to drink them."

She got in the front seat of the station wagon.

"You married to Mcrrison?" the cab driver asked, placing the bottles on the floor.

"Do you know him?" Dolores said.

"Sure, I see him around."

"I never would have guessed," Dolores said.

They drove down Central Avenue to 66th Street and stopped in front of her mother's building. Dolores carried the baby and tote bag up to the glass front door, which was open. She took out her keys and opened the inside door. She left this open for the cab driver. She walked into the dark hallway and put the key into the door to her mother's apartment. The top half of the door was made of frosted glass.

"You've got guests," Dolores called out as she stepped into the house in which she had been raised.

Her mother, smiling, stood in the hallway at the kitchen door.

"Why didn't you call? Suppose I was out."

"It wasn't necessary for you to be here."

Her mother took the baby and sat on a kitchen chair. "How long you here for?"

"For a while."

Dolores stood in the kitchen doorway and looked at her old bedroom, the small one in the back.

"Well, I got to five o'clock here. Then my sister and I are going out to a show," her mother said.

"That's fine with me," Dolores said.

Now there was the sound of the cab driver struggling up the staircase. He came into the apartment with the portable crib and the blue suitcase.

"What do I do with these?"

"Back in the small bedroom," Dolores said.

Her mother's eyes widened, and her voice was high. "What are you saying?"

"I'm going to be back here for a while," Dolores said.

"How can you do that?"

"You're seeing me do it."

"How do you leave your husband and your own house?"

"By taxi."

"What did you say to Owney?"

"Who sees him to tell him anything?"

"You're going to stay here?"

"Where else should I go?"

"Jesus, Mary, and Joseph! What if I ever decided to go with my sister Grace to Boynton Beach?"

That night, her cousin Virginia walked in and sat with Dolores during the last fifteen minutes of the six o'clock news. A black reporter was walking down a hallway of a public housing project and pointing to the spot where somebody had been stabbed.

"He knows it so well, account of he did the stabbing himself last night," Virginia said.

Dolores didn't answer.

"You want a cigarette?" Virginia said.

"Thanks."

"My mother told me," Virginia said.

"What's so secret?" Dolores said.

"She thinks it's only for a couple of days."

"She might be thinking wrong," Dolores said.

"What would you do?"

"I don't know. I've got some ideas. But I know that I'm not going back right now."

"You know that?" Virginia said.

"I know that."

"You know yourself; I know that," Virginia said. "If you tell me you're not going back, I know you're not."

They sat in silence. Then Virginia said, "What would you do?"

"I haven't thought it all out yet," Dolores said.

"You want a job?"

Dolores shook her head. "School is what I'm thinking of."

"Then you think," Virginia said. "I can offer you a show next week. I got two tickets to *Applause* from the office pool. You want to go?"

"I can't even think of going out now."

"It's all the way to next week."

"I'll see then. Right now I have to think."

Her cousin's fingernails caused the cigarette cellophane to rattle, just a slight sound, but one that filled Dolores's ears. In the kitchen, her mother put spoon to pot and to Dolores this sounded as if her mother were straightening a fender. Alongside her in the living room, Virginia's fingers dug more into the cigarette pack, and as she talked on, Dolores tried to find a chamber of her mind that held out all sound.

All the while, moving through her thoughts, light-footed, laughing, clear eyes promising, was Owney. Her instinct was to reach out and hold him as he walked up to her, to revel in the sudden ending of this emptiness and anxiety within her. And to apologize for not being home. Of course, she found herself saying that she was sorry; her first reaction to her positive act of leaving was to consider herself a defendant. Then she thought of the blanket and sheet thrown on the floor and she smelled the beer and tobacco that always signified his arrival in a bedroom dark in the middle of the night. The hell with him, she thought.

Now, she decided that she should have been smart enough before they were married to understand what was happening to him.

She thought of the night at the Arena Disco, on Fresh Pond Road, when Owney was on the dance floor with a bottle of beer and the manager walked over and said, "If you're going to drink, could you please go over to one of the corners of the dance floor?"

"I'm all right," Owney had said.

"If you spill any on the floor, people won't be able to dance," the guy said.

"I don't want to go in the corner," Owney said.

"Go there. Drink. Smoke dope. We don't care what you do in the corner. But you can't smoke on the dance floor. You'd set somebody's spandex on fire. And you can't drink here in the middle. Spill it and nobody can dance."

"The corner is too far from the bar," Owney said. He took a long swig of beer, then he spun and went a couple of steps to the bar, was given another bottle and returned with it held to his mouth.

"I guess I can't tell you what to do," the disco manager said.

"I won't spill any on the floor."

"I wish you'd go to the corner."

"I won't spill any."

That night, Dolores thought he was being outrageous and stubborn and plain mad from where he had been and what he had done, and she was excited by all of it. She never considered that he had been telling the exact truth, that he didn't want to go into a corner of the big disco room because he would have been too far from the magic of the bar. All she knew that night was that he made her laugh, that he was the only person on the dance floor with a bottle of beer, and that he kept his promise and spilled nothing.

Then, so much later, when she said hesitantly that their lives were being drowned, he listened with a nod and then went out into winds that blew him everywhere. The happiness was gone and he drank in pain.

"Want one?" her cousin Virginia said. The cellophane roared as she dug for another cigarette.

"I don't know what I want," Dolores said. She began to think about what her real mother had for insides. For Dolores, walking out on her own husband had in these first moments caused a sorrow and, immediately, a snarl. When she thought of the future, all she could see was dust. Her real mother had walked out on both the man and her own child. Dolores couldn't speak for the man but she could speak pretty well for what the child knew: the mother never glanced back, or took a step to return through all the years since. She wondered what happened to her real mother in those odd moments during a day when the thought of the child she left blinked inside her, an unnoticed mirror suddenly catching the sun's full light and turning everything blinding white.

10

FIRST, there was a creak somewhere inside the apartment. After it, the sound of several things falling at once. Then a man shouted with all his breath.

"Who are you?"

"Dolores Morrison."

"What do you want?"

"A lawyer. I looked for your office downstairs, but the doorman told me that you stay up here."

The door opened and McNiff stood in tan pajamas with a middle button missing. He clutched the front of his pajama pants. Black eyeshades were pushed up on his uncombed hair. Eyeglasses sat on the sleep shades. McNiff pulled the glasses down onto his nose.

"Oh, I know you. I was your husband's lawyer."

"That's right. The only time I ever was near a lawyer. I'd like to ask you a few things."

"What about?"

"A divorce, or an annulment."

"I knew you were mad at your husband that day you were downstairs in the bar. I told that to your husband. I knew you were mad, I knew you were mad. Please wait right where you are. I can't allow you to come inside. The only woman I'll let in this apartment is a Polish slave who will give me dinner and sex."

McNiff opened the door wider and walked back into the apartment along a narrow footpath that ran between stacks of books that went from the floor to the ceiling. He was as wide as a gunboat and had to keep his arms tight against his sides so an elbow would not knock over one of the stacks. He reappeared in a blue bathrobe.

"These books cost me nothing. When lawyers die, their wives look at their legal books and before going to Florida they call up the bar association and say they want to donate their husband's law books. I have twenty-five copies of everything. I have ten books on kidneys. It's unusual to have a lawsuit involving kidneys. But the kidney feeds into the bladder. Therefore, why be short-sighted and not have ten books on kidneys? I have all my kidney books the third from the top on a stack. That's my filing system. Kidney books are third from the top."

"I'm here to talk about a legal problem, not medical."

"What is it?"

"Marital."

"Oh, the marital, that's drinking. Drinking affects the kidneys. Why don't I get out a book on the kidneys? We both can read it here in the doorway. Remember I told your husband that you were mad at him because of his drinking?"

"I can't handle that anymore."

"Many people in the world go around drunk," McNiff said. "There's lots worse things than a drunk."

"I just want to get as far away from the whole business as I can."

"Did your husband beat you up?"

"My husband wouldn't touch me."

"Then he's not the worst."

"No, he isn't. But there's too much going on. I have to talk to somebody."

"Is he on a bender?"

"I don't know what he is. He's drowning my heart. But I have to talk to you."

"I can get you a divorce," McNiff said. "I know all about divorces. Just yesterday I was at Sutphin Boulevard for another divorce case. I was the husband's lawyer. I had an hour and I went outside. I used to go for a drink and get drunk in the hour. Yesterday I went diagonally across the street from the courthouse. There used to be a bar. Now it's a Burger King. You know what they had in there? Bargirls in yellow dresses. Bargirls at Burger King! This one girl was so gorgeous. She smiled at me. I thought she wanted to have sex. So I said, all right, I'll buy another hamburger. Then maybe she'll have sex with me. Well, I now have thirty-two hamburgers in my refrigerator and I didn't have sex."

"I'm sure the young woman still was very nice to you at Burger King."

"She was not as nice as I wanted her to be. Do you want me to get you a hamburger? You can eat it cold right here in the hall."

"No, thank you. But I have to talk to you."

"I can get you a divorce. I can prove that I can. I got one for myself. I want to inform your husband first. He was my client. I am very ethical. When can you come back?"

"I have to talk to you now. Or I'll just have to go someplace else."

"You can step right inside the door. But I have to leave it partly open. I can't have women in here behind closed doors. Unless you're a Polish slave."

He stepped back and Dolores edged into the apartment. He stood in the passageway between the books and Dolores swung the door until it was only a few inches from being completely closed.

"How long have you been married?"

"About two years. No, twenty-two. What difference does it make?"

"Because your husband is a unique figure."

"I think I'm the one who is unique."

"Don't be so angry."

"I'm not. I'm just not feeling as much as I should."

"Is this the first time you've left him?"

"That I've left him? Yes. That he's left me? Huh."

"You're through trying?"

"I don't know what that means."

"Why start an official proceeding?"

"Oh, no, that I have to do. I have to get on with my own life. I need some kind of assurances that I'll have some money. I can't go running into saloons every time he gets paid. Besides, he has so many tricks that I forget what day he gets paid on."

"Is money the problem?"

"No, life."

"Sex? Are you having trouble with your sex life? Are you having trouble with your sex life?"

"Of course."

"What's the trouble? What's the trouble?"

"Get me the divorce and I'll show you."

As his eyes bulged, she laughed, and the sound of her own laugh seemed strange to her. I can't even remember when I last smiled, she told herself.

"I wish it were something other than drinking," McNiff said quietly.

"It's a curse," she said.

"The bad thing is, that's what I do. I don't like to hear it being denigrated. I love being drunk. I love being drunk."

"I can't help him anymore," Dolores said. "Maybe if I just cut him loose and start going my own way I'll see if he wants me enough to follow me."

"Do you think he will?"

"I don't know. He can be fanatical when he has to do something."

"Then why don't you give him a clear warning?"

"Oh, no, I've no more time. I'll lose my life waiting for him. I've gone this far. Now I'm going to continue."

"Well," McNiff said wearily.

"What do I do?" Dolores said.

"I will inform your husband that you want to retain me. If he has no objections, then you come back in and we'll start filing papers in order for you to get temporary support."

"It won't take long?" she said.

"No. I have to go inside now and listen to my medical tapes. I went down to Tulane University and bought all these tapes. They tape medical school lectures. This afternoon, I'm listening to one about blood spattering on the car window in an accident. Blood spattering all over."

"One other thing before I go," Dolores said.

"Yes, but I have to listen to my tapes. Blood spattering all over."

"Do I get a divorce or an annulment? I don't know the difference."

"You're Catholic," McNiff said.

"Of course."

He went back down the footpath through the stacks of books. He returned with a pamphlet.

"This is what your church puts out on annulments. Go home and read that and think about it. I think you then ought to go over and talk to them. Then we'll discuss what you should do."

"Thank you. I'll call you."

"I liked your husband that day," McNiff said.

"I liked him too."

"I told him he had to watch himself."

"I don't know what he did. I have the baby to worry about."

"He should do what I do," McNiff said. "I go to church and take the pledge. You know what my pledge is now? That I'll only drink six Manhattans on the last day of every month. That's the only time I drink."

"I'm afraid sometimes Owney drinks that much by noon."

She left, and outside the apartment house she glanced across the street at the courthouse and thought with a dead feeling of the one morning she had been there. Then as she started up the street, a young woman walked out of the doorway marked by scarred lettering for the Legal Aid Society. She wore a black jacket over a plaid dress and carried a slim attaché case. Her eyes smiled at somebody she knew and then she took long, quick steps across the street toward the courthouse. Healthy, confident, with her brown hair shaking as she walked.

As she walked past the Pastrami King restaurant, a place with steamed windows and a narrow doorway leading directly into the crowd waiting at the counter section of the restaurant, there were a half dozen young blacks wearing huge unlaced white and blue sneakers and black sunglasses crowded at the doorway and a small white man in an apron decorated with mustard blocking their way.

"I said *ve* got no room," he said.

"Sure you do," one of the kids said.

"Ve got no room for you, *dot's* for sure."

"What you mean?"

"You coming in here just to steal something."

"We comin' from the court."

"Dot's why you're in court. From stealing."

The man shut the door on the blacks, one of whom pounded the glass with a large hand. Dolores looked across the street at the young woman lawyer, who by now was on the sidewalk walking briskly toward the entrance. A crummy world she has, Dolores thought. Then she shrugged. No, it isn't. It's life. She thought of one of these Irish lines that she had to listen to for so much of her life. Parnell passing Irish on the roadside who called out, "Ireland shall be free." And Parnell said to them, "And you will still break stones." Life. Anything is acceptable as long as you're free. Her shoulders began to move and her walk quickened as she realized she was free of alcohol, which weighs so much.

Stepping out of a coffee shop was a chubby man in a three-piece suit who kept one hand clamped onto his head, assisting his toupee in the breeze. With him was a white guy of about nineteen, who had acne, wore a leather jacket, and chewed gum as he talked. He waved a hand angrily at the courthouse across the street.

"I fuck them where they breathe," he said.

"You may not believe this," the chubby man said, "but I, too, like to fuck women. I'm not young and handsome like you. That's why I need money when I go out with girls. This explains to you why I need a retainer if I am to keep you out of jail."

She smiled—twice in a day, she reminded herself—and walked to Union Turnpike, where, by the drugstore, she got the bus down to Myrtle Avenue. The bus was crowded with airline workers going to Kennedy Airport and she had to stand. Then she had a long wait for the bus going up through Forest Park and into Glendale and Ridgewood. As she waited, she saw Owney's money sticking wet to the bar. Her foot scuffed the bus stop dirt. She had no car.

On the bus to Glendale, she opened the pamphlet that McNiff, the lawyer, had given her. Her eyes ran over the pages and stopped at a sentence that said, "In church law, and many people are mistaken about this, an annulment does *not* mean that children born out of the union are illegitimate."

She closed the pamphlet in anger. They decree on a piece of paper whether a child who comes out of my body is a real child or something to whisper about?

She still had this on her mind the next morning, when she came to the last stop of the Astoria el, which forms a roof over a shopping street that runs out from under the el and ends at a street of attached brick houses beyond Ditmars Boulevard. Dolores walked down the el steps, saw that she had a half-hour, and went into a diner for coffee.

In the next booth there were two women whose shopping baskets blocked the aisle. One, wearing sunglasses, said: "Two in the afternoon, he takes out the garbage."

The other, wearing a black raincoat, said: "And?"

"Comes back three in the morning," the woman wearing sunglasses said.

"Doesn't say where he went?"

"Nope."

"Three kids, leaves her sitting there."

"You'd think he'd try to help," the one in the black raincoat said.

"Last week, he's gone two days. For two days. My daughter says to me, 'He's going through some sort of nervous breakdown.' I asked her, 'Who told you that?' My daughter says, 'I know.' I told her, 'I sure know what part of him is nervous. And for his sake, I hope it doesn't have a breakdown.' "

Sitting in the next booth with her coffee, Dolores felt that she was listening to her own life being discussed. Listening to people speak in the open imparted a little strength to her. She left the diner and walked past the attached houses of Ditmars Boulevard until she came to Crescent Street, where there was a Greek saloon on one corner and a pizza stand on the other. She turned right and walked along a schoolyard fence. Across the street there was a row of gloomy yellow-brick apartment houses with fire escapes running down the front.

She went through a gate in the schoolyard and went past parked cars. There were double metal doors in one wing of the school building, obviously a Catholic high school, one whose name Dolores did not know. A sign on the door said, THE TRIBUNAL. DIOCESE OF BROOKLYN. The name and authority of the diocese are Brooklyn, but most of the Catholics, and most of the trouble in the diocese, are in Queens.

Originally, these marital boards were set up in Rome to keep the royal families of Europe in some sort of order so that lands owned by Catholic monks could be protected. Then, Henry VIII of England banished a wife, slaughtered another, and took England out of the Roman Church, thereby consigning untold millions of stiff English souls to Hell for denying the true religion. Rome now was left with rules written to keep kings in line and used mainly for normal Catholics who despised their spouses. In a new country, the United States, the decisions varied so much from diocese to diocese that it was obvious that some marital tribunals were being treated as profit centers and that others were bound by the narrowest use of Jansenism that Irish immigrants could inflict. Divorce was illegal in the Church: "Let no man put asunder." Only annulments could be granted. In the New York archdiocese, where the straight, cranky Irish ruled from behind rich lace curtains in the Cardinal's residence on Madison Avenue, annulments were rare, even for the supposedly powerful.

Then in Rome, the rules were suddenly opened by a deceptive man who became Pope before revealing to people that he could think. There now was less room for old hypocrisies, for there were more people, people without titles or special money, and the Brooklyn diocese's tribunal became open to all. People were encouraged to question, and even argue. At the same time, someone like Dolores Morrison, entering the unpretentious school hallway on this day, walked with the obedience to settled authority that had been placed in her during her first years in school. In grammar school, she never had worn a school uniform that didn't touch the floor when she knelt to pray. Then once, when she arrived at school with teased hair, she was made to put her head under the faucet to bring the hair down and thus satisfy the nun.

As she became older, she began to question authority. And before she entered the building on this day she was still smoldering from reading the pamphlet the day before. Nevertheless, she was a member of a religion that many people proclaim they have left, but who trust no other form for the major ceremonies of life. In moments of calamity, a sudden, searing chest pain, they reach for priest's hand before doctor's.

The sign on the wall said the tribunal was on the third floor. Dolores took the elevator up. A woman sat in a reception booth and directed Dolores into a small office along a hallway of similar small offices. A priest in his mid-forties, with black hair and a grave face suddenly changed with a pleasant smile, walked in, introduced himself, and sat at a desk.

"Before we do anything more, we recommend that you go home and prepare a written statement about your marriage," the priest said. "You write this at your own pace. You tell us essentially why the marriage is breaking up, or why you think it is."

"First, I didn't get your name," Dolores said.

"Father Resch."

"How do you do. I'm Dolores Morrison."

"Mrs. Morrison, I'll apologize for moving so rapidly, but I felt that before I even got into asking for your name, we would give you the opportunity to read something about this serious topic. Then if you returned, we could start into backgrounds."

"I already read your booklet."

"Then you know."

"I don't know. The pamphlet uses the word *illegitimate* in talking about a child. Do you still actually believe in the use of such words?"

The priest cocked his head. "It's a word used to describe a situation."

"You give a baby a bad name? For life?"

He spread his hands. "I, ah, don't write these pamphlets. Perhaps you have a point."

"I see. Now about this written statement. After I write it and turn it in, who reads it?"

"We do."

"Priests?"

"Of course. Priests from this office."

"All men?"

"They would have to be."

"That means none of them ever were married."

"That's right."

The priest was answering these questions with the confidence instilled in him by two thousand years of his church. Dolores, who had arrived in the building with the willingness to obey, found herself suddenly tense. Maybe it was the absence of cigarettes. Or maybe the two women talking in the diner had something to do with it.

"How would they know what I'm talking about?" Dolores asked.

"I think you're underrating the ability and training of people," the priest said.

"But it's still all men?"

"Yes. Certainly you don't think that a priest trained in this religion can't be compassionate and objective?"

"But you're all men. Men who never got a divorce or an annulment. A man never condemns another man. Who's going to condemn a man in here when it's all men making the decisions?"

"We look to condemn nobody."

"It's still men judging something between a man and a woman."

"We have nuns advising us."

"Maybe one of the nuns should be a priest."

The priest smiled and didn't answer.

"The booklet says that you give an annulment on psychological grounds," Dolores said.

The priest said, "We do go into the psychological factors present in both parties at the time of the marriage. We want to see if they were so dazzled that they couldn't possibly have been aware of what they were doing."

"In other words, if I get an annulment it means that it's the same as saying that the marriage never took place."

"Something approximating that."

"I'm not going to say it never happened. I'm not sorry that I got married. I don't want to deny it now."

The priest spread his hands.

"We can recommend counselors," he said.

"Some more men?" she said.

She decided it was time to leave.

"Thank you," she said. "If it's all the same with you, I think I'll come back here when you have a woman at the desk. Or maybe a married man. I think that would be nice. It also would make about half the population trust you a little more. Thank you very much."

She left with a smile and took the elevator downstairs and walked out of the school building and down the streets of attached houses to the el. The idea of a long ride on a train, and then a bus, over to Glendale, made her feel tired. She looked at a cab parked in front of the diner and started walking toward it. She stopped and looked into her purse. She had eleven dollars. She remembered her husband saying grandly that he was going to buy her a car. The trouble with him, she thought, was that he threw some of his money on the kitchen table and he spread the rest on the bar and hoped somewhere, between kitchen Formica and saloon wood, a few of the bills would take hold and grow like a bush. In her mind now she could see Owney's money on the bar, spread out like playing cards, wet, a hand with honest dirt on it moving the money around. Now a barmaid's red fingernails picked at the money and made it disappear. As Dolores walked up the el steps, she could hear saloon voices, mostly mumbles, once in a while a loud laugh at something stupid. And then somebody proclaiming, "I work for my money." Works for it and then takes it out of his family's mouth, she thought.

The afternoon light fell on her engagement ring. She began to think of the night Owney had given it to her. They were at Pep McGuire's on Queens Boulevard at a table in the back that had a candle on it and she got up and ran to the ladies' room and grabbed her hand to look at the ring. Back at the table, she and Owney sat and held hands and looked at the ring in the candlelight. He moved his glass out of the way. He knew how to make room for something pleasant, she thought. After that, he seemed to keep the glass where it was and block anything decent from reaching him.

She sat on the train and looked at the ring on the ride to Queens Plaza. She got off the train, went downstairs to the subway, and took the E train to 169th Street in Jamaica.

The man on line in front of her at the Provident Loan Office unzipped a cloth bag and took out a shotgun. "How much do I get?" he asked.

The man behind the window shook his head. "We don't take them anymore."

"All I need is fifty," the man with the shotgun said.

"We have enough trouble with guns without giving loans on them," the man behind the window said.

Dolores stepped up and shoved the ring under the glass partition.

"How much you want on this?" the man said.

"Whatever I can get," she said.

He walked away from the window with the ring. She stood at the counter and stared at the floor. She hoped she would not have to answer many personal questions.

The man came back and said, "I can give you six hundred."

She nodded.

"For how long?" he asked.

"For my life this far," she said.

He smiled and began making out the ticket. Behind her on the line now were two women. I yelled at the priest, she thought, then we all come here and wait for a man to give us money, even on a loan.

"All right," the man behind the window said. He handed her a ticket, which she signed, and then the six hundred. That's my present to myself, Dolores thought. A nice cheap car.

"Merry Christmas," she told the man. She put the money into her purse and went outside to look for a cab.

When he reached her the first time, at four in the afternoon, he thought that a visit to her mother merely had wound up as an overnight stay.

"I tried calling you this morning, but the phone was off the hook. I guess the baby knocked it off."

"I took the phone off," Dolores said.

"Oh, your mother wanted to sleep."

"No, I did."

"All right. What are you doing now?"

"I'm at my mother's."

"Why are you still there?"

"That's interesting that you should ask. You never wondered where I was before this."

"You were always home."

"How would you know? You never were there."

"Well, I'm coming home right now."

"Good for you. Bye."

Her mother, standing at the kitchen sink, was alarmed by the laconic conversation, which raised in her the terrifying notion that somewhere there actually might be the prospect of permanence.

"You two can't talk?"

"I just can't stand it anymore."

"Jesus, Mary, and Joseph, what if nobody wanted to carry their Cross?" She dried the last knife and with nothing else left, but her hands still in motion, she seemed tempted to dry the dust in the air.

The next morning, for the first time in many years, the mother did not get out of bed. "I'm all right," she said.

"She don't have to go to the doctor," Aunt Grace said. "It's just we never had anything like this in the family before."

"Where do you think I came from?" Dolores said.

"That's what I'm worried about," her mother said.

Then one morning, with a cold rain rattling on the windows, Dolores was changing from her robe to clothes for the day when the baby crawled across the hallway and, in Aunt Grace's kitchen, began tugging on the garbage can. Dolores walked out of her room. She found her mother and aunt sitting with both hands on the coffee cups.

"She'll spill everything!"

Dolores trotted across the hall, picked up the baby, and brought her back to the playpen, which was in the dining room. The tops of the tables were bare and even pictures on the wall several feet higher than the baby's head had been removed. Upon finding herself being dropped into confinement, the baby sent a wail throughout the apartment. She did not have to see the two women in the kitchen across the hall to know that their backs stiffened to the sound of crying. Dolores warmed a bottle, handed it down to the baby, and then put on her raincoat.

Seeing Dolores dressed this way, the mother gasped. "You leave me with the baby crying?"

"I'm going to the store."

"What for?"

"The butcher's."

"For what?"

"I won't tell you what I'm going to get. I'll surprise you."

The mother answered with a grunt. When Dolores returned with a half dozen loin lamb chops, her mother, unwrapping them, suddenly tried to send her voice through the ceiling. "You give a beggar a horse and they'll ride straight to Hell."

"Much too dear," Aunt Grace said.

"You're cheaper off with nice shoulder lamb chops like I told you."

"You never told me anything, Ma."

"I have to tell you something you should know?"

Her mother now spoke rapidly under her breath, which caused Dolores to say, "Will you stop? I paid for it."

"Next time you won't have money and you'll be spending mine."

That morning was proof, Dolores told herself, that she had given no thought, even subconsciously, to her returning home; that she simply had been driven out of living with Owney by his assaults on her wounded pride, for even the most fleeting consideration of this move would have caused her to sense the conflict that arises the moment anybody tries to reopen a nest. She walked through the apartment and in each room she could feel the presence of the baby. Give it just a little time, she thought, and her mother would think the baby was alongside wherever she went.

Suddenly, now that she had stepped out of a life she never had considered before and was examining each part in such detail, she found that the day had no voice; that when she went downstairs on the pretext of looking for mail, or for the newspaper, or for a neighbor, she found only silent air on an empty street and her muscle control dissolved in the blankness of the day outside the door. She got out on the stoop and then could move no more. No wonder, she thought, that they're all half dead around here. The trip to work, and the boredom and nervousness of jobs, kills men, she thought, while the silence everybody longs for descends on women who claim they revel in days that say nothing to them and have the energy drained from them, and they sit through silent days that destroy them far more than any series of subway trips in trains crowded with living people.

As Dolores sat out on the stoop and looked out at the soundless street, the wind tried to lift the lids of the garbage cans; let them go, it wouldn't even matter, Dolores thought, for the covers were made of green plastic. She shivered, not in the wind, but in realization of the days she had spent in this same kind of silence while waiting for Owney. A disease she couldn't see.

Finally, there was a small noise that came through the air. Nancy Lucarella's mother, head wrapped in a kerchief, tubby body inside a blue down coat, made her way down the street from the avenue, pushing a shopping basket.

"Half a day for me today," she said. "That's so I could shop and then come home and do floors."

"Where's Nancy?"

"Inside working, I think."

"Tell her I'll come over tomorrow."

The woman nodded and then went inside and the street turned silent again, with the row houses watching with polished eyes. Dolores was immobile in the silence. She turned and went back upstairs, where her mother and Aunt Grace and another woman from the house were at the kitchen table and as Dolores walked past she heard her mother reading the *Long Island Press* aloud to them.

"Oh, boy, look at this, Gracie, you're so right. Gang got on the subway in Brooklyn, mugged some old lady almost dead."

"Don't tell me about my subway trains," Aunt Grace said. "Where was it?"

"Myrtle-Willoughby stop. The GG train."

"That's the one they want to run through here. Can you imagine that?"

"Savages got on after school and the poor woman tried to hold on to her purse. They pulled her arm, dislocated her shoulder. A seventy-five-year-old woman."

The mother glanced up at Dolores. "What's on the agenda for today?"

"I'm thinking," Dolores said.

"Think a little faster," her mother said. Her mother and her aunt half laughed, but Dolores did not. That night, her cousin Virginia sat and watched television with her and Dolores barely heard what Virginia was saying.

In the middle of the following morning, she put her hands over her ears and ran across the empty street and into Nancy Lucarella's house. Dolores found her in the same black T-shirt, with a cigarette and Tab, and one arm on a stack of paper.

"The galley proofs for my book," she said. "You saw them when they were only typed pages. Remember?"

"That was so long ago," Dolores said. "Three years, no, four years easy."

"It takes time," Nancy said. "They don't give in so easy to our kind."

"When does the book come out?"

"Soon. You see the proofs."

"That's great. I asked so many times."

"It took so much time."

"It must be hard. I wanted to come over a hundred times. Your mother always said you were tied up."

"I sit here working every day."

"Am I disturbing you now?"

"No."

"Then let me get a Tab."

Nancy waved to the refrigerator. Dolores took one out and then sat down.

"So let me see what a galley proof looks like."

Nancy's arm suddenly tightened. "No. I don't let anybody see anything until it's all done."

"Fine."

"It's very hard when they don't want you to make it."

"Well, it better not be. Because I'm about to start out. I'm not living home with Owney now, you know."

"Everybody is against me. People like us, we're not supposed to get anywhere. Look at you, what do you do, you live in Glendale."

"I just told you, I'm going to have to start on something."

"So you have a baby and you live in Glendale. What do your friends do?"

"They're all over the place. My girlfriend Margo works as a legal secretary. Debbie Corkery works as a nurse. Couple of them got married, moved away. I don't know. They do what you do."

"When you come from Glendale," Nancy said.

The two became silent. Then Dolores said, "I'm thinking of doing something pretty good."

"You'll never make it," Nancy said.

"How can you say that when you don't even know what I'm going to do?"

"Because they stop everybody from Glendale. They stopped me from getting my mother's money."

Dolores laughed. "What money? Her sixty-dollar paycheck?"

"No. From my real mother. Marilyn Monroe was my mother."

Dolores laughed and the laugh stopped as she saw Nancy's eyes, which seemed to reflect a fever.

"Milton Green knows about it. He was the photographer who took all my mother's pictures. His lawyer told me to get a lawyer and sue the surrogate's court to get my money from my mother."

"Your mother is inside doing the rug," Dolores said.

"She's not my mother. She's nobody. My mother is dead and I want my money. Do you know where I can get a lawyer?"

"I thought you told me this Milton Green spoke to you."

"He didn't speak to me. I told you his lawyer spoke to me."

"Oh."

Hearing a noise in the living room, Nancy turned her head and glared. "That's not my mother inside. She's nothing."

"Well," Dolores said, smiling and getting up, "I think I better go back to my baby."

Nancy's fingers played with the top sheet of the stack of paper. "I don't care about this book. Why don't they just give me what's mine from my mother?"

Dolores didn't answer and as she left, she started toward Mrs. Lucarella, but the mother stood in the living room with her vacuum cleaner and a frightened look and she held a finger to her lips. Dolores nodded and left.

She sat alone and watched the baby, who by now was sleeping, watched the small back rise and fall and the hand clench and unclench, and she began to think of Owney, and immediately she felt her insides deaden, and so she thought about her clothes or the cold outside or the beach in the summer, and then she thought of Owney again. This time she saw him with those bright amused eyes and this disdain on his face for something that was going on that he didn't like. She saw him walking with that assurance pouring out of his body. Then it all became clouded in her mind and through the vapor she saw only a bar covered with old glasses. She shook her head and sat alone and thought of Nancy Lucarella. Suddenly, the unknown troubled Dolores.

That night he called—his voice full of cheer and command, and in her mind she could see him, alert and assured—and he said, "I'm coming over to get you." Then he added, "I got a bullshit call from that lawyer."

"Well," she said.

"I've had enough of this," he said.

She didn't answer.

"If you don't come home, I won't give you a dollar. I work too hard for my money to be giving it to somebody isn't even here."

"Oh," Dolores said, everything in her suddenly rising, "I was under the impression that it was your child, too."

"I don't pay anything for anybody not here."

"I think you better," Dolores said.

His voice turned into a squall and she hung up in the middle of it.

The next night, at six o'clock, Dolores went downstairs and waited for her cousin Virginia to come home from work.

"Come for a walk with me," Dolores said.

"Where are we going?"

"I don't know. Couple of places."

"I don't want to go for too long. I got to eat dinner. Then I got to iron my dress for tomorrow."

"Come with me, maybe we'll find something interesting," Dolores said.

"Find guys?" Virginia said.

"Why not?"

Virginia sucked in her breath. "Why, you're a tramp!"

"Sure, I am," Dolores said.

"We're not going to find guys anywhere around here," Virginia said.

"I can," Dolores said.

"You could find a guy around here?"

"Absolutely. Two of them."

"You're a liar."

"Then go ahead into the house. I'll go myself."

"No, you won't. Let me run in and tell them I'm going with you."

"I have to stop two places. It'll only take forty-five minutes."

"Then you're not looking for guys?" Virginia said.

"If we see one, we'll both grab him for you," Dolores said. "I don't think I want to see another man for fifty years."

"Be right back," Virginia said.

The woman who lived next door, Mrs. Kramer, now came out on the sidewalk, as she always did at this hour. "Getting my nice breath of fresh air," she said, and Dolores answered, as always, "Are you? That's nice," and Mrs. Kramer immediately said, "I wish my poor Al could be taking a breath with me." And Dolores smiled. Mrs. Kramer's husband, Al, had been dead for four years and the widow extolled him on the sidewalk and prayed for him openly in church and both she and everybody else regarded him as the finest husband a woman could ever have. Her husband's most memorable day in his many years on the street came one Saturday morning, with people on the sidewalk or peering out their polished windows. Kramer, who retired from his job as a soda truck driver, met the mailman on the front stoop, went through his mail, ripped open one envelope, and then came down from the stoop and stood looking up at his wife, who was at the window on the third floor. "My Medicare card just came," Kramer called up. Mrs. Kramer looked down at him with that tight little smile that she wore, along with her car coat. "You want to see what I think of my Medicare card?" He pushed the card into his mouth, swallowed it, then called up to the wife with her nice tight smile, "There you go! Now if I get sick, you got nothing between you and the street. I hope I'm in the hospital someplace and they pull the couch from under you to pay for the bill." When he died this was forgotten; in Glendale, once a widow, always a worshiper. Anything to disturb this memory of Kramer, a sneer, smile, or sarcastic aside, would disturb the illusion in which Mrs. Kramer and all the others on the block with departed husbands lived. Dolores, therefore, knew that she disturbed her mother's house by placing two more people under the roof and by disturbing the illusion that if it were not for death, marriage would consist of long hours of love.

The illusion got touched on me, too, Dolores told herself.

When Virginia returned, Dolores walked with her up to Myrtle Avenue, which on the winter night had little clusters of people getting off buses and into the lights of small stores and then long stretches of desolate cement.

"Do you know what you're going to do?" Virginia said.

"I'm starting to."

"What kind of a job are you looking for?"

Dolores didn't answer.

"My mother told me to look around in my place. I went to the girl I know in personnel and she said if you could come in and fill out an application, then she'd start looking through what they need. She's only an assistant but she can go through the files and at least find out what they need."

Dolores still didn't answer. She stopped at a phone booth and dialed her old number and held her breath. Five rings and no Owney. She hung up, and then became apprehensive as she saw the sign for Gibby's saloon coming at them, two corners away. When they got close to Gibby's, Dolores told Virginia, "You walk up and see if he's in there."

"Who?"

Dolores scowled at her. "Who would I be trying to duck?"

"Is this what you got me out for?" Virginia said.

"Never," Dolores said. "Just go look in the window."

When Virginia shook her head, Dolores walked boldly up to the window and looked in at the splendid scene. "There you go," she said to Virginia. "All there for you."

The owner, Gibby, resplendent in his crew cut and five hundred forty pounds, sat on a stool on the customer's side of the bar and looked sleepily at television. He was the only person in the place. As it was time for the evening news, he of course had on Lucille Ball in a rerun. It was in this same position, a year before, that Gibby was the object of a holdup. When the gunman asked for money, Gibby never turned his head from Lucille Ball. He said out of the side of his mouth, "Fuck you." The gunman said that he truly would blow Gibby away and said so with such fervor that Gibby deigned to turn his head and look at the gunman. He sneered at the gunman. "Go ahead and fucking shoot!" Then he turned away. The gunman promptly shot him in the face. The terrified barmaid screamed, "They shot my Gibby!" Gibby sat motionless on his stool. Then in the mirror he saw blood pouring down his neck. "This is good-bye, Lisa." His huge head smacked the bar. Police arrived to Lisa's screams—"He's dead!"—but upon examining Gibby, they found him breathing like a horse. Paramedics discovered a hole in the outermost part of Gibby's jowl, many inches of white fat separating the hole from the main frame of Gibby's face. Police found the .45 slug deep in the bar. Now, looking at him through the window, and seeing that the rest of the place was empty, Virginia said, "How would you like to sit there, wait to meet somebody?"

Dolores shuddered.

"I been all over. In bars, outside of bars. I never meet anybody. Do you know my girlfriend Alice Lutzen? She went to Washington, she told me it was worse than here. She met a guard at the Smithsonian building who was married. How do you like that? How do you like going all the way to Washington to chat with a married guy?"

"I don't."

"Besides, I can't go anyplace. I'm in love."

"Then what are you doing out with me? Who are you in love with?"

"The guy in work I told you about."

"The one who was supposed to take you to lunch at the Chinese restaurant?"

"I'm in love with him."

"Are you?"

"I must be. I go all the way home on the LL line thinking of him."

"Do you talk to him at work?"

"He asked me how I was the other day."

"That sounds like real love," Dolores said. "If you keep it that way you can be in love with him forever. Just don't talk much."

"That's what you think?"

"Yep."

"That means you're not going back with Owney right away?"

Dolores was looking toward the corner of 74th Street and did not answer.

"You going to get a job then?"

When Dolores kept walking, Virginia said, "Geez, you are stubborn. You got them crazy home, you're so stubborn."

When they came to the corner of 74th Street, Dolores said, "Just stay out on the sidewalk and if he happens to drive up, just let me know."

"Is he going to kill us?"

"He said he would. He said he has a machine gun left over from

Vietnam and that he'll shoot me and anybody I'm with. Now just shut up and make sure he doesn't come. I don't particularly want to talk to him. It'll get us nowhere."

"That means you're not going back?"

"I don't know what it means. I'm sure of one thing. I'm never going to be put in this position again."

"What?"

"Sneaking like this," Dolores said. They were at the house now and Dolores walked up to the front door and fitted the keys and opened it. As Virginia stood at the curb, Dolores bent down and picked up the mail on the vestibule floor, pecked through the junk mail and took out one brown window envelope that appeared to be a government check, and then her face became disappointed. "Magazines," she said. Listlessly, she went through the rest of the letters and then brightened as she found another brown envelope, this one containing Owney's check, which she put in her pocket.

"What do you do with that?" Virginia asked, and when Dolores didn't answer, Virginia said, "You don't keep his check, do you?" Dolores's answer was to keep walking. Virginia looked back at the house. "What if he's inside and he comes running out?"

"He never was there when I was home waiting," Dolores said. "What in the world would he be there for now?"

When they got to 68th Street, there was a harsh light coming from an industrial bulb that was connected by an extension cord to the inside of a house. A man in coveralls stood at the curb and looked at two cars, both of which were jacked up. On the sidewalk was a black phone. The cord ran up the stoop and through the mail slot and into the house.

"What's your best buy, Alex?" Dolores said to him.

He pointed to a two-door red Ford. The car was dented evenly on both sides. He was about to say something, but then the phone at his feet rang and he picked it up.

"Alex's Garage," he called out.

Dolores walked around the red Ford and then looked inside it. When Alex hung up, she asked him how much and when he said four hundred dollars, she nodded.

"All right," she said. Then she said to Virginia, "We'll go riding around looking for fellas."

"Where?" Virginia said.

"Staten Island. They got big strong Italian guys."

"How many?" Virginia said.

"Thousands of them."

Hearing Virginia blurt out the news of the car purchase at home, Dolores's mother sniffed. "A nice new bus to ride on is good enough for me."

The next day, Dolores dressed and the mother looked at her in alarm. "You going for how long?" and Dolores answered, "I have something I absolutely have to do."

"I was going to shop by Alexander's," her mother said. "I got to get some clothes as long as Gracie and I aren't going to Boynton Beach. I got to get good warm clothes."

"I could meet you there and drive you home," Dolores said.

"You don't have to. A nice new bus ride is good enough for me."

"I might need some clothes too. I'm going to be starting something."

The mother immediately brightened, for she interpreted this as meaning that Dolores was about to get a job. The mother said that Aunt Grace would watch the baby, in fact would be delighted to. She made a date to meet Dolores at two-thirty.

Later, seagulls squealed in the wet afternoon air, glided under a locust tree, whose bare black branches were inhospitable to webbed feet, and landed on a low cement wall. The seagulls represented nature on a school campus whose scenery consists of parking lots. The school, Queens College, rising from the banks of the Long Island Expressway, has a group of two-story buildings with red tile roofs that sit around a square of scarred grass. Once, they served as a detention center for Queens bad boys. Climbing into the dull sky behind them are buildings designed by architects with honorable intentions but hands of palsy. The auditorium, named after a dead Queens politician, Colden, is windowless in honor of the secrecy in which he lived and, probably, the bank vaults he frequented. The other feature is a gymnasium named after another dead politician, Fitzgerald, who was gifted with fast and extremely sure hands.

Dolores walked out of the science building, also windowless, and stuffed her schedule into her purse alongside the envelope bulging with legal papers that the lawyer McNiff had sent to her two weeks earlier. Driving on the expressway service road, she stopped at a candy store and went in to make a call.

Immediately over the phone came the voice of her aunt Grace. "Jesus, Mary, and Joseph! What's the matter?"

"Nothing."

"Oh, I thought something was the matter."

"Just because I call?"

"You could get mugged by one of these colored guys."

"My mother left?" Dolores said.

"She went by Alexander's. You're not going to meet her? She's waiting there for you!"

"I'm on my way there. I just wanted to make sure."

Some minutes later, Dolores found her mother standing at the front entrance to Alexander's, another windowless brick building, this one growing out of Queens Boulevard and extending for a full block. Her mother was on the sidewalk with her arms folded across her chest, pretending to be hugging herself in the cold, but as it wasn't that cold at all, Dolores knew that the arms were part of the defensive hand placement of the Queens woman. Stationed on alien sidewalk, unsure of who was in charge, she hugged herself in fear of being a trespasser.

"You got a nice job?" she said.

"Not today."

"Well, you went for a nice job, didn't you?"

"No."

"What did you do all day then?"

"I was over at school."

She was unprepared for an attack from the sky by an enemy that dived so swiftly that she was able only to unfold her arms. As she walked with her daughter through the front doors, the mother, as a reflex, sniffed at the black security guard. "Talk about a fox in the chicken coop."

In the ladies' department, her mother fingered velour tops and picked out a green and a burgundy and held them out on their plastic hangers. Small plastic clothespins kept the shoulders neatly arranged on the hangers. Keeping her eyes on the blouses, she said to Dolores, "You're going to go to night school?" and Dolores said, "Day."

Her mother started to fit the blouses back on the rack. "Much too dear."

"Ma, they're twelve ninety-five."

"I'm cheaper off going to Ridgewood."

"For what? They don't have anything you could put on your back."

"These are too dear."

This time, Dolores sighed and this sound from someone else took the mother by surprise. She again held out the velour blouses and walked around a wall, on the other side of which was the dressing room. Dolores inspected the rack for a tan blouse, intending to take at least one more blouse back to her mother, and then there was a sound and her mother was back. "Nothing fit right." The plastic clothespins were in the same position on the velour tops.

Dolores, pretending not to notice, kept looking through a rack for clothes for herself.

"You didn't even ask me what I was taking in school," she said to her mother.

"What?"

"Organic chemistry."

"What do you take a thing like that for?"

"That's what you have to take if you think you want to be a doctor."

Dolores wouldn't look at her but she was sure her mother's mouth had dropped open.

"A doctor." Now when Dolores looked at her, she stood with her hand over her mouth as if the notion of any daughter of hers attempting such a thing, or even mentioning the word, would be offensive to someone. Her hand placement was as common to Queens women as a broom. At times when she was in close proximity to any authority, and that meant a male —the women of the Kearns family all blessed themselves before so much as taking up business with the man behind the dry cleaning counter— Dolores's mother kept her hand flat against her lips and the ear had to strain to hear. Realizing this, Dolores always spoke with her chin up, her shoulders square, and her hands either at her sides or out in front of her, gesturing boldly to indicate coherence.

"How long does this take?" her mother said.

"It takes."

Her mother looked across the racks of blouses and saw years that she couldn't understand starting to stretch far down to the end of the store and then, at the point where the ceiling and the walls and the racks and the floors all came together and turned watery, she saw these two doors, at this distance the size of windows, and she realized that there was no end to anything that she was saying in her mind, and as she heard a baby's cry, she became tense, for she considered this to be fooling with eternity.

"How long?" she said to Dolores.

"But then you'll have somebody in the house to take care of Aunt Grace."

The mother's eyes flickered. "You could learn how to take care of Aunt Grace's arthritis?"

"Why not?"

"How fast could you learn? Aunt Grace got it coming down from the bottom of her neck. It's into her whole shoulder already. Remember when it was only a little crick in her neck?"

"I sure do."

"You don't hurry, she'll have it all through her arm," her mother said.

"I'll do it as quick as it can be done," Dolores said.

"Will you be able to sell neck braces?"

"You prescribe them. You don't sell them."

"Aunt Grace says so many people need neck braces that a smart doctor selling them could get rich with that alone."

The mother suddenly brightened more. "We wouldn't have to call nobody, either."

"Of course not. You call me. I'm liable to be in the next room."

"Oh, that's all right. That's perfectly all right with your aunt Grace and I. You'll be there to take care of her."

"Absolutely."

"Jesus, Mary, and Joseph. Wait'll I tell her. And she's been sitting there worried about what you're going to do."

There was a clicking sound as her mother took the blouses back off the hanger.

"You better learn about prostrates, too. Your uncle Matty got terrible prostrate trouble. For such a young man."

She walked swiftly into the dressing room to try on the blouses.

11

SEATED IN THE BACK of the hall, Owney rocked on a gray metal folding chair and looked directly up at the basketball net. He could throw it right from the floor, he thought, except that he was directly under the net and he would have to loop it out. Tough shot from this low. Then he decided that he would gather himself for an instant and then go straight for a lay-up. For sure, he would be fouled in the act of shooting and the shot would drop in and the place would explode into cheers, which would grow only louder when he made the foul shot. He looked down from the net and up at the front of the hall, where a priest was running the Alcoholics Anonymous meeting. This was at St. Stanislaus Church way over in Ozone Park, and it was something new for the parish, which had run successful anti-crime meetings and drug education nights, but never had considered there was any great problem with alcohol, except the possible shortage of it at a major function. The priest was explaining to the crowded hall that the form of these meetings was for a person to stand up, give his first name, admit that he's an alcoholic, and say what's on his mind.

"I'm Father Joe and I'm an alcoholic," the priest said, rubbing his hands together, smiling, looking around at the crowd. "You're supposed to say, 'Hi, Father Joe!' Let me hear it now."

"Hi, Father Joe."

"Good, good." He patted the sides of the halo of white hair that provided a setting for his pink scalp. His eyebrows went up and with a pleasant motion, smiling and swaying back, he pointed at two women who sat in their coats at one end of a row. Neither woman moved.

"Ladies?"

One rose. Dark brown hair shot with gray was shaggy from being rubbed by her nervous hands. She wore round glasses that were perched on her nose. Seams ran out from under the glasses and down her hollow cheeks. She spoke so slowly that at first she seemed to be retarded.

"My name is Catherine and . . . ah . . . I'm an alcoholic."

"Hi, Catherine," the priest said jovially.

"Hi, Catherine," the audience called out.

Now the woman stood in the silence as the priest looked at her and made a circular motion with his hand to start her talking.

"I don't think I have much else to say just now."

"Fine!" the priest said. "And now . . ."

The second woman, much heavier, with her hair obviously dyed light brown, stood up with both hands holding the front of her maroon coat. One hand, in a fist, came to her mouth.

"My name is Dorothy, but I am certainly not an alcoholic. I came here with my sister simply to observe."

"Wonderful," the priest said.

"I want you to know I'm not an alcoholic."

"Fine."

"I don't think you believe me."

"Of course we do."

"Well, some of these people here are looking at me like I'm a common drunk."

"Please, ma'am."

"Please? This whole room thinks I'm a stumblebum."

"Now, I think you're a little edgy. Why don't you have a seat and be comfortable."

She sat down. The priest suddenly looked at Owney. Slowly, Owney got up and stood in the overhead lights and the silence and he called out, "I pass."

"Fine, glad to have you," the priest said. He pointed to a man in a blue rain jacket, who bounced up, picking up his head so that a double chin unfolded.

"I got a name. But, I mean, can I use another first name?"

"Sure you can," the priest said.

"Well, I don't want to lie, even at a thing like this, but you see I have a business here and I don't want it to get around that I'm some drunken slob."

"Of course," the priest said.

"You see, Father, I'm liable to lose all my business. Some rumcake staggering around their house liable to take a pass at the wife while he's supposed to be fixing the faucets."

"I understand," the priest said.

"Oh, that happens, Father, believe me. You get some drunken pig he sees a good-lookin' woman and he figures what the hell, and he reaches right out there and makes a grab. He thinks he's home. But he's right in some other guy's kitchen with a tool kit. The woman lets out a holler and what do you have now? You got a rape charge, that's what you got. Oh, they do that, Father. Here comes the police and they take you down the precinct and then right upstairs to the detectives. You bet detectives. You're in there on a rape charge, no patrolman handles you. No, sir. Right up to the detectives. Oh, yes, Father, that's what happens when you get some guy got his own business and he's nothing but a real, excuse me, ladies, but a real pissbum. Now let me tell you some——"

"Why don't you just give me any name you feel like?" the priest said.

"I'd like to finish," the man in the rain jacket said.

"You'll have plenty of time for that later," the priest said. "Now just give your name. Any name you feel comfortable with."

"It can't be the right name."

"Fine."

"All right. My name is Bob and I'm an alcoholic."

"Hi, Bob!"

"Hi," he answered. Written across the back of his jacket, bright in the ceiling lights, was "Eddie Mulqueen, Ozone Park Plumbers, 82–04 Liberty Avenue."

When another hand went up, Owney slid out of the chair and walked quietly to the double doors and was through them. "Bedbugs," he said to himself.

When he stopped by the cemetery house to see how his father was getting along, his mother sat with tea at the kitchen table. Tea like hell for me, Owney told himself. He opened a twelve-ounce can of beer and took a huge gulp of what felt like a cold brook.

"I thought you were stopping," his mother said.

"One beer?" He placed the can of beer atop his right hand and balanced it there. The hand was a statue and the can did not move.

"That still don't mean you can drink."

When he finished the beer, he threw the can away noisily and swaggered off to see the father.

Later, in bed in the darkness, he thought about the plumber at the meeting. Fucking molester. He wanted to go get another beer.

In the morning, at six-fifteen, Owney stood at the table in the hog house and poured evaporated milk into coffee with an easy hand. When he saw Navy, he held the coffee container straight out.

"Is this okay?" Owney said.

"Sure it is."

"I went to a meeting last night," Owney said.

"And you didn't call me?" Navy said.

"Did I need your permission?"

"No, I just usually go with a guy the first time. But that's all right. How did it go?"

"I guess all right. I just listened. They're not like me."

"They're not?"

"No. Weak guys. One guy was a molester. Weak. That's not me."

Navy spoke softly. "If I was ever in trouble, in the tunnel someplace, you'd be the guy that I'd pray would come for me. But we're talking about something that is a lot different."

"Don't worry about me," Owney said.

"Anything I can do?" Navy said.

"There is."

"What?"

"Give my wife a call."

"And tell her what?"

"Tell her I went to a meeting and that the thing is all over."

"No."

"What's this, 'No'?"

"What you really want is a note from a schoolteacher."

"You won't even talk to her?"

"I'd be delighted to talk to her. Not on the phone. I'll go with you and the two of us will talk to her face to face."

"Good."

"Except for one thing. You may not like what I tell her."

"Hey, Navy, I'm not some baby."

"I might perform a horrible act. I might tell her the truth."

Owney's laugh brought a smile from Navy, who said, "I'll tell you what I tell everybody," he said. "You've got to realize that just because you put the glass down once, that doesn't mean you can go home and start cuddling your wife like she's some little pet. I remember one time I stopped drinking and I sat home in one of my moods. I always thought of myself as a very important guy. She said to me, 'What's wrong?' I said, 'Nothing.' She said, 'Are you sure? You act like something's the matter.' I said to her, 'If you really loved me, then you'd know what's wrong with me.' I was sure that I was that important to her. When you stop drinking, you have to deal with this marvelous personality that started you drinking in the first place. You don't do that in one day."

"Then maybe I'll go to another meeting."

"That's good."

"What else do you want off me?"

"I want you to do what you want to do. Just as long as you don't hurt yourself."

"What's that supposed to mean?"

"That we ought to sit down, go to a couple of meetings together, slide into a nice routine."

"I got into this by myself. I'll get out by myself."

"I don't think you should be thinking of doing it alone."

"What am I, a fag? I can do anything by myself."

"This is different even from a war," Navy said. "Like I say, I wish I had your guts—"

"And I'm going to use them."

The footpaths running across Navy's face remained fixed and he looked at Owney the way fight trainers do at a young kid in the gym, arms draped over the ropes and faces showing nothing as they watch for the kid to let the left hand drop after a jab and leave an opening that, some night, will get his jaw broken. As Navy looked now, he saw a green fighter, and he knew that the opponent, alcohol, was out there somewhere, old and scarred and mean, spitting out water and waiting for the chance to come out into the middle of the ring and lure this kid into mixing it up.

"Why don't you give her a call, tell her to come back?"

Navy shook his head. "I hate to tell you what I'd tell her."

"Like what?"

"I'd tell her not to come back."

"What do you mean by that?"

"Owney, I only got one thing backing me up. That I tell the truth. I tell the truth to you, to your wife, and these days I even tell the truth to myself. So I'm not going to lie to you, to your wife, or to myself."

*   *   *

"I got to put more than one of these here, *mon,*" James said. James was on his belly, his back brushing against a rock ceiling that had too much white in it. Iron rings spaced closely together, standing on heavy girders that were sunk into the floor, were tight against the white rock. The iron ring James was on, however, was about a foot short of the ceiling. The space was packed with wood planks in order to keep constant pressure against the white rock, but water dripping out of the rock at this point had so soaked the wood planks that the walking boss, Delaney, inspecting the ceiling with a scaling hook, had decided that new wood was needed. After replacing the rotted plank, James thought he needed another. Owney, on the ladder, arms full of wood, pulled out a plank and held it up. James wriggled his body into the space at the top of the ring and he had his face down, looking at Owney, who held up the plank, and James reached for it and the rock gave a small scream. Owney dropped all the wood and he threw both hands at the rock ceiling, trying to keep millions of years and millions of tons from doing as it pleased, and he knew what it was but he still put both hands flat against the ceiling and then the rock flew open and here was the woman with the wind blowing her long skirt and her arms held out. As she moaned, Owney's arms suddenly were jammed into his chest and he lost footing and fell from the ladder. The rock ceiling fell and crushed James against the iron ring and then the iron ring put its dull red shoulder into the rock and held it. Owney fell feet first and dropped hard on his hands and knees and looked up in pain and then closed his eyes against the shower of blood that came as the rock squeezed every drop out of James's body. First, the blood poured, and then it turned into a steady drip. And then Owney was on his feet and he was back on the ladder, one hand out for James, but all Owney could see above him was white rock on bent red metal that dripped blood. He kept going for the ceiling and there were shouts everywhere and he was reaching for nothing and he felt a hand clamp on his right leg.

"That's it, lad," Delaney, on the ladder, said. Owney followed him down. "You'll be able to smell him a long time before you get to see what's left of him," Delaney said.

Owney walked. He walked with a limp and bleeding hands. He walked into the darkness and stumbled and cursed and kept walking and he wasn't sure of where he was going or how long it was taking him.

"Owney!"

He was standing in the lights by the lift to the surface. He closed his eyes and somebody played a hose on him to wash off the blood.

Down the hill from the job, in Brendan's, there were two old men who wore rain jackets and coughs. The bartender had the suggestion of white hair on scalp that was blood red from alcohol. Rose light from the juke box picked out crumpled cigarette packs, and the rest of the place was almost totally dark because of windows that had been bricked up by the owner to prevent sandhogs from throwing each other through the glass.

"Yes, sir," the bartender said.

Owney's throat was frozen and his eyes focused on nothing.

The bartender said, "Whenever."

Outside on Katonah Avenue, a woman walked along, her arms filled with packages from the supermarket, and seeing her through the door of the saloon, Owney had a gnawing feeling that was on the fringes of pain. He wanted to be with his wife and baby. The woman walked into the bar as Owney went to the wall phone. When Dolores answered the phone, Owney closed his eyes in relief.

"I'm not in work because something happened," he said.

"To you?"

"No."

"Then what is it?" The tone of his voice had her anxious.

"One of the guys."

"Tell me what happened."

"I just want to come home."

"Then go. Leave right now. What happened?"

"I just want to come home with you and Christine."

"Oh."

"Dolores, the ceiling came in on a guy."

"How bad?"

"You can't do worse, don't ask me. Just let me come home."

She said nothing.

"I haven't even had a glass of water. I'm just standing here at work. I don't know what to do. I don't want to be wandering around. I want to come home to you."

He was concentrating so deeply on the phone that he did not see the woman shopper step from the bar to the rose light of the juke box.

"Play E Seven," somebody shouted.

"No," she said, dropping a coin into the juke box, "I got my own nice numbers. There." She punched two numbers and then turned to go back to the bar.

"Owney?"

"Yeah, uh . . ."

He dropped the phone and his scraped hands reached for the side of the juke box, for anything, the reject button, the electric cord. And now out of the juke box there was a blast, a foot-stomping, shouting, *"We're off to Dublin in the green, in the green . . ."*

"Dolores?"

"Did you get papers from the lawyer?" she said, her voice low.

"Dolores."

"Sign them and send them in or we'll just go without you. Have fun at your wake. Bye."

O'Sullivan sat in the beginning of the chill evening and watched the people, all black, walk out of the subway and along the walkway into the housing projects that were a block deep. O'Sullivan really saw Joe DiMaggio, who had been right at this spot, maybe a yard or so away, but that could do, you could say right at this spot, O'Sullivan said to himself. DiMaggio was here before there was a housing project, when the place was the Polo Grounds and the Giants played the Yankees in a World Series. If they hadn't pitched me inside, I would have been in a World Series myself, O'Sullivan thought. Now he stared into the night and watched DiMaggio, who was waiting in center field. With two out in the ninth inning, there was a long fly to center and DiMaggio ran across the grass with his head and body like a statue. The real big guys don't waste motion, O'Sullivan thought. Running across the grass after a ball flying through the sky. Of course, DiMaggio reached up and caught it right at the foot of the steps leading to the clubhouse. And then he never missed a beat. He just flew up the flight of stairs with the back of his gray road uniform billowing in the breeze and he disappeared into the clubhouse. The game was over and DiMaggio was gone and he left the whole ballpark in silence. That's how you do it to them, baby, O'Sullivan told himself. Put them into shock.

O'Sullivan got off the bench and stood for a moment. "All right, let's go," he said to Old Jack.

Then they got in the car, and O'Sullivan patted the shining new baseball bat resting on the front seat. He felt better with the bat than he ever had with a gun, which he had used until 1955, when he shot a man in a hallway on West 55th Street for the carpenters' union. He was held without bail for nine months awaiting a trial that his lawyer kept postponing until the two witnesses against O'Sullivan, a janitor and a night watchman on Pier 86, disappeared while O'Sullivan sat in his cell. Sat with the fucking niggers jerking off in the cells on either side. Jerking off with so much noise that it sounded like they were trying to break through the walls. The day he walked out of the jailhouse, the old Tombs, he walked away with his neck held stiffly so he wouldn't have to look back at it. After that, he went to a baseball bat. The way he swung it, it did physical damage and spread all the fear he needed, while at the same time dissuading people from launching widespread homicide investigations, as they did over guns.

"I taped the handle for you," Junior said as he started the car.

"Do you know they don't use tape anymore?" O'Sullivan said.

"I never heard that," Old Jack said.

"Everybody in the major leagues wears gloves. Nobody tapes a bat handle anymore."

"Then you got the last taped bat in the whole country," the old man said.

"I might be the last man out in the street who uses a bat at all," O'Sullivan said. He peered down at the bat. Thirty-three ounces. Too light for a big guy like me, he thought. Then he decided that, no, that isn't right. Stan Musial used a thirty-two-ounce bat.

"Every time I come around here, I think of that rat kid," Old Jack said.

"That's personal," O'Sullivan said. "You do what you have to do with him. He don't live but ten blocks from you. I'm only thinking of business. We're supposed to get our end, every week from that job. They try to give me nothing. Morrison cries."

"He's stealing the money," Old Jack said.

"Of course. He must be taking four thousand dollars home, nobody knows about it. He says he couldn't come up with anything. They were screaming about ghosts. He had to put in full crews. He said. The fucking liar. I told you, Jack. I checked. They had full crews for a couple of weeks until everybody calmed down and then he started ghosts again. But he told me that the crews still was full."

"He thinks you wouldn't check?"

"He's a fuck."

As Junior drove toward the Bronx, Old Jack said to O'Sullivan, "I'd love to get that rat bastard kid of his right here tonight."

O'Sullivan held up a hand. "I told you, that's personal between you and him. You want him, he lives ten fucking blocks from you. I'm here on business. I'm going to pick on one of Morrison's silent partners and that's the end of this here particular job tonight."

"What time is it?" Owney said to Danny Murphy.

"Quarter to six."

"The fights start what time?"

"Seven-thirty."

"They got a bar there?"

"Big bar."

"Then I'm going there now."

"I'm having one more," Murphy said. When he opened his mouth to swallow, he showed missing teeth.

"You got your car," Owney said.

"Absolutely."

"Then I'll bring these to my father," Owney said, tapping the fight tickets in his shirt pocket, and he left the bar.

A couple of minutes after Owney's car pulled out, it was replaced by another, which shuddered to a stop a full three feet from the curb; parking was never Junior's strong suit.

One drink later, Danny Murphy walked to his car in the shadows of a side street. He unlocked the door and paid no attention to the footsteps coming along the sidewalk and out into the street after him.

O'Sullivan did not break stride. He walked up to Murphy and with the same motion brought the bat whizzing in the darkness and against the side of Murphy's head. Leave them in shock, baby, O'Sullivan told himself as he walked away.

When Owney arrived out in Queens, at Holy Child High, the school parking lot was filled and the streets facing the school were solid with cars. He parked a few blocks away. Bayside was a neighborhood of attached, two-family brick houses that ended at streets of old, expensive frame houses that sat under high, full trees. The Golden Gloves boxing show was being held in the gym, with the added feature of a bar one flight downstairs, which consisted of cafeteria tables tended by men from the Fathers' Club, who wore plaid wool shirts and white aprons. A couple of steps away was the entrance to the school locker room, which ordinarily was a sanctuary for lithe bright white Queens young men.

On this night, though, the locker room was being used for the Golden Gloves fighters, which created the sight of young black kids in mirror sunglasses and huge sneakers with the laces untied bouncing the length of a bar crowded by Bayside whites, bouncing along as if they belonged in the place, the more sensitive of them trying to show that they owned the place, causing the crowd in the bar, both Holy Child Fathers' Club bartenders in their white aprons and Bayside men drinking in basketball jackets with names of their parishes on the back, to shudder with their beer, jerk actually, as standing on a power line suddenly turned live.

Owney's father and Chris Doyle, from the job, were at the end of the bar along with Willie Clancy, Owney's cousin. Clancy had a good job with the Fire Department, driving a battalion chief. Owney always hoped that Clancy would have an accident, and the battalion chief emerge unscathed. As Owney approached them, he told himself not to talk, that he had been drinking too much, and so he went into his shirt pocket and took out the tickets and gave them to his father. A small bandage covered a butterfly stitch in the corner of Jimmy Morrison's right eye. It was the last of seventy stitches that had been put into the face, which now looked like a cracked windshield.

The father held a soft drink in his hand.

"Want one?" he said to Owney.

"Not one of those. I want a beer."

"Hey. We said we'd both lay off everything, even beer, until you got straightened out with her."

"I tried that."

"You called her?"

"Today."

"And it's no good?"

"No good."

"Then what am I doing with this in my hand?" the father said. "We went and stopped drinking and she still didn't care, did she? Well, that takes care of that. Hup! Give us a couple of beers."

They had the beer first and then Chris Doyle ordered shots with the next beer. Willie Clancy signaled that he wanted only beer. Now he looked at Owney haughtily and said, "Too much drinking for her, huh?"

"No," Owney said.

"Had to be," Clancy said.

"Never."

Clancy pointed to the shot glass. "You don't have the control."

"What do you mean?"

"One time you had the most control in the world. I'm telling you now, you got none. She might have seen you going to pieces on her."

Owney wanted to smack him in the face. Instead, teeth clenched, he said, "You don't know why she left, so why do you keep talking?"

"I can see why she left."

"Your ass," Owney said. "She left for another reason." Now his mind was as hot as his eyes and his only desire was to beat this Willie Clancy somehow.

"What are you talking about?" Owney's father said.

"She's got a personal problem with herself," Owney said. "She wouldn't sleep with me because of it."

"She told you that she wouldn't sleep with you?"

"Told me? She wouldn't come near the bed."

"So she's frigid," the father said.

"She wouldn't come near the bed," Owney said.

"Never happened before in the whole family," the father said.

The cousin ran a hand through his red hair as he thought. "We don't know that, account of there's things people don't talk about. Even in the family."

"She just got mad at me," Owney said.

"Over sex?" the cousin said.

"She sure did."

The father jammed a cigarette in his mouth. "We never had a woman leave the house."

"Didn't Uncle Richie bust up with Aunt Eileen?"

"That was him doing it," the father said. "I'm talking about the woman leaving. This is the first time I ever heard of the woman walking out. You expect that from a guy. The woman never should leave."

"She should be home in my house with my kid," Owney said.

"I thought she was a smart girl," Owney's father said.

"So did I," Owney said.

"She shows me no fucking sense at all," the father said.

The cousin, looking around, saw that they were being overheard by others. He put his head down and had Owney and his father lean over.

"I got to ask you one thing," the cousin said to Owney.

"What?"

"You been running around on her?"

The father's head went straight up. "That got nothin' to do with it!"

Owney turned in disgust from the question and held his hand out to the bartender.

"I got to have a beer to get over *that*."

"The woman's supposed to be home and that's all there is to it," his father said.

"She's supposed to be home in my house with my baby," Owney said.

"Absolutely," the father said.

"Now she's so smart, maybe she doesn't get me back so fast," Owney said.

"That's one way," his father said.

"She's not home in my house with my baby, then I don't go home to her," Owney said.

"Do her good to fucking wait for a while," the father said. He took a large swallow of beer and stared at the plastic glass, shook it as he thought, then drained the glass, put it down, and placed a hand on Owney's shoulder.

"As long as we're talking, we might as well go all the way."

Owney listened.

"I'm going to ask you one question and that's all."

Owney nodded.

"You're telling me she left you because you wanted her to sleep with you like a wife should."

"Yes."

"Now I got to ask you something and I want you to think before you answer."

"All right."

"Has she been seeing a lot of women?"

Owney frowned. "You mean are people telling her things?"

The father shook his head. "No, no, you don't listen to me. Has she been spending time maybe with one particular woman and now she don't want to go to bed with you?"

Owney slid his shoulder from under the father's hand. "That's nuts."

"I said I'd ask you once. Say no more about it."

"That's really demented," Owney said.

Suddenly in the doorway to the locker room was a small black man in his sixties who wore a red trainer's sweater. He had both hands up and was talking to somebody inside the room.

"Yab!" the trainer said, in a Puerto Rican accent.

A black fist covered with bandages came out of the locker room and slapped one of the trainer's hands.

"I say, 'Yab,' " the trainer said. "You didn't yab. You push. Snap the yab."

The fighter inside mumbled something, which caused the trainer to drop his hands in disgust and walk back into the room.

A priest, dark hair slicked straight back, stepped through the crowd and touched Owney.

"Excuse me. I know who you are. The lad from West Point said he'd certainly be honored to meet you."

"He's here already?" Owney's father said.

"Oh, the lad's in the first fight. He has to drive all the way back to the Point."

"Oh, boy, are we counting on him tonight," the father said.

Owney looked at the full beer in his hand.

"Go ahead, I'll be right in."

"Oh, no, you come now with us. He wants to meet you, not us," the father said. He took the beer from Owney and handed it to the bartender. "Here, hold this for him."

The priest led them down the hall to an office. The priest walked in first and immediately a big kid with light brown hair, wearing a black robe with gold trim, jumped up. A bandaged hand saluted Owney. Two West Point cadets, in white T-shirts and gray uniform pants, stood at attention and saluted.

"This is Cadet George Lenane," the priest said.

"Good luck to you," Owney said.

"I don't know if I can live up to you, a Medal of Honor, but I'll try," he said.

"Sure you can," Owney said.

"Whack the guy around like you're supposed to," the father said.

"Who are you in with?" Owney asked him.

"I believe his name is Winston Sheffield."

"Some big nigger," Owney's father said.

The priest shook his head. "We like to think we talk a little better than that. We also like to think that dignity and order will prevail out there tonight and set an example for our youth."

"Yeah, let 'em see a good West Point Irishman ready to put down his life for his country insteada wrecking it can punch out any nigger alive," Owney's cousin said.

The cadet smiled. "Oh, I don't know if it makes much difference what he is. Once you've run plays against Notre Dame, with those big black bears they had playing front four, then I don't think anything matters. If I could gain ground in a football game against Notre Dame, then I don't think a Golden Gloves bout is going to be too much for me."

"We gave you the only private place in the building for a dressing room," the priest said. "Now just win one for us."

The fighter smiled and one of the cadets stood behind him and kneaded the muscles in the back of his neck. Lenane rolled his head.

"Let's go, I want to see this one," Owney's father said. He and the cousin left and went to the staircase. "I'll be right up," Owney said. He wanted the beer he had left at the bar.

He had the plastic glass to his mouth and was swallowing hard when he saw Navy, eyebrows up, looking for somebody.

Owney brought the glass away from his mouth.

"You don't want me tonight."

Navy smiled. "I'm not bothering you. I was just looking for Danny Murphy. I owe him."

"I saw him six o'clock at Brendan's. I thought he was coming right here."

"If you see him, tell him I'm here and I got my money for him," Navy said.

"You're mad at me," Owney said.

This caused Navy to smile. Someday, he told himself, he was going to have a new conversation with a drinker. "I'm not allowed to get mad at anything. Because if I get mad at you, then I got to reach out for a drink. If I get mad at you, I kill myself."

"I got a little trouble at home, that's why I'm like this tonight," Owney said.

"Hey, you don't have to tell me anything. You mentioned it to me before, you know."

"When I get through tonight, I think I'm going to stop drinking for a while," Owney said.

"Good," Navy said. "If I can help you, just give me a wave."

"Don't worry, I'm going to stop by myself," Owney said.

"That's a little hard," Navy said.

"I got the guts to do anything," Owney said. "I'm tough Irish. I can do anything I put my mind on."

"Oh, I know the Irish are tough," Navy said.

"Bet on it," Owney said. "Bet on me being tough."

"Oh, I know that."

Owney glanced over Navy's shoulder as one of the cadets walked past. He carried a gleaming pail that contained a green water bottle with a fresh tape around the neck. Then came Lenane, the fighter, in the imposing black robe. The cadet behind him was massaging Lenane's shoulders. Lenane's eyes closed, and he rolled his head.

"Here we go," Owney said.

Lenane's eyes opened and he winked broadly at Owney. Then he went upstairs to the auditorium.

"See that?" Owney said. "That's tough Irish."

"Oh, I can see he's tough," Navy said. "Now let me get upstairs and watch him show it to me."

"What does he have to show?" Owney said. "You just saw for yourself."

"But I want to see the man fight."

"You couldn't see just standing there that he's tough?"

"Oh, sure. But let me see the man demonstrate it."

"You probably think I'm not tough," Owney said.

Navy laughed. "No, I think you're a pretty tough fella."

"You hang around me like I need a nurse," Owney said.

"Owney, I want to go upstairs. I don't want to hang around here. Let me go. In fact, I'm going right now."

Navy walked away. "I can do anything I want by myself," Owney said. "When you see him fight upstairs, think of me. He's a tough Irish and so am I."

Out of the room alongside the bar came the black trainer in the red sweater and behind him a big lazy-looking black in a cheap red bathrobe. On the back, a couple of letters were missing from his club name, "Brownsville Housing Tenant Patrol."

"What are you doing?" Owney said to the trainer.

"Walking my boy."

"Why don't you rub his neck muscles like they do for the other guy?"

"A good fighter don' need a rubdown, a bad fighter don' deserve one."

"This guy a good fighter?"

"Who know?" the trainer said, starting up the staircase.

Owney finished his drink and he was reaching out to put the glass down so he could go up to the Golden Gloves fight when at this moment his own fight began. The opponent was there, all right. A lot older than these Golden Gloves kids upstairs; a nose broken and bent, the front teeth long missing, the scar tissue over the eyes turning pasty in the fluorescent lights. Old soggy gloves beckoned. Owney was alone at the bar, with customers and bartenders gone up to the fight, and nobody saw or heard the punch that Owney took. He stumbled behind the bar and got a hand on a bottle of Fleischmann's and he was about to pour it into a glass and then he simply began to drink from the bottle, as if it were a soft drink.

Upstairs, there were a couple of great roars. Then a long wail. Suddenly out of the silence there came footsteps pounding down the stairs. The big black, his red robe over his arm, came jumping out of the staircase.

"Go get mah *pussy!*"

He went into the dressing room. The trainer, smiling, now appeared.

"I say yab, he say laf hook," the trainer said to himself. He shook his head. "He wins. Laf hook hurt. Wow!"

Now Owney heard somebody talking in the hall. "Watch yourself now," a young, clean-cut voice said. "Just a couple of more steps and we're all right."

Owney's eyes went over the top of the bottle he was drinking from. The tough Irish fighter, Lenane, with liberal support under each arm, still walked haltingly. His eyes, numbed by the left hook, looked at Owney, and Owney, the wires in the back of his eyes short-circuited by alcohol, looked at the cadet and neither of them saw each other.

Sharon picked up the glasses that Owney, his father, and three others had used for their last drink.

"Geez, they were mad," Chester Doolan from the Post Office said.

"So mad they went home so they could drink more beer and tell each other how mad they are."

"You think that's all?" Doolan said.

"No. Then they go to bed because they can't even walk."

"And this is the same guy did it to you?"

"Baseball bat. Same guy, same thing. Baseball bat."

"Do they know where he is?"

"They say they do. You know, you think about it. When it happened last time, his old man told me, Owney went flying over to the city with a gun, to that bar the guy hangs out in on Eleventh Avenue. He didn't want to know from nothing. Now, you seen him here tonight. He's mad enough to kill the guy but the guy has to be right here. Owney's drinking so much he can't even get over to the city to do to this guy what he should do."

Doolan reached for his rain jacket, which was hanging on a wall hook, and took out cigarettes. As he did this, straining to get the cigarettes without leaving the barstool, the handle of a small pistol showed from inside the back of his pants. Doolan, the night supervisor of the Post

Office substation down the avenue from the bar, was not required to be armed while supervising night mail, and had no means of obtaining a licensed gun. As Doolan imagined himself a stagecoach driver and thus entitled to wear a gun like a real man, he had purchased this weapon in Fort Lauderdale, in a shop that sold air conditioners, television sets, and handguns.

"Whatever," Sharon said, staring at the gun.

"What's that?" Doolan said.

"Nothing. I just said, 'Whatever.' That's the story of my life. Even the words I say don't mean nothing."

"Things are better than that," Doolan said.

Sharon sighed. "You know how bad it is? You know what I done last night? I hung around this place in Ozone Park until it closed and then I took a ride out to Long Island to buy beefsteak tomatoes. I drove all the way out to Orient Point and parked there on the road until the guy came out and opened his stand. It was so early he was sleepwalking. I told him I wanted beefsteak tomatoes. He said, 'You got to come back in about six months for them.' 'All right, give me the cauliflower and I'll come back someday for my beefsteak tomatoes.' Then I rode all the way back here to my house and went to bed. It was the best couple hours I had all week."

She took a long drag on her cigarette and looked up and down the bar. "I was so tired when I went home that I forgot to take the cauliflower out of the car. It's still sitting there on the front seat. A whole big bag of cauliflower."

Doolan shook his head as he finished his beer.

"What are you doing when you finish?" Sharon said.

"Going home to my wife and family."

"What about poor Sharon? Are you leaving her alone?"

Doolan smiled. "I'm afraid so."

"Oh. I wanted to go out tonight," Sharon said.

As Doolan realized that Sharon suddenly was offering what might be the greatest promise of them all, he stood uncertainly, a man suddenly thrust from the wings and into the lead role.

"You really want a drink?"

"Absolutely. I want you to take me out."

Doolan swallowed. "I don't get off until twelve."

Sharon made a sour face. "I thought you was the boss in there."

"I'll be here by ten," Doolan said.

"That's good," Sharon said. "We'll have fun."

* * *

Sharon chewed gum, smoked a cigarette with her left hand, and kept in front of her a drink that she did not want. The right hand rested on the large bag of cauliflower from Long Island, which was on the next stool. Inside the bag, wedged between heads of cauliflower, was the gun she had taken from Chester Doolan, who was her boyfriend for the night. Now, at eight in the morning, Chester was still asleep in Sharon's bed and Sharon was in the Green Fields bar with Chester's gun. Next time he wakes up early, Sharon said to herself.

"Dead," Sharon said to the bartender.

"Out shopping early," he said.

"Out shopping early," Sharon said.

"Where were you?" he asked.

"I don't know, some store over on the next block."

"They got good stores on Ninth Avenue," he said.

"To tell you the truth, it's the first time I've ever been here."

"I know you're not from around here," he said.

"I'm from Jersey."

"I didn't think I'd seen you here before."

"Never. I was out last night and I met this guy. He told me come around here today, he'd buy me a drink. I'm coming for the first time and I seen these stores and I figured, let me stop and buy something nice. Take it home with me."

"That was good," the bartender said.

"Yeah. Only now I'm sitting here with nice fresh cauliflower and nobody buying me a drink."

A smile came over the bartender's tired face. "Somebody will."

"Guy said he'd buy me a drink. I'm here and he's not. O'Sullivan."

"Oh. Well. I don't know about him. This is early for him. He stops around late in the afternoon. You never see him before then. When he's in town, he makes a lot of stops all day. He gets in here late afternoon. Then he goes over to theatres."

"He in show business?"

"He goes around the stagehands; I don't know what he's got to do with them. I know he goes there. He's got a sister works there, too. Works usher. He always stops by to see her. She was working at the Lyceum, but that play closed. She's working at another one of them. The one got *Sleuth* playing at it."

"What am I supposed to do, sit here all day?" Sharon said. She slid off the barstool and picked up the bag of cauliflower with both hands and hugged it. This caused the heads of cauliflower to rearrange themselves and the gun that Sharon originally had shoved into the middle of the cauliflower was now pressing against her chest.

"If he comes in," Sharon said as she went to the door.

"I'll tell him," the bartender said. "What's the name?"

"Tell him Sharon from last night."

She went out into the cold air. A flatbed truck, chains slapping against crates piled too high, rushed by. Next door to the bar, a man opened the door to an old appliance shop and the burglar alarm went off. Sharon flinched at the noise. She stood hugging her package, with the gun against her and an indoor look, the pile of black hair and thick make-up out of place on the morning street. At the corner, Puerto Rican men stood in leather jackets and talked to young women. They waited for the freight elevator doors to open and start them on a day of work upstairs on a factory floor.

Sharon knew that she had many hours to wait. Fair enough, she thought, so I could wait a few hours for him. She remembered how once, going to the first job of her life, a day waitress on Flatbush Avenue down in Brooklyn, she was shoved as she stepped off the bus at Myrtle and Wyckoff in Ridgewood to change to the el. She fell into a deep puddle of slush. The guy who shoved her, a round-faced man who wore a blue jacket with his name, Lou, written over the pocket, went by her without glancing. He ran up the el steps. Two weeks later, he ran up the same el steps. Sharon, waiting on the platform, only had to step out and give him one good shove. The action of the guy running up the stairs and Sharon's hands moving at his chest caused the guy to give an extra flip as he went backward and started tumbling down the steps.

Now, standing on Eleventh Avenue in Manhattan, in front of the Green Fields bar, Sharon said to herself, And this guy hits me with a baseball bat and he's supposed to walk around?

Sharon went to her car, placed the bag of cauliflower on the front seat, and drove to a cousin's house in Astoria. She carried the cauliflower into the second-floor apartment. Her cousin said, "You got for me?" Sharon said, "No, this is special for me. I'll get something for you next time."

The cousin watched as Sharon took the cauliflower into the spare bedroom. It was nine-thirty in the morning. Sharon slept until three. Before leaving the apartment, she looked in the newspaper for the play, *Sleuth,* and saw that it was at the Music Box on West 45th Street.

At four o'clock, she was back in the Green Fields. O'Sullivan was not there. Sharon never had seen the man. He had hit her with his baseball bat and she went out cold and he was gone. But for the last few months she had repeatedly asked Jimmy Morrison to describe him. Asked so many times she now could do a painting of O'Sullivan.

She went back to the car and chewed gum to the music on the radio. It was almost six o'clock when a car pulled to the curb in front of her. O'Sullivan got out and walked quickly into the bar. Sharon calmly turned off the radio. She juggled the bag and put the gun on top of the cauliflower. She had the car door open and was about to get out when O'Sullivan came striding quickly back across the sidewalk and got into his car.

Sharon pulled her door shut and followed O'Sullivan's car. It went down to the parking lot near the Martin Beck Theatre on 45th Street. O'Sullivan got out and started up the block. Sharon put her car in the same lot and walked after him, hugging her package. O'Sullivan kept walking quickly, and Sharon began to run. Past the theater, at the corner of Eighth Avenue, there were two cops. Sharon stopped running. Her mind was not on witnesses, but stopping at the sight of uniforms was a reflex. The first groups of people were on their way to dinner before the theatre, and O'Sullivan weaved through them quickly. Sharon saw him enter the Music Box. As she got up to the theatre, she bumped into a small, dark-haired man who was about to go in the stage door.

"Excuse me, my dear woman," he said. Then his eyes widened as he looked at the top of the bag and saw the gun.

"Will you tell me what in the name of anything holy you need that for?"

"None of your business," Sharon said.

"If it goes off in me belly, it would be," he said.

"In case I get mugged," Sharon said.

He put his hand on her shoulder and spoke softly. "My dear, lovely young woman. Murder begets murder and always in the cause of honor, peace, and justice. And so it will continue until the gods grow tired of blood and breed a race of better men."

"That's very nice," Sharon said.

"It's Shaw," the man said.

"Oh."

"It's just my offering to you on a night that I hope will be so much better for you than your day. The idea of your carrying a gun while you shop for food causes my face to become snowy white."

Sharon nodded and the man said, "All the best." He walked into the stage entrance and she remained on the sidewalk, waiting.

Ten minutes later, O'Sullivan walked out of the theatre. He was smiling to himself about something. At first, Sharon wanted to say something to him. Then she put her hand into the bag of cauliflower and gripped the gun and held it straight out. The paper bag tilted and the cauliflower bounced onto the sidewalk as she fired the gun inside the bag three times into O'Sullivan's back. The paper bag caught fire. She smothered it against her chest and kept walking.

She just kept walking. She went all the way to Ninth Avenue and turned the corner and nobody bothered her.

The next morning, Sharon brought a container of coffee and the newspaper into the bar on Jamaica Avenue to start her day's work. The porter was in the back, mopping the men's room. Standing at the far end of the bar, hands trembling, eyes desperate, was Chester Doolan. He wore a black raincoat over his gray postal worker's shirt.

"Chester, you got anything to say, you go home and tell it to your wife. Tell her you slept with Sharon."

Sharon took off her imitation leopard coat and hung it on a hook. Without talking, she walked past the man, went behind the bar, stuck the newspaper underneath, and opened the coffee.

"Dead," she said.

"Is he?" the nervous man said.

"I don't mean anybody else. I mean me. I'm dead. I'm the only one that counts."

"It says in the paper he's still alive," the man said.

Sharon didn't look at him. "Chester, what are you worried about?"

"Because the guy could be dead by now."

"Did the paper say that Sharon could have been dead the way he hit me with his baseball bat?"

"The guy could die right now," Chester said.

"What's that got to do with you?" Sharon said.

"It was my gun."

"You told me yourself that you got no license to have a gun on your job," Sharon said. "You told me you went out somewhere and bought it someplace. What are you so worried about?"

Chester backed away. "You're acting like someone crazy."

"I'm acting like someone who got good and fucking even."

She reached for her shoulder bag on the back bar. "You're yellin' so much, I want to give it back to you."

Chester was about to run. She reached into the bag and took out a pack of cigarettes. "I told myself I never was going to talk about this today. If anybody asks me, I'll tell them that you did it and gave me the gun to hold."

She walked out from behind the bar and went to the ladies' room. "I don't want to see you here when I come out."

When she stepped out, Chester was gone. She told herself that she truly would never think of him again. She sat on a stool at the end of the bar nearest the window and smoked several cigarettes and sipped coffee. She thought about turning on the juke box and listening to Sinatra records. Sinatra sure wouldn't of been so insulted if I took a gun from him, Sharon thought. He would of given me a hug and said, Are you all right, Sharon? That's what he would of done. In the smoke in the air in the empty saloon, she saw Sinatra rubbing a hand on the side of his face and saying, Well, baby, you got to do what you got to do. Now Sinatra reached out and patted Sharon on her cheek. You're all right, baby. You're a stand-up broad. Sharon shrugged. So what do I get around here? I'm sitting here and the best I got is a guy scared to death that he's in trouble. Never mind Sharon. He doesn't even mention Sharon. Sharon can't get a break, she told herself. She grimaced as she saw Owney's car pull in front and Owney getting out with a face flushed with whiskey.

"What are you up to?" she said as he walked in.

"I just heard on the radio."

"What did you hear? Pearl Harbor?"

"The guy's dead."

"That's a shame. Who died?"

"We heard on the radio, they found cabbages—"

"Cauliflower."

Owney stared.

"My radio said cauliflower," Sharon said. "Cauliflower. Do you want to see what else the woman had in the bag? Do you want to see?" Sharon reached into the shoulder bag and pulled out the gun as if it were the American flag.

She held it to her nose. "It still smells."

"You used it?" Owney said.

"Did I use it? You know I did. Here, you want to see? Here." She handed Owney the gun.

"Smell it. You could smell the real Sharon there. Gunpowder. That's my new name. Sharon Gunpowder."

Owney sat dazed, with the sour taste in his mouth.

"What was I supposed to do, wait for you people?" she said. She picked up her coffee.

"I hope it's all right," Owney muttered.

"You hope what?"

"I hope you're all right. Are you all right?"

"At least," she said.

"What?"

"I thought Frank Sinatra was the only one ask me that."

"What are you talking about, Sinatra?"

"Forget it. Don't listen to me. I forgot you know your way around, too. You're good and fucked up, but you got a little style anyway."

"I'll take this." He was befuddled by what she said, but he knew he couldn't leave the gun with her. Owney put it into his pocket and walked out of the bar. As he got to the car, Sharon stood in the saloon doorway with coffee in one hand and the cigarette in the other.

"Owney?"

"What?"

"He shouldn't of done that to Sharon."

Then she smiled at a man passing by on his way to work.

As Owney drove away, he careened around a postal truck. The sides of the street rose and became the sides of a toboggan. Then the pavement began to climb, fall, and twist. He blinked in a futile attempt to clear his vision. He assured himself that what he was doing was right; she had taken over the peril that belonged to his father and him. Now he was taking away the one sure way they could trace a shooting to her and he was going to bury it. He went to the cemetery, but there were too many people—workmen and funeral directors. Instead of throwing the gun into a grave, the way he wanted to, he took it upstairs and shoved it into his dresser. When he came back down, he knew enough not to drive. He wandered out of the gates and headed for the streets.

On the newsstands the first edition of the *Post* had a huge headline about the murder. It was replaced in all later editions by the marriage of a rock star. The murder was not mentioned again anywhere for months.

It was still morning when Grandma opened the door and let Owney into the Gold Key, which was on Palmetto Street in Ridgewood.

"Beer," Owney said.

"Too chilly in the morning for just beer." She reached for a bottle of Fleischmann's. Owney stepped slowly to the bar with his hands rubbing together. Instead of rubbing together briskly, the fingers were slowly braiding, pushing his nerves back into their catacombs. From the other side of the bar, just this least bit hazy, were the spotted old hands of a fight second who was leaning through the ropes and yanking up the gloves on the opponent, alcohol, who stood in the corner and waited for the bell.

The first drink brought water to Owney's eyes. The second went down easier. Owney took only half the beer chaser and then put the glass down. He never heard the bell as the opponent walked out of the corner. The face was smeared with Vaseline, so punches would slide off. The opponent jabbed.

Grandma poured another shot, then put the bottle in the gutter. Walking on old legs, she went to the dimness at the end of the bar where her latest boyfriend, Louie, sat with his cane hooked onto the bar. She raised her shot glass to Louie.

"I can't do it, Louie, and you can't do it, so let's get together."

She had a white sweater around her stooped shoulders and eyeglasses hanging on glass beads around her neck. She was seventy-five and was supposed to be the oldest barmaid in Ridgewood.

The el line runs well over Palmetto Street, the city buses barely fitting under the rusting el trestle. Owney watched the big buses crowded with people going to work swing out from under the el.

"Are you working today?" Grandma asked.

"Tomorrow."

"Why not today?"

"I got a lot to do today," Owney said.

"You got union and all that?" Grandma asked.

"Doesn't mean anything if you don't work one day," Owney said.

"You don't get no benefits for being off?"

"No."

"Don't somebody come up with something?"

"Nope."

"I thought unions were supposed to do everything," Grandma said.

"I need the day," Owney said. He sat in silence and suddenly became comfortable with the squeaking sounds of boxing shoes on a canvas as the opponent began to move as he pleased, the left hand snapping.

An old man in a black overcoat, with dandruff-whitened shoulders, came in and read a newspaper over a beer. The Con Edison meter reader came in for rye. Two Budweiser beer truck drivers came in next. They had a beer, then the heavier of the two handed Grandma the yellow slip.

"We got ten cases for you."

"Ten? I'm supposed to get thirty."

The beer truck driver looked at the slip. "It says only ten here."

Grandma shook her head. "I'm supposed to get thirty. I got to think about this."

"What can I do, Grandma?"

"Have a drink while I think."

Owney fingered his change on the bar and looked out the window. Now, a bus with seats vacant in the midmorning pulled around the corner in a turn so wide the front of the bus seemed to be coming through the bar window. The driver was in a black sweater. On a hook behind him, the orange lining of his zippered jacket showed. Owney's eyes followed the orange lining as the bus swung past the window and went up the street. He remembered walking into school late and everybody sitting at desks and their clothes hanging on the hooks in the back of the room.

The shot glass dropped out of Owney's hand.

"Don't worry about it," Grandma said.

"About what?"

"Don't worry about it. You're supposed to drop things." She was wiping the bar in front of him. He had knocked over the beer too.

Owney went to the men's room.

On the way back, the squeaking became loud and now alcohol came off his toes and stood flat in the middle of the ring and threw a flurry of punches. He ended the combination perfectly, with a left hook, and Owney, his hands down, stopped at a table in the back of the barroom.

He decided he wanted to sit down alone and rest. He knocked over the first chair and slumped onto the chair against the wall. He put his shoulder against the wall. Behind him were stacked cardboard cases of Rheingold beer. He sat there and listened to Grandma and Louie talk to each other about getting fucked. After a while, Owney heard a small noise, a pop, and felt something pushing out of his pulse. A worm had broken through the skin on the inside of his wrist and was starting to wriggle out of the vein. Dark brown, a hint of red, the worm bunched fat in the opening. Just a little of the worm was coming out of the skin. Then the worm was getting as much of its body as possible through the opening, pulling up its skin like a pair of socks, trying to get the rest of the body, down inside the vein, to just slide through the vein like a tail and come out through the opening in the skin.

Owney plucked at the head of the worm, trying to catch it so he could pull the whole worm out of his wrist. The worm began to roll inside itself, the outer skin running over the front lips and then going down inside. Owney wondered how the worm saw his fingers coming. Does a worm see? Perhaps the follicles around the front lips serve as some kind of eyes. As Owney got his fingers on the worm, the head withdrew into the body, the worm skin rolling rapidly inside, the bunching of the worm's body becoming noticeably less in the opening of the skin at Owney's pulse. Inside his wrist, Owney could feel the worm going back through the vein, back up into his arm. He pressed his thumb hard against his wrist, a half inch above the opening the worm had made. This trapped the worm. The head of the worm, with a fat roll of escalator-motion skin, sat in the mouth of the open pulse. Owney worked his thumb so that he pushed the skin on the inside of his wrist down toward the heel of his hand. The fatty roll of worm head now came out of the hole in his wrist. Owney worked his thumb more. The worm came higher out of the hole. Enough worm so that Owney could pick it off with his thumb and index finger. The head of the worm now was touching the first creased line between the bottom of Owney's wrist and the start of the heel of his hand. Owney plucked quickly, too quickly for the worm. He caught the worm by the fatty roll and pulled. He could feel the worm coming through his vein. Long, wet, brown wrinkles. Pull easy, he told himself, don't rip it off and leave the tail inside. As the worm came out, he worked his fingers down the worm so that he couldn't pull the top half off, and he kept pulling carefully until it all came out. The worm was four inches long.

Owney held the worm in one hand and lit a cigarette with the other. He held the cigarette against the worm. The worm shriveled as he crushed the cigarette against it. Carefully, Owney folded back the skin flaps of the hole the worm had made coming out of his wrist. When he had the flaps of the skin in place, he pressed a thumb against the skin so it would begin knitting. It's a good thing, he told himself, that I heal so fast.

He got to the diner early, took one look inside, and went across the street to a big place that was empty, except for a man with watery blue eyes who was at the window. Owney ordered a beer and then decided to have a shot with it.

Five days, he said to himself. So I'll do five days.

Sometime in the middle of the night, he couldn't remember when, he knew he had tried to call Dolores and she had snarled and hung up on him. And then he had called Navy; he agreed to go away with Navy. Now he sat at the bar and swallowed his drink. Outside, the traffic on

Fourth Avenue in the Bay Ridge section of Brooklyn was heavy. Across the street was the diner, on the corner of 69th Street. At night, the entranceway to the diner, and the sidewalks right outside it, are the scene of the most fistfights of any place in the entire city except Madison Square Garden. In the morning, there are bewildered men, the coffee shaking in their hands, who wait for union alcoholism counselors to pick them up and take them off to dry-out centers.

Owney pushed money at the bartender and went out into the street. He walked into a delicatessen and bought nine bottles of beer. Then he walked down to a liquor store and bought a small bottle of Mateus white wine. It would taste good in the morning if it was chilled, he thought. Maybe if the car window was open on the ride down to this place in New Jersey, the cold air would chill the bottle.

He went over to the diner. Navy sat in a booth alone with coffee and a nervous cigarette. "We have to make one stop on Staten Island. You know Pete Toner?"

"He works the Sixty-third Street tunnel?"

"That's him. I got calls from him all last night. The last time was three in the morning. This is about the fifth time I've had him." He paid the cashier and led Owney out to the car.

On Staten Island, in the middle of a row of two-story attached houses, a woman was at the upstairs window. She had a mattress hanging halfway out the window. A man on the front stoop stood up unsteadily. He had on a white golf cap and clutched a small paper bag. He looked up at the woman.

"Go ahead," she said to him.

Then she called down to Navy, "Thank God you're here." She pushed more of the mattress out into the air. "If you didn't come today I was going to make him start wearing Pampers."

On the stoop, the man yelled up, "Would you shut up? Everybody will hear you."

"It's good everybody wasn't sleeping in bed with you last night."

The man on the steps snarled something.

"The big shot," she said. "Now he's going to hit me." She pointed at the mattress. "I go all through this business with three kids. Now I got him."

"It happens," Navy said to Owney.

The man in the white cap, Toner, walked to the car and flopped into the back seat. He immediately went into the paper bag and brought out a can of beer. The car was moving when Toner suddenly wailed, "It's frozen!"

"She's got to get back at you some way," Navy said.

Toner raised his right leg and shoved the beer cans under it. He brought the leg down and settled himself with a hen's grunt. "I'll just wait till they get warm," he said. His chin dropped onto his chest and he fell asleep with a cigarette burning down between his fingers.

"Driving drunks," Navy said.

"He's not doing anything," Owney said.

"I'm driving you, too," Navy said. On the Jersey Turnpike, Owney pulled out a bottle of beer.

"How long does it take to get there?" he said.

"Another two hours," Navy said.

Owney began to measure the trip. Nine bottles. No, better make it eight, this guy Toner will be taking at least one of them for sure. That leaves eight bottles for two hours. A bottle every fifteen minutes. He looked at the one bottle in his hand. It was nearly gone. Owney started getting nervous. I'll never make it, he thought. Then he remembered the wine. He relaxed. That'll take me through the last half-hour, he thought.

Toner woke up a short while later. "Where are we?" he said. His hand went under his leg for the beer he was trying to hatch.

"Soon," Navy said.

Toner took the tab off one of the beers and moaned, "It's still frozen." He swallowed the small bit of foam that had collected at the top. He licked the amber ice underneath. Then he held the can between his hands, trying to warm it. Whenever some of the ice melted into the foam he brought the can up and licked it.

Navy said, "I took four guys down here once. When I left, I wouldn't have given any of them more than two weeks. But three are still sober. That's two years later. They're sober. And you're the only one that's still drunk."

"Yeah, well," Toner said.

"I guess it's tough for him," Owney said.

"He's not alone," Navy said.

The car swerved to pass a bus. The bottles between Owney's legs clinked.

"What's that?" Toner said. His head hung over the front seat and his eyes widened as he saw the beer on the floor between Owney's legs.

"Why didn't you tell me?" Toner said.

Owney opened one for Toner and one for himself. They drove in silence for a while and then Owney asked, "What is this place, a hospital?"

"No, detox and rehabilitation. Mostly rehabilitation. They keep you the first five days in a separate section, then they move you over."

"Five days in?" Owney said.

"That's right," Navy said. "Then twenty-three days with the others for rehabilitation. It's AA. Nothing else works."

"Let me ask you a question," Toner called from the back.

"Go ahead," Navy said.

"Did you ever drink cold duck?"

"Of course. I always thought that when I had that drink I'd have on a nice velvet robe and I'd be drinking it out of a snifter. Like a gentleman. But one morning I came down in my underwear and I drank two quarts of it out of a Welch's jelly glass."

Later, Navy got off the turnpike and went onto a road that ran through South Jersey farmland that was brown in the cold weather. Toner now became nervous.

"I need cigarettes."

"You'll get them," Navy said. "Just about now you're wondering why you called me."

"No, in two days I'd of been dead," Toner said.

"Well, I'm wondering a little," Owney said.

"That's normal," Navy said. "Just concentrate on what you can do for yourself here. Think ahead."

"Is it far from anyplace?" Owney asked.

"Pretty far. That's why you're only allowed to have ten dollars for cigarettes. As long as people don't have any carfare, there is no way that they can leave the place. It's too far."

Owney took a couple of fierce slugs of white wine. He had a hundred dollars stashed in his shoe. He wondered if they would search him.

They went down a road that had only one farmhouse for half a mile. Then they came up to a long white fence and Navy turned into the driveway of what had been a private estate. There was a large white house and behind it was a long, low building of gray wood.

Navy parked the car and went into the white house through a side door. He stood in an office and talked to a man with a round face and thick glasses. The man laughed in greeting as Toner and Owney came in.

"Hey! Hiya!" He looked at Toner. "Where'd you get the hat?"

"Staten Island," Toner said.

"Boy, it sure looks like it," the man said. He laughed uproariously.

Toner and Owney sat down and a secretary took their names and addresses and asked questions about their medical history. They turned over their personal belongings and Navy gave her twenty dollars to buy cigarettes for the two. Then he took Owney aside.

"I'll call the wife. I'll go to the house and pick up any clothes she wants to send down. You think you're here to get out of trouble at home. If you think a little bit, you might realize that you're here for more than that. That's all. I'll see you around."

The man in charge took Owney and Toner over to the gray dormitory building. The man showed Owney into a room that had four neatly made beds. Dull red bedspreads were unwrinkled. The shades were drawn. There was a small television set in the center of the room.

"We don't have single rooms here. We believe in people helping each other. We allow television only in the detox unit. After you get over the first seventy-two hours, we don't feel you're here for television. We have too extensive a rehabilitation program to allow time for television. Let me show you something else we have."

Owney followed the man out a door and through a small gate that led into a large garden.

"Isn't this perfect?" the man said. "You stand here and it reminds you of how much you have forgotten about God. People come here and think about a power greater than themselves. It's very important to rehabilitation."

"It's nice," Owney said.

They walked back to the dormitory building. "I'll just step down the hall and see how Toner is doing," the man said.

Owney stepped into the doorway of his room. Restful. If you have to be someplace, it's not a bad place to stay at all. He walked over to the window and lifted the shade. Outside, on this side of the dormitory, the afternoon sun was falling on empty farm fields that ran as far as he could see. He walked out of the room and went to the door that led out to the gardens, which sat silent under the trees. He walked slowly down a path. When he came to a low wall, he stepped over it and into a field on the other side. It was a corn field, and the nubs of stalks crackled under his feet as he walked. Crackled louder as he began to pick up the pace. He figured he had a long walk until he hit someplace that would be fun.

He kept walking through dirt fields for what seemed like an hour and then one field ended at a crossroads where there was a silver corrugated diner. Owney's eyes picked out the blue neon sign in the window that meant there was beer inside. A trailer truck and a couple of cars were parked in front of the diner. Owney came out of the field and walked briskly across the road and now he could read the blue neon sign. SCHMIDT'S. A Philadelphia beer. He was that far down from New York. Something, he told himself. He walked briskly across the road and into a vestibule that was decorated with color snapshots of truck cabs, the owners posing proudly in front of them. Reds and blues, with big gleaming metal fronts and painted decorations. Maybe there would be a couple of them around to have a drink with, Owney thought. He grabbed the sliding door handle and pulled it and walked into the diner.

"You got here fast," Navy said. He sat in the first booth with coffee and a cigarette. He pursed his lips and looked at his watch. "Twenty-two minutes, from your room to here. Last guy I had here took a whole half-hour."

"He must've got lost," Owney said.

12

As a child she never had realized that her mother snored at night. Her mother fell asleep with the suppleness and consciousness of a cinder block dropped onto the bed; within moments, her mouth opened and she snored with extraordinary velocity. Dolores's baby slept in the crib against the wall; Dolores, denied sleep, her foot switching back and forth as it investigated her empty bed, felt trapped in the small room by the noise. On the first night that she had returned to her mother's house, Dolores had walked into her mother's bedroom and shaken the woman by the shoulder. As this was the first time since her husband's demise that she had been touched in bed by anything more than an old dream, the woman awoke with a yelp. "I got my own way to sleep, after all these years. You don't like it, you don't have to listen." Dolores, standing barefooted, as she had on so many nights of her early life, suddenly realized that she was a stranger under the roof.

On many nights, she lay awake and waited for the noise to diminish, or for exhaustion to cause her to fall asleep. Never had Dolores envisioned the passion that noise at night could produce. Prisoners in large penitentiaries understand the reasons for strict rules of silence after the night bell; there have been too many murders over prolonged whisper. A wife leaving her husband to return to her family home has no such lore. In bed each night, Dolores was furious at her mother and gave the sheets an extra kick as the sound keeping her awake caused her to become furious.

She put her hand flat on her midsection, which was a mistake at this hour, for she could feel the new fat; she had accepted the notion that she had gained ten pounds from late-night eating, but now her touch told her it was more like fifteen. When Owney is in a bar, he drinks up at least three thousand calories and he weighs less than when I met him, she thought. I watch him drink and I gain weight. Immediately, she thought of the Baby Ruth in her purse: big red lettering on white paper. The peanuts delightfully resistant against the teeth. She reached into her purse, gladdened as she felt the Baby Ruth bar and pulled it out. She stared at the darkness above her with the candy bar in her hand. I have to stop doing this, she told herself. I don't even like it now. She knew the eating came out of a disorderly mind and her success depended on her mind's eye collecting orderly sets of thoughtful pictures, and not these sudden blowups of Baby Ruth bars. Of course she took another bite.

The absence of money in a woman's life, Dolores realized, does as much to deform a woman's figure as having children. There are no sit-ups that can reduce the effects of missing money, an ailment that goes right to the jawbone. Only the most stringent discipline, which she could not summon, could prevent this. Through the month before this, while Owney sat in a dry-out home in New Jersey, and received no pay, Dolores found herself grabbing cold ravioli in the morning. Then, two weeks into this month, when she went around to their old apartment on 74th Street to look for the check that Owney received for his medal, she found only a sheaf of white envelopes, junk mail, on the vestibule floor under the mail slot. She put them atop the radiator and looked on the floor again for the brown window envelope, and finding it missing, she walked immediately up to the Glendale Bake Shop and bought four charlotte russes, two of which she ate on the seven-block walk home, where she called Owney's parents' house and got his mother.

"He isn't in yet," she said.

"Of course."

"I wish you wouldn't talk like that. He went to a special meeting of his union."

"That's fine. I'm wondering why he didn't leave any money for his child and his wife."

"He wasn't workin' for all that time."

"He's been working for the two weeks, hasn't he?"

"Oh, yes. Every day. Dolores, you have to stop yelling at me."

"Mrs. Morrison, I still love you, but why doesn't he support his wife and child?"

"He had to pay the rent on the apartment this week, I know that."

"Why did he do that? We're not living there."

"Oh, but you need a place."

"For what?"

"Oh, you do, you need to keep that place."

"No, we don't. At least I don't. And why didn't he leave me the government check?"

"Oh, I don't know about that. I know I saw him with it here."

"That was supposed to be mine."

"But that was his check for having the medal."

"No, that was my check for having a family."

She remembered now that when she hung up on the mother that night, she immediately pulled open the refrigerator and took out another charlotte russe. Two days later, while Dolores was in school, Owney stopped by and handed Dolores's mother an envelope with two hundred dollars in it. He then was able to come up with two hundred a week for the next five weeks, followed by one week in which he left a large amount of dust. Dolores called the cemetery house and the sound of her voice blew the bravado out of Owney's father, who committed the error of answering.

"He . . . he's not around, I think," the father said, with enough pure fear to supply the dying.

"He hasn't been around here, either."

"What can I tell you?"

"You can tell me why he doesn't leave any money for his wife and child."

"Oh, I don't know about that."

"He's only your son."

"I'll tell him."

He hung up, and she dialed McNiff, the lawyer, who took two days to get back to her.

"We'll have to go into court and get a judge to order him to pay you so much every week," McNiff said.

"Why haven't we done that before now?" Dolores said.

"Because you told me you didn't want to. You started off with papers and a time schedule but then you told me you didn't feel like going into court. You said you trusted him."

"That's how smart I am."

"No, you're a nice person. And he's a nice person. But life intrudes. That's what courts are for."

"What do we do now?"

"We go into court and get a judge to order him to pay you so much every week as support for your child and for you."

"When?"

"I can request a hearing tomorrow."

"Then when will it be?"

"Next month."

"That long? And how long after that?"

"Month."

"But he never answered the papers you sent him. Doesn't that mean he's—"

"In default. That's for you and me. In a Queens courtroom with a Queens judge, it could mean anything. If he were in trouble for shooting thirty-five people in a saloon argument, I could walk in and get a judge to burst into tears and try to help him. But if I came in and said, 'I have to get this hero to pay his wife some money,' the judge might want to take your husband out for a drink. Judges don't like to see men forced to pay women anything. You could have six kids who were so hungry that they were crying in the hallway and the judge still would feel sorry for the poor father. A woman? Let them shut up and go back to their mother's."

Beautiful, Dolores now said to herself. She took a last bite of the Baby Ruth candy bar. She hated the Baby Ruth and assured herself she never would eat one again, and then she remembered sadly that she didn't have another one anyplace in the house. Her mother's snoring still came through the wall. On many nights such as this, she simply got up and took her books into the kitchen and ate until she was ashamed of herself and read until the pages turned blank. Then she would go to bed, the hour now past the time for full snoring.

This time, on a Monday night, tired, and with her longest day coming up, with school until ten-thirty at night, with a cold February night wind blowing a tin can along the alleyway under the window, Dolores gave one last thrash at the sheets, swung out of bed, and stepped silently into the hall, then slowly, noiselessly, opened her mother's door. Now she slammed it shut. Dolores stood motionless in the hall as inside, her mother's head flew off the pillow. Her mother coughed and sighed, then her feet pounded on the floor, signifying a move to the bathroom. Dolores eased back into her room, and was quickly asleep.

"I hardly slept." Her mother's voice burst out of drowsiness as she saw Dolores using a normal amount of coffee from the yellow bag that had no brand name and came straight from the sale at the Pathmark store on Myrtle Avenue. "You're puttin' in too much. Give you nerves all day."

Her mother's hands got between Dolores and the pot and began spooning coffee back into the yellow bag. "Don't have to make the supermarket any richer, either. Use a little less. Nice cup of coffee at home doesn't have to cost a fortune."

Dolores left the kitchen, showered, dressed, and was brushing her hair when she heard the phone ring. "It's that Marissa!" her mother yelled. Dolores grabbed her books and car coat and walked into the kitchen. She took a swallow of her mother's coffee, which this time seemed to be tan-colored hot water.

"What can I do for you?" Dolores said to Marissa.

"I'm in so much trouble. I need your help." Although it was seven-fifteen in the morning, Marissa's voice was loud with emergency. Of course, Dolores found it cheerful. She had discovered Marissa on one of the first days of school: a cricket topped by jet-black hair, and thick mascara highlighting green-gray eyes. Earrings made of stiff wire bounced gaily with each move of her head. She carried a leather purse that was so large it should have been carried by a strong porter. She chewed gum and hummed as she went into the purse and brought out notebooks, whose covers, neatly encased in plastic, gleamed. She then took out a set of pens, all of different colors, chewed gum furiously, and waited for the professor to speak. When he did, she wrote down what he said. If he talked for the whole period, she wrote for the whole period. She was nineteen, but she functioned in school as if she were some old trusted employee, who would do the job whether the owner was peering from his office or vacationing in France. Dolores found her comforting, for on the first days of the term she had been bewildered, completely forgetting her earlier successes in these same classrooms, when these new Queens public high school products, mostly Jewish, walked in and began looking rapidly around the room, eyes passing over Dolores without a flicker, counting themselves, and then, comforted in their numbers, talking to each other excitedly, their conversations leading inevitably to the medals won in an important high school science fair that Dolores, raised on Catholic streets, never had heard of.

Suddenly, Dolores thought she was too old, and carrying too much weight of an unsettled or even a losing life, to keep up. Once, she had walked into this school with no trace of the usual fear of competing against Jews that is carried around by most graduates of Diocese of Brooklyn high schools. She had just taken her seat, done her work, and received marks that indicated that she was a prospect for anything she wanted to try. If she had feelings of resentment at first, they were against her mother, who never had wanted her in college. She subdued the resentment with prayers and with such personal success that she was able to forgive anything.

Then she met Owney and from then on the only inner voice she heard came from her heart. She walked away from it all, from a future that seemed so assured that she could see it, hanging right out there in the air in front of her. Now, returning three years later, she listened to a young woman talk about driving her younger sister to Westhampton to buy duck eggs for a grammar school experiment in embryonics, and Dolores suddenly despaired and then immediately was calmed by the sounds of Marissa slapping open her stiff notebook a few seats away.

When she had first noticed Marissa, she had been pleased by her style, and assumed that she was also Jewish, from Forest Hills High, probably, but then noticed that the other eyes swept past Marissa, too. While some outsiders no longer can differentiate between Queens and Brooklyn Jews and Italians, as the two, living alongside each other for so long now, begin to look like so many from the same breakfast table, the Jewish heritage of being slaughtered allows them to know their own at any distance and in any setting. So Dolores, attracted to Marissa at first by stubbornness of approach, now felt for the first time that she could control her apprehensions by her proximity to someone with not only a similar style, but the shared background of a Diocese of Brooklyn education. When Dolores spoke to her one day, Marissa brandished her notebook and said, "I take this home at night and learn it like you learn the Hail Marys. Once I know it so that I don't have to think about knowing it, then I can sit down and learn what it means. I do my work." Dolores, who usually was in the school library until nine at night, began staying until closing time, at eleven. Staying with some confidence, for which she silently thanked Marissa.

Who now was saying to her on the phone, "What goes with chartreuse sweat pants?"

"Marissa, I'm trying to get out of here."

"So am I. But I have on chartreuse sweat pants. What do I put on the top?"

"Marissa, what do I know? Chartreuse. Something fuchsia, I guess."

"Oh, good. I'll go inside and try on something. Hold on while I go."

"Marissa, I can't. I said I'm leaving."

"Then let me ask you about one other thing."

"No, I don't have time." The swing in Marissa's voice, causing her to go from teenager in chartreuse to a young woman with something on her mind, alerted Dolores.

"I got to ask you."

Dolores sighed. "All right."

"I was just watching the television."

"I can imagine what was on."

"I know it bothers you, but I have to know."

"Go on."

"I was just watching Vietnam on the news and they had this film on from, you know . . ."

"The place."

"That's right, Vietnam. Now a lot of the fellows were hurt, right as I was watching. It doesn't matter if they actually were hurt a few days ago and the parents already were notified. All I know is that they were hurt right in front of me. Hurt? Dolores, I screamed. A guy got killed. I'm just thinking, I know about the Constitution, but I also was trying to picture myself as this young guy's mother. Sitting home watching my son get killed on the television set. Do you think that's right? Do you think they should let your son die in front of you just because you have a television news show?"

Dolores was thinking of Owney's father on a barstool, gulping proudly when his son was mentioned.

"I think the parents should be flown over so they can see the battles themselves," Dolores said. "They could all get up on a hill and look down and see their son carrying his gun. If there isn't a hill, the fathers could get up in trees so they could call down to the mothers, tell them what's going on."

"The mothers could bandage their sons," Marissa said.

"Run right out there and be the first ones there," Dolores said. "There would be only one trouble with my mother-in-law. She would moan so much that you wouldn't know whether she was the one wounded or not."

"Dolores, you're crazy."

"No, I'm not. I'm experienced."

"Dolores, you should see on the television what all these poor fella——"

"I don't want to talk about it anymore."

"Then do you want to know why I'm wearing chartreuse sweat pants?"

"No."

"You'll love this." She was back to being a teenager.

"Good-bye, Marissa."

She hung up, took a swallow of her mother's tan water, and left.

At Myrtle Avenue, she pulled in front of Prine's candy store. The usual place for breakfast would be Bob's Diner, eight blocks down, but she was fearful that if she walked into the place, she might find Owney, sitting there with his cup of coffee between his hands as if it were a bowl of rice; if he was in the diner at this hour, seven-thirty in the morning, it would only mean that he had been out all night. She walked into Prine's and sat at the nearest place along the short, cluttered counter. At one elbow was a display of the most popular newspapers, the *Staats-Zeitung und Herold,* the tabloid *Il Progresso,* and the *Irish Echo.* On a stand against the wall behind her was a low stack of the *New York Times* newspaper, which was quite popular with schoolteachers traveling into the area to work, and then, rising to shoulder level, the *New York Daily News* newspaper, known in Queens only as "the paper."

Dolores took a Drake's coffee cake out of a wire rack on the counter and ordered coffee from the owner, Prine, who had not shaved yet and wore a black sweater with his white shirt showing through the elbows.

Dolores glanced at the *Staats-Zeitung,* an eight-column paper printed in German and still quite popular in Ridgewood, where the results of the last two world wars have had no effect on bloodlines. The headline, she knew from the German learned while growing up in the neighborhood, had to do with issuance of new postage stamps. *Il Progresso,* a tabloid printed in Italian, had stories from Trapani in Sicily and Naples, with the word Mafia in each headline. The same Italians reading the paper on Myrtle Avenue would be the first to scream if they saw or heard the word Mafia in American papers or on television. Dolores refused to glance at the *Irish Echo.* She knew the format by heart: stories of fighting in Northern Ireland on the front page, and then on the inside pages five- and six-column pictures of silver-haired men surrounding a priest at a dinner, and on their table in front of them were glasses half-filled and ready to be drained the moment the camera shutter became still. Of course she would not look at the dailies, the *Times* or *Daily News,* for at this time, in 1972, anything she watched or read turned into a tale of young men with smooth faces from neighborhoods like Ridgewood who were being honored at great military funerals.

Two gaunt men, collars pulled up around their chins in the raw morning wind, crossed the avenue toward the store. Dolores flinched. They were brothers, in their late fifties, Matty and Walter Guerin, who opened the church for the seven o'clock Mass each day, and then went to their hardware business over in Maspeth. Along with sainthood, they also were heroes, or at least they managed that impression while marching in Memorial Day parades as leader and co-leader of the Lieutenant Arthur J. Foley Post, Catholic War Veterans. Dolores had attended a couple of functions at the post, housed in a new brick building on Metropolitan Avenue that had raised gold lettering over the door and a bar inside that could accommodate the College of Cardinals. At each occasion, Owney was honored with a flock of toasts, after which the members, particularly the Guerin brothers, talked so much of the most horrible violence that they had been called upon to perpetrate in the name of God, country, and the dead generations from which they received their heritage, and, probably, thirst, that on the one night that Owney had not felt well, and therefore did not put himself into a haze where he accepted everything, he whispered to Dolores, "I don't think any of these fellas ever were around a shot being fired."

Now, she felt uneasy at their appearance, for she could sense their eyes locked on her.

"Cold," Matty said, walking in.

"Yeah, cold," the brother Walter said.

"Cold?" Prine, the owner, said.

"Canada got nothing on us," Matty said. He suddenly pretended to notice Dolores. "Hey. How are you?"

She kept the coffee cup to her lips.

"How's Owney?"

She held the cup an inch from her lips and stared straight ahead. "I hope he's fine."

Matty ran a hand over his face. "Geez, you got to forgive me. I forgot for a minute."

Dolores drank the coffee.

"I forgot that the two of you ain't together."

She still said nothing.

"It's a shame," he said.

"Yeah, I was sorry to hear it," the brother Walter said. "I just heard it the other day."

"News must get to you last," Dolores said. "It's been months now."

"Oh, I'm sorry. I didn't know that," Walter said.

Dolores put the cup down and began going through her pocket for change. She could feel the two of them looking at her, straining at the tongue to say something to her before she left.

"Is there any way any of us can help?" Matty said. "I remember standing in the back of the church in tears and I didn't even care who knew it when the two of you got married."

"That was very nice of you," she said, and started for the door. "Have a nice day."

"What about helping him?" Matty said.

Dolores sighed and took the door handle.

"The guy deserves something," Matty said.

"Did anybody say he didn't deserve help?" she said, staring at the street.

"Isn't that your job?"

"I think I was fired from that job."

"Look out that you didn't quit."

"Why don't you buy him a drink and tell him what you just told me?" She wanted to turn around and look at their faces as she said this, but she was suddenly in tears and went out the door with a hand over her eyes. She cried all the way to school.

She needed Marissa, and found her, in chartreuse sweat pants, seated in the front row of the first class, calculus, a course that Dolores had found excruciatingly hard at first, although never before had she experienced any difficulty with mathematics, and it was Marissa's presence that had comforted her. Now, Marissa took off her heavy gray coat and revealed a fuchsia blouse as top for the chartreuse sweat pants.

"Lovely," Dolores said. Inmates would have protested the combination, Dolores thought.

"Thanks," Marissa said. "You know why it's so important, don't you?"

"You started to tell me this morning."

"You wouldn't let me finish."

"Because you wanted to talk about the other thing."

"Oh, the television on Vietnam. But this is more fun. I never told you this before. I got this old man, he has to be seventy, in Garden City who walks the dog every morning and he gets so excited when he sees me that I'm afraid he'll die. I don't want him to do that right now. I come over from West Hempstead to get the train and this old man stands there waiting for me. He just looks and you can see him losing his breath. The ticket man in the station told me the guy is loaded. He has a fortune. He lives alone in a big house. His wife died a couple of years ago. He's lonely and rich. And, Dolores, he's so old! You know what I'm going to do? I'm going to make him into a sugar daddy for me. He can pay my way through medical school. Then he can die."

When Dolores said nothing, Marissa said, "You think I'm talking, don't you? You should see what my father makes. I told you, he works in a lumberyard. What could my father make? Enough for the house and car, right? Where's he going to get thousands and thousands to pay for me at some school? What these schools are charging. I know what I'm going to do. I'm going to turn this nice old guy into a sugar daddy."

"How do you know he's such a nice old guy?"

"Because he can't breathe when he sees me."

"How do you know he'll want to pay bills for you?"

"I'll make him happy to pay. I got to the station five minutes early today. When I got there, the man was way down at the other end of the block, walking the freaking cocker spaniel. He saw these chartreuse sweats of mine, all right. Did he start pretending the dog was making him run up to the station! You should have seen him yanking that dog along the street, trying to make it look like the dog was doing the pulling. He's lucky that I'm only going to make him pay for medical school."

"How old is he?"

"I told you. I bet he's seventy."

Dolores shook her head.

"Do you think that's so bad?" Marissa said.

"I think it would be very bad if the man lived until he was eighty-five."

"Oh, don't say that. He has to die right on schedule. The day my last bill is paid, for the medical school, I want to take a couple of dollars and buy a nice black dress for his funeral. Sugar daddy, nice to have known you."

Listening to Marissa's discourse allowed Dolores to put Owney out of her mind. The class, calculus, had taken so much time at home that she would have regarded a distraction now as criminal. The hour, on integration of three-dimensional shapes, went by in silence and in hand, as did the hours that followed.

In midafternoon, however, in a comparative literature course, the instructor referred to a Hemingway novel, *To Have and Have Not,* and began a discussion of transitional devices, and Dolores, who had only skimmed the book once, stopping cold when she reached a point, early, where the hero was able to see vividly the colors of the muzzle flashes of his submachine gun, now dug the paperback out of her shoulder bag and opened it to a passage where the wife was awake and thinking to herself, as the instructor read aloud in a thin voice, " 'Look at him, sleeping just like a baby. I better stay awake so as to call him. Christ, I could do that all night if a man was built that way. I'd like to do it and never sleep. Never, never, no, never. No, never, never, never. Well, think of that, will you. Me at my age. I ain't old. He said I was still good. Forty-five ain't old. I'm two years older than him. Look at him sleep. Look at him asleep there like a kid.' "

The instructor suddenly stopped to clear his throat and then there was this little smirk. Dolores knew that she'd best stay out of it, but she found her hand going up anyway. "I don't think the person who wrote this ever had much experience with a woman."

"This is *Hemingway.*"

"I just don't think he ever slept very much with a woman."

"Why do you say that?"

"Read the last couple of lines on page ninety-three," Dolores said.

In them, the man and his wife were at the boat dock. Dolores reread them to herself:

> He said: "You aren't worried, are you?"
> "No."
> "Good."
> "You know I lay awake almost four hours just thinking about you."
> "You're some old woman."
> "I can think about you anytime and get excited."
> "Well, we got to fill this gas now," Harry told her.

Dolores had a picture in her mind of Marissa in her chartreuse sweat pants staying awake four hours for a man who then reached for the gas hose. Dolores said to the instructor, "He was longing to put something into the gas tank. That doesn't sound like somebody who has such a great life with females."

"What does it sound like to you?" he asked.

Dolores looked around the class. There were a couple of Chinese men behind her who were gay, and a young woman in front who wore her father's shirts and seemed mainly interested in other females. Dolores didn't want to make them uncomfortable, but at the same time she wanted to answer the question. "What does it sound like? The man might have been a little gay."

She watched the two Chinese gays. They showed no unease.

The instructor now said, "Perhaps you don't understand the sort of man he is writing about. Harry is a man who lives a dangerous life. An old-fashioned man of action. Perhaps the blood courses a bit differently in such people. Hemingway certainly was that type. He lived quite an adventurous life, so he was able to capture this style of man. I am not taking a position on whether they are so desirable to us here or not. I am saying that perhaps they did, or still do, excite women that much."

"I never stayed awake for four hours for any reason in life except a baby crying," Dolores said.

"We won't get personal," the instructor said.

"I don't think what I just said is personal. I don't think there's a woman who stays up four hours. The man who wrote that simply doesn't know what he's talking about."

"Well, all of us here are from some Queens neighborhood. Probably pretty bland. Hemingway and his people were out on the sea. Men of action in dangerous places. This was the literature of their times."

Dolores shook her head. "The main character never lived. The man who wrote it never lived this way. And I wonder if the man who wrote it knew what he was sexually."

"What would you call him, then?" the instructor said.

"A man with the best writing style who comes out with a little gay in him."

The instructor laughed.

"Which happens to be his business," Dolores said emphatically. "Except he does wind up in a classroom discussion, so I do think it's pertinent."

"It's not uncommon for people to dislike his violence," the instructor said.

"I sure hate it."

"There you are."

"Only I have a reason. A person capable of great violence starts believing that he's impervious to everything, and he refuses to see that the things that can cripple the rest of us do it to him, too. And they sure do."

"Such as?"

"Alcohol. The bravest war hero who can't handle alcohol becomes just another drunk. Like anybody else."

"Well."

"Well, I don't see Hemingway saying that. So I don't think he can see very much."

"But he isn't dealing with alcoholism here."

"Then he isn't dealing with life."

The instructor shook his head. "This is about a woman's thoughts and desires about the hero."

"Four hours for a guy who couldn't wait to fill a gas tank?"

Later, she sat in the cafeteria alone and had coffee and was grateful when they began putting out the lights at ten after six, for this signaled that it was nearly time to start the last part of her day. Dolores went outside and stood in the cold evening air and waited for the last class, organic chemistry, which started at six-thirty and went through until ten-thirty. Suddenly, an ambulance, purple lights flashing from its top, rocked down the driveway and she stepped out of the way as it moved up to the building. The back door opened and an attendant stepped out. When his head moved, she saw that he was a lanky guy with shaggy black hair who was in the organic chemistry course. There were three ambulance drivers who always sat together in class, with at least two of them usually in the uniform of white shirt and green field jacket and pants. This one's name was LaVine, which, as he explained cheerfully to Dolores one day at the start of the term, had always been Levine until he had a grandfather who learned to play golf at Dyker Heights public golf course in Brooklyn and who then decided to get away from a course littered with old cars and, worse, young Italians, and take what he felt was his extraordinary backswing out to some private club on Long Island that didn't mind his golf game but sure did his name. Enter LaVine with a backswing.

"Here we are," the lanky grandson now said to Dolores cheerfully.

Propped up in the back of the ambulance was an old white-haired woman with skin so pale that in the harsh light she seemed to be an albino. Her eyes opened in great alarm as LaVine left her.

"You're supposed to take care of me!"

"I did. You're fine."

"What does that mean?"

"That you just stay where you are. I'm off duty now."

A short guy got out of the front of the ambulance and walked around to the back.

"See ya," LaVine yelled to the old lady. The doors closed and the ambulance started off.

"Where does she go?" Dolores said.

"Home. She lives alone in Rego Park. She takes a drink and then you get her calling nine one one for the cops. They turn her over to us right away. Usually, we take her to St. John's Hospital. Some nice Catholic girl brings her ice water and they got a priest in the morning. She stays there a day or two. Gets pampered and goes back home to Rego Park. She never has anything so wrong that she can't care for herself at home. She's lonely, just wants somebody to talk to, hold her hand. It's a beautiful thing for her. But I have to tell you, we can't do that anymore. We have people shot, thrown off a rooftop. We can't use up an ambulance run on a lonely woman. What we're doing tonight, we're taking her right down the street here to the Queens Hospital Center. That's how they could drop me off here. It's on the way. When she gets into one of those wards with a hundred percent blacks—half of South Jamaica comes up the hill to use that hospital—this old Irish lady will get frightened to death. She won't be calling nine one one so quick anymore."

"What happens if you have somebody who's really sick?"

"I wouldn't have been here. I just went with her to get the ride. My car is the one that's sick tonight."

"Have you been doing this long?" she asked him.

"Four years. I finally decided to improve myself."

"Are you going to try medical school?" Dolores asked.

"Sure. Just like the rest of them. My father's a doctor, too. I got to uphold the family tradition."

"That's nice."

"Sure it is. He's a doctor. He's a doctor in the meat market. He cuts up veal all day. If I'm lucky here, I'll pass a course and somebody in Health and Hospitals will make me a supervisor."

He said it with a lifeless voice that made her laugh. He smiled, ran a hand through his hair, and went inside. Dolores followed him; in the four-hour night course, Dolores always sat somewhere near the ambulance drivers because at this point in the day she became annoyed by even the smallest sounds; from about eight on, the simple moving around of the college-age students caused her body to stiffen. The ambulance drivers knew to sit motionless. The class had forty-seven students, half of them regular full-time students, eighteen and nineteen years old, who had signed up for the course on the theory that the chemistry department courses during hours of daylight were the school's most demanding and that the night courses, accommodating older and slower minds, weary from a day's work, would be much easier. Thus they were moved to a common wail when, on the first night, there was a change of teachers and the chemistry department's most demanding professor, Steiner, walked into the room. Right away, Dolores noticed that the professor was highly annoyed by this moaning and at the same time seemed slightly intimidated by the size of the class, and by the presence of so many others who were anywhere from twenty-four and twenty-five, like Dolores, through the late twenties, which LaVine certainly was, all the way up to a man who was at least sixty, a retired courthouse stenotypist who used short-hand to take down the lectures. One night, he had explained to Dolores, "My wife goes to her Eastern Star meeting Monday night. Then I'm here Tuesday. I swim at the Eastern Queens YMCA Wednesday night. Then I'm back here Thursday night. If I could only get something going for Friday, Saturday, and Sunday, my life would be complete."

As the class started on this night, a chubby young woman, with red hair and freckles and only a large Star of David around her neck to set her off from being Irish, said loudly to her friend next to her, "I study better at home than I ever could here. I'm taking off. I'll be here for the tests. Save my seat." She walked out, causing laughter among her friends. The professor, Steiner, licked his lips in agitation and then went on. Somehow, Dolores thought, a man in his position of having the power to mark, and particularly to mark these young people who needed high grades so desperately to fulfill parents' wishes that they become doctors who earn big money, might be unable to forget what these people had done to him all term.

"On the test," Dolores said, aloud, to herself.

"What's that?" LaVine mumbled.

"I think he gets a little mad at these kids behind us."

"You got no idea what the inside of his stomach must be like, four hours at the end of a day like this."

"I think he'll get even on the test."

"I never thought of that," LaVine said.

"I'm thinking of it now," she said.

Over the next few weeks, Professor Steiner kept his eyes fixed on a point in the air and his body motionless no matter what indignities were perpetrated by the students before him. When somebody talked during his lecture, the right side of his mouth gave a twitch, which at first seemed involuntary but as the twitch presented itself night after night, it became clear to Dolores that it was studied. Then one night Steiner flushed at the sound of young laughter up in the back of the room. His mouth gave that twitch and now, under his breath, but not that far under, Steiner said something that came out to Dolores's ears as "ajabaday." When he muttered this again, Dolores wrote it down. After class, she showed it to Marissa, who frowned and then copied it in one of her gleaming books. "My father might know." The following Tuesday, Marissa came into the room and handed Dolores a sheet of paper with the words *"a giaviada,"* and under it, the translation: "We're going to see."

"My father says that you don't say that unless you mean it," Marissa said.

"Oh, I'm sure he does," Dolores said.

At ten-thirty that night, Dolores stood in Steiner's way as he left the room. She pretended to yawn. "I can use a rest," she said.

"We all can."

"Do you plan your summer this early?" Dolores said.

"My wife and I go to Italy every year."

"Really? Where?"

"Sicily."

"How exciting!"

His eyes closed in an expression of ecstasy. Then he spoke softly. "The orderly tranquillity of it all. We sit in the morning in Taormina at this outdoor café and here is this man who is in charge of the town. The Don. They really have them, of course. He sits alone with his coffee and these people take their seats at tables all around him. Then he beckons them, one by one, to come to his table and present their grievances. Or their excuses. Then he rules. And his rule is the law. The Don simply gestures or whispers. After that, there isn't a murmur. Oh, the order! The police of the town? They sleep all day in the sun." Steiner chuckled. "Of course you never ask what happens to any of the people who have to sit at the Don's table. Heh. That's all part of the order. So medieval. And so magnificent. My wife and I were there for three summers before we understood what was going on each day. Your average tourist sits there and doesn't have the slightest idea. I do. The people trust me. I can't wait to get there again this summer."

As he talked, Dolores thought, there was somewhere in him, somewhere in his life of compounds and formulas, a secret compartment where he was a controlled but ferocious gangster killer; revenge is a dish best taken cold.

Outside, in the parking lot, she saw LaVine and mentioned this to him. "Of course!" He nodded toward younger students. "If you told them that, they wouldn't know what you're saying."

For simple conversation, something to say before putting keys into a car lock, Dolores said, "Have you your usual ambulance coming?"

"Not tonight. Everybody is watching the Lakers game. Don't get sick in Queens tonight. I got to hurry up and catch the last quarter. You want to stop off?"

"Thanks. I'm going home."

"You live in Glendale, don't you? We watch the game right up near you. Everybody from my job hangs out in the Trotters. It's right on Fifty-ninth Street in Maspeth. It's two blocks from our garage. Stop by, see the end of the game. Plenty of women are there from the job."

"Is that my protection?"

"Well, I don't know. I'm just asking if you want to see the game. It's up to you. I don't want to know your business."

"What do you mean by that?"

"I don't know whether to talk to you or to run away from you."

"What makes you say a thing like that?"

"I heard. The guy you're separated from. Forget about it."

"Where did you hear this?"

"Around."

"You mean around Marissa."

He laughed.

"And what did she tell you?"

"She told me who your husband was."

"What else did she say about it?"

"That the guy was so mad at you that he was going to come here some night and blow up the school."

"That's what Marissa said?"

"Yes."

"What else did she tell you?"

"Not to say anything."

"Is that all?"

"You won't be mad?"

"No."

"All right. This is what she told me, not what I'm saying. She told me that your husband was out there in the parking lot one night with a gun or something and that she had to talk him out of shooting you when you came out of the school."

"She's nuts."

"What can I tell you?"

"You tell Marissa that I'm going to start telling people some things about her. Tell Marissa to stop bothering senior citizens. She'll know."

When he laughed, Dolores said, "Because of that, now I don't know whether I want to come tonight or not."

It was pleasant to talk to him, and with the pleasantness came a light feeling, which she did not identify as slight excitement until she was at the 59th Street exit. She wondered if he could have been a quarter step or a half step beyond being merely cordial when he asked her to watch the game. Then she was in front of the Trotters, which was a low cinder-block building next to a gas station. She looked once in the big front window and saw ambulance drivers in white shirts crowded against the bar. She watched glasses catch the barlight as they were lifted. Thank *you*. She started driving home slowly, through side streets.

At the end of Cypress Avenue, she pulled to the curb. She looked over the tops of low factory buildings and saw the East Side of Manhattan, its riches, white in the night, strewn across magenta. That "the city" can be seen, that there are bridges and tunnels going to it, and subways rushing through the dirty underground air, is the only thing that prevents Queens from being as completely rural in its thinking and emotions as any Arkansas hill town. As it is, people born in Queens, raised to say that each morning they get on the subway and "go to the city," have a resentment of Manhattan, of the swiftness of its life and success of the people who live there. Those of Manhattan are the brokers on Wall Street and they talk of people who went to the same colleges; those from Queens are margin clerks in the back offices and they speak of friends who live in the same neighborhood.

At this point, the East River separates Queens from Manhattan. To the eye, it is gray on one side, the Queens side, where it runs past the old pilings of the Pepsi-Cola storage plant, and a delightful seafoam green as it glides past the United Nations buildings and the riches of the East Side. Here the river is three hundred yards wide and forty-one feet deep and its effect on a couple of million people in Queens is as much as an ocean of the world.

During the week before this, her cousin Virginia had waited for Dolores to get home and, eyes leaping with excitement, said she had spoken to Conlon, the man around the corner with the red-headed kids, and he knew of an odd-hours job in his back office at a Wall Street brokerage. Conlon was the chief margin clerk, Virginia said. "You can go there when you're not in school. You won't have to rely on stealing Owney's checks." These were words that Dolores treated as flying glass, but she decided not to contest the notion that the check was not hers. After she had her daughter bathed and in her crib, Dolores walked around to Conlon's house.

"Mister Conlon—"

"Dan."

"Fine. Dan, my cousin Virginia told me that—"

"We got an insane asylum where I work," Conlon cut in. "The head of the company doesn't trust machinery. He tells everybody to buy IBM stock, but he won't let an IBM salesman into the place. We still do our work as if we got Jack Sprat—is that his name?—working with an eyeshade. The margin clerks are working from six-thirty in the morning until midnight. All hours. We have to send them home by cab. We need help at all hours. Do everything by hand. You're in school again, aren't you?"

"Yes. And I don't know how much time I could spend working. How much would I have to put in?"

"Well, I mean. It's only back-office work. You're not a rocket scientist. It wouldn't fatigue your head so much. You could fit in five days. That's the job."

"I just don't know if I could do anything. I can barely make it as it is."

"What are you taking that's so hard? School, how hard can it be? My nephew goes to school."

"I'm taking pre-med courses and they're quite demanding."

"What are you taking them for, nurse?"

"Oh, I don't know. Doctor, maybe."

"What's a girl want to be a doctor for? Girl's supposed to be a nurse. You'll have another baby sometime, you'll never finish anyway."

"I'm going to try."

"I think that would be very hard for a girl that's married. I know Doris Roehmer next door was trying to do that, but between the house and then getting pregnant, she gave it up. She's got a nice thing now. When she needs a few extra dollars she puts in a shift night nursing, St. John's Hospital."

"I think I want more than that."

"Suit yourself. I just told Virginia that if you wanted something—"

"I think I'd rather starve than give up. In fact," and she patted her middle, "I think I better start starving."

Now, sitting in the car, Dolores thought about LaVine. Pure Queens, embarrassed to admit his own dreams. The night wind blew against tin somewhere on the street, the sound of which put a chill inside the car. Dolores pulled her car coat around her, which caused the collar to rise on her neck, and at first brush, against the right side, she immediately remembered Owney's lips against her neck. Wistful. Then she thought of him alone in his room at the cemetery. Wistful, sad. The feeling, however, didn't clutch and cause pain, for now she thought about him in one of his bars. Thanks.

When she got home, she saw the light in Nancy Lucarella's window and walked across to the house.

"Still trying?" Nancy said, her arm draped on her stack of paper.

"Why not?"

"Because you can't do it. Nobody can do it. Go from here to anyplace else but a knitting mill." She slapped her hand on the desk, which caused the can of soda to spill. Nancy's elbow sent many pages to the floor. "I'll get it!" she shrieked. Dolores was bent over and she had the first blank pages in her hands, cover pages, she thought, but then as she started to pick up more, she noticed they all were blank. Suddenly, Nancy's hand was pushing Dolores out of the way. Dolores straightened up as Nancy picked up her paper.

Dolores now glanced at the pile left on the kitchen table. The top page was blank. Dolores made a pass at the middle of the stack. The kitchen fluorescent light struck another blank sheet. "You came here and made me nervous," Nancy said, standing up. "They had me nervous all day. I went to the ASPCA lawyer today. I asked him to help me in surrogate court to get my money from my mother. He said to me, 'Why are you coming to me to sue for Marilyn Monroe's money?' And I said, 'Because if they are treating me like a dog, then I might as well use a dog lawyer.' "

"I'm exhausted," Dolores said, walking to the front door.

In bed she moved her leg across the emptiness. Once, this would cause him to stir and a hand to reach for her. Now her leg just felt the sheet and through the wall came the sound of her mother's snoring. She lay awake thinking of Nancy Lucarella, who left this block too late in her life and now was across the street in pieces.

At five-thirty, she got out of bed, put on a robe, picked up her book and set of highlight pens, and walked out to the kitchen, where she turned on the light. Then she opened her book and started reading.

On another morning, Marissa called while Dolores was in the midst of changing the baby. "She says *Today* show right now," her mother said, and Dolores said, "Tell her I can't."

"She's screaming."

Carrying the baby, she went out to the television. On came a commercial for Dannon yogurt, which made Dolores think of eating a container of maple walnut ice cream on her way to school.

On the phone, she said to Marissa, "What are you talking about? I hate yogurt."

"You turned it on late! When I say something you got to do it right away. You should have seen it."

"What?"

"They had people on from colleges about scholarships. There were two of them that had scholarships for people like you. Older women."

"What did they say?"

"I didn't hear it all. I had on my hair dryer when they started. I know there was one from Smith and another woman from someplace else. The rest were men. But why I wanted you to catch it, the one from Smith said they even had day care for babies. I don't know what the others were saying. One was from Texas A and M and they had one other woman. From Syracuse."

"Smith had day care?"

"That's what she said."

"Interesting."

"Yeah."

"You at least should ask."

"I'll call right away," Dolores said. Standing in the kitchen with the baby, not even dressed herself, the idea of a phone call to someplace strange seemed overwhelming. Beyond that, there was no time for exotic contests that were unwinnable; she had to get through each day. When Marissa asked her about this at school, Dolores told her that of course she had called and that the scholarships were only open to minorities, which took care of the subject. And then it rained on a Saturday, rain that started early, before anybody woke up, and drummed on the windows and in the gloom of the house the baby immediately was cranky. Her mother, standing at the front windows, gave an enormous sigh.

"I got cataracts."

"What gave you that idea?"

"How would I know, I been to the doctor's."

"This is the first time you've mentioned it."

"You been so busy, I wouldn't bother you."

"That's ridiculous. We're going to have to do something about them right away. Why didn't you tell me?"

"We all got enough to do."

"Mother, we're talking about your eyes."

"You just do your job. Maybe someday you'll know about cataracts. I won't even have to leave this room to have my cataracts looked at."

"They'll be gone by then."

"There'll be something else for you to look at. I'm at that point now where I've started dying."

"So has everybody else. Now tell me how much they bother you."

"I can't thread a needle."

"Well."

"You said it. Well."

"I meant that I hardly call that a catastrophe. A lot of people can't thread a needle at your age."

"It's a pretty big thing to me."

"Well, what did the doctor say to you about it?"

"He said come back. I'm going to call up Jewel Feeney. She had it done. She said it was wonderful."

As Jewel Feeney lived in Boynton Beach, Dolores felt the conversation, whether her mother realized it or not, was an expression of fatigue with the present circumstances.

At the window, her mother sighed again. "Can't go anyplace in the rain."

"Of course you can." Dolores went over and put her head on her mother's shoulder and looked out at the street. "You just go for the day."

"Where? Go jump in the lake?"

"Get an umbrella and go."

"I can't take the baby out in the rain."

"I'm not leaving here today."

"I thought you go by the library today."

"No, I'd just rather stay home."

She relinquished the day to a fretting baby, and, when the child fell asleep at two in the afternoon, she sat at the kitchen table with her books. Immediately, her cousin Virginia walked in.

"Did I sleep! Just got up. What are you doing?"

"I was trying to do some work."

"I have an idea," she said.

"What?"

"That there isn't half the sex in this city that everybody says there is. There are girls walking around this city who have absolutely nothing happening. They don't have a date. Nothing."

"What about the boys?"

"What boys? There aren't any in New York."

"They're not all in Vietnam."

"Who knows where they are. Dolores, I go out and they're either married or they're fags. Where are they all?"

"I'm sure I don't know."

"You talked big. You told me just go out and look. Well, I looked. You know what I found? Girls. Do you know what?" Virginia said.

"Tell me."

"All the stories you read about sex are made up. There are no guys in the whole city. If girls answer questions in a poll, they make up the answers. If they told the truth, there'd be no more magazine stories about sex. Because there isn't any sex in New York."

Now Virginia took a seat across from Dolores, who reluctantly put her books away. She went to the front windows and stared out, as Virginia kept talking.

Dolores discovered the buildings across the street suddenly seemed so close; she could feel them. When she glanced around the apartment, it now seemed miniature. I'm always living in a corner, she thought. Outside, the rain fell steadily and heavily. She went to the phone and called Marissa. "That show you called me about was the *Today* show, am I right?"

"Barbara Walters," Marissa said. "Call her up."

In school on Tuesday, Marissa said, "You call Barbara Walters?"

"Yes," Dolores said.

"What did she tell you?"

"She said, 'Good morning.' "

"I was serious," Marissa said.

"I know. I just can't put anything like that together right now."

Some weeks later, on a Sunday morning, Marissa called again and told her to look in the *Times* education pages. Dolores found a story out of Syracuse about the program. It gave the names of the people from Smith and Syracuse. On Monday, Dolores called Smith and the woman said she could fill in an application and then, if it interested the school, she could come up for an interview.

"You're where now?" Dolores said.

"We're in Northampton."

"And how far is that?"

"About three hours from you."

"Oh, I could never go that far."

When Dolores called Syracuse, she was told that an application blank would be sent and that interviewing of New York prospects could be done in Manhattan. When the thick envelope arrived, her mother said nervously, "What's that?"

"They have some sort of a scholarship."

"What if you get it?"

"I'm not going to get anything. Don't worry."

"But if you do, you'd go up there?"

"I said, I'm not going to get it. Don't worry."

"But what if you did get it? What would you do with the baby?"

"She'd come with me."

"I never heard of such a thing. What would Owney say?"

"Mother, let's totally forget about it. There is no way I'll get anything." Even an offhand thought of taking the baby away from the father caused guilt to churn in her stomach. How could you consider such a brutal thing, she told herself. She had the application for a week and was about to throw it away at the end of a night. And then she suddenly filled it out. One night two weeks later, her mother said, "The school I don't like wrote you again."

The letter this time said that interviews were being held in Manhattan at a Syracuse University building on East 61st Street. There was a date given for late in the afternoon two weeks from then, and Dolores called Syracuse and confirmed it. On the day of the interview, she came home early from school and changed into her only suit, a navy wool, and a white blouse.

"Where are you going?" her mother said.

"To my interview. But only because they were nice even to give me the appointment."

"There'd be hell to pay if you took that baby away. My God in heaven. Don't you think of that?"

"All the time. That's why I'm just going to see them. I won't do anything."

At four o'clock, she found the place, a red brick building across from the side entrance to the Pierre Hotel. She sat in the waiting room next to a black of about twenty-five who had his hands clasped.

"How are you?" she said, brightly.

"Anxious."

"Then I hope you get what you want."

"I was in Syracuse before this. Two and a half years ago. Too bad I didn't keep going."

"I feel the same way. But I stopped to get married."

"Then why you coming on back?"

"Oh, I don't know."

"You got hassles at home?"

"Maybe."

"That's what I had, too. Hassle with my stepfather. He was beating on my mother."

Dolores didn't answer.

"We live in Poughkeepsie. The lawyer told me no jury ever would convict me. He sure was wrong. They put my ass under the jail."

Dolores didn't know how to continue the conversation and sat in silence. "Mr. Dixon?" A man with sparse light hair and heavy jowls, and a large smile, held out his hand. Dixon stood up and the man clapped him on the back heartily and they walked out of the room. Another door opened and a woman with short dark hair and round glasses perched on her nose stood at it and said, "You must be Dolores Morrison. Come in."

Inside, the woman sat on a couch and motioned to Dolores to sit with her. "I'm Susan Bradley. I'm in the university grants office. Your record certainly is good. How did you happen to hear about the program?"

"On television first. Then I saw the paper."

"Then you know about the Smith program?"

"I read about it."

"Have you applied?"

"No. For the interview, I would have had to drive all the way up there. That might sound silly to you, but my mother is taking care of the baby and I can't take any more advantage of her right now than I am. It would just be too much."

"I certainly don't think it's silly. I had someone to take care of mine, but I can imagine what it would be if I had to rely on my mother." She rolled her eyes. "No, strike that. I can't imagine what it would be like. *My* mother? I can't *possibly* imagine."

"Well, I've got my mother."

"Let me tell you why I wish you'd look into the Smith program. The emphasis here is so much on males. They would prefer a man who plays what they consider a minor sport to the most brilliant woman you can find. As for a major sport, well, they don't need grants. They get scholarships pretty quickly. Would you believe me? I'm the only woman in this office. When I mention a woman to them, all they do is smile. For someone like you, for the day care alone, Smith is worth trying for."

"Don't you have day care?"

"Oh, we have it for faculty members. I'm sure it could be included for you. But I have to tell you, our grants are just so male oriented."

"But you specify the pre-med. That isn't exclusively men."

"Someday it won't be. Give people like us another ten years. But for this program, all they're thinking of is men. Who else could have the strength to take on a massive thing like this after they already have started in life? Why, only a man. That's how they think around here. Now the medical school up there adjoins our campus. It's separate. It's part of the state system. But we work together on some projects. With our engineering school, for one. There you go. Mostly men. And then we place our undergraduates in summer lab jobs at the medical school that do help in getting a person admitted. The man who runs the grants programs can't see anything in his mind except a deserving young man."

"I'm still going to try."

"I hope you have other options."

"I don't have much time to think of them."

"Look. It's terrific that you want to try. Better yet if you ever make it. But there are so many things that you can do with your life. I just want you to keep that in mind. What happens here isn't the end of your life."

"I guess not. And I'm going to get what I want." Suddenly, all the doubt and guilt had been replaced by a fierce need to resist even the gentlest suggestion that she was unable to compete.

"I must say, you've made it this far, haven't you?"

"On my first try."

"I still want you to try Smith. It's all women, and I think the atmosphere would be much more supportive. You could do as well in pre-med at Smith as you could here. I know how hard it is going to be for me to sell a woman pre-med."

"Does Smith have the summer lab jobs that you have?"

"Oh, I guess they have something. They don't have the medical school adjoining their campus the way we do. I don't think so, anyway."

"And you have the lab jobs and all that?"

"We do get them, yes."

"That's all I need to know."

"I certainly admire your spirit. I just want to point out that the emphasis is so much on men."

"That guy I met outside doesn't sound like he's had so much of an advantage on me. Where he's coming from."

She smiled. "You're wrong. That's what you're up against. He's a male. He's been in prison. The men at school will get all puffed up. Save a convict for the world. That's their idea of what a scholarship like this should be. God forbid a woman with a baby would be involved. My advice to you is to go out of here today and try Smith. I even know the person up there in charge of the program. I'd be happy to call her for you. She understands the situation here."

"Why did you even bother calling me in?" Dolores said.

"So I could talk to you and hopefully direct you to someplace that would work out. I'm just saying it's all so male dominated here. A black male ahead of a woman. It all comes out of the war." She laughed sarcastically. "That's the only way I could think of helping you. If you had something to do with Vietnam."

13

O N SATURDAY NIGHT, she was in front of the television set for the night, but then her mother said she felt too tired to go out and Dolores got dressed and went with Virginia to the Midway movie on Queens Boulevard. After it, they walked down to the Wine Gallery on Austin Street, which was packed with young people. "Great!" Virginia said, and Dolores answered, "There isn't one person in there who isn't still in school." Virginia said, "Well, that makes it all right for you, and I'm with you, so then it's all right for me, too." Dolores shook her head. "Well, I'm going in," Virginia said; in answer, Dolores placed a hand against her back and pushed her in the direction of the packed bar. "I'll take a cab home," Virginia said.

Dolores walked up to the candy store alongside the subway stop at Queens Boulevard; the Sunday *News* first edition was in stacks and she took one across to the T-Bone Diner, which is a Greek rebellion against public health. She ordered coffee and grilled cheese and opened the paper, whose headline across the bottom of page three said: MEDAL OF HONOR HOLDUP MAN KILLED IN DETROIT IN SHOOTOUT. Her eyes moved across the type swiftly.

DETROIT—Army Sgt. Dwight W. Johnson, 22, the holder of the Congressional Medal of Honor for heroism in Vietnam in 1968, was killed while he was attempting to hold up a food market here tonight. The store manager shot Johnson four times during a scuffle. Johnson was dead on arrival at Ford Hospital. According to police, Johnson came into the store at 11:40 P.M. and asked the manager for cigarettes. Johnson offered a bill for the cigarettes. When the manager opened the cash register to make change, police say Johnson pushed the manager aside. The manager, who was licensed to carry a weapon, shot Johnson three times in the chest and once in the cheek. Police searching Johnson's body found papers showing that he won the Medal of Honor. A relative of Johnson's summoned to the hospital stated that Johnson had gone out unarmed and was attempting to get someone to shoot him.

"What did you do with Virginia?" Her mother watched a *Lucy* rerun.

"Nothing."

"Where is she, then?"

"Stopped to see somebody. She'll come home in a cab."

"And you left me sitting here like this all night?"

"You told me you weren't going out."

"Makes no difference. I spent half my life waiting up for you before you were married. I'm not going to do it now."

"I was all ready to stay home. You were the one who said you weren't going out."

"All I know is that I sat up like this once for you. Now you got me sitting here with another baby."

"How can you say that?"

Dolores was walking out of the room when her mother said, "Sometimes I think."

Dolores said nothing.

"Sometimes I think that maybe you and Owney didn't try all that much."

Dolores sat on the edge of her bed and stared at the baby. She was certain that her mother knew about the story in the paper. Of course. The television news. And now, from nowhere, from the silence of a listless living room, there came a sudden threat: she felt positive that there would be a push to get her to return to Owney. She began to tremble.

At seven-thirty on Sunday morning, bringing the baby into the kitchen, she found her mother gone. "She went to early Mass, St. Pancras," her aunt said. "Virginia's still asleep. What time you keep her out till?"

Dolores said, "I hope, all night."

When her mother came in from church, she was carrying the *Long*

Island Sunday Press, which was delivered to the house. Her mother did not have the *Daily News.*

"You didn't get the papers?" Dolores said.

Her mother shook her head.

"Want me to bring them?"

"No," her mother said, "there's nothing in there that I want to see today."

Later in the morning Dolores deliberately walked to church on the opposite side of Myrtle Avenue from the candy store, and she glanced at it with apprehension that turned into alarm as Prine, the owner, suddenly called to her from the doorway. Dolores waved a hand and tried to keep going. Prine walked rapidly across the street toward her.

"I just want to tell you one thing," he said.

Dolores sighed. "Go ahead."

"That you have some mother. She was in the store before. Just coming from church. Those two brothers from the Veterans Post were in here and they said something smart. Your mother took them on. I haven't seen anybody go after somebody like that in a long time."

"What did they open their mouths for?" Dolores said.

"Exactly what your mother said. She told them, well, I don't want to tell you what she told them."

"She did?" Dolores asked.

"She sure did."

"She told them what they should do?"

"You know it."

"Then she must have told them to go fuck themselves."

"That happens to be exactly what she said," Prine said. "And I thought you should know it."

"Thank you, Mr. Prine."

She walked another two blocks and she was almost at church when she stopped at the outdoor phone booth in front of the Victorian House.

Owney's mother saw the story first and tried to put the paper away, but her nervousness attracted Owney's attention and he waited until his mother finally put the paper down and then he grabbed it and sat at the kitchen table with the coffee cup in his hand as he read the story.

He put the coffee down and got up and went to the refrigerator. He was looking out the window at the cemetery headstones and spires in the chill morning and his hand was on the cold cans of beer in the top of the refrigerator and then the phone rang.

At one-thirty, Dolores Morrison and Owney Morrison stepped into a smoky ground-floor room in Park Slope. A gray-haired woman with her coat on leaned over and said, "This is the first time you come here?"

"Yes," Owney said.

"Where do you usually go?"

"Nowhere."

"Oh." She was elated. She waved. In front of the room, a man nodded to the woman. "It's first time ever!" she said, pointing at Owney. The woman looked at Dolores. "You, too?" Dolores nodded. "Her, too!" Somebody clapped and the man immediately held his hands out for silence. "Ah. Here we let people decide for themselves whether they want to be recognized or not." Owney and Dolores sat in silence. The man looked over the crowd of people who sat on folded chairs and drank coffee out of containers and smoked cigarettes. "Would any new people like to introduce themselves?" he said. Dolores's hand tensed and she was about to touch Owney. Then she stilled herself. But right away, she was disappointed that he had ignored the chance. A man in a red sweater stood up. "I'm Eddie and I'm an alcoholic," he said.

"Hi, Eddie," the people in the room called out.

"Care to say anything?" the leader said.

"Yeah. You know what I did for Christmas? I lost my house for Christmas. That was my present to my wife and kids. I lost my house. You know something else? I hadda look at the newspaper this morning to see that it was almost April. That's all I got to say. I'm banged up. Yes, sir, banged out. I'm just going to sit here and listen, if you don't mind."

"You do whatever makes you comfortable," the leader said.

In the seat next to Owney was a thin man whose face needed shaving. He reached into a leather pouch and took out a roll of thread and a shiny needle.

Owney whispered to Dolores, "Is he actually going to knit?"

"Crochet," Dolores said.

Now, on the side of the room, a short, light-skinned black with a trim mustache and an easy voice began talking. "I have to tell you about a gig I had. Took me to China. I went spinning all through China. I looked at the Great Wall and I told myself, I don't like this at all. What do I need with something like this—all these Chinks build a wall I don't care about? But I knew I could make it all right if I got myself back to the hotel and got ahold of that bottle of brandy I had stashed there." He sat down.

The leader pointed to a man who had thin red hair. "I'm Don and I'm an alcoholic."

"Hi, Don."

"I just got to say that they don't want you to live. Now the whole world knows that I'm a drunk. I live in a town in Jersey and half the people there have had to help post bail when my wife didn't have any money in the house and I got myself arrested for drunk driving or something silly like that in the middle of the night. You know? I'm not secret."

"I don't think any of us are secret," the leader said. "We keep it all anonymous to help you over any personal fears you have about coming here, but I have to tell you, in the town where you live, I don't think there are many secrets."

"Course not," the red-haired man said. "So what happens? We got a big family party for my sister's kid. He graduates out of high school. Fine. I can take a party. Give me a glass of Tab, maybe a cup of coffee, and as many cigarettes as I can smoke. I'll enjoy myself. I'll be a good guy for everybody else, mostly the kid, who happens to love me."

"Oh, you've got to stand up for kids," the leader said.

"You know it," the red-haired guy said. "And I did. Then what happens. I got to tell you. I sit down for the meal, right? Here's my sister mixing a salad in the middle of the table. My own sister, right? What is she using? She got a whole great bottle of wine vinegar. She drowns the salad in it. So I hold up my hand. I know myself. One taste of wine vinegar, crying out loud, I drink the vat. So I hold up my hand. None for me. No salad with wine vinegar. What does my sister, my own sister, do? She starts making fun. In front of the whole table she tells them to look at me, that I'm afraid of wine vinegar. I got so nervous that you know what I thought of right away. My hand was starting to shake. Get something in it."

The leader said, "You just got to be firm. You let them know and then you let them know again and you let them know every single time if you have to."

"Oh, I do."

"That's great."

"Could you imagine giving me wine vinegar? You might as well give bombs to the Germans. I'm still upset with my sister."

"You have to understand that they don't understand."

"Boy. Wine vinegar. That's all I need. I didn't eat salad because of it. On a leaf of lettuce, I would've been in Detroit by morning."

At first, Owney had been smirking as the guy talked of evading the clutches of salad dressing. Owney could taste the salad dressing; it was far too sour for him. Suddenly, his tongue remembered the taste of a cold beer, which was sweeter than whipped cream.

A woman who didn't bother to give her name called out, "I've been sober for seventeen days." Everybody clapped. Now the leader pointed to a young guy in the front. He was dark haired, wearing a light gray suit, and had a campus face, except for eyes that seemed to be looking for a rope on a washy deck. "Hi, I'm Jimmy and I'm an alcoholic."

"Hi, Jimmy."

"I've been sober for three weeks now." They all applauded. "I'm glad I came here to talk to you because I'm afraid I used to drink my whole paycheck up on the day I got it. I even had to borrow money in the bar to get home."

Owney's legs moved. Dolores made a sound in her throat to tell Owney that the young guy was plagiarizing from him.

"I lost my job and my apartment and now I'm living in a room. I'm afraid of drinking. That's why I'm thankful I'm with you. Because I need someone to share my fear with."

Owney muttered, "What is this being afraid?"

"Maybe he is," Dolores whispered.

"Afraid of what? The man talks like a moron. If somebody comes after your life, you can be afraid. Otherwise, forget about it." Dolores put her hand on his arm to call his attention to the man leading the meeting, who was saying:

". . . that fear, well, we're all afraid. People are afraid of looking at themselves. People are afraid of saying that they're afraid. All right now. Let's see who else. Newcomers?" He looked at Owney, who tried to sink his chin into his chest. When the man looked at Dolores, she stood up. "I'm Dolores and I'm an alcoholic."

"Hi, Dolores!"

"I came here because I'm afraid, too," she said. "I think that I've found that you can be the strongest person on earth and then the moment you have to face a glass on a bar you become weak. I even think you can be a hero in every place in life, say in a war, and still be afraid of that glass. Afraid of leaving it alone, I mean. That's what I've found out about the fear part of drinking."

"Oh, it sure is something," the leader said. "It's too powerful for anybody. You need an awful lot of help and support. No one-man-gang act can save you." The leader looked at Owney again and Dolores sat down and now she simply poked him. He stood up with his eyes down. He said softly, "I'm Owney. I pass."

"Fine," the leader said. He nodded to a man of about forty, dressed in a dark business suit, who got up. "I'm Cliff and I'm an alcoholic."

"Hi, Cliff!"

"I can't tell you how relieved I am to be here tonight. I find that when I miss coming to meetings, I get frightened. When I was drinking, I had a lot of trouble controlling myself. One night, I went into my eighteen-year-old daughter's room and beat her up . . ."

"He was looking to do more than beat her up," Owney muttered. Dolores was irritated. Now he talks.

". . . You know how I found out what I did? When the cops woke me up in the cell and told me. I've been in the program for five years now. I'm doing fine. The other day, I had this little scrape with the police, but it wasn't my fault and I'm confident that it will be resolved."

"He's a cop fighter, blames it on whiskey," Owney said, and Dolores said, "Bullshit."

"What do you mean?" Owney said

"Just what I said. Bullshit. Why didn't you talk when you were up?"

The red sleeve of a woman sitting in front of Owney went into the air. The leader pointed. "My name is Alice and I'm an alcoholic," she said, waving a cigarette.

"Hi, Alice!"

"I want to thank you very much for recognizing me. Like Cliff, I have been in a highly nervous state for the past couple of days. I find myself looking at darkness. I needed to come to this meeting today. You see, I'm having my first date in two years tonight. I couldn't go out for the two years because I was afraid. Tonight, I'm going out with a man who drinks. Right now, I'm standing here terrified of the moment when he asks me to have a drink. I honestly tremble when I think of having to face that question."

The man running the meeting said, "Why don't you just say that you don't feel like drinking tonight?" The other people nodded. They smiled, placing a tone of gentleness into the room. The woman sat down.

Owney put a hand on her arm and spoke quickly. "Let me tell you something. Why don't you just look this guy in the eye tonight and say that you are an alcoholic and that you can't have a drink, and that's it? Tell him, 'Don't even ask me to have one.' Don't be afraid of what anyone thinks." Her smile had the gentleness of the room. "Thank you."

"Don't thank me. Just do it."

"But if I did what you say, I'm afraid he would say to me, 'Hey, you're no alcoholic. You can take a drink.' I know I can't."

"Listen to me. Just tell the guy."

"Thank you. But you're new, aren't you?"

"First time here."

"Then perhaps I could help you."

Dolores nodded vigorously at the woman.

"Thanks no," Owney said.

The meeting was over and people stood up and held hands and bowed their heads and prayed for the strength to go through another day without drinking. Dolores took the hand of the woman next to her. Owney, terrified of the man who had been crocheting, kept his hands stuffed in his pockets. He edged out of the room as the prayer ended. He was the first one out of the room.

In her car on the way back to Queens, Owney said, "Where are we going?"

"I'm going to the library," she said.

"You spend your life there."

She didn't answer.

"I'm doing good with it," he said.

"It didn't look like it in there," she said.

"Why? Because I didn't say anything?"

"Could be."

"That's you."

"No, that's you," she said.

"I don't make a fool out of myself."

She didn't answer.

"And what was that thing you had to say? You'd think you'd help sometime."

"I think I just did. Try to, anyway."

She said nothing else. When she stopped in front of the cemetery, he said to her, "There was something in the paper today."

Whatever you do, please don't use that, she said to herself.

"No, it was nothing," he said. "Forget it. I'll see you. Thanks for the ride."

As she drove away, she glanced back once to see him walking, framed by headstones, and she suddenly wished that she had been more forceful with him at the meeting, and made him talk. Then she began to realize that this was the only feeling she had had about him all day: responsibility.

*   *   *

"You realize," the lawyer said to the assistant district attorney, who was annoyingly young, "that these kind of people don't talk. And I, of course, have nothing to do with people who do such a thing."

"I'm familiar with that," the young assistant said.

"Therefore, he has nothing to say to you," the lawyer said.

"You realize that with twelve other defendants it is going to be a long trial," the assistant said.

"I do," the lawyer said. He tried desperately not to sigh, but of course he did.

"I hope your client pays you well enough to tie up your services for four months."

"That's my business," the lawyer said.

"I'm just bringing it up because we're in the same field. And I'm looking at this case, where your client stuck his nose in because he was trying to collect six hundred and ten dollars from a man selling pills on the street. Strikes me he may not be such a sport."

The lawyer went to the door and beckoned. Old Jack entered the assistant's office. He looked at the municipal green walls, the leather chair with cracks all over it, and the untidy stacks of paper everywhere. This kid lives in a slum, Old Jack thought.

"We were just saying that there's a chance that I can cut you loose from this trial," the young assistant said.

"What can I tell you?" Old Jack said.

"You can tell me that you don't want to go on trial for extortion, drug selling, and conspiracy and then go to state prison for twenty-five years."

"What can I tell you?" Old Jack said.

"State prisons are about ninety percent black," the young assistant said. "No, excuse me, they are seventy percent black and twenty percent black Hispanic."

"You know us, we don't say nothin'," Old Jack said.

"He would never talk and I would never stand here and become a part of an arrangement whereby somebody does talk," the lawyer said.

"Then why am I supposed to let a man out of a trial that would take as much as four months out of my life, and out of yours, counselor?"

"We can't trade our way out of here," the lawyer said. "I would never do such a thing."

"The prisons are all black," Old Jack said.

"I didn't say that. I said they were seventy percent black. I said the other twenty percent are black Hispanic. That means they're not only black but they don't speak English. They play Puerto Rican music loud all day in the cell blocks."

"What can I tell you?" Old Jack said. In a whisper.

"I don't know. You tell me," the assistant said.

The lawyer coughed. "I think I have to go to the men's room."

Old Jack, not looking at the lawyer, said, "Go to the men's room."

"You're not going to speak in my absence?" the lawyer said.

"Of course not," Old Jack said.

Fifteen minutes later, the assistant walked into his superior's office. "I cut that mumser from Queens loose."

"*You* cut him loose? There goes your megalomania again. We got no real case against him. The judge was going to throw it out of court on Friday."

"He didn't know that today. So I took something out of him on the way out anyway," the assistant said.

"Took what?"

"Just a little piece of him. He gave me some homicide. Actually, he couldn't wait to do it. It was obvious he thought he was getting even with somebody. I wish I could've pushed him for more things, but I was afraid he would stop altogether. I settled for the homicide. Whatever it's worth."

"I wouldn't worry about him," the superior said. "He has a federal strike force case coming against him that will bury him in January. Want to get lunch?"

Two days later, a supervisor of detectives in the station house on West 54th Street in Manhattan hung up the phone, looked at the notes he had just made, and then bawled, "Give me the file on this O'Sullivan."

A detective named Webster brought a folder, with black marking pen on the cover proclaiming that Charles O'Sullivan had been shot dead near the Music Box Theatre on West 45th Street.

"How many witnesses do you have?"

"None," Webster said.

"Why don't you have any witnesses?"

"Because nobody saw it."

"How come I got something and you don't?" the supervisor said. He handed Webster the notes.

The supervisor stood up and left the room. Some time in the next ten days, Webster knew, the supervisor would go on vacation. By the time the supervisor returned, he, Webster, would be in Pompano Beach, Florida, for three weeks. The O'Sullivan case, which was never going to get solved anyway, would be under a stack of fresh and more easily solved cases. Webster was a gaunt man with a brown toupee that was so obvious that the others at work called him Rughead. A policeman for seventeen years, he was so busy counting the days to his twentieth year, and pension, that he rarely spoke about anything else. His partner, Eagen, was young, but the job itself, and then being around Webster, had soured him so quickly that he thought like a man of sixty.

Webster looked at the notes. "Three of them got beat up. Two sand-hogs and a barmaid. They were in hospitals."

"I hate hospital offices," Eagen said. "People work in them are a pain in the ass."

Webster kept looking at the notes. "Hunh. Something here with an Owen Morrison."

"From where?" Eagen said.

"Queens."

"All the way out there?" Eagen whined.

14

STEAM FILLED the bathroom until she could not see the mirror. Good. Helps get the hair a little fuller. She wrapped an orange towel around her and thought about a silver necklace to wear with her shirts in the fall. Sure, that was a long way off, but not that long when you think of the time it takes to find what you want: they might have necklaces like that on Austin Street in Forest Hills, she thought, but the sure way was to take a Saturday and go to St. Mark's Place on the downtown East Side of Manhattan. Jewelry from New Mexico. What could it cost, seventy-five dollars? Whatever it is, I deserve it, she assured herself, and the money had to come from her husband and not as something left on the kitchen table as a contribution, some sack of coins tossed to the ground by a knight riding through a hamlet of huts.

Then she thought of Christine's feet. The wonder of miniature toes had turned into pink shoots that now barely fit into their socks and shoes. If I don't take the time to get her new shoes this weekend, I'll have a child walking barefoot, she thought. She began brushing her hair fiercely; at each moment such as this, as she thought of some stark failure to attend to her daughter, she became so susceptible to guilt that her body moved in dashes rather than with the ease of full lines. Now she saw herself as a little girl again as she walked the streets behind a woman she felt was her real mother, following the woman down the streets with a hope trying to burst out of her chest, and then standing on an empty sidewalk in the cold late afternoon as the woman went up to her own house and pressed her flesh against that of her children and Dolores had to turn again and carry her weeping insides home. Now she shivered in the steamy bathroom. She had to press her baby against her right now.

She wiped the steam off the mirror and inspected her hair once more and then turned to start out of the bathroom and walked into Owney, who stood in the doorway holding the baby, who was silent and then wailed as Owney suddenly held her up over his head. His eyes were clear and his blue shirt smelled of fresh air. He was annoyed that his daughter didn't trust him and Dolores, taking the baby away from him, said, "She hardly knows you." She calmed the daughter as she carried her out to her mother, who was not there.

"She said she was going out," Owney said, and this caused Dolores to holler louder than the baby. "She wasn't even dressed when I got into the shower. How could she do this?"

"I told her I'd take the kid for a couple of hours."

"And she left just like that?"

"I think she thought we could be alone if she went out."

"At seven-thirty in the morning? You're catching me in the middle. I have to keep moving."

"I'll drive you."

"No, because then somebody from school would have to drive me home. And maybe I wouldn't be able to find a lift."

She put the baby in the highchair in the kitchen and pointed to the coffee for Owney and then went into the bedroom to get dressed and the emptiness of the apartment suddenly became ominous. Without turning around, she said, "Just stay where you are. I have to get dressed." The small sound of his foot in the hallway just outside the bedroom told her that her timing was of the sort that wins wars. Then she counterattacked. "Why aren't you working, anyway?"

"They had an accident last night. The wires caught fire. Nobody can work today until the electricians get through. The whole place got knocked out. Five o'clock in the morning we had a meeting downtown at the union. Four, five guys were caught in there for a while last night."

"You can't keep working there. You'll get killed."

"I've got a couple of moves figured out with Kellerman and then we'll see what's what. The big thing is, look at this." He stood in the doorway and held his hand straight out.

"Great. Now let me get dressed."

He walked in and put his arms around her and she could feel the desire in them, and she had no reaction to it except to strain to get away. "Take the day off," he said, and this caused her to push harder. "I'm going to school. Would you mind letting go of me? I have to get out of here in five minutes." He did not let go. Where is that fucking Marissa on the phone? she said to herself. That gave her enough energy to force his arms to drop away. She reached into the closet for a blouse. "Would you mind? I have about five minutes." She dressed in a white blouse and jeans, picked up fake pearls, and, without bothering to look at herself, went into the kitchen. Why be standing in front of the mirror as a temptation? Owney was at the table, placing his hand over Christine's face and then pulling it back, which each time first frightened and then delighted her.

"This is no good," Owney said. Dolores was busy looking into her purse. "She doesn't have me and she doesn't have you. What kind of a life is this for her?"

The pain rose so rapidly that before she had finished a breath she was stricken. There was not a day, an hour, a moment that she was away from the baby, that she was not conscious of enormous guilt that she attempted to keep battened down somewhere inside her, and never successfully, for it always rose and consumed her at the odd moment. This time, the only method of expelling it was to attack immediately.

"We have to talk about money. You're going to make me go to court the way it's going."

She knew that she was appropriating the thing she liked least in her husband—when cornered, attack—but she assured herself that she was correct in what she was doing because he most certainly was dreadful with money.

"I get my vacation bonus early this year. I get it next week. They hand it out now in case somebody wants to put up money ahead of time for a vacation. When it comes, I'll give you the whole thing." His hand went into his pocket and placed folded bills on the kitchen table. "That's all I have."

She sighed. "We're back to this. I don't want money that way. It has to be on a more orderly basis. I would take a job if I could. But I can't. You're going to have to do better."

"I'll do the right thing with the money. Where does that leave her?" He was looking at the baby, holding her hand.

"With her mother."

She leaned down and hugged Christine and then left with the guilt now at its fiercest.

At noon in the cafeteria at school, she scolded Marissa for not calling.

"You told me not to bother you," Marissa said, and Dolores answered, "I said that yesterday. I didn't mean today." She went to the phone and called the house and when nobody answered she became nervous, and it wasn't until the third call, an hour later, that she got her mother and found that she merely had gone for a walk with the baby. When Dolores got home that night, she found that Owney had left $315 on the kitchen table. If he can leave that much once, then he best do it every week, she muttered. She then found that Owney had spoken to her mother about taking the baby on Sunday. "I told him maybe the two of you could have her together," Dolores's mother said.

That Sunday morning, Dolores was up before seven and put on clothes that gave her a dull feeling: a brown vinyl jacket over a yellow shirt and purple skirt. Ugly colors, she thought. As she drove into the cemetery she spotted Owney's father walking up the roadway toward the house. He turned his head once and saw her and then picked up his stride. Dolores rushed the car past him, waving once, and at the caretaker's house she let Christine climb up the staircase on hands and knees. Owney's mother stood in the doorway and looked with elation as Christine squeezed past her and went into the living room and had to be followed. Dolores went upstairs with the father right after her and Dolores swung into the kitchen and found a can of beer alongside the ashtray, where the father reluctantly took his seat. Caught dead.

The father tapped the newspaper. "I just read a story in the paper about walking. Maybe I'll walk to the racetrack today. In the paper it says that in Mexico they have this place where you can walk up the pyramid and see the place where they used to cut the people's hearts out. Offering them up for a sacrifice. They had a real terrible religion. What can you expect from pagans? Let me go get Owney."

"Not as long as you got that around," Dolores said, waving disdainfully at the beer can.

"This is only beer," Owney's father said.

"To me, it's drinking."

"You think we stand still for him drinking?" The father rose, making a great deal of noise with his chair as emphasis for the magnitude of the act he was about to commit. He took a bottle of J&B Scotch, a third full, from a shelf and poured it down the sink. "There'll be no more drinking by anybody in this house."

"What's that?" Dolores said, pointing at the beer.

"That's beer," the father said.

"What do you think that is?" she said.

"Beer isn't drinking."

Owney walked in with a T-shirt, wrinkled pants, and bare feet. His eyes were hooded with sleep. "I was coming to the house myself."

"I got here first. And I have to leave now," she said, walking into the living room, suddenly sulking but her mind not grasping the reason: never before had she left the baby outside of her own house. She heard the noise from Owney's bedroom and walked in hesitantly and found Christine on her stomach on the bed and trying to get off, with Owney holding her. When the baby saw Dolores she became more determined and started to cry and Owney had to let her go. She tumbled off the bed, got up, and fell against Dolores's legs. "Well, this isn't starting off so well, is it?" Dolores said.

"She'll be fine," Owney's mother said from the doorway. Dolores did not talk. "Won't you be fine?" Owney's mother said to Christine, who now hugged Dolores's legs. Owney swung from the bed and reached for Christine, who wailed.

"You shouldn't of let her see you before you left," the mother said. Dolores gazed at the deep, dark, concentric rings around the mother's eyes.

"I wouldn't leave her like that."

"Maybe you should just run out right now."

"Yes, go ahead, I'll hold her," Owney said.

Dolores shook her head.

"It's all right. She's with her father," Owney said.

Dolores picked up the baby, who buried her face in Dolores's shoulder.

"You only made it worse," Owney's mother said.

"Put her down and get going," Owney said.

Dolores patted Christine. Clucking, Owney's mother reached for the baby. Dolores kept her eyes on the woman's fingers as they reached out. The fingers grew longer and closer to the baby and Dolores took a step back. The fingers simply lengthened and spread to the baby and Dolores took another step back. The fingers jabbed boldly and almost grabbed her baby. Dolores's mouth was open and her eyes were wide with fear. She stepped to the right. Owney's mother stepped to the left and this brought her even with Dolores. The hands were so close to the baby. The baby clutched Dolores's blouse. Her gums were wet against her shoulder. Dolores sensed the wall behind her. A step and a half back. Straight to her left was the window, about four steps away. Ahead was the bed. Between the end of the bed and the wall, in the space where she now stood, there were about three paces in which to move. On the left of the bed was the bureau. If she turned to the right, she was facing the door to the living room, four steps off. On the right of the bed was the closet, whose door was open, and, a pace away, a closed door into the bathroom. Owney stood between the bed and a chair. He started forward and his hands, too, began to raise. Dolores stepped quickly to the outside of the chair. She knew she was acting queerly and attempted to disguise this by talking and soothing the baby; when the mother moved on her from the left, Dolores, murmuring to the baby, began to use the room. Moving suddenly, going to the left, passing Owney's mother, who was standing still for the moment, going toward the windows, she lengthened her stride as she used the room and came to the window and looked out at the fields of headstones in the pale morning sun. "Here," Owney's mother said, walking to her. Dolores moved away from the window, shoulder blades brushing the wall, and then she found herself in the corner and Owney's mother had both her hands out and Dolores's breath caught and she took a step to the side, turning her body and bringing up an elbow between herself and the mother. She walked across the entire room and pretended to inspect Owney's closet.

Owney reached past Dolores and she pulled away because she thought he was trying for the baby, but he simply closed the closet door. Dolores held the baby in front of her now, protecting her with both arms, looking directly into the face and small eyes that trusted and now she saw the blue veins of the mother's hands that were so raised that they seemed to be throbbing. Clinging to her baby in a room with an unmade bed, with beer in the kitchen and a poisoned vision of a night in the first days of her life, she became motionless. Cornered, she screamed with her mouth shut.

There was thick planking over the hole and they were putting metal braces around the top. They stood on the thick planking, which had spaces between the boards, an inch at the most, but enough for the eyes to peer through and see the darkness below. There was a small hole in the center of the planking. Feet moved with care about the hole. The shaft was a new one, on the fringe of the Van Cortlandt Park golf course. Someday, water would rise up the first five hundred feet of the shaft and enter a main. Now, it was a deep hole that had to be lined with concrete.

Blaney, who had dressed for underground work, a light shirt underneath a rain slicker, now found himself doing a morning's work outside in the cold spring air. He shivered.

"This is as bad as Letterkenny," he said. He was illegal Irish, who had arrived in this country on a piece of paper good for two weeks; he was now in his second year in the Bronx. He was chunky, with a square face.

"Will I be able to see Danny Murphy out here?" he said.

"Is that all you got on your flamin' mind?" Delaney, the foreman, said.

"I was in two places last night where they had the signs from the Fire Department up. In the restaurant it says, only one hundred and eighty-seven is allowed in. Then I go to the Litram House on Jerome Avenue and it says right over the bar, only one hundred and eighty-seven is allowed in."

"Two places, you say?" Delaney said.

"With my very own eyes, I saw the both signs."

"Then you'll be fucking seeing Danny Murphy," Delaney said. "One hundred and eighty-seven."

"I'm going to be dancin' in the Bronx tonight with my money."

Owney left the conversation as he saw Navy getting out of his old car out on the street. He walked down to meet him. "Can I talk to you?" Owney said.

"I'm up for grabs."

"I went to a couple of meetings again," Owney said.

"Sounds good."

"Then yesterday I was over at my mother-in-law's. I had the baby there all day. Dolores had to go to the library and she brought the baby over for the day, but I thought, well, it's better for her if I keep the baby at her mother's. I stayed there all day."

"That's what Sundays are for. Everything go all right?"

"Fine. I took the baby for a walk. I sat and watched the Mets game. I get along good with the mother. When Dolores came home, we had dinner. Then I had to go home. I'll tell you, I decided that was the last night I'm going to do that."

"Go there to see them?"

"No. Sleep alone at night. I loved holding my daughter yesterday. From now on, I want to hold my daughter whenever I want, and I want my wife in bed with me after that. I didn't get married to be alone. Know what I mean?"

"People discover that at odd moments. The first time I decided to hold my daughter was at her wedding. I went out onto the dance floor and said, 'I want to hold my little baby.' I wouldn't let go of her. Twenty-four years old, she was. First time I ever really held her, I guess. The husband put his hand over my face and pushed me away."

"That's not me anymore."

"For today."

"You could give her a call for me. No, better yet, you could go over and see her for me."

"Certainly. What am I supposed to say?"

"Tell her I went to meetings and I'm not drinking."

"We've had this conversation before."

"It's different. She could see for herself yesterday that I wasn't drinking. If somebody tells her I'm not drinking at work, either, that could straighten it out. I'm going to be back with her soon anyway. Why do I have to wait?"

"That easy?"

"Well, it's the truth. I told you she came and took me to a meeting. From nowhere she showed up one day. Then on Sunday, I told you, she had me come to her mother's house. So it's only a matter of time. Why don't you tell her something good?"

"I thought we agreed that I'm no schoolteacher giving out notes. What I will do, I'll go to a couple of meetings with you." When Owney made a face, Navy said, "Why haven't I made any meetings with you, anyway?"

"I go."

"But what do you get out of them? Do you put yourself up there? Say anything about yourself?"

"You see for yourself, I'm all right."

"Today. Rather, this morning."

"Isn't my word any good?"

"A drunk's word?"

"I'm not a drunk."

"There's your problem right there. As long as you talk like that, I can't give you much help. When you put down the glass once, that doesn't mean official retirement. Ray Robinson retired five times that I know of. You get a good drinker, lifetime, he makes a retirement announcement maybe seven hundred fifty times."

By now, they were standing alongside the excavation and Blaney, hearing this part of the conversation, said, "The people who want to take the drink away from a man would steal the Cross from Christ's back and leave him hanging in the air." With a shout, he jumped onto the scaffolding. "You can deprive the man of a drink. Not me. Tonight, I'll be dancin' in the Bronx." He took a step. The joy in his shout turned into a scream as his legs went into the small hole in the center of the scaffolding. His body caused the boards, with the spaces between them, to click together. The hole in the center now was wide enough for a body to fit through.

Owney threw himself at the wood. He landed on his stomach, with his chin on the wood, seeing blackness and hearing Blaney's long, single scream as he fell down a shaft eight hundred feet deep.

In Brendan's, on Katonah Avenue, the day bartender was suddenly so busy that he had to throw his cigarette away and work with both hands. He looked out the window while he drew beer. "Danny Murphy."

"He'll be here," Delaney said.

"The fookin' number is going to turn up," the bartender said.

"Sure as we're here."

"If he isn't here in ten minutes, I'll call up for him," Delaney said.

Owney tried to drown out the sound of Blaney's scream by placing two dollars in the juke box and punching numbers randomly; he heard only Blaney. Beer tasted sour, but he kept drinking it. "I don't want to insult you."

Navy's creased face smiled sadly. "That can't be done."

"Tastes lousy."

"It always does when you need it," Navy said. "Alcohol is nothing but a traitor."

"I need something."

"Just don't expect me to stay."

By now, the place was filled with bellies and reaching arms and then the bartender called out, "Hup," and Danny Murphy, the left side of his face still discolored from his encounter with the baseball bat, pushed in. The barman slapped a hand into the cash register and pulled out a bill, which he held out for Murphy. "One eighty-seven!"

"Put me in for one eighty-seven. Ten dollars," Delaney said.

"Twenty dollars," Chris Doyle said.

"On?"

"One eighty-seven."

"It'll fookin' come in," the bartender said.

Danny Murphy nodded. "That's the way it always happens."

Owney said, "Put me in ten dollars a day for the next two months. One eighty-seven." Murphy held out his hand. "Mark me down. I'm good for it," Owney said. Murphy nodded.

"I want another ten. The man's death has to stand for something," Delaney said.

Murphy was being pressed to the wall; hands that had been reaching for glasses now held out money, which Danny Murphy snatched.

"One eighty-seven!"

"What's so bad if you win and give the money to his family?" Delaney said.

"The fookin' number is going to turn up," the barman said.

Owney pushed the beer away. "I don't know if it's the beer or the number. It's making me sick. Probably the number."

"Then you ought to hang out in a funeral parlor," Navy said. "Play every dead stiff's pet number. You're liable to wind up rich and sober."

On the way home, Owney stopped in a place in Flushing, but he couldn't get Blaney out of his ears. He stopped at Gibby's on Myrtle Avenue and looked at a beer and then went to see Dolores, who was not home. He played with the baby and left. When Dolores got home, she said nothing when her mother told her that Owney had been around.

"He was very quiet," the mother said.

"And?"

"He didn't have anything to drink in him. He said he'd be over to see you and Christine tomorrow maybe."

"Fine."

Now he decides he's married to me, Dolores said to herself. Just like nothing ever happened, dissolved consequences. I guess bringing him here Sunday was a mistake. She shuddered and went into her room.

That Thursday night, at about nine o'clock, in the organic chemistry laboratory, she heard cellophane crackling somewhere around LaVine, at the next station. She looked up in time to see him pulling Lorna Doone cookies out of his pocket.

"Give me one of those." She pressed her hand against her stomach. "I'm starved."

"My dinner," LaVine said.

"So you'll eat a diet meal." She grabbed a cookie.

"Don't you eat dinner home?" LaVine said.

"I've been here since nine in the morning," she said.

"Oh."

"And why didn't you eat?"

"How was I going to eat if I'm carrying a woman who was hit by a Sanitation truck? After something like that, I can't stand the sight of gravy."

"That's too bad if you're so squeamish." She took another cookie out of his hands and went back to her station.

At ten twenty-five, with people starting to pack up, LaVine said to Dolores, "Can you get home without something to eat?"

"No."

"Neither can I."

"I guess we'll both be found on the roadside," she said.

"I'll get you something," he said.

"No, I appreciate it very much, but you go to that place of yours. I'd prefer going home."

"What place? We'll go anyplace you want around here."

"No, thanks. I'd like something to eat. But I just don't feel like eating in a bar."

"We won't go to a bar."

"Don't be silly. You're exhausted, too. You go have something to eat and have a few beers to relax."

"I don't drink," he said.

"You do so."

"No, I don't."

"You invited me into that horrible place near where you work."

"And you didn't show up."

She was surprised that he mentioned that. "It looked like a dungeon."

"You think the place was that bad?"

"From what I could see from the street, it was at least seedy."

"The only reason I'm in there is to watch the games with everybody from work. I don't go into bars, otherwise. I don't drink. I was raised in a house where nobody took a drink. So I don't. That's some case for genes. I don't drink and I live in Queens. I'm the only one in the whole borough who doesn't drink."

"There's one other," she said. "All right. Where do we go for something to eat?"

"The pizza stand on Parsons."

"Fine."

She drove to the pizza stand, whose signs proclaimed "Real Sicilian," and which served squares of wet cement that, if offered in the city of Palermo, would cause the counterman to face a unique negative reaction. They sat at a counter along the back wall and Dolores went for a moment to a phone out at the curb.

"Everything is all right home. I worry when it's this late."

"Who's home?"

"I have a baby."

"Oh. That makes it tough, doesn't it? With your husband and all."

"We're bringing nice modern complications to Glendale," she said.

"They like families there," he said.

"They love the idea of them. Sometimes I think all the families don't like each other so much, but they stay together because everybody loves to see families together. They stay together for holiday pictures. Wait'll they hear that I put in for a divorce."

"You did?"

"Yes."

"You Catholic?"

"Of course."

"I thought you weren't allowed."

"That's why I went to a lawyer."

He didn't say anything.

"You're married?" she asked.

"No, not close."

He pushed half of the slice into his mouth.

"You'll choke."

He shook his head and chewed.

"Where do you live?" she said.

"Over in Long Island City. It's close enough. But I don't have any food home. I only have myself home. I have the second floor of a small factory. I'm two doors from the river. I look out the window at Manhattan. Then people in Manhattan look out the window and they see me. For ten thousand a month they see David LaVine in the window of his factory."

She noticed that her square of pizza was disappearing virtually as quickly as his. She was anxious about this because it meant that soon she would have nothing in her hand to eat.

"Do you hear from that woman you had in the ambulance?" she asked.

"Her? She lives for the next twenty-five years. And she's not the star. You know what we just had to do? In East New York, we had this one family who kept calling us all last weekend for a grandfather who had a toothache. A guy from Haiti. They want an ambulance for his toothache. So we said to the family, 'It costs you two hundred dollars out of your welfare check if we pick up your father and take him to the emergency room for a toothache.' "

"They must have loved that."

"What did they say, they said, 'My grandfather is a baby when something hurts him. We don't need any ambulance. He can just sit and let his tooth hurt him.'"

The two of them laughed. She found his laugh pleasant and his open face appealing. The eyes were heavy and tinged with red from the long day, but she thought there was friendliness kindled in them.

Later, when she got home, she went directly into her aunt's apartment. "Wake up, Virginia," she called.

"She's in the shower," Aunt Grace said. "Been in there half the night. I call her, she won't come out. How come you're so late?"

"I stopped off for pizza. Where is that girl?" Dolores went into the bathroom and found Virginia sitting in the bathtub with the shower raining water on her. Virginia had her head hanging.

"What do you call this?"

"I'm so depressed I could kill myself."

"What happened?"

"Nothing."

"No, what happened? Something must have."

"I said nothing. And that's the reason I'm depressed. Nothing happens in my life."

"What do you mean by that?"

"I want a man."

"What do you want one of those for?"

"Because nobody else in the whole city has one, either. There isn't one girl I know has a man. They're either married or gay. Where the fuck are they?"

"I know where one is. I found him for you tonight."

Virginia's head snapped up. "Where? What did you find?"

"I think he's a terrific guy. He's at school."

"Is he married?"

"No."

"What is he, the janitor?"

"No. He goes to school."

"How old is he?"

"Your age exactly."

"He's white?"

"Absolutely."

"You're lying. He's a big black, scare my mother to death."

"Nope."

"If he's a spic, it's all right. I'll meet him outside the house. He doesn't have to come here. Maybe if he's a black that's all right, too. As long as they don't want to come home."

"He's all white."

"Then he's some crip. That's what he is, right? A crip in a wheelchair. Roll right up to the door and then he can't even climb my stoop."

"He is a good-looking guy who works for the Emergency Medical Service. He's an ambulance driver. He wants to be a doctor. I don't know about that. I do know that he's appealing and he's fun. And he doesn't drink."

"Well, get him for me."

"I'll have to talk to him a little."

"I'll talk to him myself. Show me where he is. I'll come to school with you."

At the start of the long class on Tuesday night Professor Steiner appeared to be particularly annoyed when one of the young women used the wrong term. Flustered, she corrected herself, but this did not seem to satisfy him. "Nomenclature," he growled. "We have to be careful of nomenclature." When he used that word for the third time during the night, Dolores looked at the faces in the room and was amazed to find that the point apparently failed to register on them. After class, she said to La-Vine, "You heard the key word, didn't you?" His answer was a vague look and then embarrassment that he had not grasped something so obvious. "I can't make it. I can't work and do this right. I'm a dead man." He refused to listen to encouragement.

Out in the hallway, Dolores called to Marissa, who waved. "I can't wait to talk to you. I'll miss my ride. I'll call you when I get home tonight. No, it's easier in the morning. Bye." She ran out the door.

When the phone rang the next morning, Dolores was still in the shower and she called out to her mother to tell Marissa to call back and the mother said, "She says you got to come right away." Dolores protested and then, wet, wrapped in a towel, got out, and on the phone Marissa said, "Dolores, you think I could wear red hot pants to school? Then a nice pink shirt. You think so?" When Dolores thought about this aloud, and seemed to be leaning toward something more student, Marissa said, "I like them," and Dolores said, "Then wear them," and Marissa said, "Maybe you don't like them for school, but they drive Harry crazy, I think. Sees everything moving on me."

"Harry?"

"Yeah, Harry, the man from the railroad station in the morning."

"So now he's Harry?"

"Harry likes me. He wants to take me to Colorado."

"What's out there?"

"He likes to look at mountains."

"I guess it's a nice place."

"I don't know how to go there. What am I going to tell my mother, 'Ma, I want to go to Colorado with a guy twenty years older than Daddy.' "

"Don't ask me to help you make up lies," Dolores said. "Why don't you just try dinner in Nassau County first. See if you can even stand him through a salad."

"I need Colorado."

"Why?"

"Because in a couple of years, when I don't need a sugar daddy anymore, I'll take him to Colorado and instead of looking at mountains I'll make him climb them. He'll die trying to get on a rock that juts out over his head."

"Where do you get these things from?"

"I saw that on *Wide World of Sports*. Guys climbing mountains. I always think when I watch television. I don't just sit there like a chair. I watch so much television. I keep what I want. I don't keep every single thing I see. I don't keep every little fact. I got to remember the nomenclature, you know."

"Oh, why would you do a thing like that?"

"Because he used the word so much last night that it went off in my ear like a bank alarm."

Over the last weeks of the term, Dolores worked late in the library many nights and returned to find, on an average of twice a week, Owney sitting in the living room with her mother and sometimes the baby, and his face seemed to have its old energy spilling out of it. He made a point of saying that on the nights that he did not stop around to see the baby, he was attending AA meetings and had resumed his labor courses. "What have you told them at the meetings?" Dolores said.

"Not much. I listen."

She said, "I have to tell you, I truly believe that you are better off joining in."

Then she walked into the bedroom and closed the door. She could feel him closing in and she knew that her mother was delighted that he came. Which was one topic she made certain not to discuss. The second was the apartment on 74th Street, which kept reappearing in her mind at night and whenever she passed the street. Now that she had no need to raid it for his government checks, she turned her head so as not to look at it. Sitting in her room now, with Owney out in the living room, she felt as if she were in a closet at the end of an airless passageway.

In the third week of May, Steiner gave his test. He began it by standing in front of the room and speaking in a voice that had far more carry to it than at any time in the term thus far. "I consider this test tonight the beginning of a weeding-out process. I will know and perhaps many of you will know if we are all heading in the direction you feel you want to pursue. Or, is it the one your parents decided upon?"

With that, he spun and left the room and the teaching assistants took over. The chairs in front, where Dolores usually sat, were taken, and there was confusion among the young teaching assistants and she wound up in the fourth row, next to a dark-haired young man with thin lips who settled in his seat and glanced down to be certain that he could read the pages of white notes he had between his legs. Dolores reached into the pocket of her sweater nearest the guy and took out her change purse. This immediately caused him to shift in his seat.

"Am I in your way?" he said.

"No."

"Then you didn't have to move it."

"I'm more comfortable with it on this side," she said. "I'm merely doing what your mother must have to do. She does hide her purse on you, doesn't she?"

The test was mimeographed and the first glance showed that it was indeed Steiner's revenge. The questions, dealing with synthesis, were in a naming system that is almost never demanded from undergraduates. As Dolores looked over the test, nodding to herself, she heard a moan in the back of the room. She glanced back and saw the red-headed young woman standing up and crying uncontrollably. The other young people seemed too much in shock to bother with her. In tears, the red-headed girl simply walked out of the room. Dolores saw Marissa, head down, chewing gum, starting to work. Off to the right, LaVine's legs stretched and he slumped in the seat. "No way for me," he said. When Dolores looked at him, he made a face and looked down. There was no reaction next to her. The kid was catatonic on two counts: lack of knowledge compounded by an inability to cheat. Later in the night, on one question about a synthesis of trichlorophenol, her back became tired and she forgot herself and stretched. As she did, the kid in the next seat put his head so close to her paper she was afraid he was going to eat it. She put her hand over it as if they were in grammar school. Then she bent her neck and went back to the test that could have something to do with the rest of her life.

"Look at me," LaVine said in the parking lot.

"I am."

"Take a good look."

"All right."

"Now close your eyes until I'm gone. I want you to remember me like this. It's the last time anybody ever is going to see me."

"Oh, come on."

"No, that's it. I'm truly dead."

Four days later, the postcard came from school. The mark in organic chemistry was an A. Dolores made a small noise and headed for the phone. She called Marissa first; when there was no answer, she called the Emergency Medical Service number in Maspeth and left her number for LaVine.

She was sitting home at seven o'clock at night when Owney walked in. Just like he lives here, she thought. He swung the baby over his head in the living room.

"My daughter tell you her mark?" her mother said.

"An A," Dolores said.

"In what?"

"Organic chemistry. That's the hardest."

"My daughter's smart."

"She sure is," Owney said, keeping his attention on the baby.

Later, they were watching a movie on Channel 9 when her mother answered the phone. "It's David LaVine."

Dolores got up too quickly and immediately felt Owney's stony look.

LaVine shouted "Great!" when he heard Dolores's mark. "Now you got me crazy. I haven't been home, so I don't know if mine came or not. I'm standing in Howard Beach right now. We got here second on a car accident. Waiting for the priest."

"They made you *wait?*"

"There's no reason to leave without him. He's only coming for—what do you call it?—*ex*treme unction."

"Oh, David."

"What can I tell you? Kids. They went into a tree. Bridge abutments and trees don't move. You ought to see it. The tree doesn't have a piece of bark missing. I mean it. The car, forget about it. The car and two of the kids who were in it."

The noise around LaVine's phone booth now grew louder. "That's your nice crowd here. They hope there's another crash right now."

"Awful."

"They don't know. They need thrills. They have boring lives. So I'll wait for the priest. He should be here any moment now. The church is right down the avenue."

"At this rate, what time will you finish?"

"I'm on till, what, two. It's all right. Except, because of you, the rest of the night I'm going to be in torture."

"I shouldn't have told you."

"Not only the mark. It's your face. I see it all night."

"I know. At every accident."

"First time."

"What?"

"First time I'm nervous about school. Right here. I feel like leaving here right now and running home."

"Now I'm upset. I should go to your house and see if it came. I could call you."

"Stop it."

"No, I'm going to."

"Why bear horrible news?"

"Will you cheer up? You probably got a wonderful mark." Out of the corner of her eye, she looked at Owney. If LaVine had the confidence that Owney had in one finger, he would be different. She smiled. Some confidence. If he had it, LaVine might be calling from a bar.

"I am going to go to your house. Where do I go?"

"Nowhere."

"Don't be silly. I said I wanted to do it. I have nothing else to do. I need the air."

"I'll get it when I get home."

"What time is that?"

"I told you. After two."

"Nonsense. I want to get it to you right now. I want to call an ambulance service and inform them tonight somebody started living. What's the address?"

"No. It's all the way over by the river in Long Island City. You'll never find it. It's surrounded by weeds."

"So? I'll have somebody with me."

"Who?"

"My cousin Virginia. I want you to meet her some night. You'll love her."

"You're sure?"

"I'm waiting for her to come home from work now. She'll love taking a ride with me."

"Write it down, then. It's complicated."

Walking back into the living room, Dolores said, "LaVine. That's the guy I have for Virginia." Owney, who had pretended indifference through the call, immediately brightened.

"I had to tell him about the mark."

"It was great," Owney said.

"I've got to go the whole summer for the second half of the course. And then we'll know."

"Know what?"

"Know what we know." Not one step more into this conversation, she thought quickly. "All right. Let's get going here." She picked up the baby. "It's late for a bath. But don't you still want one? Sure you do."

Owney stood up. "I'm on the go the whole day tomorrow. Be at work early, then some union thing in the afternoon."

"Really, what?"

"Something to do with tests for veterans. It's not just my union. It's the central council."

"That sounds like fun. All right." She picked up the baby and walked into the bathroom. Don't dawdle, she told herself as she walked in. What kind of a life is this, anyway? she thought. Nobody leaves you alone for five minutes. If he was out drinking, I certainly wouldn't have him all over me. See him once a week. She regarded the bathroom—a room so small that she had to move sideways between the tub and the wall—as a plaza of freedom.

When Virginia was not home by nine o'clock, Dolores went in to change her clothes, a yellow T-shirt and jeans, and she found herself looking at the bathroom mirror, brushing her hair and trying an earring; she frowned at herself, put the earring down, and went out and sat and waited for Virginia, who walked in at ten-thirty.

"Where were you?" Dolores said. "Let's go. We're going to get in touch with this fellow from school."

"Where? I'm exhausted. I was shopping, Manhasset. Then we stopped and had something to eat."

"We're going to Long Island City."

"At this hour? Are you crazy?"

"Virginia, we're going to get something from his mailbox, then you're going to call him and if you have any brains, you're going to meet him when he gets off work."

"Do we have to do it tonight?"

"Absolutely."

"Oh, I can't."

"Virginia, will you stop it!"

"I said I'm too tired."

"You said you'd go to school to meet him. Now I'm getting him for you right now."

"I didn't say at an hour like this. Dolores, I'm so tired from shopping."

"I don't care what you are, you're coming."

"Dolores, what's the matter with you?"

"I want you to go."

"I'm not deaf. You told me that ten times right here. You're making this the only important thing in the world."

Dolores went into the kitchen to call the Emergency Medical Service number and leave a message for LaVine to tell him she wasn't coming, but instead she impulsively picked up the car keys and walked out. "I'll be back in forty-five minutes," she called in to her aunt's apartment, where they all watched television.

At Long Island City, she noticed an outdoor phone booth at the subway entrance on 51st Street; I'll call him from here, she told herself. Then she drove down a street lined with row houses, which ended at the start of a short block that was dark and lined with factories. She stopped and reread the directions. So far, perfect. At the end of the block were the remains of a pier and high weeds, which combined to block any view of the river. Looking up, she could see over to the Empire State Building, which climbed into the night and sprayed light across a magenta sky. The car rocked like a small boat as it went over the broken street. On the left was the corrugated box factory and next to it, the two-story building with the sign proclaiming a metal stamping business. The windows on the second floor had shades drawn halfway down. She stopped under a streetlight. The street around her was a cellar. How could he have let me come to a place like this? Peering out, she saw advertising mail stuck out of a box at the metal door leading to the second floor. She got out and, apprehensively, pulled out the letters. The postcard nearly fell out. Flipping it over, she saw the mark, a B minus.

Told me it was the end of his life, she said to herself. If he ever had stopped moaning for five minutes, he would have wound up with an A. She shrugged. Maybe he didn't moan all that much. Just acted it out. He couldn't have been so uncertain if he could work all that time and still do this. She walked out to her car and got in. She glanced at the mirror and saw a car moving down the deserted street and immediately she could tell it was LaVine's old Buick. He told me not until two o'clock! She adjusted the car mirror to her face and ran the fingers of her right hand through her hair, puffing the front. I can't believe I'm doing this, she thought. She laughed. Her fingers went back to her hair. Make the front a little fuller. Then she was out of the car and standing in the street with her thumb high in the air as LaVine pulled up. She shouted the mark to him and he got out slowly and walked up to her and then stopped a pace away.

"Why didn't you tell me you were going to be this early? I wouldn't have come over here and scared myself to death."

The light from the lamppost was full on her face and he said to her, "You look terrific."

"Thank you."

"No, don't thank me. Thank yourself. You are pretty."

"Thank you again. Don't you want to see your mark?"

"I'd rather look at you."

"Come on." She went to the mailbox and pulled it out. She found he was still standing by her car. "Don't you want it?" she said.

"Only if you stand in the same place. Right where you were."

Laughing, she walked back. He held out a hand and said, "Stop right there," and she stood in the light from the streetlight with the postcard and he stepped up, took it from her, and didn't look at it. "You're absolutely beautiful."

"Thank you."

He kissed her on the forehead. Then he stepped back. He did it so quickly that there was no implication to it. She found it delightful. He stood in the street and looked at the postcard. "All right."

"All right, what?"

"All right, let's get something to eat."

"What?"

"Anything. I'm starved."

"All right."

"I have to go up and change. I had so much blood on the sleeve here." He held it out.

"I'd rather look at the view you told me about. All I can see is the top of the Empire State."

He faced Manhattan and shouted, "Here I am, everybody! David La-Vine is on deck." He waved his arms. "Hiya! Thank you. Good night to you, too."

"Who could see you?" Dolores said.

"Everybody over there. I told you. They pay ten thousand dollars a month to look at me."

"I can't see anything but the top of the Empire State. Does that mean the only people who can see you now are the cleaning women?"

"You don't like it here?" he said.

"Yes, I do. I like you. I'm excited about how well we both did. I just don't think as much of this view you kept telling me about."

"You don't like my view?"

"So far it's a fraud."

"Huh."

He went to the metal door and, making as much noise as a jailer, opened it. "Wait until you see this." He held a hand out, and without considering it, she followed him up the dark staircase. He opened another lock, flipped on the light, and stepped aside. As she entered the room, she cracked her ankle against one of the cinder blocks that was supporting a bookcase along the wall.

"You all right?"

"I broke the bone."

"I don't want to turn on the lights. I want you to see out."

As she bent over to rub her ankle, her eyes fell on a book that sat in the hall light atop the pile nearest her: *Last Exit to Brooklyn.*

"When I read that book," she said, "it was the first time I ever found out how homosexuals had sex."

"That's because the guy wrote it was a whacked-out faggot himself," LaVine said.

"Must you talk like that, too? I could've stayed in Glendale to hear that."

"I can say anything I want," LaVine said. "What do you think I work with? Half the drivers are gay. They talk, I talk. Say what we please. The ones that aren't gay are black. You think we call them 'blacks'?"

"It still sounds dumb."

"I'm not so dumb. I can prove it. I'm with you." He put a hand on her arm. "Don't move." He stepped through the dark room, past a couch covered with green corduroy and two large chairs that didn't match. At the end of the bookcase, alongside the windows, was a stereo set and speakers. At the windows, he raised the shades and unlocked one window. "Look at this."

She stepped to the window and the breath went out of her. Beyond the weeds and the old pier, she saw the river water black in the night and, suddenly, out in the middle, the river turning into a silver fire that ran with dazzling impact up to the foot of the night-bright buildings on the Manhattan side.

"Ten thousand a month just to see me."

"Don't talk," she said.

"Why?"

"I want to listen."

A horn blared in the distance, perhaps from up on the Queensboro Bridge, that went over the water to Manhattan. Up LaVine's street, a truck bounced hard on a hole. A helicopter thumped in the sky. Otherwise, silence. But a different silence from the one in Glendale. That was permanent. This was a prelude. The air had a heavy smell of river water. Not clean salt air, as you get at the ocean, but a mixture of salt and city streets.

"No sound," she said.

"They let the money talk."

"No, it's because it's a dream. A dream doesn't have any sound."

He didn't answer.

"Don't you stand here and dream ever?"

"A little."

"What about?"

"Sometimes I think I'm living there. What building do you want to live in? I'll buy it for you."

"No, it's more than money. It says to you, come here, this is the way it ought to be. You can carry the idea of it with you. It doesn't belong to them. I'm not afraid of them. I think I might be better than them."

"How are you going to take a place like that and go anywhere else on earth?"

"I can take the lights with me wherever I go. I can keep them inside me. I've spent my life on two blocks. In both places, all people ever did at night was turn lights off. They turn the lights off in the room and then inside themselves."

"Save money," LaVine said.

"They don't even save that much. And they lose whole parts of their lives inside. It's some sort of fear of being discovered. They are so uncertain of their own lives that they can't bear the idea of somebody looking at them when they don't have this façade on." She hugged herself with her arms, imitating her mother. "And they keep the lights out inside because they can't bear to look at themselves. They won't even stare at the darkness. Afraid their eyes will become accustomed and they might see something."

"Maybe they just want to walk around comfortable and don't want people seeing them," he said.

"Oh, Lord forbid somebody should be seen walking around the house in a slip! Oh, they'd die. No, I think it's more than that, really. They regard themselves somehow as being misshapen. They would prefer an outsider to feel that nobody is at home. A little lamp in the window is the most they want to show the world. And then nothing to themselves."

"I don't know. What do you call your husband?"

She sighed. She thought of Owney and his parents sitting in the cemetery house. Even in a cemetery, with nobody possibly able to see them, they presented only the tiniest light to the dead around them and to the few living passing in cars out on the street. And they presented utter darkness to themselves. She thought of them refusing to discuss anything about themselves outside of being wet in the rain. "He is reassured when there is something he can do with his body that requires bravery. Something where he can use his hands and his reactions. Something that threatens him. He is absolutely fearless. But he can't deal with an interior enemy. Talk about keeping the lights out. If he thought he could see even a vague outline inside him, he'd drown his eyes."

"Is he still doing it?"

"I don't want to talk any more about it. Let's talk about you. What do you do with yourself?"

"You're seeing it."

"Oh, I doubt that. A single man in this city. Nothing else?"

"Where am I going to meet so many people, on a stretcher?"

"Somehow I doubt that."

"It's true."

"If it is, it's too bad."

"No, it isn't. I met you."

She smiled.

"No, I met you and you're beautiful."

She laughed. "It must be getting late. You're telling me the same thing all over again."

Quickly, he stepped over to a lamp. "Here, I don't want to keep you so long. Just give me a minute."

"Don't be silly. I love to hear you say something nice."

"Then I'll tell it to you again. Just give me one minute."

"What for? I better get home, don't you think?"

"I just want to change. Don't worry, I'll do it quick. In and out of the shower."

"A shower? Oh, come on, let me go home and give you time."

"Never. You stay here."

"What are these, orders?"

"All right. Please. I have to get you something to eat."

"Here?"

"I don't have a can of soup here. We'll go up to Sinatra's. Place on the corner from the police station."

"It's so late to eat."

"The food is good even this late. That's because of the cops working shifts."

"But I don't want to make you rush."

"Forget it. I'll be right out."

He walked out and she remained at the window. Then she looked over the stack of records. He had a new John Lennon album in the middle.

She was holding the album and trying to turn on the stereo when she heard LaVine in his room.

"I'm out of the shower. One minute, and I'll get you something to eat."

"Take your time. I'm just trying to figure out how to turn this set on."

"What?" He came walking out in a white terry-cloth robe. His dark hair was wet. "I'll do that." He brushed up against her and put the Lennon album on.

"Put side two on," she said.

"You don't want to hear the first side, 'Give Peace a Chance'?"

"I want to hear 'Imagine.' I don't want to hear anything about the war, no matter what it is. 'Imagine.' "

As the music started, she went back to the window. He was standing directly behind her and he leaned over her shoulder.

"You look over at the lights and you imagine. See? I said that before.'

"Your hair is beautiful."

"Thank you."

"I would've told you the same thing the first night I saw you."

"Really? Why didn't you?"

"I was standing outside and you came into the building. You walked right past me and I just looked. I said, I hope I see her again."

"And you saw me five minutes later in class."

"No, I didn't. This was way back in the winter. We weren't even in the same class. I just said, I hope I see that girl again."

"Hardly a girl."

"All right. Woman. I still wanted to meet you."

"You thought about me and you didn't even talk to me?"

"I've thought about you more than that, but I heard you were married. The guy was famous. When I found that out, I forgot about it."

"When you asked me to come to the bar, was it before or after you found out I was separated?"

"After. I'm not crazy. No, it's more than that. I wouldn't ever make a move like that."

She nodded. She didn't tell him that after she drove past the bar that night she sat in the car and thought about him while she looked at these same lights. She worried about his nerve then. Now, she saw him differently.

He leaned forward in the music and had his chin on her shoulder, against her face, and it had been so long that she had had the feel of anything like this that she ran a hand gently against his cheek. His hand came around her waist and touched her middle. She tensed. She hated the feel of her extra weight. The movement caused him to withdraw his hand. She kept her hand on his face.

"I'm getting so heavy."

"Never."

"Yes, I am. I eat everything," she said.

"And here I'm taking you out for something," he said.

"I really don't want to go out," she said. She thought she was telling him this because she didn't want to eat, but suddenly he clasped both hands on her middle and as he kissed her neck, she turned into his arms and his mouth covered hers. The front of his robe opened and now he was full and hard against her and her breath became short. It had been so long since she had been noticed and now she let the anger and the loneliness drop onto the floor with her clothes. They walked into the bedroom where he ran his fingers lightly across the bottom of her stomach. It had been so long since she had been so comforted. She could have remained just doing this all night. She sighed loudly when he entered her.

She got home at four o'clock in the morning. She made no noise and in the morning she decided that her mother had not known the hour. She took the baby to Rockaway, where the sand had been cleaned for the first time. She watched Christine toddle up to the water, and when it ran spring-freezing against her feet, the baby turned and wobbled back slowly, causing Dolores to laugh aloud. She thought for an instant about LaVine. His touch had lasted through the night. She shook her head quickly. The gentleness and need and innocence of the night before turned into guilt. What are you doing with yourself? she thought. Never in her life had she thought that she would wind up of a night with a man while she was still married. If she was this mixed up by her life now, and she felt the dangers of any more of this were incalculable, then there was only one thing to do: just get out, she said. She looked at the water and thought that she could not survive with Owney no matter what he did.

At nine o'clock, while she was getting dressed, LaVine called.

"You were supposed to call me when you got home," he said, his voice a roadbed.

"It was too late for me even to pick up the phone here."

"You all right?"

"Of course."

"Everything good?"

"Sure. It's a lovely day. I'm going to the beach with the baby."

"I'd say something nice to you, but I got to steal some sleep," he said.

"Then sleep."

"Yeah. See you. The next time I see you, I'll say something nice."

She began to estimate the meaning of the call, and then found this disturbing and stopped doing it.

15

AT FIRST LIGHT, five-thirty in the morning, he was as clear as polished glass, with grapefruit juice, coffee, and the first cigarette of a day, which he thought might stir a wind and disperse some of the ground fog in his life. The day before, late in the afternoon, Kellerman had called excitedly to announce that he had maneuvered Owney into something that was sensible: an appearance at a meeting of the Central Labor Trades Council about men returning from Vietnam. Owney saw this immediately as assistance to his personal life; by now he told himself that he was torn by the long separation and he was, he assured himself this morning, ready to make his way back.

His mother said, "You went by her mother's house again last night?"

"I went to see the baby."

"I know you. You got your mind set on something."

Owney didn't answer.

"How long until the three of you go back to your own place?" When he said nothing again, she said, "Well, I know you will. You're going to stay at it until you wear her down."

Looking out the window, Owney considered the notion that the only way to resume his marriage would be to have another baby. A simple, beautiful way to ensure that it was not a matter of instant needs: for Dolores, a husband, and for him, order and, yes, he thought, comfort.

Lock each other forever with a second baby. That would take care of everything for me; you can't be in a bar with two kids.

"We'll probably all be moving out of here almost the same time," the mother said.

"What do you mean?"

"I'm leaving my wonderful rock garden."

Owney made a face.

"No, this time even I have to say that I think it's real. We saw a nice raised ranch, Exit Sixty-three. We had a nice talk with the man in the sales office."

"What's talk?" Owney said.

"Oh, no. Your father showed him the bank book. There's a ton of money, put a down payment on a raised ranch. Your father did pretty good with his overtime and all this last year. The salesman said it could be done. This'll be the first roof over our heads that this family ever owned."

At work, Owney stood in the puddles and thought nervously about his mother's enthusiasm for a bank book. Where did this come from again? he asked himself. Guilt rose in him as he thought of all the days he hadn't been around; who knows what goes on when you're flopping in some sanatorium? He looked up at the rock roof over his head. Gray and oppressive. And then there were white spurts going through the rock. Iron supports were up, yet the iron seemed thin to Owney as he walked along, looking up at the cracks. Maybe that was because the supports were placed too far apart. All the line in the rock looked jagged, like the teeth of something attacking.

At one o'clock, he went up to the hog house, where he showered and dressed in a shirt and tie. He drove downtown to the offices of the Central Labor Trades Council, on the sixth floor of a building on Park Avenue South. The "South" is added to the name for purposes of realty values, always more important in Manhattan than the next heartbeat; this was a neighborhood of lofts and cafeterias and was not to be confused with the golden street to the north, the real Park Avenue.

"We haven't seen you in such a long time." The receptionist had a maternal attitude. "How *are* you?" There was so much solicitousness that Owney was uncomfortable. She walked him down a corridor that was lined with pictures of men with jaws out and dull eyes; the labor leaders all try to imitate John L. Lewis in posing for photos and, lacking his eyebrows, try to make up for it by sticking the chin out. The dull eyes, however, remain with them after the picture is taken.

"Brother Morrison!" Kellerman, loud and nervous, stood, not too well, at the end of a long table, around which sat a dozen people. Kellerman indicated a seat near him, which Owney took. He looked around and immediately recognized Allingham, who ran the central council while the figurehead, McGrath, was in bed with liver trouble. Allingham sat with the business agent, Callahan. Both of them nodded. Sitting next to Callahan was the young prince, Donnelly, who smiled greasily.

Four blacks, each in T-shirts and sunglasses, walked in after Owney and sat together at the end. "Samuel Gompers sent them," Kellerman muttered under his breath. Allingham nodded, somebody closed the door, and Kellerman had to turn around and cough up phlegm into a handkerchief. He then said, "As education director of the City Central Labor Trades Council, I want to raise the moral obligation we have for fighting men who return from Vietnam. Every maj——"

"We got a question to start off with," one of the blacks said.

"Sure."

"We nominally from Eleven ninety-nine, hospital workers' union. We tired of hearing that all we can do is run around with bedpans. We got to provide our brothers with more. We interested in making exams like Fire Department fair for our brothers. If they could fight Vietcong, they could fight fires, right?"

"Brother, we are with you," Kellerman said. "But tests are up to the courts."

"We know better than to trust some white-bread judge. We want a new man writin' questions for the next test. Someone give our people an equal chance."

"You can't expect them to lower standards," Kellerman said.

The black suddenly held up a booklet and said, "Here's a Fire *De*partment test asking which one of these names don't belong together: de Gaulle, Montgomery, Rommel, Bach. I don't know none of those names. Imagine some brother back from Da Nang lookin' at this."

Kellerman smiled and spoke quietly. "De Gaulle, Montgomery, Rommel. World War Two generals. Bach, a German composer. Of course Bach doesn't fit. I don't see where that's so unfair."

"I never seen his name in print. I never heard of him. Most of my people have *heard*—that's all, they just *heard*—of the Beatles. Nice white kids. But my people don't know what the Beatles ever sung. So this Bach. How can you expect a black from Brooklyn to read about him? Man, you just put a history book anywhere near a black kid who got any heart and this kid, he jes' turns his head. We got no place in history, so why we bother learnin' it?"

Kellerman mumbled an answer and started to go through his papers. From the center of the table, smiling, leaning between Callahan and Allingham, Donnelly suddenly spoke. "Then you tell us the name of a composer."

"Billy Strayhorn. James Brown. Listen to James Brown songs, man."

Donnelly got aggressive, showing off for Callahan and Allingham. "How can you mention these guys, whoever the hell they are, in the same conversation with Bach?"

"Who the fuck is Bach, man? We don't know who he is."

"Come on," Donnelly said.

"Tell you what," the black said, holding the book out, "look at this next question."

He handed the book to Donnelly, who read aloud: "The Tet offensive was the result of (a) superior fighting ability of the Vietcong; (b) American combat soldiers' reluctance to fight; (c) massive Chinese Communist aid while America was busy fighting a rearguard action against 'peace' groups at home; and (d) tactical errors by our generals." Donnelly cleared his throat. "The answer in the test is 'c.' I sure agree, too."

The blacks laughed.

"What's wrong with the answer?" Donnelly said, hesitantly.

"Bullshit answer, man."

"What do you think the answer is?"

"Fightin' people for no reason in their back yards. Homeboys always win."

"Yo, homeboys," one of the other blacks said.

Now one of them, fat pouring out of the bottom of a T-shirt, said, "We know. We in Nam. You in Nam?"

Donnelly gave a half smile. "No. I have to tell you I wasn't."

"Well, I was there," the fat guy said. A little too quickly, Owney thought. "So how you answerin' a question like that to us? See? We right about what we sayin'."

Owney looked directly at the smoked glasses. "I don't think that was the reason." His voice drew everyone in the room.

"You tell me? I there."

"Where?"

"Nam."

"Where in Nam?" Owney asked.

"*Viet*nam."

"What Corps?"

"Army."

"No. I asked you what Corps you were in."

"Man, I told you. I was in Nam."

"Were you in Eye Corps or Two Corps or what?"

"What co'? I don't know no co'. I was in Nam."

"You were in bed."

"I nearly die in Nam."

"Then tell me the Corps area you nearly died in."

"Fuck you and your co'."

"You fought blankets in bed," Owney said.

"Blue-eyed motherfucker."

Owney knew he had the guy now. "Look at these eyes. What color do you think they are?"

The face said nothing.

"They're brown, just like yours," Owney said. "If you'd been in Nam, you would know that. All white guys don't have blue eyes. You don't learn that by sitting in bed all day and eating potato chips. Look at the shape you're in."

Allingham suddenly cleared his throat and took over. "Clearly, we have some sort of impasse here. Or a misunderstanding. I'm sure you know that Brother Morrison here has quite a record in Vietnam. Holder of the Congressional Medal of Honor. I think somebody should have mentioned that right at the outset and we would have saved ourselves a lot of unwarranted animosity in this room. I think we better study this situation more before I can make any recommendations."

He set the date for another meeting and the blacks filed out sullenly, without looking at Owney, and Callahan clapped Owney on the back and presented him to Allingham and said, "He's coming along, coming along."

And then Owney said, "I think they were right about the test."

"What do you mean?" Allingham said.

"I lived with a lot of blacks. They come from a different world and we don't know it."

"Well," Allingham said.

Owney said, "The guy was right. I just got mad because he was lying."

"And you think that he's right about the test?"

"Absolutely."

Allingham shook his head. "You got me screwed up. But that doesn't mean I'm not listening to you."

Then Owney shook hands and walked away from Allingham and Callahan. He saw Donnelly behind them, afraid to move one step away from Callahan. As Owney walked out, he knew everybody was looking at him.

"Now that was leadership," Kellerman said to Owney after his class the next night. "True union leadership." He stood on the corner of Jamaica Avenue as a bus bounced past. He waved to the driver.

"Hello, brother."

His head followed the bus as it went. "Surface men in the Transport Workers Union, the last real union men left. Once you go downstairs into the subways, the make-up of that union changes. Gets pretty dark. All right. Here we go."

Kellerman started across for O'Looney's and Burke's bar. When Owney didn't move, Kellerman stopped and waved his arm impatiently.

"Come on."

"Not tonight."

"Do you have a flu?"

"I'm just not drinking."

"What do you mean by that?"

"Want the truth?"

"Yes."

"I need a layoff. Just a little. You know I was out for that whole month."

"You had a virus."

"Whatever. I'll tell only you. But I've been going to a couple of AA meetings."

Kellerman's arms flapped. "Who told you that you drink too much?"

"Nobody, actually."

"Because nobody can! You're no alcoholic. What are you, crazy? What put that in your head?"

"I still better get home."

"You're coming with me. Who do you think maneuvered you into that thing yesterday? I'm going to see that you replace George Meany."

He took Owney by the arm and walked him across the street. Kellerman held the door to make sure Owney went in, then followed with an old briefcase under one arm and his pants flopping around his shoes and his free arm waving in the air.

"Brother trainmen!"

The bartender put a shot glass down with such force that it sounded like a hammer. When he saw that Owney was with Kellerman, he put a second shot glass down.

"Remember the Ludlow Massacre!" Kellerman shouted.

Owney went for the door. "I forgot something in the car."

Owney's campaign was as subtle as advancing tanks. On one day, he went to the supermarket for Dolores's mother and aunt. On another, right after work, he drove the mother to the bank. And late on a Saturday afternoon, in the rain, he suddenly showed up and found only Dolores and Virginia home. Dolores, who had made a deal with Virginia to watch the baby while she went to the movies, walked sullenly into the bedroom and when she came out, Owney was still there.

He said, "I could use a movie, too. I'll drive you."

Dolores said, "Who said I was going to a movie?" and Owney said, "Virginia."

Dolores felt the room narrowing until the walls touched her shoulders. Reluctantly, she went with Owney, sitting close to the car door so their legs didn't brush, over to the early showing of *The French Connection* at the Midway on Queens Boulevard. She sat stiffly, maintaining space between them, and she was certain that he would do something, a touch, a hand carelessly draped on her shoulder, and she knew that she would have to react. Push him away like we're back in high school, she thought sourly. Right away, with the Three Degrees performing and, suddenly, the eerie Don Ellis big band music as the detective saw the drug peddlers in the nightclub, the film caused the audience to become tense and motionless. Somewhere during the picture, she realized that she was at least comfortable sitting next to him. Or was she really?

After the movie, she thought about this in the ladies' room as she brushed her hair vigorously. How could Virginia have trapped her like this? What was she doing with him in the first place? She was getting a divorce and every time she walked through a room, he was sitting there. Anyway, Virginia would serve one purpose now. She could say truthfully that she couldn't even stop for coffee with Owney because Virginia was at home with the baby and was counting on going someplace at nine o'clock.

Then she and Owney were walking out through the lobby. Down at the doors, the usher stepped aside and the crowd started in for the next show. Almost past her before she saw him was LaVine, who was smiling and talking to a man and a woman with him. He walked right past her. Dolores stopped and wheeled.

"David."

LaVine, still talking, walked on.

She stood with surprise and disappointment running through her. Then irritation. What is he, afraid? She shrugged and started walking again. Owney, who had stopped, caught up with her. His face was blank. He kept looking straight ahead and said nothing. He walked with Dolores up to the glass doors leading out to the street. Dolores pushed her door open. Owney came up to the door alongside and then his right leg whipped straight out and kicked out the glass. He pushed the brass-colored door frame open and walked through the broken glass. He said nothing.

A porter, looking at the door, said, "It must have been some kid. Threw something right through the window on us."

It was eight-twenty on a Saturday night in Queens, when, in silence, he let Dolores off and then drove to Gibby's on Myrtle Avenue, where, when he walked in, Gibby was inspecting the mouth of a customer, who had his lower lip pulled down to reveal a lack of teeth.

"He done some job on you," Gibby said.

"Give us a beer," Owney said.

The customer then released his lower lip. "Imagine that? An usher at Shea Stadium doing that to me? How come they have ushers like that? Go to the ball game at Shea Stadium, an usher punches you in the mouth."

"You ought to sue the whole ball club," Gibby said.

"Oh, I am. I can't work because I got punched in the mouth."

Gibby now said to Owney, "You said a beer?" When Owney nodded, Gibby stood at the tap and as he poured the beer he spoke to the guy with the punched mouth. "When did this happen to you, anyway?"

"Last week."

"You take a day off from work to get punched by some lousy usher."

"Oh, I didn't take the day off. I was working there as an usher, too."

Gibby put the beer in front of Owney, who backed away from it and went into the men's room. When he came out, he headed straight for the barstool, put a hand on the beer, felt its icy cold, and then pulled the hand away and walked to the phone. He dialed Navy. "I think I need you."

"That's what I'm here for."

"I'm in Gibby's on Myrtle Avenue and I'm about ten seconds from taking a drink. My wife just got me crazy."

"Here's what you do," Navy said. "Don't take a drink yet. Wait there for me. Don't go anyplace else. Smoke a cigarette. Have some coffee. Whatever. Just don't drink until I get there. If you still want a drink then, we'll talk about it. But please do me one favor. Just sit there until I get there."

Owney hung up and went back to his seat at the bar. The beer was still in front of him. "You got any coffee?"

"You want a diner, then go to a diner."

Owney sat and smoked. He saw in the smoke his wife Dolores, whirling around in the Midway lobby, calling to this guy. Brown-haired woman in a blue sweat shirt, the shoulders falling in disappointment when the guy didn't turn around. Now, as he saw her whirling in the theatre lobby, her feet made this squeaking sound on the floor. In the smoke over the bar, suddenly here was the opponent, head bobbing, body dancing to Owney's left, and lumpy arched eyebrows telling Owney, come on, let's go. Come on, where are you? Owney's hand came out to the glass. Still cold and gold. He stared at the glass and thought about Navy and his fingertips touched the glass.

"She nearly made me drink tonight," Owney said when Navy walked in.

"You didn't need her for the five million drinks you had before tonight," Navy said.

The next morning, Sunday, Owney drove to Brooklyn to meet Navy in the diner on Fourth Avenue for purposes of reinforcement: coffee, a smoke, and those warm but strong glances that Navy used to cause the desire for whiskey to disappear. "How did you sleep?" Navy said, and Owney said, "Good. After I left you, I just dropped out."

Navy smiled. "I got none. I'm not home fifteen minutes and I get a call from one of our brothers. The first call was from a bar. The second was from home. He was just trying to calm himself with a few pills. Well, the next call was from the Flushing precinct. So I got up and drove all the way past your house and picked him up. I got him out in the car."

"Now you have to drive to Jersey?"

"Not with this man. I've got to stash him good. I take him to Maryland."

"Do I know him?"

"What's the difference? You shouldn't even look at the poor guy. I have to tell you the truth: I had to truss him up. I don't want him strangling me on the drive. You'll think I'm a kidnapper, you see him."

"On a weekend," Owney said.

"People drink then, too."

"Then I guess I shouldn't have bothered you last night, but I was about to go. My wife doesn't say anything to me and, I told you, I see this guy."

"You never can be sure because you're so paranoid from alcohol as it is. I told you, when I stopped drinking I used to sit there in a stew and my wife would say to me, 'What's the matter?' and I'd say to her, 'If you cared about me, you wouldn't have to ask.' "

Owney laughed.

"Now you're starting a day on the right foot. Why don't you make sure by going to a meeting and talking it over with them?"

Owney didn't answer.

"See if you feel like it. You're giving yourself a chance if you get up and say something at a meeting."

When Owney nodded absently, Navy said, "I have to tell you. Otherwise, I think you'll have constant trouble."

"I can take care of myself," Owney said. "I get a little help from you, that's all I need. I don't need a public ceremony."

"If you wouldn't be so stubborn, you'd listen to me."

"I do. But I know myself."

Navy smiled. "That, sir, is a very good topic to discuss someday. Well, I'm not going to be coming back until tomorrow afternoon. I'm too tired to drive down and back. I'll stay over someplace."

"Don't worry about me," Owney said. "Any trouble, I'll handle it."

"I'm more worried about a laugh," Navy said. "That can do it to you. A good laugh. For our set, that can be harder to handle than all the trouble in the world."

As they left, Navy patted his pockets. "I better get myself another pack of cigarettes. I got a long haul."

He went back into the diner and Owney now saw Navy's car across the street. The back of a head was up against the window in the back seat. The window was lowered halfway. Remembering his own ride in the car, Owney decided to go over and give some encouragement to the guy. As he walked up to the car, the head moved. Owney put a hand on the half-open window and now the head stirred and rose and here came Kellerman, eyes rolling, with his hands tied behind him, growling like a dog, and he got his mouth up to the window and sank his teeth into Owney's hand.

"Pinkerton!" Kellerman screamed.

* * *

In the morning, two weeks later, Danny Murphy, the numbers runner, walked through the mud, smiling as Owney came in to work.

"How do you want it?"

"Want what?"

"One eighty-seven. It hit. It took exactly forty-five days. There you are."

"That's the hand of the Lord," Owney said.

"Not at all. The Devil's hand."

"At least Blaney gets something."

"It's a shame the man isn't here to enjoy it," Murphy said. "But if he's here, the number doesn't turn up. This is a death number."

"Send it to the family."

"Where? The man lived alone in a room on Gun Hill Road."

"To his family in Ireland."

"Who knows where he lived?"

"Look it up in the office."

"And then what?"

"Then send the money."

Danny Murphy took out a roll of bills and examined them. "I don't near have it here. You get five thousand. I'll have to see you this afternoon."

"I have to go downtown again."

"Why don't you let me bring it down to you?"

"Because it's Blaney's money. It's not my money."

"Suppose I send it to somebody in Ireland doesn't know who the hell I am or how I make my living?"

"Oh, fuck it. I gotta go to work. Give it to me tomorrow."

At one, Owney went to get dressed for the meeting downtown. As he was leaving, Delaney said to him, "You'd think you'd do something for us."

"I'm not keeping the money."

"I don't care who keeps it. All I know is that you won."

When he got off the lift, Owney walked down to Katonah Avenue, where the idea of a drink waved from every window. He went into a liquor store and bought a bottle of VO. Next door in the delicatessen, he bought two cases of beer and asked for a dozen steak sandwiches. The counterman said it would take a few minutes. Owney went outside and stood against the plate glass window in the sun. Next door was Brendan's, where an old man was sweeping at the doorway. Behind was the dimness of a place with bricked-up windows. A loud squeak came from inside the place. Owney flattened the palms of his hands against the front of the delicatessen and waited. Finally, he heard the counterman call and he went in, paid, and carried the bags to the cage.

On the phone in the shack, he told Delaney, "Twelve steak sandwiches and plenty to drink, coming right down."

"Twelve? Who are the others for?" Delaney said.

"I got you twelve."

"We're nine."

"Nine?"

"That's right. Nine guys working."

"We're supposed to have twelve."

"Well, we're nine today. Didn't you look while you were down here?"

"Are we back to that again?"

"Don't bring that up to me. See somebody else."

Owney didn't answer. He walked slowly over to the hog house and leaned against the wall and remained there until he saw he was late for the meeting at the Central Labor Trades Council and had time only to put on a shirt and pants, wash his hands and face, and drive downtown with dirt-caked body and workboots.

The meeting began with Kellerman's absence pointedly unmentioned. There were, however, no blacks there, which made the meeting unnecessary, because nobody ever was going to block a white Vietnam vet from a job, but the blacks had to be discussed at length because of their natural inability to perform tasks, the most important of which was to turn themselves into whites.

When a phone call came for Allingham, and he never returned, the number in the room began to dwindle. The receptionist looked in and said that Owney had a call.

"He's here for the second time and now he takes calls," Callahan said. The laughter of the three men around him had a resigned quality: young guy on the rise who probably passes them.

At the phone on the receptionist's desk, Owney heard Danny Murphy screaming over the street sounds.

"Where do I meet you?"

"I told you tomorrow."

"I can't do that. Suppose something happens? I'm responsible. An amount this big."

"Leave it with my father," Owney said.

"You're sure?"

"I . . ." Owney's voice became uncertain.

"I'm at the train. I'm getting a three-fifty. I'll be sitting in Grand Central at four-ten. Sitting right there."

"Where."

"Bar."

"Where?"

"I don't know. I been there twice in my life. Big bar. Big drink in a big bar."

When Owney went back to the room, Callahan said to him, "We're getting nothing done here. I feel terrible making you come all the way down here. I won't forget this, though. What we got to do, we got to sit down and have a talk and see where we're going. Why don't you get the wife and bring her up some night and we'll have dinner and talk about things?"

"You're on." Owney poked a finger into Callahan's chest to press the point. Standing here in this room he saw his life coming together. "I'll come up with my wife."

"One thing, can you stand working on top or are you sucked in with that life you got down there?"

"Whatever made you think I wouldn't work on top?"

"Talking to Donnelly. He's our young guy and he told us—"

"Donnelly's full of shit."

"Well."

"About everything. You saw him here last time."

Callahan sighed. "I have to tell you, I wasn't the only one saw that."

He looked at Owney's eyes closely and Owney said, "If you're looking for whiskey, you're going to be looking for a long time." He slapped Callahan on the shoulder and walked out, body swinging, confident, his chin up, and he knew the ones in the room, again, were following him out.

"How do you want it?" Danny Murphy said.

"In money."

Danny had claimed an area for himself at the end of the long, splendidly polished bar, which was in the saloon part of a place called the Oyster Bar, a large old room with high ceilings, filled with reedy businessmen in severe three-piece business suits who carried slim attaché cases. The businessmen tripped down a staircase coming from the main level of the station and had to brush past Danny to move into the bar and dining area. Danny did not like them brushing him. Arranged on the bar in front of him were Danny's cigarettes, old metal lighter atop them, his wet bar money, and his drink, a shot and a beer, and on his right flank, the ashtray with cigarette. He had a foot on one stool, which he indicated was for Owney, and on another stool he had an Alexander's shopping bag, which he clutched in one hand, much as government agents must do when flying with attaché cases containing national defense plans to bomb Russia. The place smelled of horseradish and cocktail sauce. Tables of people eating cold seafood appetizers with their drinks before leaving for Connecticut and Westchester spread so far out that they seemed to disappear under the curved ceilings. Danny, who clearly felt he was drinking in a great arena, rose to the occasion. He sat with his back to a tall man with short gray hair and a mouthline that was firm to indicate command. Danny drank his shot and beer and reluctantly ordered a tomato juice for Owney and, at the same time, listened to the gray-haired man, who on his second drink was searching for conversation, say to another man, "My father took me here the first time for oysters. It was a real thrill for him."

"Oh, I'll bet it was," the other man said.

"Yes, to bring his son in here. The young don't like oysters that much."

Danny muttered. "Guy eats an oyster."

"I want a martini," Danny Murphy said to the barman. "I don't know if I ever had a martini." Then he cautioned the barman, "I don't want no ice in the drink."

The man behind him, in an attempted pleasantry, said, "You mean straight up." Right away, Owney knew that the voice was all wrong. And without turning to look at the man behind him, Danny Murphy said, "I don't care what the glass looks like. Straight glass or a goblet. Just don't put ice cubes in the glass. I never saw a martini with ice cubes."

"That's what you call straight up," the man said.

"And you're what I call a real ball breaker," Danny said.

The man pursed his lips as if to say, Well, and Owney, who had a tomato juice he didn't want, and certainly didn't think he should participate in a fight while drinking such swill, said to Danny, "Let's just give me the money and we get out of here."

"Good enough." Danny went into his shopping bag and pulled out a handful of money. It was in fifties and hundreds.

Danny began counting out money and putting it on the bar in front of Owney.

"That's three thousand."

As he resumed counting, the gray-haired man was elated to see a group of men come bouncing down the steps, swinging attaché cases.

"What did you do in the board room last night, make a fool of yourself again?" the gray-haired man asked.

"Yeah, I did it again. Danced all over the table."

Now one of them, who was pushed right against Danny Murphy's back, sniffed.

Owney knew his own body smelled of stale underground dirt, but Danny Murphy's odor was worse than that of a sweating cow. Suddenly, the one man, and the others, attention caught first by the odor, now looked wide-eyed as they focused on the piles of money that Danny was making on the bar in front of Owney.

Each set of eyes then showed amusement at the tableau.

"They think we're assholes handing out money like this," Danny Murphy said.

"Don't talk because then you lose count and we'll be here till tomorrow."

"All right. That's forty-five hundred, right?"

"Right."

Danny now had tens and twenties out.

"Don't you have any more big bills?" Owney said.

"Is the money no good?"

"We'll be here all night."

"It's a nice enough place. Forty-six twenty, forty-six forty . . ." Danny turned to the bar and took a great swallow of his new drink, the martini. ". . . Forty-seven thirty, forty-seven forty, forty-seven fifty. Done."

"You're two-fifty shy. You owe me five thousand," Owney said.

"What about my end?" Murphy said.

"What end?"

"Let's stop jerking each other off. I don't care if the guy dropped fucking dead right in front of me. I still get my fucking end. The runner gets five percent of the bet, no matter what happens to the winner. You wanted me to send all this to the auld country. Fuck the auld country. Who would have given Danny Murphy his end? I'm hanging on to my five percent right here."

"You're taking blood money," Owney said.

He was interrupted as one of the men in the group behind them, younger than the others, with smooth cheekbones and a sort of smile, said: "Do you mind?"

"Mind what?"

"If you're not using the stool." He indicated the stool with the Alexander's shopping bag on it.

"What do you think I'm doing with it?" Danny said.

"You're not sitting on it."

"It'll be sitting someplace, all right. It'll be sitting on your head."

"I had imagined that we were all civilized."

"Maybe you are, but I'm a fucking animal," Danny said, still counting.

"You're certainly trying to act like one."

"Sure am." Danny turned and swallowed the rest of the drink, which took a lot of swallowing, and he immediately banged the glass down.

"I really don't have to take abuse," the guy said.

"Yes, you do," Danny said. He grabbed the young guy's drink and took it in two swallows. The young guy shrugged, as if to make allowances. Owney also thought the guy was considering retaliation.

"Danny, you do me a favor," Owney said. "We're wasting time on nothing here. Leave them alone." Now Owney noticed how beet red Murphy was from alcohol. "Where were you all day, anyway?"

"Getting ready."

Danny put his cigarette down carefully. "Getting ready for this quiff."

He turned around—pivoted, actually—and hit the guy directly between both smooth cheeks. The smacking sound was loud in the room. A woman in a business suit and maroon attaché case screamed. The bartender was reaching across the bar and now the gray-haired man who had been there from the start put his glass down and didn't seem to think for a moment about what he was going to do: go straight for Danny Murphy. The man had his hands up. He also had his chin coming forward. The chin rocked right into Danny's punch in an explosion.

There was much grumbling in the bar and Owney saw the barman reach for a blue wall telephone and waiters begin to gather for an attack. Danny grabbed the money and Owney grabbed Danny and they went up the flight of stairs, against the stream of people coming down, with Danny first, hugging his shopping bag full of money, and Owney behind him.

And then Owney heard in the commotion at the foot of the stairs somebody saying, "Let them go. They're not worth chasing. Scum."

Owney turned and came running down the stairs and the guy at the foot of the stairs, whoever he was, thoughtlessly came right up and Owney kicked the guy right there in the V of his slate-gray pants. The guy made a noise and, clutching himself, fell back on his shoulder blades.

Owney went back up the stairs, and he and Danny moved quickly through the fields of commuters coming out of passageways that seemed to be everywhere. They were moving toward the huge color picture of kids in a corn field when they decided to veer onto an escalator going up. When they reached the top, people with lips tight in annoyance were pushing around a fat blind man with a dog. Danny Murphy held out a hand and blocked people from walking around one side of the blind man. "Now come on with me, pal," Danny said to the blind man. "Watch your step. Ha ha. Hear what I said? I said, Watch your step. Ha ha. Look sharp." The seeing-eye dog waddled to the top of the escalator. Danny Murphy, holding people back, watched the blind man and his dog go down the escalator.

"You're some fuck, you don't even say good-bye to me," Danny said.

They now were in a building lobby, where off to the right was a bar. Danny bulled his way in and ordered a double martini. Immediately, the young, splendidly dressed people reacted to the smell of Danny Murphy, who was closest, and then Owney Morrison. As the place was too crowded for Danny anyway, he left, holding his drink.

Outside they stood in front of the Grand Central building, at the base of Park Avenue, facing straight uptown with its flower plots dividing the avenue that runs between buildings housing the greatest wealth in the history of the earth. Traffic heading downtown runs up to a ramp on one side of the building, which, like some stone whale, seems to suck in the traffic. Then, on the other side, traffic heading uptown comes spitting out of a huge stone mouth and into the splendor of Park Avenue. One cross street, 46th, cuts in front of the building entrance and serves to promote traffic tieups.

It was at this spot that Danny stood with his drink and with Owney Morrison next to him. Danny switched the shopping bag to his strong arm, the right, so nobody would steal it from him. Danny watched the traffic as it came on and off the ramps of the Grand Central building. He stood in front of the glass doors and looked straight up Park Avenue.

"They think they're important."

"They're not bothering you," Owney said.

"Yes, they are."

"Why?"

"Because they're all quiffs."

Owney chuckled.

"Look at them. Millions of quiffs."

Danny walked into the building and came back out carrying the elevator starter's straight wood chair. With the timing of a devil, he walked out in front of the stone mouth that sends out uptown traffic at a moment when a red light kept the traffic stuffed back inside the stone whale, and on the cross street, a white van was attempting to turn around the flower plot and go ahead of the waiting traffic onto the uptown lanes. Danny stepped in front of the van just before the van finished the turn. The van stopped so that it was perpendicular to the traffic waiting on the ramp inside the building.

He placed the chair in the middle of Park Avenue. He sat and slowly lit a cigarette.

The van driver was too astonished to talk.

The sound of laughter caused Owney to look up. The sidewalk was two deep with people watching, all of whom anticipated what happened next: the light turned green and the traffic came jumping out of the ramp, like horses out of starting gates, and then the first cars had to squeal to a stop for the van that was being blocked by Danny Murphy in his chair. New York rush-hour traffic. The horns started. Danny Murphy raised his hand gently.

The van driver yelled in an accent that seemed to be Haitian.

"Mon, I got to go, *mon."*

"Fuck you, *mon,"* Danny called back.

Now a cab appeared from behind the van. There was an Israeli accent. *"Meester!"*

"Up your keester!" Danny yelled.

He was so proud of that that he jumped up and placed the glass on the chair and clasped his hands over it, like a priest saying Mass. Then he turned and faced the traffic and held out his hands and gave his blessing. He whirled for his drink.

Which Owney held high. Standing in the middle of Park Avenue, in the dusk of rush hour, with his body shaking with laughter and the glass in his hand, right in the middle of Park Avenue, with horns honking for blocks and people laughing uproariously, Owney drank the drink, all of it, while Danny Murphy wailed. Laughing, clouting each other, they left the traffic and went down the street toward Lexington Avenue, where there were good bars, and Owney had this fire in his throat.

"Where are we going?" Danny Murphy said.

"To Queens. Maybe."

It was nothing, just an old clock on a dresser somewhere in the bedroom, a clock with heavy insides that caused a loud ticking. It also was wrong that the clock was there at all: Owney kept no clock in his bedroom. He tightened as he listened to the sound.

He was lying on his right side. Allowing his eyes to open, he saw a wall that was wrong, too. Yellow. In his bedroom in the cemetery house, the wall was light blue.

The body on the other side of the bed moved.

"Dead," Sharon said.

Her hand fell on Owney's bare shoulder.

"Do you have to go by your job?"

Owney sat up, fuzzy sick. Somewhere at the bottom of his throat was a pool of mucilage. There was complete remorse as he looked at Sharon, who had one bare hip and leg stuck out from under the sheets. Tangled black hair covered her forehead. Eyes had wide rings of mascara under them.

"Work, baby," Sharon said.

"I wound up here," Owney said.

"I think so."

Owney shut his eyes and blew breath out of a sour mouth.

"There was no way you could make it home, baby. You were a carcass."

"What did I do here?" Owney said.

"What do you mean, what did you do?"

"With you, what did I do with you?"

Her head came off the pillow. "How can you ask me a thing like that?"

"Because I want to know."

"You're asking me that? You're in Sharon's bed, you don't even know what you did? You're some freaking hero. You sleep in Sharon's bed, you don't even know what you did."

"I don't know anything," Owney said.

"Do you know about Jamaica Avenue?"

"Stop playing."

"Sharon doesn't play. You know where Jamaica Avenue is, you don't even know what you did when you were in bed with Sharon all night. This is a man? They give him medals?"

"I want to know what I did."

"I wouldn't tell you if the doctor says I got twenty minutes to live. I never heard of anything like this."

Owney glanced at himself. He had on shorts and his black loafers and socks. He looked at the floor and saw his pants and shirt. Utter defeat.

"Talk to me," he said to Sharon.

"You're wrong again. I say things, but I don't talk. There's a difference. Sharon says things like Hello and Do you need a match. But Sharon doesn't talk. You're the one does the talking."

"What did I say?"

"You talked on the phone half the night."

Owney's head snapped around. "What do you mean?"

"You called everybody. You told the world off last night."

"Who?"

"What do I know, who? Who could listen?"

"Did I call my wife?"

"How do I know?"

"Didn't you hear me?"

"I told you, who could do that? You were yelling at everybody."

"Tell me if I called my wife."

The leg covered by sheets kicked them off. Sharon got out of bed and stood naked and yawning in the dim room.

"You're asking me? Ask your wife if you called her. I told you, you spoke to so many people who knows who they were?"

Owney looked at the loud clock on Sharon's dresser. "I'm going to work."

"Good. Maybe at the end of the day you'll know whether you worked or not."

Sharon walked out of the small room and went into the bathroom. Owney grabbed his pants from the floor and began to put them on. Right away, his right foot, with the loafer on it, got stuck in the pants leg. He tried to shove it through, but nothing moved. When he started to pull the foot back, the heel remained caught in the pants leg. He wondered how he got the pants off in the night. Shoes were on all night. Then he thought of the phone. He looked around for it. Old black phone on the table next to Sharon's side of the bed. He stared at it and waited for the scene or the whisper in his mind to tell him whether he spoke to his wife or not. When nothing came to him, he felt a single small hope. Then he reminded himself that he couldn't remember the other calls either.

Sharon came back from the bathroom in a pink wrapper with a frilly front. It was open and she walked lazily, as if the room were empty.

Owney pulled the pants off his shoe and dropped them on the floor. He went past her toward the bathroom. "Let me think," he said.

"So think," Sharon said. She put a knee on the edge of the bed and fell into it. She stared at the ceiling.

"Dead," Sharon said.

Owney had trouble bringing the shower curtain across the tub. The water started cold and he opened his mouth, caught some of it, and gargled. The crop still was thick with phlegm. When the water turned warm, Owney let it rain on the back of his neck. He looked at his feet in the shower and suddenly realized how sick he felt. Now a scene came to him. Throwing up on the sidewalk outside Sharon's bar. He wondered how much he had been drinking. Had he called Dolores? You can't even remember if you laid a broad. How can you remember a phone call?

The two words, *phone call,* were lethal. If I got her on the phone, I lost my life.

Then he remembered the dream during the night. In Nam they had a dog who had a German shepherd for a father and a small Vietnamese mutt for a mother. The dog, Brutus, had a German shepherd's face and fur mounted on a frail body. Whenever anything happened, the instant it ended, here was the dog running around looking for a chunk of some-body's body to bring back in his mouth. A guy from the outfit was caught by a mortar round. He was in pieces in the hot sand. Brutus sniffed at the remains, grabbed a foot and brought it back in his mouth, proudly, the boot seared in half and stuck to the foot. Tail wagging, whining happily, the dog pushed the foot against Owney's thigh. A guy's foot in the mouth of a dog smiling with blood foaming out of the sides of his mouth. Stand-ing in the shower, he could feel the foot pressing against his thigh.

He was amazed at how sick he felt. The alcohol in his cells caused suffering in every part of his body.

Get a beer, he told himself. Total defeat.

The bathroom door opened and Sharon stepped in. "There's some fuck at the door," she said.

"Who?"

"What do I know? I don't let anybody in. Who comes to tell you something good at this hour?"

Owney turned off the shower. Loud knocking on the door filled the apartment. Outside, an el train went along the old loose Jamaica Avenue tracks. The train noise could not drown out the knocking.

Owney got out of the shower and went to the living room.

"Telephone company," a voice came through the door. "We got to check the neighborhood."

Owney stood in silence.

"I heard you were in the shower. Then I heard you turn the shower off. What am I, deaf?"

When Owney didn't answer, the voice said, "What do I have to do, knock the door down?"

"If you do, you won't like it when you get in," Owney said. "Call nine one one," he said to Sharon.

"Save yourself the call," the voice said. "I'm Detective Webster, Manhattan South."

"How do I know?" Owney said.

"I'm standing here with a badge."

Owney went to the front room. Standing away from the window, he looked down at the street. At the curb under the el was a black Plymouth. Detectives, all right. He walked back to the door.

"And?"

"I just want to ask the girl something."

Sharon, standing in the bedroom doorway, said softly, "And I got a good answer."

"I'm only trying to help," Webster said through the door. "We can get rid of this thing right here."

"You got a warrant?" Owney said.

"What warrant? I just want to talk to her for a minute," Webster said.

"Get a warrant."

"Now you see what you're doing?" Webster said. "You're making me go to the boss and tell him I got to take hours off to go to court to get papers signed. My boss'll get mad at me and then he'll make it tougher on you. If I get a warrant, I'll make everybody mad."

"You do that," Owney said.

He went into the bedroom and sat on the edge of the bed. Sharon handed him a cigarette. The first smoke went down with a whine.

"Let's stop worrying," Owney said to Sharon.

"What are you saying, worry; I shot the sonofabitch, you didn't," Sharon whispered.

A few minutes later, he went to the door. The hallway was silent. Then he looked out the front window. The car was still there. Sharon stood at the bedroom mirror and put on mascara. "Do I bring the cop to work with me? I am going to work, you know."

"I'm thinking that we walk out of here, don't even look at them, just go right to the car. They can't do anything without a warrant. Then we go right to the lawyers."

"What lawyer?" Sharon said.

"I know one guy over on Queens Boulevard. He helped me out once. He also got my wife suing me."

Sharon kept brushing mascara on her eyelashes. "You could remember a lawyer, but you can't remember if you did anything in bed with me last night."

At seven-thirty, Owney opened the door. The hallway was empty. Going down to the street, he said to Sharon, "Don't even look at them. Go right to the car. They can't stop you."

He pushed the street door open and walked out into the summer morning under the el. Sunlight came through the tracks and covered the sidewalk with orange oblongs. The detective, Webster, pulled himself out of the passenger seat. His partner, Eagen, sat at the wheel.

"You're only hurting yourself," Webster said to Sharon.

Owney, holding her elbow, started to the right. Some dim recollection told him his car had been left at the corner during the night. Sharon pulled her arm away. "No, this way, Owney." She led him in the opposite direction.

"Owney . . . Morrison?" the detective said.

Owney kept walking. Webster slipped back into his car. "Look at this," he said to the other detective. "If you had to pick out somebody who could blow a guy away right on the street, you wouldn't have to look much past him."

On Queens Boulevard, the doorman pressed the buzzer for McNiff. There was no answer. "Try yourself," the doorman said. "He's in Fourteen-Y." Getting on the elevator, Owney saw the detectives parked at the curb.

McNiff did not answer the bell. Owney then banged on the door. He did it many times, increasing the sound, and finally there was a bellow from inside.

"I'm eating," McNiff called out.

"It's Owney Morrison. You represented me in court."

"I can't see you," McNiff said. "Your wife came to see me. I'm going to represent her against you in a divorce. I sent you some papers. She must hate you, she's going to divorce you."

"No, she isn't," Owney said. "But right now I have this girl here who needs help. She might be in some trouble."

McNiff opened the door. He was in a hooded bathrobe. His eyes bulged as he looked at Sharon. "What did you do?" he said to her.

"Nothing I shouldn't of done," Sharon said.

"Detectives followed us here," Owney said.

"Yes, but I'm eating my breakfast," McNiff said. "I'm having prunes and orange juice and eggs and toast. One slice. I eat very intelligently. Unfortunately, I eat ten times a day. You can come in if you don't stop me from eating."

He led them through narrow alleys between books that were stacked to the ceiling. In one room, the windowsills were left uncovered by book stacks. McNiff stood at a counter and began eating scrambled eggs.

"What are the detectives following you for?"

"They want to ask her about a man got killed," Owney said.

"Really? You're the second woman I've met this year who has difficulty over a murder. A blonde wanted to kill her husband. She met this guy Bad Roger in a bar. A pants presser. So he went out and killed the husband. But the blonde went to another bar and met a rich guy. He put up twenty thousand to try and save her. He wanted her out of jail so he could have sex with her. She was so sexy. If she even looked at you, she drew a sexual response. She's in jail now. She's so gorgeous. And she loves so gorgeous. Are you the same way?"

"I'm better. I'm not in jail and I'm not going there," Sharon said.

"That's terrific. Do you like jargon? I have a book on jargon I always read. In fact, I may have an extra copy for you. I bought six copies."

McNiff looked around the book stacks nearest him. He shook his head. "Look at that. I made a mistake. I put all the copies on this open stack. Right in the middle. I usually don't do that. I have textbooks on the large intestines in four different places. Do you want a book on large intestines?"

"You live like this all the time?" Sharon said.

"Yes, I had prostate trouble and when I went to the doctor, he said, 'Can you have sex?' I said, 'I don't know. My wife left me.' Maybe you can replace her. That's if you don't get put in jail for murder."

Sharon sat on the windowsill and took out a cigarette. She looked around at the stacks of books. "I guess there's worse places to be than in a homemade library."

McNiff's fork made a loud noise on the plate as he ate. "Tell me the problem," he said. "You're supposed to tell the truth to the police. But the last time a lawyer around here told that to a client, the judge said that the lawyer was incompetent."

Owney recounted only what had happened to them that morning. Sharon smoked and nodded.

"Do you know this O'Sullivan they want to talk about?" McNiff asked Sharon.

She shook her head.

"Never met the gentleman," Owney said.

"I'll go down and talk to the police," McNiff said. "I'll tell them that I can't help them because I have to help my client. I'll tell them that I believe that when the crime occurred, my client was in Alaska. Then if they want to see you, they'll have to get a warrant."

McNiff went sideways between the books on his way to the door.

"Is that how you're going?" Sharon said.

"I'm not getting out of this robe all day," McNiff said.

"I like that. That's the way you're supposed to treat them," Sharon said.

They sat in silence for fifteen minutes. When McNiff came back, he went past them and disappeared around a stack of books. "Excuse me, but I have to take a pill. I have Antabuse mixed with aspirin in a bottle. They look the same. I swallow one every day. Particularly when I feel like drinking something. It could be aspirin or it could be Antabuse. But I have to act the same. If I have Antabuse and I take a drink, I collapse. You're lucky. I'm not drinking this week."

There was the sound of water in a sink. Then McNiff came back. "I spoke to the cops. Cops are funny. I was in New Orleans. They have terrific prostitutes on Canal Street. And no cops there. Did you know that in the old English law, if a maiden got accosted by a knave or a boy from the lower class, the maiden was allowed to kill him? I was just thinking. Anyway." He looked at Owney. "The two cops were more interested in talking to you right now."

Owney shrugged. "I got nothing to do with it."

"I got them talking and they gave me the impression that they wanted to look in your house for a gun. Do you keep a gun home?"

"Not me." He stopped when he realized that he had been thinking in dusk, that he had Sharon's gun home.

"You seem worried," McNiff said.

"Well."

"I told you they were talking about searching your house. I don't have to say much more. All right." He looked at Sharon. "I'll talk to you now."

"I don't talk. No, why lie? I talked this morning. I said Owney's name right in front of these creeps on the sidewalk. That's the only way they knew to come here after us. I'm through. Dead."

16

I**T WAS LATE AFTERNOON** when Owney arrived at the job, with his mouth as dry as paper, and nerves leaping, and he went into the lunch wagon for a Coke. He sat on a box, drank one, and asked the woman to hand him another. He saw Navy through the doorway.

"Four times," Navy said.

Owney said nothing.

"Four calls in the middle of the night. Let me sleep, will you?"

Owney clutched his fatigue jacket under his left arm and felt the gun pressing against his ribs. The right hand went around the gun handle and then he put his hand completely over the gun and began walking with his head down. He went only a few steps and he saw the black Plymouth parked between two cement trucks. Fuck it. He kept walking, a man who didn't even know he was taking a chance, walked right up to the shaft, without glancing at the two detectives standing in the doorway and talking to Chris Doyle, who immediately pretended to be scratching his neck, a motion that told Owney to get on the lift. As Owney opened the small gate to the lift, the clicking noise caused Webster to look up.

"Hey."

Owney stood on the lift and said nothing. He had all the feeling of a Formica table. Webster ran out of the shack and then vaulted over the gate and onto the lift. Which suddenly groaned and dropped into the darkness.

"Look out for something dropping on your head," Doyle called. "We got no roof on this thing."

Webster looked up and saw the darkness chase the light and he jerked and stood so close to Owney that their shoulders touched. He inhaled quickly as the lift shuddered. "Where does this go?" His voice was tremulous.

"To the bottom."

"How far is that?"

"Nine hundred feet. That's about ninety stories down."

"How long does it take?"

"A long time."

Webster became silent. The lift scraped and growled its way into the earth and then broke into the light and noise and foul air at the bottom of the shaft. A motor swayed over the rocks at the shaft's entrance. Its fumes blew into the lift. Owney stepped out into a puddle of water.

"Hold it." Webster was rooted to the lift and he reached out for Owney. Now the motor threw more fumes and Webster covered his mouth. Suddenly, his eyes went to the rock roof. His mouth opened in pure fear. His legs took him backward. Bells began ringing, and as the lift started up, Webster's head jerked straight up, exposing a chicken neck, giving the appearance of a man being hanged.

Owney rode through the tunnel from the Bronx to the face, which was hundreds of feet under the sidewalks of upper Manhattan. As the motor ran through the tunnel, the rock overhead became mean and the steel supports on some places were only a couple of feet apart, but in others, with similar dirty white lines shooting through the rock, there appeared to be too much space between supports. When Owney got off, he found his father walking along the tunnel and muttering about uncovered hoses running along the walls. "These things are supposed to be covered. We'll shoot and the rock'll break the lines."

Owney just walked away, going under an area where a shaft went up hundreds of feet, to 155th Street and Amsterdam Avenue, where it was sealed on the street with a large metal hatch. Past the shaftway, the tunnel was wet and strewn with rock and much of the walking had to be done sideways. He moved to the face, where they were loading it for a shot. Rolling up the fatigue jacket, he shoved it as far as he could into the large center hole, the burn hole, his hand feeling the gun inside. He stepped back. The blaster came up and began stuffing the holes with explosives. Owney became wary: he waited until he saw that the hole was loaded. He was the last man to leave the face, walking behind the others up the tracks, where he stayed until there was the *pop-pop-pop* of explosives going off in sequence. As it was the end of Friday, and there was no night shift coming in, all along the tunnel things were being shut off and Owney complained loudly about air and water hoses that were left uncovered by plywood.

"Why don't the men do it?" Owney said to his father.

"Because men today are too lazy. I asked three people to do it today."

"Where are the three? In your head?"

His father looked at him blankly and turned and walked up the tunnel. "I'm going to sit here until you tell me something," Owney called after him. He sat down on a bench along the wall. His father came back carrying wood. Owney's eyes drooped; he stretched out on the bench. "Go ahead, keep fooling around. For once, I'm not going away," Owney said. His father began dropping wood over the hoses. He kept walking back and forth nervously. Owney fell asleep with the wood the only sound in the empty tunnel.

Until the rock overhead made its sound. *Caw.* Owney's father dropped the wood and began to run. Owney was behind him, the two of them moving along the side of the tunnel, half sliding along the rock, half stumbling. *Caw.* Now they were past the sealed shaft and at the section of the tunnel where the rail tracks began. Now they were running along the tracks, splashing through water in the darkness, and for a moment Owney remembered that he had done this once before with his father, when he was a kid, only that time the father was running behind him, and it was fun, and Owney was thinking that he was too young to have life repeating itself on him, and then the gray rock with ugly white lines screamed.

Tons of ancient rock crashed onto the floor of the tunnel, forming a pile that was a small pyramid. The rock crashed and then there was total silence in the tunnel, except for the loud, endless moan from Owney's father.

"It's very nice here today," her mother said.

"Beautiful."

"Nicer than there." They were at one end of Rockaway, where there are houses on the beach. She was pointing to the boardwalk, which was twenty blocks down and whose sands attracted Puerto Ricans who cooked on the beach.

Then her mother said, "It would be nice if it was like this all year."

"It is in Florida. Go there."

"Oh, I don't know yet."

"Sure you do. You know I'm going away in September," Dolores said.

"When will I see the baby?" Her mother lifted the baby from her.

"You will."

"And what about Owney? Did you tell him yet?"

"No."

"When are you going to do that?"

"I don't know. Soon, I guess."

"You're taking her away from everybody. I never said I didn't like the baby."

"I just recognize that sometimes it is hard."

"What's the poor child going to do in the snow?"

"She'll be well taken care of."

"Where? In this care place?"

"Day care."

"I don't like day care. The mother is supposed to do day care."

"The mother can't be there all day."

"Then the grandmother does care. I don't like day care."

"Do you like being in a strange place with six feet of snow and ten degrees below zero better than you like day care?"

"Weather don't make no difference when you're inside."

Her mother put the baby down. Christine was on her stomach in a gulley that the water had formed in the sand alongside the old rocks. The last of a wave ran over the sand and the water lapped at the baby's side and then enough of it got under her to lift her. As the water ran out of the gulley, ran swiftly out alongside the rock jetty, it carried the baby with it. Christine was in water that was only ankle deep and her small hands could still clutch wet sand. The water, however, was pulling her out. Dolores took two long steps and had her baby, swooping her up from the water, and Christine gave a delighted cry. And Dolores looked at the rock jetty, at rocks with white lines showing through black glistening sea moss.

"What's the matter?" her mother said.

"I don't know."

"You shivered."

"I guess just thinking about the snow made me cold."

Owney was up on the pile of rocks in the tunnel and trying to work his way down to his father, who was in there somewhere, and whose moans filled the tunnel. Owney felt that he was climbing high and that his father was on the far side of the rock pile. He started to lower himself. Now there was the sound of men coming on the other side of the rock pile. Suddenly, through a space in the rocks, Owney could see flashlight beams jerking in the darkness as the men holding them stumbled over rocks. Then he heard the voice of Wozniak, one of the Poles from Greenpoint. With it, the singsong of a West Indian. Maybe Lazarus. Peering through the rocks, Owney saw that there were three men. They had their flashlights on his father's face. Now the face was gone as they were throwing clothes over him to prevent shock. Hands dug under the shoulders of Owney's father and tried to move him. The face under the pile of clothes screamed.

Wozniak was talking in a whisper. Then the whisper grew to a shout. "We can't move as long as his foot is here. The foot is wrapped around the rocks."

"We'll have to wait for a doctor," one of them said.

"Wait? Nobody waits here," Wozniak said. He threw a flashlight up at the roof. There was a great cavity left by the rock that had fallen. The cavity was shot full of white.

"We're getting out of here," Wozniak said.

Owney yelled through the hole in the rock. "Wait until I come around."

"Come around? Take you all day to get here. We got to go."

"What about the foot?" the West Indian said.

"Comes off." Wozniak scrambled forward on his knees and put his face against the pile of clothes covering Owney's father. "It's all gone, anyway. I can see it. You can't. I hate to say this to you, but it's got to come off so we can get out of here."

"Do what you have to do," Owney's father said.

"They could sew it back on," Owney called. "You take it off, he never has a foot again. Why don't we get him out with the foot?"

"It would take weeks to get his foot out of here," Wozniak said. "We're going now."

"They got surgery," Owney said.

The cavity in the rock roof settled the argument by squeaking.

"We're going!" Wozniak shouted.

He had the flashlight on the father's foot. Owney crept through the hole in the rock. He could get part of his face and one arm through. He looked down into the light and saw a band of skin on the outside of the rock. It was holding the father's foot to the leg. It was also holding the father to the rock. Owney could reach down and touch the band of skin.

"It goes," Wozniak said. Suddenly, in the light, his hand held a penknife.

"Give it to me," Owney said.

Wozniak gave him the penknife. Now Owney's nerves went down, down, and his voice was flat and low.

"There's no way?"

"None," Wozniak said. "You see for yourself."

"Pop. No way, Pop."

"Just do what you got to do."

Owney's hand reached down as Wozniak held the flashlight right on the band of skin. The rock under the skin served as a cutting board and the small penknife went through a band of skin that was much thicker than it appeared.

And now the skin was gone as Wozniak and the others were tugging and they had Owney's father out and were carrying him away in a basket. Somewhere overhead, there was a sound in the cavity of the roof and something small dropped and then the cavity screamed and Owney dived into the blackness. A slab of rock fell. It had to be an enormous slab, for its thud was exceptionally loud.

As the accident occurred at three in the afternoon and rushing a footless man to the hospital was the first duty, it took an hour before a search could be organized for Owney Morrison. The first people to reach the cave-in shouted through a bullhorn and flashed lights. There was no sound. A wall of rock stood between them and anybody on the other side, if there was anybody. Moving the rocks could be done only with dynamite and then only over many days.

The only chance, they decided, was to open the shaft at 155th Street and Amsterdam Avenue and send a bucket down. As the shaft at that point was five hundred feet deep, a crane with that much cable on the reel was needed.

At this hour, four-thirty on a Friday afternoon in the summer, the New York construction trade was on the highways going to Hampton Bays and Lake George and Breezy Point. Sitting in his shack, Chris Doyle called two construction equipment yards and in each found only a watchman. Both watchmen made calls, and a half-hour later, Doyle heard from Al Bessing, who had a construction equipment company in Yonkers and was starting his weekend in Sea Bright, in New Jersey. It took Bessing almost two hours to round up drivers and equipment.

Dolores Morrison arrived at 155th Street and Amsterdam Avenue at eight o'clock. There were lights turned on inside the fence. The yellow metal door covering the shaft had been pulled open. Sandhogs stood at the top and looked down.

Navy took Dolores by the arm and led her to the edge of the shaft. She looked down into the darkness.

Navy said, "We have to drop a line down. Just like we're fishing. I think we'll have a catch for you today."

Dolores said nothing and walked slowly out onto the street. Queens, she told herself. She must have seen a hundred pictures on television of Queens wives being hustled through crowds to the hospital where dead police husbands or firemen were. She walked down the hill alongside a gloomy stone church, turned the corner of Broadway, and climbed the church steps. It was closed. A Presbyterian church. She walked down the stairs. A woman was arguing with a cab driver. Going back up the street, she passed a man walking a sheepdog, a woman struggling with supermarket bundles, and a young boy on a skateboard. She crossed the street to another church. This one was almost opposite the shaft. These doors, too, were locked.

She turned and walked deliberately across the street and over to the shaft, and peered down again. If there was a way out, she knew, Owney would find it. Maybe that's what he's for, she thought, big emergencies. What good is all the courage if it's something you can use only in a great emergency? You're supposed to place your hands on life every day. Then she told herself, Maybe that's what it's for. Big emergencies. So his life floated from one calamity to another. What about most people who could handle nothing and would clutch his arm if something went wrong? Maybe I should have realized that and tried to fit it all in. She shook her head against the brooding thought.

As she was thinking of this, somebody ran up and took her picture. She felt strange being alone. It's true, she told herself, you don't feel comfortable in a picture unless you have a husband standing next to you.

Navy stood alongside her and said nothing for a while. Then he said in a low voice, "How have you been doing in school?"

"Fine. I'm making it on my own."

"In the meantime, your husband is the first in the family to practice medicine. His father's foot."

She said nothing. A few paces away, she could hear Danny Murphy saying to somebody, "Geez, these accidents are terrible. Billy Kennedy died six months ago from a massive heart attack. Down in Long Beach.

He was at a fire. His wife got married four months ago. Jesus, she didn't give him time to turn in his coffin."

Horn blaring, the flatbed truck carrying a crane pulled around the corner. The truck backed up and the crane was placed over the shaft. A motor sounded and threw fumes into the hot evening air. A guy with light curly hair and a red face jumped off the crane and held his hand out as a bucket lowered. The curly-haired guy and two sandhogs got into the bucket. The crane dropped them down the shaft. Chris Doyle held up a lamp.

Dolores watched the lamp drop down the shaft, the light turning into the smallest match flame. The cable slowed and the crane became still. Somebody said that they would be trying to signal with a horn from the bottom, but the traffic on the street made it impossible to pick out the sound. Everybody concentrated on the small light.

Dolores prayed. Around her was silence and still air. Then a light wiggled. Dolores looked at the light as it grew in the darkness. She prayed and hoped that Owney was alive for himself, and her daughter, and yes, for her too.

If he's dead, I am not going to let myself feel guilty. She stared down the shaft. At her back, the crane motor made a racket and the cables squealed. No one talked.

The men around her leaned farther out over the shaft, trying to pierce the darkness, and they still said nothing and the wires squealed and then the breath and prayer caught in her throat. There was no sudden movement or sound. The cables just smoothly pulled the bucket into the light. She saw the curly-haired man first, because he was laughing and he had most of his body around Owney's in a hug. Owney stepped off and pushed through to Dolores. He covered her mouth with his and pressed her against him. She felt nothing. Then Owney let go of her and quickly turned and began accepting grabs from the other men.

It had not been an embrace, she realized, for there had been no passion. It had been a thanksgiving kiss. He walked over and took her hand, gripped it, and started walking her away, and she felt the hand trying to wrest the future from her. One moment she had been filled with compassion and now fear whirred in her. Had she, by standing still at the edge of a pit, abandoned the chance to change her life?

At Columbia Presbyterian Hospital, at four in the morning, they were with Owney's mother, seated on wooden chairs outside the intensive care unit.

"You eat anything?" the mother said.

"I don't even remember," Dolores said.

"I left pot roast on the stove," the mother said.

"It'll still be there when you get home."

"I left a whole pot roast just sitting there."

A doctor the size of a jockey came down the hall. He looked at Owney, indicating he wanted to talk to him, but Owney shook his head. "It's all right," he told the doctor, indicating he could speak in front of the mother.

"He lost the foot, you know," the doctor said.

"I was hoping they found it—and maybe sewed it back on."

"Afraid they didn't."

Without looking at his mother, Owney put a hand on her arm. The mother stared at the wall.

"Can't do anything about it?" she said.

"I'm sorry."

"Then I guess you can't."

The mother stood up.

"Where you going?"

"Just for a little walk down the hall."

Dolores said, "I'll go with you."

"No, I'll just take a little walk by myself."

The mother's step was firm and she seemed relaxed as she walked.

"She'll be all right, won't she?" Dolores said.

"Yes, she will. That's her way. She can take things. That doesn't mean she doesn't feel it. She just can take things."

They sat in silence. Dolores put her hand over his. She wondered if by touching him she was merely trying to give comfort, or if she was also actually expressing remorse, confirming to herself what had already happened, that a sudden tragedy was decreeing that she should return to the life for which she had been raised.

"So we wind up here," Owney said.

She did not answer. Nor did her hand move. Did it remain because it was obeying a heart that had decided that it no longer had redress?

"I know I figured out one thing," he said. "We should have had another baby."

Her hand raised. "What are you talking about?"

"I'm talking about what I know about myself."

"I don't know what you mean by that." She stood up. "I know that I best be home to take care of the one I've got."

"We've got."

She nodded.

"What do you think I did sitting six hours in a cave maybe I wasn't going to get out of? Sit there thinking that I wanted to live without my wife and daughter?"

"Did you think of that because of where you were?"

"That's not me," he said, and she knew that it wasn't.

"Then were you thinking that way because that's the way you were supposed to?"

He made a face.

"Do you really want all this responsibility?"

"I just told you that I thought another baby would've straightened me out."

"Do you mean that I'm supposed to give birth immediately so you can stay out of bars?"

"No, I mean before. Forget it. I'm grown up now. We'll put a lot into every day and make up for what we lost."

He said this as dryly as the recitation of a ledger and she found herself standing in the hospital hallway and accepting it.

When his mother returned, he held each of them by the arm as they walked toward the elevator. On the way home, Dolores tried to deal with her inner confusion. Danny Murphy, who sat in the front seat and talked incessantly, saved her from the trap of any conversation. When they came up to the cemetery house, Dolores got out of the car and stood with Owney and his mother. She kissed Owney's mother on the cheek and then brushed her lips across his cheek.

"What time tomorrow?" Owney said.

"I don't know," Dolores said, hesitantly.

"I'll call you from the hospital and come around the house then."

"Which house?" Owney's mother said.

Dolores said nothing.

"You pay all this rent for a house you don't live in," the mother said.

Dolores's foot almost slipped and brought her to another level and some impulse to surrender. She heard herself saying, "Well, right now, I have to get to the baby."

On Saturday, Owen Morrison was allowed to see his father for ten minutes. Then as he headed for the car, a block down, he passed a bar whose window was filled with faces, and one of them moved quickly and flung open the barroom door. Danny Murphy stood there. "The whole mob is inside. We're here to see your father if they'll let us."

On the hot street, the opponent, grunting like an old cow, tried to dig a left hand into Owney's stomach. With dirty sweat on a pasty face, eyes looking out from a circle of scars, bandy legs that would not buckle, the opponent dogged Owney. The opponent looked for that greatest opening, uncertainty. He stood in the center of the ring and the crowd's derision of Owney rang to the rafters. The opponent motioned with his gloves for Owney to come out and mix it up.

"We're everybody here," Danny Murphy said. The noise of the bar came out the open door. Cold beer in a clean glass in the morning sunlight. "Come on," Danny Murphy said.

An hour and a half later, Owney and Dolores Morrison were at a table in the AA meeting in Park Slope, listening to a man say that because of trouble with his children the night before, he had nearly gone to drink and that he was thankful that everybody now would listen to him, as seeing their faces alone was of great assistance to him.

The man running the meeting pointed at Owney, who stood up with cold beer in his mind and his opponent only inches away; the opponent became more agile as the fight grew tougher, and he was here to let Owney know it in front of all of those who sat in the low-ceilinged, smoky room. Now the opponent got in a good shot. Owney standing, looking at a blank wall in the front of the room, became embarrassed and resentful. What he was doing was an exercise to please the others in the room. Pathetic wrecks. He stood in doubt and said nothing. Then the opponent threw the punch that would knock Owney back into the seat, humiliated and angry, and send him out for that cold beer. This one time anyway, Owney bent his body and let the punch go around his neck.

"I'm Owney and I'm an alcoholic."

"Hi, Owney," the people in the room called out.

Owney felt the hand on his arm and he looked at Dolores, who now was standing next to him.

"I'm going to go so you don't have to talk in front of me."

"Don't worry about me. I can do anything now," he said.

"I know you can," she said. If there was one thing she knew, it was that. If he had made a vow to himself, and he certainly had, right in front of her, she knew that it became an issue of life and death to protect it. In one tiny space in life, with these few words wrung from his soul, he had returned to himself his own fortune. And suddenly, she felt her anxiousness smoothed. She wanted to go for a walk in the sun. "You are going to be all right now. And I have to tell you that I have a lot to do for myself. I'm going."

At first, it didn't register. "How are you going to get home?" he whispered. Then, looking at her, he felt it: a sense of elation, of freeness, a sky somewhere inside her that caused her to soar as she stood next to him.

"Aren't you going to listen to what I say?"

"Owney. The whole last three years?"

He said nothing.

"Owney. Yesterday makes me tired."

She pointed to the front of the room, where the leader patiently waited for Owney to talk.

"Take care of your business; don't worry about me."

Nodding, smiling, she left the old room, the wooden floor creaking under her tiptoe, and she was in the vestibule when she heard Owney's voice. She hurried through the door. She walked the wrong way, away from the subway and down a street of brownstone houses on a street blinking with sun.

On the drive to Syracuse on Tuesday, the baby lasted all the way up to Exit 23 on the New York State Thruway before she became carsick. At the rest area, Dolores walked to the cafeteria to get a couple of wet towels for the baby.

"Dolores!"

"What?"

"Bring me back something," her mother called from the car.